STORMLESS

NICK STITLE

BOOK ONE OF
THE STORMLESS SERIES

ISBN (eBook): 979-8-9878962-0-4
ISBN (Paperback): 979-8-9878962-1-1
ISBN (Hardcover): 979-8-9878962-2-8
ISBN (Jacketed Hardcover): 979-8-9878962-3-5

Library of Congress Control Number: 2023904061

Cover Artwork & Design by Jeff Brown Graphics

Title Production by The Book Whisperer

Published by Blazecrest Publishing, LLC

For my mom and dad, who brought this book to life

Auris
Freyfall
Orrinshire
The Ice Fields
Utrya
Elos
Telenaris
Hirane
Celes
Elan Taesi
The Highlands
Fairfrost
Hythe
The Wastelands
Etherus
Arvendon
The Salarin Sea
Goldenleaf
Suchara
Asari
The Dunes of Despair
Cyfalion
Jaskye
Ayria
Ashos
The Blazing Circlet

CHAPTER ONE

ARRIVAL

Velarus Ravamoira stood in the stark yellow light of the Blazeday, staring into the dim chamber ahead. He strode into Summerglass Palace, passing through the massive white-marble doors as the guards heaved them open. Velarus's voluminous black robes whispered across the smooth, white floor. He glided across the Royal Entry Hall, making for the second set of marble doors at the far end of the atrium.

Lavish furniture decorated the sides of the chamber, resting below grand marble statues of kings long passed. A magnificent crystal chandelier hung in the center of the entry hall, its light staining the entire corridor. Hallways broke off to the left and right, leading to the rest of the palace. Pairs of golden braziers lined the walls, orange flames dancing wildly within. Torches hung at intervals between them, casting feral shadows on the walls beyond.

Four guards stood before the closed doors, each bearing a torch and a silver-gold spear. Scorchers. The abundancy of open flames in the room would give them an undeniable advantage should conflict arise.

King Avenos Titansworn was known to be a powerful Scorcher, Velarus knew that much.

But will it matter? he wondered. Velarus was not here to test the King's strength; no, Velarus had come for another reason.

The guards took note of Velarus's robes and began whispering to one another at his approach. The guards stiffened as he neared, raising the spears held firmly in their armored hands. Their orange uniforms were decorated with Arvendon's insignia: a golden blaze-crest circling a flame.

Velarus's robes bore a much different look, consisting of only the darkest of blacks with slender veins of a deep blood-red cloth weaving amongst the folds and curves of the cloak.

"Not any closer!" one of the guards called from behind a steel faceplate.

Velarus stopped.

"The King is not currently taking appointments," the guard called.

"And yet here I am, seeking an audience with him nonetheless," Velarus said, folding his hands into his robes.

The guard turned back to his companions, who shrugged slightly.

"We are under strict orders to only let in those with a missive signed by the King's Council," the guard said, straightening. "We cannot grant you entry. Please be on your way."

"Well then," Velarus sighed. "That is quite a shame. I only arrived this afternoon, and I was hoping that I would be given an opportunity to share the information that I have been sent to pass along."

The guards showed no reaction.

"The message I carry is intended for the King himself, might I add," Velarus continued, pacing closer. "And, if he does not receive it, I fear that there may be... consequences." Velarus trailed off.

"You have been ordered to leave," the guard said, stepping forward. "You would be wise to do so."

"I had hoped it wouldn't come to this," Velarus sighed, grimacing. "But, as it happens, I will be seeing the King this afternoon, one way or another." Velarus was now only a few paces away from the lead guard. "You see, there is another method that I can take to grant myself entry to this throne room." Carefully, Velarus bled one of the Crystals within his robes. Power seeped into his veins, infusing his body with energy. "And, unfortunately for you, that method involves a bit more *force*." He raised his hand, initiating the spell.

An immaterial weight manifested in Velarus's palm. Velarus twisted his fingers, readying himself.

"You—" the guard started.

Velarus didn't let him finish. He squeezed his fist, calling upon his abilities to cut the blood flow to the boy's brain.

"I... wha—" the guard stuttered, stumbling backward. The other guards shifted into a defensive stance.

"Move, and your friend dies," Velarus said, raising his black eyes to meet those of the other three guards.

They hesitated, giving Velarus all the time that he needed to take control of them as well.

Velarus closed his other fist, bleeding several more Crystals. He forced the men to the ground with a wave of his hand.

They crumpled to the floor—incapacitated—almost instantly.

"Pitiful," Velarus spat, releasing the guards a few seconds later. Velarus stopped bleeding the Crystals hidden within the inner pockets of his cloak and made for the entrance before him. With a heave, he pushed open the colossal marble doors to the throne room.

Dozens of marble pillars lined the chamber, a golden brazier sitting before each one. No chandelier hung in this room. In its place was a massive hanging pendant made of pure gold bearing an overpowering hearth that cast the tall ceiling in a fury of dancing shadows.

Before Velarus lay a long stretch of marble flooring leading to the throne at the end of the room. Guards lined the walls, each wearing the same suit of vermillion armor.

"Who dares venture into my throne room unannounced?" Avenos bellowed, rising from his royal seat. There was something to his voice... a sort of *regal* weight. The guards raised their spears. Orange Crystals hung from their waists. Scorchers.

Advisors, cloaked in the shadows of the throne, watched Velarus. *Whisperers.* They were attempting to manipulate his emotions.

With a slight bleed of a Crystal, Velarus shrugged off their effect. Velarus's abilities allowed him to stabilize his mind, preventing it from being affected by outside influence.

"Velarus Ravamoira, and, might I say, it is wonderful to finally meet you." Velarus smiled, bowing. "Surely your men have informed you of my presence already, your majesty," Velarus began, striding forward. "A man wearing the robes of a Blood Sorcerer entering the city... That is most certainly a piece of information that would have reached even your ears."

The King's eyes wavered ever so slightly.

"I understand your apprehension in believing that one with my powers could truly be standing before you today," Velarus continued. "Which is precisely why I am here now: to confirm that I am that which I claim to be."

"Guards!" the King started.

"I have come bearing a warning and a threat," Velarus interrupted. He was now perhaps twenty feet from the King. The guards were no more than a few dozen yards away in any direction. Velarus would need to position himself very carefully in order for his plan to work.

"Guards, seize him! Get this man out of my throne room!" the King commanded.

Just as the guards moved to apprehend him, Velarus flung open the sides of his robe, revealing rows upon rows of blood-red Crystals.

The guards froze.

"I am a Blood Sorcerer, and I am one of many," Velarus said. No one dared move as he pulled back his hood, revealing his shaved head. "My Sect has returned, and my Master has sent me to your disgusting city with a message: You will surrender control of your army, and your country, to our organization... or it will be taken from you."

The King stood for a moment, as if pondering his words. Then, the King laughed.

"You come into my kingdom, into my castle, and now you command me to hand over my city?" The King chuckled. "You must be mad!" The King slapped his knee, still bellowing with laughter. He raised his eyes back to Velarus. "But if that is the game you wish to play..." Flames drifted from the King's crystals, swirling around his hands as he wove them together. "Well, we have a special place in the dungeons for your kind." The fires licked the King's fingertips. "I will not give up my armies. And I certainly will not surrender my country to you." The King guided his hands through careful, well-practiced motions, and Velarus soon found himself surrounded by brilliant tendrils of flame. "Besides, even if you were a Blood Sorcerer —as you claim to be—my answer would be the same." Swaths of golden flames surrounded the King, giving him an almost divine aura. "I have always thought the powers of your kind were a bit... exaggerated."

Velarus smiled, subtly bleeding his Crystals. This would be a display that the King would not soon forget.

"Exaggerated?" Velarus snorted. "Well, we'll see about that."

The King lunged.

Velarus closed his eyes, diving into the depths of his soul. His power awaited him, *begging* to be unleashed. Velarus grabbed hold of it, and then the blood came.

The King's flames vanished as the room exploded with black-red energy.

Torrents of blood flooded the chamber, scattering the contents of the throne room. Darkness surged within the air, warping the blood and causing it to levitate. The terrible power thrived, rivers of blood and darkness ravaging the chamber.

Velarus knocked the guards to the ground with nothing more

than a thought. The hell-storm raged, knocking down braziers, tearing apart the soft carpet, and wreaking havoc on even the pillars themselves. Dark energy smashed into the walls, causing the whole palace to quiver.

The cyclone of blood magic quickened, growing stronger with each passing second. Velarus smiled. With a wave of his hand, the frenzy of horror receded slightly before him, leaving in its place a single person...

The King writhed on the marble floor before Velarus, his vermillion robes flapping in the raging storm of blood magic. Velarus approached him, forcing the King to his knees with a twist of his finger.

"You are nothing," Velarus whispered, his face mere inches from the King's. "You will *always* be nothing. You cannot even imagine the power my people hold."

"Please." The King wept, trembling beneath the spikes of pain Velarus pulsed through his body. "Why are you doing this?"

Velarus paused. "Auris is in danger, and it seems I am the only one who can save it. You and your people have made it clear that you only respond to *force*," he breathed. "We are your last hope. Even your most powerful Summoners don't stand a chance in the face of the Resurgence." Velarus released him. The cascades of blood and darkness vanished in an instant, fading into nothing.

The King fell to the floor. He was mostly unharmed—as were the guards—but Velarus had no doubts that this would be a day they would never forget.

"You have six weeks," Velarus said. "Surrender the city by then... or suffer the consequences."

The King offered no response.

Velarus turned, gliding toward the doors through which he had entered. As Velarus passed through the entrance, the only sound in the enormous chamber was the gentle crackling of the flames, a reminder to the King that, even surrounded by the very element which he controlled, he was powerless.

CHAPTER TWO
THE SOLDIER

Castien Varic took another step forward. The large chamber was quiet and empty save for the two guards who now stood behind him. Castien turned, finding them standing perfectly still in their orange armor.

He spun back, shifting his attention to the doors in front of him. The massive white-marble body and golden handle of the middle door marked it as the most important. With a slight pull, it opened.

Castien stepped back, his footsteps quiet on the red carpet beneath his boots. It almost felt criminal that he was still wearing his muddy soldier's shoes on the beautiful rug, but he had bigger things to worry about. It wasn't every day that someone like him was summoned to the royal palace for yet-to-be-known reasons.

He closed his eyes for a moment, syncing his breathing to his pulse. *Five beats in, six beats out, hold for three. Repeat.*

Both his heart rate and his respiration slowed, effectively easing his anxiety. Castien looked up, clinging to the newfound confidence rising in his chest.

The marble door finished swinging open, revealing a man

wearing hooded dark gray robes. *Whisperer's robes.* Castien frowned, tilting his head. *Why would they bring me here?*

"I want to begin by easing your worries, Castien," the Whisperer said. His age was rather apparent in his raspy voice, though in a way that projected wisdom, not weakness. "You are not being interrogated, and you are not being punished. We have simply called you to Summerglass this evening to... talk."

What good conversation ever starts with that?

"If this is about the skirmish in The Highlands, I've already told you, I don't know what more there is to say," Castien said, his voice shaky.

The Whisperer tilted his head, seeming to smile beneath his hood. "It is about that, actually." The Whisperer looked up, then lowered his gaze once again. "Although we have nothing more to ask you regarding how you were able to resist the Whisperer's spells." The Whisperer turned around, waving to Castien as he started back into the room he had come from.

Castien hesitated, but followed. He looked around, bidding goodbye to the marble walls and white pillars of the waiting room.

The Whisperer shut the door behind Castien, effectively trapping him in the office. A large wooden desk lay before him, complete with one chair on each side. One of the seats was leather, the other was made of wood. Castien didn't have to ask to know which one was meant for him.

He slid into the wooden chair, settling down against the uncomfortable backrest, then looked around at the rest of the room. A bookshelf covered the entirety of the back wall, filled to the brim with tomes and volumes that Castien didn't recognize. To his right was a wall decorated only with a painting of a Mistveil. It was made up mostly of random gray swirls, but so were Mistveils, Castien supposed. On his other side were a series of hooks and hangers, many of which were occupied by gray robes that matched the ones the Whisperer wore.

The Whisperer slid into the leather chair, and placed his hands on the desk, lacing his fingers together. A single lamp stood to his right, the bright gray Whisperer Crystal glowing beneath the translucent shade.

"Are you comfortable?" the Whisperer asked, raising a gray eyebrow.

"Not really," Castien admitted.

The Whisperer huffed a laugh, lowering his hood to reveal the balding remains of an aging man's hair. "I assumed as much. You don't exactly seem at ease." The Whisperer gave a knowing smile.

Castien raised an eyebrow. Of course, the Whisperer was referring to Castien's emotions. The Whisperer was likely reading his thoughts at this very moment. Castien looked to the side, letting his vision trail off. Indeed, he felt a slight fuzz at the back of his mind.

"I assume that, if you know about the skirmish, then you know that Whispering doesn't work on me," Castien said, turning his attention back to the Whisperer.

"Remarkable," the Whisperer breathed. "Who would've thought that such abilities hide behind those bright blue eyes? I have, of course, heard the stories. But I had never thought that one could truly be so... resistant. Especially a Stormless," he added.

"Could you please tell me why I've been brought here tonight?" Castien asked, his voice still unsteady. "I don't mean to be rude, but, as I'm sure you can tell, I'm made quite anxious by members of your Sect."

"Hmm," the Whisperer said. "Now why would that be?"

"Forgive me if I'm not too keen on having my emotions constantly read and analyzed, but I'm also not terribly fond of having someone else put thoughts in my head."

"Yet you can resist such inputs, correct?"

"I..." Castien trailed off. He closed his eyes, taking a deep breath. He found his heartbeat, attuning his mind to the steady rhythm. Opening his eyes, Castien forced himself to speak. "Listen, I'd really just like to know why I'm here. Please."

The Whisperer's brown eyes twinkled in the dim light of the

room. "You have made yourself quite well known among Arvendon's troops," the Whisperer started. "And it is because of the stories that we have heard that we have brought you here tonight." The Whisperer extended his wrinkled hand over the table. "My name is Estmar, and I will be conducting your interview."

"Interview?" Castien raised an eyebrow again. "I'm already in Arvendon's army, aren't I?"

"Ah yes, but you are being considered for a *special* mission of sorts, you see. And my superiors would like me to conduct a few tests to see if you are up to the task."

Could this have something to do with the commotion at the palace earlier today? Castien turned around, still feeling the slight fuzz at the back of his mind. The door was closed, but he had no doubt that the guards stood just beyond it. It would seem that he didn't have much of a choice when it came to whether or not he wanted to continue.

"Am I allowed to ask what this mission pertains to?"

"If you pass my tests, then you will be given all the information you need, I assure you of that. However, until then, I'm afraid that I must keep those details under wraps," Estmar said, offering a warm smile.

Castien did not smile back.

"Now, if you wouldn't mind, I'd like to begin by asking you a few questions," Estmar said.

"Of course."

Estmar leaned forward, his wrinkled brow furrowing as he produced a piece of paper from the desk and began reading it. "Can you tell me about the events of the skirmish that you were involved in?"

"The one in The Highlands?" Castien asked.

Estmar nodded, smiling once again.

"Well," Castien started. His thoughts drifted back to that cold night many months ago. "The Frostfall that day had ended, and the camp was beginning to settle down for the evening, no different from any other night."

"And then?" Estmar prodded, lowering the paper slightly.

"I began to feel something strange in the air," Castien said, keeping his gaze forward. "I quickly recognized that our squadron was being influenced by a Whisperer who was trying to…" Castien trailed off. "It was almost like he was trying to force us to sleep."

"The Lullaby, also known as the Sleeping Curse. Yes, I am quite familiar with it," Estmar mumbled. "Please, continue."

"I called for our captain, told him that I was worried about an ambush," Castien said. "And he told me that we had nothing to worry about, and that I was imagining things."

"Because you would have no way of knowing if there was a Whisperer in the mountains that night, right?" Estmar tilted his head, his eyes not quite hostile. *No, just curious.*

"Right," Castien said. "The others didn't feel a thing."

"Yet you did," Estmar said. He stared into Castien's eyes as if searching for something. "If you wouldn't mind me asking, where did you learn to not only detect, but to *resist* the influence of Whisperers?"

"I didn't," Castien said plainly. He kept his face solid, forcing his heart rate to slow. "I didn't learn it from anywhere." Castien steeled himself, catching the slight change in Estmar's composure.

That was a lie, wasn't it?

"I'm not lying," Castien said firmly.

Estmar's eyes unfocused, then refocused on Castien once again. "Fascinating," he whispered. "Never have I seen one of the *Stormless* bear such remarkable abilities."

Castien snapped his gaze back to Estmar and glared. That was not a term he was particularly fond of.

"Now," Estmar continued, "I would like to try to plant some thoughts in your mind. Would that be alright?"

"Do I have a choice?"

Estmar laughed again. "You catch on quickly, don't you, Castien?" Estmar's withered lips cracked into a full-toothed grin.

Castien had to keep himself from rolling his eyes. He wasn't exactly in the mood for jokes. "Yes." He sighed, trying his very best to keep his composure. "You may do what you please."

"Very well," Estmar said. He lowered the paper once again, this time setting it on the table. Estmar let his hands rest before him and closed his eyes.

Castien called back to his training. He closed his eyes as well, falling back into the smoke and mirrors of his mind, steeling his thoughts in preparation of the battle ahead.

Can you hear me, Castien?

"Yes," Castien said, keeping his eyes closed.

Ah, interesting indeed. So far as I can tell your mind feels quite the same as the others I have infiltrated.

"Take a look around if you want. I have nothing to hide."

Precisely what I figured. However, I would actually prefer it if you tried to keep me from your thoughts.

"And why would that be?" Castien asked.

I simply want to see if you are truly as "special" as I have heard.

"Very well then," Castien said, keeping his eyes shut. He synced his pulse to his breathing once again. *Five beats in, six beats out, hold for three. Repeat,* he told himself.

Castien centered his thoughts, focusing on the synced rhythm of his respiration and heartbeat. His thoughts melted into picture. He unraveled them, slowly. One by one, he felt them release within his mind, his conscience coming undone as he continued focusing on his heartbeat. His breaths echoed in his thoughts, radiating through the endless caverns of emptiness.

The pulse focused upon itself, undulating and twisting in his mind's eye. Castien saw his shadow standing in a dark room with his hands raised above himself. He felt the beating of his heart as it swam alongside his breaths. He had power. This place within himself... it was unlike anything he would ever feel in the real world.

He unwrapped his thoughts, feeling a slight pull. It was as if something were altering them, if only slightly. He held his thoughts firmly in his phantom hands, continuing to count the synced inhale and exhale of his respiration and peeling the thoughts from his conscious mind. It was working. The tension in his face faded. His body began to sag. His eyes relaxed, now hanging open in the dim room.

And, finally, he let go.

Darkness enveloped him. The only sound was that of his own heartbeat, echoed by his timed breathing. Time passed slowly, and it wasn't until several minutes had gone by that Castien felt the pull dissipate.

He peeled his eyes open, finding Estmar grinning widely across the table. Castien smiled uncertainly, though he felt a strange sense of pride.

"I must admit, I am truly astonished." Estmar tossed his hands up. "You mean to tell me that you truly didn't feel a thing?"

"Not enough to constitute any sort of response, as you have seen." Castien smiled once again, this time the feeling of warmth and pride within him growing into full-fledged excitement.

"Well then," Estmar said, leaning back in his leather chair. "I have exhausted my trials it seems. You have passed. The King will be pleased." Estmar slipped the paper back into the desk.

"The King himself called for me?" His heart picked up, the steady drum in his mind increasing its pace. He felt a rising excitement in his veins, born of adrenaline.

"I told you that this mission was special, did I not?" Estmar raised a gray eyebrow, his face taking on a strange seriousness. "This afternoon our King was attacked by someone who claims to be from one of the Lost Sects."

"Wait," Castien said. "There were rumors of someone posing as a Blood Sorcerer roaming the city this morning."

"It seems that this person may not have been *posing* after all," Estmar said. "He threatened His Majesty, and fled the city before we could capture him."

"How in Niventia's Light could he have fled the city unnoticed?"

"Don't," Estmar said, raising a wrinkled hand. "I know. I am confused as well, but I promise you that all of your questions will be answered soon."

Castien settled into his chair, allowing his eyes to wander back to the painting of the Mistveil hanging on the wall. "The King is sending an expedition to follow the Blood Sorcerer and track down where, exactly, he came from," Estmar continued. "That is all I can tell you now—for it is all I know."

"An expedition?" Castien asked, tilting his head.

"Indeed," Estmar said. "He has already sent Commander Knyvet to pursue the Blood Sorcerer and keep track of his whereabouts. Tomorrow morning you are expected to report to the palace at the eighth bell. General Surge will meet you and the others assigned to your crew there. He will be leading your mission."

"General—" Castien gaped. His heart quickened once again. "General Surge?"

Estmar laughed. "He's not as cold as his reputation may have you believe, though, between you and me, he's not exactly the kindest man I've ever met either."

Castien slid back into his seat, eyes wide. He exhaled, his mind almost rejecting it. *General Surge...*

"The guards will escort you back to your barracks. Your presence is expected tomorrow, so don't be late." Estmar stood up.

Castien remained in his chair for a moment. It wasn't until Estmar opened the door that Castien came to.

"Well, come on then." Estmar said, waving Castien out the door.

Castien stumbled to his feet, his legs feeling unsteady. He passed the pair of guards who had been waiting outside. The room beyond seemed smaller now, somehow. Castien started forward, a heavy fog still smothering his thoughts.

"Oh, and Castien," Estmar called.

Castien turned, meeting those soft eyes once again.

Estmar tapped his head, smiling.

Castien frowned, then began to feel the slight tingle in his thoughts once again.

Estmar winked. *Good luck.*

CHAPTER THREE
THE SHADOW-SWIFT

Two years ago...

The cold mountain air was quiet this evening. Frozen winds howled through The Highlands, echoing across the countless peaks around him. There was a sort of silence tonight, a kind of silence that only exhibited itself on nights of bloodshed. A shame, truly.

Lucien had no intentions of killing these men, but the storms did not lie. A few weeks of distant kinship could do wonders to one's bloodthirst. Lucien had been following these soldiers for quite some time now, though it was only recently that he understood their purpose in venturing so close to his home.

A Silver Sun... Violet wings... Lucien shook his head slightly, pushing the thoughts away.

A half-dozen soldiers wandered the slopes of the mountain, aiding three scholars in the search for a secret door. They had spent nearly two months searching The Highlands, uncovering clue after clue. Their investigations had led them to this very mountain, a mere half-mile from Erydon.

The soldiers and scholars alike were unaware of Lucien's presence, just as they always had been. If they were to find him, they would likely assume him to be an Arvendi spy, and Lucien wouldn't blame them. The Arvendi had been sticking their nose in Freyfall's research for almost a decade now, trying to determine what it was that the Northern City found so fascinating about The Highlands.

The Silver Sun glowed solemnly overhead, emanating a soft white light. It was barely enough to see by, but Lucien's enhanced eyes allowed him to overcome this issue. His heightened vision was a gift of Izara's, as were all of his abilities. Unsurprisingly, it was these same powers that allowed him to follow the soldiers without being noticed.

At the present moment, Lucien was levitating above the mountain, watching the soldiers through the inky air of the Unbound, peering between Realms. Only Shadow-Swifts could Transcend to the Unbound—a hidden plane of reality that mirrored Auris. It was here that Lucien hid, watching the translucent shadows of the soldiers as they milled about. Lucien could still interact with the real world from the Unbound, meaning that, if he were touched, he would be discovered, hence why he opted to levitate rather than stand.

"I'm still not seeing anything," one of the soldiers said in Utryan. "Are you sure this is the right mountain?"

"Positive," another voice called back. "The writings all point to this location, it has to be here somewhere."

"Damn scholar," the soldier grumbled. He spoke softly enough that the other man—the scholar—had not heard.

"Tyrs," the scholar called, shouting the name of one of the other researchers. "Anything over there?"

Lucien shifted his gaze, allowing his body to drift through the shadowy skies of the Unbound toward the other scholar. He found him quickly, exploring another landing a few dozen feet below.

"Maybe," Tyrs shouted back. "There appears to be some sort of...

oh, I don't know." Tyrs trailed off. "Whatever it is, there's something down here. The stones aren't cut naturally."

The first scholar, along with the other soldiers who had been on the upper landing, made their way down to Tyrs.

Lucien watched curiously. Indeed, the stones were perhaps a bit too flat for something that was supposedly formed naturally. Strange how these academics picked up on things that Lucien and his kin had ignored for centuries.

One of the men shivered, though Lucien felt only warmth within his black Shadow-Sand armor. The man, who was a scholar judging by his uniform, was approaching a cleft in the face of the mountain. He seemed to take a few more steps, and then he *disappeared*.

Lucien advanced, dropping to the ground a few feet behind the soldiers.

The man reappeared—the third scholar of the nine-person crew —and started waving the others over. He was saying something in Utryan, but his words were too bent with excitement for Lucien to comprehend them with his minimal understanding of the language.

The six soldiers and two remaining scholars walked over to the man, who was eagerly motioning for them to follow.

Striding forward, Lucien kept pace. If they had looked back, they would have seen the snow parting to make footprints of a man they could not see. Blessedly, they kept their eyes forward.

Indeed, as Lucien neared the cleft, he found that it was not a cleft at all, but instead a *passage*. What had seemed to be nothing more than a cleft in the ice and rock was in fact the entrance to a small cavern.

Trailing the rear soldiers, he passed through the crack, entering the small chamber beyond. The soldiers and scholars stood quietly for a few seconds as Lucien searched for a hiding place.

"Light the torch," Tyrs said in the darkness.

Lucien backed into the corner nearest to the exit, nestling into the shadows of the small cavern. He raised his eyes as the torch was being lit, his enhanced sight uncovering something *remarkable*.

The spark caught flame, igniting the end of the wooden torch, revealing the secrets of the chamber.

A large stone door stood at the far end of the chamber, a soft arch lying in place of the upper-right corner. Hundreds of lines were carved into the wall, seeming to flow like rivers across the entire cavern. They twisted and turned relentlessly, passing by strange markings at every junction. Complex symbols were chiseled into the stone door. Runes. The Runed-Lines wove themselves all throughout the intricately carved door, each of them linking back to a distinct square symbol in the center of the construction.

Runes had been forgotten by mankind, though the power that they were imbued with persisted, even centuries after their creators had vanished. These Runes were square, meaning that they served as locks for the door.

"We found it," one of the scholars breathed. She stepped forward, dragging her gloved fingers along the delicate twists and curves of the Rune-Door. She paused at one of the smaller square Runes, staring at the symbols inside. "All of our work, everything that we have done…"

"It is all paying off," Tyrs said, tugging at his beard. He took the torch from the soldier, then approached the door.

"I can hardly believe it," the third scholar said. "We've been searching these damned mountains for months, and we're finally here."

"Yes," Tyrs said. "Though now it is simply a matter of getting inside."

"This is what we practiced for, isn't it?" the first scholar asked. "We've been picking our way into Runed-Lockboxes for years now. How could this be any different?"

One of the soldiers approached Lucien's corner, rubbing his eyes. His hands dropped to his waist, his fingers fiddling with his belt.

Don't do it, you damned fool, Lucien thought, willing for the man to turn back.

The soldier continued forward, seemingly preparing to relieve himself in the corner. He started whistling while the others talked, finishing the belt, unbuttoning his coat, and loosening his pants.

Lucien cursed him silently, readying his Shadow-Sand swords. If the soldier took any more steps forward, he would bump into Lucien. There would be no turning back if that happened. All Lucien could do was pray that he stopped.

The man paused, seemingly having trouble unbuttoning his pants.

Lucien let out a sigh of relief.

The soldier chuckled to himself, freed the button, and took that final step.

Lucien closed his eyes, feeling the man's left foot bump into Lucien's shin. He knew that he had not misread the winds. The scent of violence was in the air tonight after all.

"Well... shit," Lucien muttered.

The inky film that coated the world shattered as Lucien crashed back into Auris, phasing out of the Unbound.

"Arvendi spy!" the soldier screamed. His eyes went wide as full moons.

Lucien grunted, ripping his curved black blade across the man's chest. Lucien drove his other weapon—one that was shorter, and straighter, perhaps more akin to a dagger than a sword—through the same soldier's throat.

Blood poured out of the wounds, covering Lucien's pristine armor. The man fell to the ground, slumping across Lucien's now dark-red boots.

It didn't take long for the rest of the party to notice him.

"Spy!" someone shouted, but his words didn't matter, for anyone whose ears they could reach would be dead before the minute was out.

Lucien worked with surgical precision, weaving in between Auris and the Unbound as he danced through the chamber. He took one man in the chest, using his longsword to sever the head of another. Phasing into the Unbound, Lucien easily passed through the ax that one of the soldiers swung at him. Lucien dashed forward, moving with inhuman speed through the Unbound before phasing back to carve through the attacker's chest.

Lucien sensed the *whish* of a flying ax, and phased once again. The weapon passed *through* him as if he were nothing more than air. Lucien whipped back to reality, sliding toward the man and knocking him down with a swift blow to the stomach.

One of his Crystals emptied.

He was going to have to hurry. Phasing expended a *tremendous* amount of energy, and, if Lucien wasn't careful, he wasn't going to have enough power remaining to return to Erydon.

A scholar charged him from the left, wielding nothing more than a dagger.

Lucien plunged his longsword into her heart, killing her instantly. Blood showered him as he pulled the sword back.

Growling, Lucien hurled himself at the next man, not even bothering to phase. He expertly avoided the Utryan's ax, delivering a firm blow to the man's sternum while driving the other blade through his neck.

Sensing another blow from behind, Lucien ducked. The ax missed, and Lucien quickly stabbed the man in both knees. The soldier dropped to the ground, which allowed Lucien to finish him off with ease.

Lucien rolled to his feet, hurling his dagger at the falling corpse of an earlier victim. He impaled another writhing body, finishing one of his earlier targets off.

A cry of fury sounded amongst the screams of pain. Lucien whirled around, facing the final man—Tyrs—who was charging toward him. With both of his weapons lodged in the dying bodies of other men, Lucien was left unarmed... At least, that was what the soldier must've thought.

Calmly, Lucien raised his hands, pressing them together as he called upon his divine abilities. Just as the burly man was about to reach him, Lucien opened his fists.

Darkness exploded from Lucien's outstretched hands. It hit the scholar with a sickening crunch, shattering the man's bones and flinging him backward. He crashed into the far wall of the cavern and slumped to the ground, unmoving.

Lucien breathed heavily, allowing himself a moment to recover. To his horror he found himself *smiling*. His sentiments regarding violence had been subtly changing over the past few years... but smiling? Smiling felt wrong.

Either way, what's done was done. He had been left no choice. He had eventually been caught, and mistaken for an Arvendi spy—just as he had predicted. But he had what he needed. Not only was the party taken care of, but they had led Lucien to one of the most significant discoveries of the last century. Asteros would need to hear about this, whether Lucien wanted to tell him or not.

One could only imagine what was beyond that door. Knowledge that had been lost for over a millennium could finally be recovered. The scholars had been guided to this cave by clues—inscriptions left by the Ancient Stonemasters who had colonized these mountains. If the Stonemasters left clues to one of their hideouts, they had likely left clues to all of them.

It was not lost on Lucien how significant this discovery was. Whatever lay on the other side of that door would be felt all across Auris.

The Shadow-Swifts themselves had been searching for chambers like these for centuries, chasing ghosts and following rumors. They had assumed that the fabled Stonemaster Strongholds were nothing more than a myth. But tonight... Tonight, the Freyfallion scholars had found one, and they had led Lucien right to it.

CHAPTER FOUR
THE EXPEDITION

Castien Varic swung the pack over his shoulder. He crept quietly past the still-slumbering members of his new squadron. He almost woke them to bid his goodbyes, but he didn't bother. He had been transferred a few weeks before anyways. He wasn't particularly attached to these men.

Following his stunt in the Freyfallion skirmish, Castien had been promoted. And now he was being promoted *again*—well, not officially. He wasn't quite sure whether this was a promotion or not, but, given that General Surge would be leading the expedition, he was inclined to believe that this change of station was a good sign.

Raising a hand, he brushed aside his short, dirty-blond hair, fixing it neatly into place. He straightened the orange, armored vest he wore. It was lightweight enough so that he would be able to travel in it without tiring himself out. The pack he carried contained several days' worth of stormroot rations as well as a few canisters of water.

Castien turned, satisfied with his appearance, and continued his quiet walk through the barrack. The neatly arranged bunks made for somewhat of a maze, which took him several minutes to navigate quietly.

He stopped by the door, walking along the engraved wooden slab that held up a series of hooks. A crooked "C" was carved into the space above one of them. Castien smiled to himself, recalling fondly the day he had scratched his initial into the wood. It was an old Arvendi tradition, for the Stormless Corps at least. He reached for the hook, taking off his Ghost-wood bow and strapping it over his pack along with the quiver of arrows.

The dark bow was a little dirty, but Castien found it beautiful nonetheless. It had been a gift to him from his mother, upon his departure to join Arvendon's ranks. At least, that was what he told people.

Castien carried no Crystals, and possessed no divine abilities. None of the Stormless did. Not that it mattered, given their separation from the Summoner's Legion. This expedition would put him in far more danger than his six years in the Stormless Corps had. Summoners traditionally led the more important missions, while the Stormless were assigned to patrols and small skirmishes. But if he was going to be with General Surge on this mission... he would be right on the front lines of whatever they were facing.

He peeled open the door, greeting the cool, damp air of the Mistveil. Castien smiled, breathing in the wet fog. Mistveils were among the more pleasant Tempests. They were fairly mild, with the only drawback to their ubiquitous mists being the reduced visibility.

People milled about Arvendon's streets already, despite the early hour. Castien started the walk to the palace, walking cautiously on the slick cobblestone roads to avoid falling. Buildings stretched out in blocks around him, mostly made of red brick or stone.

The roofs were either flat or tiled, constructed from a mixture of dusty-orange rocks. Occasionally he passed a mansion made of white marble—built after the style of the palace—yet Castien snorted at these.

He took note of the gray Crystals hanging in open fishnet bags from the high gates of the mansions. Summoning Crystals were somewhat expensive, hence why Castien found the fact that they were used in simple lighting fixtures in some of these homes frivolous. The gray Crystals soaked up the mists eagerly. They were even beginning to take on a dull glow despite how early it was.

Peddlers shouted their wares as Castien neared the market district. He ignored them. On nearly every corner merchants were drawing out their posts to full length and raising their signs. Mistveils were tame enough that banners wouldn't be destroyed by any strong winds or cataclysmic lightning.

Castien hurried his pace just a bit as the clocktower came into view. It was nearly eight o'clock, and he needed to be on time. The white stone of the clocktower came alight, cast in the dull golden glow of the rising sun as its rays fought through the mists. The Mistveil would persist through most of the day until all its energy was either soaked up by Crystals or returned to the sky. By dusk the skies would be clear once again, allowing for a peaceful night before a new Tempest formed tomorrow.

Castien listened to the distant crash of the waves, syncing his breathing to the ocean's melody.

Before long, he found himself at the base of the palace hill. The palace sat at the top of a fairly steep incline, with a zigzagging path that led up the hill toward it. It overlooked the rest of Arvendon, which, Castien supposed, not only made for a wonderful view, but also a strategic advantage.

He passed several guards—as well as a few nobles—on the way up, but they ignored him. He was used to it. The Stormless were often ignored. By the time he reached the top of the hill, his legs had started to ache. *Zephyr's Watch, I hope we're not going to be walking this whole way,* Castien thought as he wandered around the summit.

Summerglass Palace loomed over him, the white marble sparkling despite the heavy fog. Several Whisperers walked about, each paired with a Scorcher. Castien shook his head, then continued wandering toward the palace. *Surely someone will show me where to go, right?*

"Out of the way, Stormless," someone said. A woman wearing orange armor marched by. She walked gracefully despite the mountain of weapons she carried in her arms.

"Pardon me, ma'am," Castien muttered, stepping aside.

The short woman glared at him. Her eyes were a curious dark brown, and her deep tan skin marked her as Sucharan.

Castien frowned. *What is a Sucharan Scorcher doing here?* Castien looked around. Finding no other help, he figured that he would follow her. From the looks of it, she was important. At the very least, she would know where this "Expedition" was meeting.

The clocktower bell rang through the fog, again and again until it had rung eight times. Castien cursed, then hurried after the woman.

She was walking toward the Eastern Wing of the palace, though she kept to the outskirts. She turned a corner, wrapping around one of the outer spires of Summerglass.

"Uh, excuse me," Castien called, quickening to a run as the slick stone turned to soft grass. "Ma'am!" Castien shouted, turning the corner. He spotted a faint impression of an orange cloak a couple yards ahead. "Excuse me!" Castien shouted once again. A couple of guards turned to him, but quickly looked away. He was Stormless. They didn't need to pay him any mind. Finally, the woman turned around.

"Are you talking to me?" she asked, taking a few steps back toward Castien.

"Uh," Castien stuttered. "Yes?"

The woman rolled her eyes.

"I was wondering if you could help me find something."

She sighed. "Alright. Out with it."

"I'm looking for General Surge, I've been summoned for an expedition of sorts," Castien explained, careful to keep from sharing too many details.

The woman's eyes widened. "You're Castien, aren't you?" the

woman asked. Castien nodded. "Tarathiel's Stones, you're even worse than we thought."

What? Castien frowned.

She turned around, and started walking again, then stopped after a few feet, turning back to Castien. "Well, come along then," she said, motioning with her still-full hands.

Castien jumped, breaking into a slight run to catch up to her. "How do you know who I am?"

"I'm going with you and the General," the woman said. "I've heard about you. It's not every day that a Stormless gets sent on a mission as important as this one."

"You're telling me," Castien muttered. He stole another glance at the woman's amber skin, finding himself wondering why a Sucharan was being sent with them on such a mission.

"Saevi Embrore, by the way," the woman said, nodding to the side.

Castien turned. "What?"

"It's my name," the woman said, shaking her head. "You know, even though you're Stormless, I would've expected that the King would've selected someone who was at least a little brighter than a divebrisk."

"Sorry," Castien said, lowering his head.

Saevi looked at him again. "It was a joke, Castien," she said, smiling slightly.

"Oh."

They continued walking in silence, then rounded another massive white-marble spire.

"You don't talk much, do you?" Saevi asked after a moment.

"Eh, I'm usually a *little* better," Castien explained. "Just... overwhelmed this morning, I guess."

"Hmm," Saevi said. "Understandable, I suppose."

"So do you know what exactly we're going to be doing?" Castien asked, quickly diverting the subject.

"I assume I know as little as you," Saevi said, the weapons in her hands clinking against one another. "The King himself is supposed to address all of us before we leave. I'm hoping that he'll tell us a little more then."

Castien heard voices up ahead as they rounded yet another shadow of a towering pillar.

"I know he was told to come here, but he's clearly *not* here, is he?" a low voice said.

"Did anyone tell him that we were gathering behind the castle?" another voice asked.

"I don't know what Estmar told him, but he should be here. We can't get started without him," the other voice responded.

"Relax, everyone," Saevi called through the mists. "I've found our lost Stormless."

The mists began to clear slightly as the group came into focus. Castien instantly recognized the massive, hulking figure in red and gold: Elias Surge, Voltarian, Master Summoner, and General of Arvendon's Summoner Legion.

"Ah," Surge said, stepping forward. A collection of bright white Voltarian Crystals rattled with electricity at his waist. His hair was grayer than Castien would've expected. Yet, despite the man's apparent age, he didn't appear to have been weakened by time. He stood easily over six feet tall and had muscles that made Castien's own arms look like twigs. Surge smiled deeply, his stubble of a beard twisting around his crooked teeth and cracked lips. A long scar ran down the side of his face, and his short hair was nearly completely shaven. Surge extended a huge hand.

Castien took Surge's hand and found himself met with a very strong grip. He shook weakly.

Another man stepped forward, making to shake with Castien. The man's skin looked strange... almost scaled.

"I'm Luka Delmorian," the man said. His bald head had a sort of dry, tattered look to it. *Curious.* "Special agent of King Avenos," Luka said, smiling. His lips were cracked and reptilian as well. Patches of skin here and there on his face were covered in scaled flesh. Castien recognized these features as being those of a Cryostalker—a manipulator of ice.

"I'm Castien." His voice sounded weak even to his own ears.

Luka smiled warmly, despite the icy Crystals that hung at the waist of his brown-red vest. A long, slightly curved blade with a narrow hilt sat in its sheath beside the Crystals. *An unusual blade,* Castien thought.

"Now then," another voice said as someone approached the group. A gray robe became clear through the mist, and a Whisperer approached. This man seemed younger than most of the Whisperers Castien had seen, though his face was beginning to crease with wrinkles in a few places. "If everyone's here, I suppose that we can get started, correct?"

"Castien, I would like you to meet my new least favorite person: Arthion Aldrich, Whisperer and servant to the King." Surge raised one of his massive hands and motioned to the Whisperer as he approached.

"Oh hush, General," Arthion said, turning toward Castien. "Surge is just upset because he knows that I'm the only one honest enough to report *him* to the King." Arthion smiled, extending a gloved hand to Castien.

Castien shook it, meeting the warm brown eyes beneath the hood of Arthion's gray cloak.

Saevi abruptly dropped the weapons, causing a terrible clanging noise as they fell atop one another. "I'm done carrying these things," she announced. "Pick whatever you want and let's get moving. The King is waiting." She knelt down and picked up a twisted, metal pike —a Sunspear—the kind of weapon carried by Arvendon's guards. Castien recalled learning that the gold and silver spears conducted heat without burning up themselves, thus making them the perfect weapons for Scorchers.

Arthion reached down to the small pile of sheathed blades and picked out a pair of daggers, holding them clumsily. Given that he was a Whisperer, he had likely never trained with common blades.

Castien looked to Surge, noticing the large greatsword hanging on his back. He turned to Luka, eyeing his sword once again.

"Well, go ahead and pick something," Surge said, motioning with his hands. "You'll need more than just a bow if we're heading into The Wastelands."

"Right," Castien said, dropping to his knees and scanning the small collection of weapons. He picked out a simple sword and a dagger without thinking, little things that wouldn't add too much weight.

"Good, we mustn't keep the King waiting," Surge said, waving Castien forward. They strode through the mists as a group, nearing the back side of the palace once again, until they came to a large wall.

Doors opened. Castien looked up, finding a small balcony hanging off from the castle. A man in voluminous vermillion robes walked out. There was a certain... regal air to him. *The King,* Castien realized. He had never been this close to the man, not in his entire life.

"Welcome," the King said. Surge dropped to one knee, as did the others. Castien followed suit, only a little late. "You may rise," the King boomed.

His voice, Castien thought. *It's so... strong.*

"Your Majesty, let me start by saying that we are honored that you have selected us for this expedition," Saevi said, dropping to one knee once again.

"She doesn't speak for all of us," Surge interrupted. "I, for one, was enjoying my leave."

Castien gaped. He was talking to *the King...* like *that?* Yet, to Castien's surprise, the King simply chuckled.

"As you all know," the King continued, pacing around on the small balcony which hung perhaps ten feet above the ground. "Our palace was infiltrated by a Blood Sorcerer yesterday. He not only threatened our kingdom, but he *showed* us his power." The group remained silent. "I am sure you wonder what I hope to accomplish with this expedition, as well as why there is a Stormless among you," the King said, his long brown hair dusting his shoulders with each turn. "And the answer is simple: I wish to know *who* this Blood Sorcerer is, and *how* he was able to create such a convincing illusion."

"Illusion?" Luka asked, raising his head.

"Illusion." The King nodded. "The Blood Sorcerers could not have truly returned—that would be impossible—thus, I am inclined to believe that there is another explanation for the events of yesterday afternoon." The King paused. "I believe that what my guards and I saw yesterday was a trick, of sorts. In fact, I believe that none of it happened at all."

"Whisperers have long been one of the most mysterious Sects— perhaps even the most secretive, save for the Shadow-Swifts," the King continued. "I theorize that a Whisperer, or a group of Whisperers, infiltrated the palace and directly planted memories into our minds, making us recall events that never happened."

"With all due respect, your Majesty." Arthion stepped forward. "Planting memories is not something that we are capable of."

"If you are speaking in terms of ordinary Whisperers like yourself, you are correct," the King said. "However, the most likely explanation for yesterday's events seems to be that the Whisperers of some other nation were able to find a way to do just that. Hence, the reason you have a Stormless with you. I take it you have all met Castien?"

The others nodded.

"Castien has proven himself to be resistant to the abilities of the Whisperers, and therefore I have deemed him worthy of accompanying you on this expedition." The King's eyes settled on him.

"Thank you, your Majesty," Castien squeaked, falling to one knee again. He gathered as much dignity as he could muster, and rose once again, his legs trembling.

"Your orders are to follow this 'Blood Sorcerer' and find where he came from," the King said. "Once you do that, I give you permission to eliminate him, if you deem it necessary. I have sent Commander

Knyvet ahead to mark the trail for you. Set out along the eastern highway and follow the markings he left behind. You'll know them when you see them."

Surge stepped forward. "Your Majesty, if you don't mind me asking, why are you sending not only me and Specialist Delmorian on this expedition, but Commander Knyvet as well? Why send three Master Summoners?"

The King straightened his back again and spoke. "If my theory is correct, then you will be facing one of the strongest Summoners the world has ever seen. And if my theory is incorrect... then you will be facing a Summoner from a Sect that has been extinct for the better part of a thousand years," the King said. "I am erring on the side of caution, and I think you would be wise to do so as well."

"Understood." Surge nodded.

"Well then," the King said. Life poured back into his voice. "You have no time to lose. Commander Knyvet is already several miles ahead of you, and your team must not fall too far behind."

"We will not disappoint you, sir," Luka said, bowing.

"I do not think that you will." The King's eyes rested on Castien. "Make sure to take care of that one. And good luck."

Castien forced himself to stay focused as Surge led the small group away from the balcony. Fear crept into his muscles, plaguing them with instability and tiredness, but he could not surrender to nervousness now. This was the chance he had been waiting for. Finally, after nearly six years in the Stormless Corps, Castien had a chance to truly make a name for himself. If he was lucky, he might even be able to go home.

CHAPTER FIVE

THE PRINCE

Faelyn Titansworn glided across the marble dance floor of Summerglass Palace, searching for an excuse to get another slice of pie. He brushed past pair after pair of spinning nobles, barely dodging the dancing couples as he slithered through the crowd. Someone bumped into him, slightly crinkling the gold ruffles of his vermillion vest. He grimaced, but bit his tongue. He slipped past another pair, narrowly avoiding them as they carried out their well-practiced routine.

Faelyn snorted, turning back toward the dessert table at the far end of the ballroom. He ran a hand through his long golden hair, scanning the dance floor.

His father sat atop his throne at the head of the room, his bellowing laughter reaching even Faelyn's distant ears.

Faelyn shook his head. Just yesterday his father was practically begging for his life before an Ancient Summoner, and now he was hosting a ball as though nothing had happened.

Of course, that was the intention. Faelyn's father had made it exceedingly clear that no one was to so much as *mention* the events of yesterday afternoon. An incident like that would strike fear into the hearts of the Arvendi, and fear... fear was dangerous. Not to mention that there were rumored to be Celesian or possibly Freyfallion spies in Arvendon's royal court, and keeping news of the confrontation as far away from them as possible was vital to Faelyn's family's safety.

Which was why Faelyn was understandably surprised when someone whispered, "It's fascinating how your father's men are able to act like there's nothing wrong, isn't it?"

Faelyn whirled, flames sparking to life between his fingers. He relaxed. It was only Reluraun. He silenced the flames, ashes sprinkling to the floor like falling snow.

"Rel," Faelyn said. "You can't joke about that."

"Oh, simmer down, my prince. You know that I understand just as well as you how vital it is that we keep our secret safe," Reluraun said a little too loudly.

Faelyn reached out, grabbed the slender boy by the wrist, and pulled him from the dance floor.

"Hey!" Reluraun said, stumbling after Faelyn. "You almost made me spill my drink!"

"Of course," Faelyn muttered, glancing at the crystal glass in Reluraun's hand. Faelyn shook his head, realizing now why Reluraun had been so careless in his mentioning of the Blood Sorcerer.

They now stood by the dessert table, which had been Faelyn's intended destination from the start anyway. Faelyn leaned down, picking up a berry-filled pastry. He took a bite. Sweet flavors exploded in his mouth with a satisfying *pop* as the berries broke.

He and Reluraun were only a few years apart, and they were both set to inherit a position in Arvendon's royal court, for better or worse. Reluraun was a Cloudwalker, like his father Captain Elric Knyvet. Faelyn looked around, searching for Elric in the crowd, though he could not find him.

"Are you sure?" someone said, their voice hushed, as they passed by. "Who told you that?"

Faelyn's eyes snapped to the red-cloaked noble. He observed as the man walked by, whispering to another noble.

"The whole palace is denying it," the other noble said. "No one knows for sure what happened."

Faelyn clenched his teeth. He began scanning the room. His father wouldn't be able to hide news of the Blood Sorcerer's attack from the public—not for long, at least.

"Looking for a lovely lady to bed this evening, are you?" Reluraun guessed.

"Some of us have bigger things to worry about," Faelyn grumbled. The Blood Sorcerer had deeply disturbed his father. It had been over a day now, and he had yet to hear his father even start discussing options.

Reluraun put his long, thin arm around Faelyn, taking another bite of the pastry as the nobles spun in mesmerizingly perfect routines across the dance floor. A small orchestra sat on the opposite side of the ballroom, playing an infectiously upbeat melody.

"You think I'm not worried about the threat?" Reluraun asked, tilting his head to the side, trying to meet Faelyn's gaze.

Faelyn rolled his eyes, Reluraun was taller than him, yes, but he didn't need to be *that* dramatic about the way he leaned down.

"Well, given what you carry in your right hand, I'd argue that you aren't worried about much of anything right now," Faelyn said, glancing at the dark gray liquid in the glass Reluraun held.

Reluraun lifted the glass between himself and the massive Scorcher-Crystal-chandelier hanging overhead.

"Why do you think I'm drinking tonight?" Reluraun asked, his long face turning solemn.

"Because you're an aspiring alcoholic?"

"Because I wouldn't be able to do all of *this* tonight without something to take the edge off, you know?" Reluraun said, lowering the glass and turning back to Faelyn. "The dancing, the flirting, the gossip, the politics... To say that it's challenging when one is already stressed is an understatement."

"What do you have to be stressed about?" Faelyn asked. "It's not like your family has to deal with all of this mess."

"You're not the one whose father is out there right now, following the very man who threatened our city," Reluraun shot back.

Faelyn frowned; he scanned the room again. "What do you mean?" Faelyn asked, his gaze settling on the King.

His father bellowed another laugh. His booming chuckle echoed between the white-marble pillars of the ballroom.

Reluraun raised an eyebrow. "I would've thought the King would've told you."

"Told me what?"

"The King sent my father to follow the Blood Sorcerer," Reluraun said, his brow furrowing. "Not more than an hour after he departed, your father ordered a Cloudwalker to pursue him from a distance, not with the purpose of interacting with him, but to find out where he was going." Reluraun paused. "My father—being that he is the most powerful of our Cloudwalkers—decided to volunteer himself for the mission," Reluraun finished. "Did he seriously not tell you about this?"

"No," Faelyn said, turning back to his father. "No, he didn't."

Reluraun shrugged, reaching down with his free hand and taking one of the pastries from the glass platter.

Faelyn shifted his gaze to the shadows of the ballroom, where white-marble pillars lined the walls. Shadows moved there. Many were servants, though some were undoubtedly his father's Whisperers. There were more of them tonight.

"How long is Elric supposed to be gone?"

"However long it takes for him to track down Velarus's hideout," Reluraun said, taking another sip of the gray wine. "I wouldn't be surprised if it takes a few weeks, especially given that my father has to mark his trail."

"For what purpose?" Faelyn asked, feeling his face heat up. He glanced at his father, who was cackling heartily once again. *How much have you kept from me?* Faelyn wondered.

"I'm not sure," Reluraun admitted. "I overheard something about the King sending an expedition to follow Velarus and confront him, though I can't be certain. Personally, I think that—"

Faelyn didn't hear the rest. He was already storming through the ballroom, marching toward his father.

"Hey!" Reluraun exclaimed, running after him. "What are you doing?"

"It seems that I'm being left out of the loop," Faelyn simmered. "I clearly haven't been told *nearly* as much as you have, and I'm the one who's going to be taking the throne in a few years' time."

Reluraun fell silent as they approached the upper landing at the head of the ballroom. The King sat in the middle, of course, positioned atop his extravagant throne, which was decorated with Scorcher Crystals.

"Good luck," Reluraun muttered, stopping as Faelyn climbed the four steps up to the dining area. A red carpet covered the white-marble floor here, and it took Faelyn several minutes to weave in and out of the countless tables that dotted the upper landing before he reached the King's section. There had to be at least forty people seated at these tables, all of whom watched his father.

That's going to be you soon, Faelyn, his mother's voice rang through his head. Her lessons had been more effective than any Whisperer when it came to hijacking his mind, before she left, anyway. Faelyn shook the thought away, looping around the table.

"And so I said, 'Why would I surrender? I'm the one with the Crystals!'" His father boomed a laugh, the sound echoing through the massive chamber as the others at the table joined him in laughter.

Faelyn had heard the story about a thousand times by now, but, due to the weekly rotation that determined who had the "blessing" of sitting with the King, it was new to the ears of the nobles who sat here tonight.

"Father," Faelyn whispered, running another hand through his long golden hair as he slipped behind his father's throne.

The King did not react.

"Father!" Faelyn whispered, a bit louder this time.

The King looked over at him, his face softening as he met Faelyn's eyes. "Excuse me for just a moment, my friends," the King said, smiling widely. "My *son* wishes to speak to me." He almost sounded proud. He turned away from the table, stepping down from his throne and into its shadow before a heavy frown came over his face. "I told you that you were not to interrupt me while I am dining with the nobles."

"Did you send Elric after the Blood Sorcerer?" Faelyn asked, ignoring his father's words.

The King's face twitched slightly, then his brow furrowed as he fell into thought. He pulled Faelyn aside, distancing them from the crowded table.

"I should've known that Knyvet boy would say something to you," his father said, shaking his head.

"I would've found out eventually anyway," Faelyn said. "Why didn't you tell me about that? Just last week you were saying that you would like me to get more involved in the politics of the royal court."

"This is not merely politics, my boy," his father hissed. "The arrival of a Blood Sorcerer is not just another common occurrence in the world of Arvendon's court. I am not sure what any of this means, but I have a feeling that it could be the start of something *very* significant."

"Then why leave me out of your decisions?"

"Because I don't know where this is going," his father said. His brown eyes burned brightly despite the darkness. Flames sparked at his fingertips as he spoke. "I don't know where this is going," he repeated. "And, if something happens, I want you to be as far away from the situation as possible."

"Dad," Faelyn said, raising a hand.

The flames on his father's fingers faded.

"You can't keep me away from this sort of thing for much longer. You realize that, don't you? We agreed that you were going to pass the crown to me in *six years*. That's not that far away."

"Forgive me for saying so, Faelyn, but your twenty-first birthday seems *very* far away at the moment, especially given that I was only given six *weeks* by that damned Blood Sorcerer," his father growled.

Faelyn sighed, allowing his ears to drift to the steady beat of the orchestra, letting silence fall between him and his father.

"Come on now. Be a man," his father rumbled, meeting Faelyn's eyes once again. "I understand that you probably feel 'left out' and everything, but this is *real*. I can't afford to let you get mixed up in all of this, even if your *feelings* are hurt."

"I don't feel left out, father," Faelyn said, his eyes falling to his father's orange armor. "I'm just concerned about the fact that we were threatened by a man that should not exist. Not to mention that we may've already sent one of our best Summoners to his death as a result."

The King took a deep breath. "Elric is one of the most powerful Cloudwalkers on Auris. He will be fine," his father said. "Besides, his purpose is to serve us, and that is exactly what he is doing. What is the point of putting together such a formidable force of Summoners if we are never going to put them to use?"

"I..." Faelyn trailed off. "I don't know. Something just feels *off* about all of this."

"You're telling me." The King shook his head. "Trust me, this is part of what being a leader is all about: being able to make decisions when everyone else is too scared or shocked to do anything," his father said. "These people rely on me, and soon they will rely on you too. They need us to show them strength and confidence. They need to be able to trust us to do what is right even when they don't trust themselves." He paused. "I know that it may seem intimidating right now," his father continued. "But trust me when I say you will be the greatest king Arvendon has ever seen." His father grinned.

Faelyn looked away.

His father laughed gently. "And, if you're not, well, I won't be around to scold you, will I?"

Faelyn smiled a little.

His father laid a warm hand on his shoulder, his hearty smile turning into another full-bellied laugh. "Run along now, boy," his father said, patting him on the back. "I will ensure that our city, and our family, stays safe."

Faelyn smiled one last time, turning away from the royal table as his father sat down in his extravagant throne once again. Faelyn started through the impossible maze of chair legs and tables, aiming for the dance floor once again as the orchestra started playing a particularly upbeat tune.

His father was right. What was the point of gathering and training Etherus's greatest Summoners if not to put them to use when the time came? Besides, Faelyn trusted his father. Maybe it didn't matter if he was kept in the loop or not, maybe he should stay out of this—as he was instructed to—and just take this time to enjoy himself.

Not to mention that it was the start of the Gold-White Harvest, meaning that the next two weeks would be filled with festivals and parties ending with a massive celebration on the Solstice. Perhaps Faelyn's father was on to something... He still had six years before his ascension; he should just enjoy himself.

CHAPTER SIX
ERYDON

Lucien Shade slowed to a stop before the jagged summit of Telenaris, one of the most remote peaks of The Highlands. He found the small nook in its rocky slopes, using his umbrakinesis to propel himself forward. He slipped into the opening, finally safe from the tyrannical fury of the Frostfall outside.

Phasing out of the Unbound, Lucien jumped through the passage, landing in one of the back hallways of Erydon: The Hidden Fortress of the Shadow-Swifts. The walls of black rock were carved by Ancient Stonemasters before their Sect had gone extinct. Even Erydon's entrances were sealed by Runes conjured by the Rune-Writers themselves, before they *too* died out.

Runes like the ones that guard the door I just discovered, Lucien thought. He strode forward quietly, his Shadow-Sand armor softening his footsteps.

Shadow-Sand was native to the Unbound, and served as the primary resource for the weapons and armor of the Shadow-Swifts. The sand could be melted and then hardened into metal, which was then able to shift with its owner back and forth between Auris and the Unbound, allowing Shadow-Swifts to unlock their full potential as Summoners. Lucien entered the grand atrium, which was empty at the moment. He breezed past the complicated carvings that decorated the walls.

The inscriptions apparently told the legends of the Ancient Shadow-Swifts—warriors beyond even the most powerful modern Summoners—though Lucien had never taken the time to read them himself. They painted the walls all throughout the chamber, even reaching the massive dome-like ceiling of the room. Lucien remembered when Asteros had first taken to transcribing them. The poor fool had spent weeks hovering around the atrium only to realize that Haldir had already deciphered them decades ago... before Haldir had passed, of course.

Whispers in the wind... A flash of light... Lucien grimaced, pausing. The thoughts vanished as quickly as they had come, disappearing like stars at dawn.

Lucien passed through the large room and moved throughout the hidden fortress in search of Asteros, who would be awaiting his return.

Various Crystals hung in place of Incendiary-powered torches throughout the caverns. Their illumination was much more permanent than that of the barbaric flames used in the rest of the world. Although Lucien supposed that the civilizations of Auris knew very little of the nature of their world in comparison to the Shadow-Swifts, which made their simplistic practices seem somewhat appropriate.

Lucien strode through the curved passages of Erydon, wearing the blood of his recent slaughter as if it were a medal. Asteros would not appreciate it, but, then again, that was the point. He followed another turn of the passage, seeking out Asteros's personal library. The damned fool spent more time in there than he did out in the real world, lost in the words of ancient philosophers who seemed to have a strange obsession with being unintelligibly cryptic in their ramblings.

"Lucien," a voice said.

He stopped, a devilish smirk spreading across his face as he turned his head slightly. A shadow waited behind him, apparently having observed his return. Sometimes, Lucien forgot how perceptive the boy had become.

"Hello, Asteros." Lucien bowed, swiveling around to face his master.

Asteros Silverglade floated toward him, carried by the phantom limbs of his umbrakinesis.

"I was hoping to find you in the library," Lucien said. "But it seems that *you* have found *me* instead."

Asteros's gaze lingered, a flicker of recognition lighting in his eyes. "You found something, didn't you?" Asteros asked.

"I did." Lucien bowed once again, showcasing his bloodied armor to his master.

"The Freyfallion scholars... I take it you found what they were after?" The boy appeared young, with his remarkably sharp features and jet-black hair, but that was nothing beyond the result of the near-constant draining of Shadow-Swift Crystals. He was perhaps in his fiftieth year now, though he was still not even half Lucien's age.

"In a sense," Lucien said, once again flashing a grin.

"Why the smirk?" Asteros asked, tilting his head. "And why the... blood?" Asteros lowered his gaze to Lucien's armor, the stench no doubt drawing his attention.

"Do you really have to ask me that?" Lucien asked, raising an eyebrow.

Asteros stepped back, his face neutral. "I hope you had good reason to kill them," Asteros said softly. "The loss of high-value researchers like that will not simply go unnoticed by Freyfall's King."

"Who said we were going to claim responsibility?"

"Who said we would have to?" Asteros paused. "I don't suppose you're going to tell me what you found? Or what *they* found—I assume."

"See," Lucien started. He began pacing through the narrow hallway. "I could tell you. Or I could *not* tell you."

"Now is not the time to play games, Lucien," Asteros growled. "You and I both know that Freyfall's researchers are venturing deeper and deeper into these mountains with each passing day. If you know something, you owe it to our order to tell me."

Lucien waited. He knew Asteros hated when he did this. But, then again, that was part of the game they played—always locked in a delicate dance of verbal jabs and calculated political moves against each other.

"Why do you hesitate?" Asteros hissed. "I act only in the best interest of our clan, withholding information from me serves no one, not even yourself."

"That is where you are wrong, Asteros." Lucien smiled. "When I know things that you do not, that gives me power. And you know how I feel about *power*..."

"Is that what this is?" Asteros advanced. "It's *over*. Haldir is gone. I am your master now. Your foolish games won't change that."

"Not even if the very thing that I've discovered comes from before the Vanishing?"

Asteros froze.

Lucien narrowed his eyes. *I have you now.* Lucien continued pacing around Asteros, watching the boy process his words.

"They found one of the chambers, didn't they?" Asteros started. "That's what they were looking for: The Ancient Stonemaster Sanctuaries of The Highlands." Asteros trailed off. "And they found one."

Lucien nodded.

"Where?" Asteros demanded.

"Give me one good reason why I should tell you." Lucien crooned. "All I would be doing is giving up my lead."

Asteros fell silent for several moments.

"Oh, this is a delight," Asteros said. "Beautifully ironic too, might I add."

"What is?" Lucien stepped forward. "What are you talking about?"

"My inheritance, of course," Asteros said. He advanced. "You followed the scholars to the door, and presumably killed them, but you couldn't get inside, could you?" Asteros raised an eyebrow. "Your lead means nothing because you don't have the means to open the door you've found. Unlike..."

"What? You?" Lucien snorted. "Please, spare me the bullshit. You're just as helpless as me when it comes to unlocking the Runes."

"And what if I said that you were incorrect?" Asteros turned.

Lucien frowned. Asteros's parents were killed before he became a Shadow-Swift, meaning that whatever inheritance he was referring to wasn't left by them, it was left by—

"Haldir," Lucien said. "Haldir left you with something, didn't he?"

"A key," Asteros said. "He created a device that was capable of opening Rune-Locks. I don't know how he made it, but, when he passed, he bequeathed it to me."

"Giving you a way to open the door," Lucien finished.

"You and I seem to be at a bit of an impasse, my friend," Asteros preened. "You know the location of the door. Oh! But you can't get inside. Whereas I have a way in, but..." Asteros trailed off.

Lucien considered it. This could be an opportunity to gain Asteros's favor. Not only that, but it presented a means to reconcile, finally putting an end to their petty rivalry. On the other hand, he still held a *slight* advantage, and he would be foolish not to make use of that.

"Fine," Lucien said. "On one condition: We do this on *my* terms, and whatever we find is mine to make use of."

"The two of us will decide *together* what is to become of our findings," Asteros countered. "We will work alongside each other, for once."

"I find it amusing that you think I would trust you."

"I have given you no reason to be mistrustful of me," Asteros said firmly. "It is you who I am worried about." Asteros paused. "Either way, I fear more Freyfallion scholars will begin venturing into our lands before long. We would be wise to open the door sooner rather than later."

"Tomorrow night," Lucien said. "Let us meet in the grand atrium. We will go then."

"So it is." Asteros turned away, starting down the hall. His footsteps echoed through the corridor, signaling the end of the conversation.

Lucien began walking in the opposite direction, aiming for his rooms. While their encounter had yielded unexpected results, it had given him a path forward. Working alongside Asteros would be unusual; they hadn't worked together since Haldir had passed.

"Oh, and Lucien," Asteros called.

Lucien spun, facing the young leader.

"Shalheira will be coming with us," Asteros said.

Lucien started. *"What?"* Lucien advanced.

"She is well versed in the Ancient tongue; we need her there."

"And what of Keries, Malik, and Lyseria? I don't suppose you'll be wanting to bring them as well?" Lucien snorted.

"No," Asteros said calmly. "Just Shalheira." Asteros levied his gaze. "She could be valuable to us, Lucien. Only you and I will have a say in how we move forward, but I want her there nonetheless."

"Fine," Lucien growled. "But if she gets in the way—"

"Don't bother," Asteros cut him off. "She won't."

Lucien grumbled but nodded anyway. There was no point in arguing with him on this. Asteros and Shalheira were close allies. He wasn't concerned about Shalheira's competence, quite the opposite, actually. She was cunning, that was what threatened him.

Shadows... A Silver Sun...

Still, however, Lucien found himself with a unique opportunity to finally claim his rightful place in this clan. If he acted carefully, he might find himself not only in control of Erydon, but also with more power than ever before.

Keries Nightbloom sat atop the ridges of Telenaris. He did not think. He observed. Here, above the raging Frostfall below, it was quiet. It was peaceful. The stars were stunning. Nebulas of color and light were laid out in undulating waves. Constellations of distant suns drew pictures in the sky, populating the vast planes of the heavens above.

A slight breeze gusted over the mountaintops. Strange, how Tempests of fury battled endlessly below the clouds, while above them... There was only silence.

Keries sat upon a jagged segment of rocks, staring into the moonlight above, the eerily peaceful glows enthralling everything that dared rise above the clouds. The twin moons of Lotius and Oria shined brightly this evening—Lotius with her pale gray color and Oria with her turquoise hues. He rubbed his short, graying beard, his long brown hair wavering slightly in the face of another breeze.

Silence. It was beautiful—the most beautiful of life's sounds. Silence meant solitude. And solitude meant peace. When one was alone, there was no war. There was no fighting. There was no *killing*.

Yet, the second he passed below those clouds, he knew that he would be forced to raise his blade once again. The sickness would take him again, smothering his thoughts, haunting his bones and weakening his muscles. Nothing waited for him down there. Only more pain, more *death*. But here... here, he was free. Here, he did not have to worry about such things. Here, he could simply *be*.

But that was not the way of the rest of the world. Auris demanded constant supervision, and Niventia had bestowed these gifts upon Keries for a reason, even if he didn't quite understand her purpose in doing so. Hundreds of thousands of people lived on the continent, and, for some reason, he had been chosen.

He and five others, as it stood, although his companions refused to believe that such an occurrence could be credited to a divine source. They tried to explain to him that there was a hereditary system that could explain the origin of the powers of every single Summoner on Auris. But Keries knew better than that. Keries knew that the six of them had been carefully chosen, imbued with both the capacity and the duty to protect the Auris, and ensure that Niventia's Will prevailed.

Keries liked to fancy that he was the only person in the entire world who fully grasped the true beauty of the night sky. From the rest of Auris, below the clouds, one could only see a few stars mixed in with the dull glow of distant galaxies. But here...

It was almost as if he were staring directly into the eyes of Niventia herself. It had long been said that the Goddess of Light had ascended to live among the stars after creating mankind and gifting them the powers of Summoning. She still watched over them now, subtly guiding her children through the chaos of the world, ensuring that they did not deviate from the path of salvation.

But he allowed himself to forget all of that, if only for a moment. One *glorious* moment. A star fell from the cosmic waves above, soaring over the boundless planes of space and reality. It vanished beneath the clouds, leaving a bright streak of light in its wake.

Ripples of green and blue swirled above, painting a canvas that no artist could ever capture. Mountains crested the cloudscape below, their rugged peaks framing the sky above. Glittering stars danced amongst the aurora, intoxicating Keries once again, halting his thoughts.

Sometimes, he forgot that five other bloodthirsty murderers lived within this very mountain. They were not all bad, but they were murderers nonetheless, like him.

The thought brought with it a flood of overpowering emotions as the weight of his duties collided with him once again. *No,* he thought. *Not yet,* and, with only a simple thought, it was all washed away. Replaced by the peaceful calm of one who was above the petty ways of the violent savages below. A state of peace that only one who was among the *stars* could achieve.

Keries rarely left his quarters, and often when he did so it was only to come here. The others resented him for it, and that he understood. Yet he forgave them. For they had been bestowed with the greatest of Niventia's gifts, and they held the interests of the greater good at heart—despite their sadistic tendencies.

Perhaps he might someday be able to enlighten them to the error of their ways. Perhaps he could show them Niventia's path, and prove that she was more than just a "facade of hope and light masking a deep-seeded desire for answers to questions that men were not meant to ask."

But, alas, that day was not today. Keries was aware that the others would soon retire to their beds, and that he would be expected to do the same. For the moment, however, he found himself unable to pull his eyes from the divine grace of the rolling plumes of light overhead. Someday.

Someday, he would find out what was up there. Someday, he would leave this world behind and join Niventia in her City in the Stars. He would look back on this world as nothing more than a fond memory, basking in the glory of a higher conscience.

Someday...

CHAPTER SEVEN

THE DEXTERIS

Castien Varic glanced back at the thick iron gates as they slowly closed behind him. A low rumbling signaled that the barricade was being lowered; seconds later, the door was sealed. He was officially beyond Arvendon's walls.

The city sloped toward the Salarin Sea on the other side of the stone ramparts, the distant crash of the waves and ring of the ships' bells forming a soft melody in the evening air. The cool fog of the Mistveil had dissipated, giving way to what had turned out to be a rather pleasant evening. The sister moons, Lotius and Oria, shined overhead, lighting the way for their journey.

"Keep up, Stormless," Saevi called out from up ahead.

Castien spun, realizing that he had fallen several yards behind. He jogged lightly, catching up. "Sorry."

Surge led the group, his short graying hair reflecting Lotius's pale gray light. "Leave the boy alone. I'm sure he doesn't get out of the city often," Surge said, his voice low.

"Why would they send him with us if he's never been out of the city?" Saevi asked.

"I have been out of the city, actually," Castien said quickly. "Several times," he added.

No one bothered asking when.

Castien looked around, scanning the rolling hills of Arvendon's outskirts. They were still within the protective wards of the city—though the land outside of the walls was dedicated to the farming of stormroots and stoneblossoms, for these were the crops that sustained Arvendon. Divebrisks were brought in from the sea almost daily as well, accounting for the other portion of Arvendon's food supply.

Castien's bag clunked on his back, the condensed stormroots and dried krellin shells rattling around in their cans.

"How did you end up here anyway?" Saevi asked, pulling Castien from his thoughts.

"Huh?" Castien turned. "Oh, I uh..."

"He's famous in the Stormless Corps," Arthion interjected. "He saved an entire squadron from an Utryan ambush a little over a year ago."

"Yeah..." Castien trailed off. He wasn't aware that Arthion knew of his past, but how could he not? Castien supposed that the prospect of a Whisperer-resistant Stormless would likely be an alarming thought to Auris's Whisperers.

"I didn't know we had your biggest fan in our group." Luka laughed. He offered a warm, cracked-lip smile.

"I wouldn't say *that*," Arthion said, smiling back. "Although I must confess that I find Castien's story to be quite intriguing."

"How exactly did he manage to prevent an ambush anyway?" Saevi asked.

Castien looked up, taking this as his cue to explain. "I was able to detect a Whisperer's influence on our camp," Castien said, his voice sounding small. "I noticed that he was trying to lull us to sleep so that his crew could attack, and I raised the alarm." He stumbled over his own feet, the cobblestone road beneath them taking on a subtle incline as they began to climb one of the many small hills of Arvendon's outskirts.

"And you knew that the Whisperer was influencing you... how?" Saevi raised an eyebrow, her tan skin looking even darker in the night.

"Just a trick I learned, I guess," Castien said.

"Ah, he's even more humble than I could've imagined!" Arthion laughed, seemingly delighted. "Did you know that he was tested by Estmar yesterday? And, not only that, but he *passed* the test. He proved that he is somehow able to resist the influence of my kind!"

An uncomfortable silence fell over the group. Well, Castien wasn't sure if it truly was "uncomfortable," but it certainly felt that way to him. Castien turned his head to the side, trying to find something to occupy himself. The dark dirt of the fields stretched out on either side of the cobblestone road. The fields were marked with a crisscrossing pattern, meaning that stormroots were being grown here.

It was a bitter, uncomfortably fibrous plant, though Arvendon's scholars claimed that the root was good for the body, and it certainly did fill one's stomach. Castien was used to eating it anyway. While he had been away in Utrya, he had been forced to eat mostly stormroots to survive—save for when his team hunted an occasional snowprowler.

A few dark squares dotted the fields—farmhouses, Castien recognized. Flickers of light glowed within them, slowly going out one by one as the families of the city closed their curtains for the night.

The expedition's departure had been delayed by an unnamed disturbance within the palace, which was what had given Castien the freedom to get some sleep before they left. Whatever the disturbance was, it had been resolved, or at least forgotten.

"What exactly are we looking for?" Saevi asked, interrupting the silence.

"Nothing yet," Surge said. "The King said that the markings would begin once we left the wards."

"At which point we will be subject to the undiluted tyranny of the Tempests," Luka added. "Though you needn't worry." Luka turned to Castien as they walked, smiling. "I've spent most of my life outside of the wards where there's nothing but ghost trees and nrekuma. I know the ways of the wilderness."

"Not to mention the fact that he's Arvendon's most powerful Cryostalker," Surge said. "If that doesn't give you a sense of safety, then nothing will." Surge walked on.

Castien looked down, trying to focus on his thoughts. He was walking *right next* to General Elias Surge, the most legendary general in this generation of Auris's armed forces. And just ahead of him walked Luka Delmorian, a Cryostalker and special agent of the King. Not to mention Arthion and Saevi, though the Whisperer and Scorcher were only Lesser Summoners.

"For a group with a lot to talk about I'd say it's pretty pathetic that we couldn't even keep up a conversation for the first ten minutes of our journey." Arthion chuckled.

Surge bellowed a laugh. "I suppose you're right; it is pretty pathetic."

"It is unfortunate that you're all so unbelievably boring. If not for me, you'd probably end up walking in silence," a new voice said.

Castien jumped, spinning.

A woman walked behind him, seemingly appearing out of nowhere.

"What in Izara's Shadow—" Surge stopped, turning around. His eyes settled on the woman.

She wore a blue-gray cloak, her colors mirroring that of Celes's army. Castien stepped back, putting Arthion between him and the stranger. The woman's tight cloak wrapped around her body quite beautifully. Castien raised his eyes, catching sight of her face.

Pointed lips, sharp cheekbones, slightly pointed ears... This woman was Elosian. *Elosian!* Castien's hand instinctively inched toward his bow.

"Who are you?" Surge asked, unsheathing the massive blade on his back.

"Calm down, Elias," Luka said, stepping forward. "She's on our side… I think."

The woman smiled.

Castien looked up, catching sight of two strange hilts protruding from the top of her back—Elosian swords.

"But she's Elosian!" Surge said. "Is she from Celes?"

"Yes, but her allegiance is to Arvendon; our King seems to think so, at least."

"It's good to see you again too, Luka," the woman said, extending a gloved hand.

The Cryostalker didn't take it. "What are you doing here?" Luka asked.

"And how did you sneak up on us?" Saevi snapped.

"She's a Dexteris. Sneaking up on people is what she was born to do," Luka said, his hand shifting to his sword. "And you still haven't answered my question, Ilyana."

The woman sighed. She lowered her blue-gray hood, revealing a head of long, straight black hair. "You didn't think that the King would send you on a mission this important without his favorite Dexteris, did you?"

"I did." Luka glared. "Which is precisely why I'm confused as to what you are doing here."

"Wow," the woman—Ilyana—breathed. "Five years apart and you suddenly don't trust me anymore."

"Your kind should not even be in our city," Luka shot back. "Especially not *cheats* like you."

"I won that duel fair and square." Ilyana shrugged, shaking her head. "Besides, it doesn't matter if you want me here or not; I've been ordered to join you." Ilyana opened the robe of her cloak, revealing a tight black shirt. She fished around in the pockets of her clothing, pulling out a tightly rolled piece of yellowing paper which she handed to Luka, her curved lips twisting into a smirk.

Luka skimmed the page, using the moonlight to read. He looked up. "Damnit," Luka muttered, handing the paper back. "She's not lying. The King's seal is even on the page."

"So what?" Saevi folded her arms.

"Only the King has access to this seal, meaning that he's the only one who could've signed the note," Luka said, shaking his head. He turned around, motioning to the rest of the group. "Everyone, this is Ilyana Xirel. Yes, she's from Celes. And no: I do not like her very much."

"If you're wondering why, just know that his claims are totally unfounded," Ilyana said, raising her arms as if in surrender.

"Unfounded! You literally *ignored* the King's summons," Luka said.

"I ignored a summons to a job that I did not want," Ilyana said. "Can you honestly blame me? Look at how you turned out."

"*I* turned out far better than you ever will," Luka snapped. "You're an outcast now! Your decline was a foolish humiliation for both yourself and our city!"

"You're the one who was humiliated—you lost to me," Ilyana said.

The group stared at one another blankly.

Luka sighed, turning to face the group. "After my predecessor's passing, the King gathered Arvendon's greatest Summoners and held a series of trials to determine who to appoint as his new personal agent," Luka explained. "After a few weeks, Ilyana and I were the top two, and we were forced to duel to determine the champion, but she *cheated* to win—only to end up not taking the job anyway."

"I played by the rules. You just lost, it was nothing more than that," Ilyana snorted. She fluttered her sharp, thin eyelashes.

"Then why didn't you answer the King's summons?" Luka challenged. "You knew ignoring him would make you an outcast, yet you did it anyway. Only guilt can lead someone to do something like that."

"Have you considered the fact that I don't *want* to work for the King?" Ilyana folded her arms. "Some of us don't like to be kept on a leash."

"Then why even enter the trials at all?" Luka shouted. "You made a mockery of our King and showed the entire city how much of a krellin you are."

"To prove that I could win." Ilyana smirked, walking past Luka with an almost admirable confidence.

"It's wonderful to meet you, dear. I am Arthion." The Whisperer extended a gloved hand.

"Charmed!" Ilyana shook his hand, smiling back at him. She turned to Saevi, who kept her arms folded. Ilyana shrugged, turning to Surge.

"You'd better not cause any trouble," Surge warned, eyeing her as he shook her hand.

"I wouldn't dream of it." Ilyana curtsied. She finally spun around, noticing Castien. "Oh!" Ilyana brought a gloved hand to her mouth. "You must be the Stormless."

Castien felt his face heat up. He closed his hand into a tight fist, but kept his mouth shut.

"I had almost forgotten that you were going with us as well," Ilyana said, turning back to the road ahead. "Well, so long as you keep up, I don't think we're going to have any problems." She laughed and took off running.

Castien jumped, picking up to a jog as he tried to keep up. The others didn't bother, and then Castien saw why.

Ilyana's legs were a blur in the night, her body trailing a dark blue essence as she sprinted down the road.

Right, Castien thought. *She's a Dexteris—a master of speed and dexterity.* The others started walking again, the group now up to six, apparently. Ilyana stopped, laughing in the distance as she waited for them to catch up.

Castien cursed under his breath; she didn't even look winded.

He had never seen a Dexteris in person before. Most of them lived in Celes. Yet, somehow, he could already feel himself understanding why Luka despised this woman so much. She jumped up and down, pulling out one of her strangely shaped blades and swinging it around at phantom enemies.

The blade itself was both elegant and terrifying. It had a circular hand guard that branched out from the hilt, and a short, thick blade that had a deep crease straight through the middle.

Butterfly sword, Castien realized as Ilyana pulled an unseen trigger on the blade's hilt. Half of the sword unfolded, turning the thick blade into a long and thin one. She twisted her arms, showing off her Dexteris-enhanced skills as the group caught up to her.

"She's a bit of a showoff," Luka whispered.

"Yeah, I can see that," Surge said.

Castien rolled his eyes, trying to keep his breathing steady. His anxiety crept to the surface again. He synced his heartbeat to the steady rattle of the krellins as they walked.

Five beats in, six beats out, hold for three. Repeat, Castien thought to himself, focusing on the rhythm of his pulse. Steadily, the path faded away, as did the night sky, and Castien found himself falling into the folds of his own mind. His body kept walking, though his thoughts had now drifted somewhere else... somewhere far away.

It was a technique Castien had learned from his mother at a young age, one that was very similar to the technique he used to resist Whisperers. A sort of mediation where one vacated their own mind—through the syncing of their heartbeat and their respiration—to take control of their thoughts. And so Castien walked, only one sentence cycling through his mind as Ilyana continued dashing off ahead:

This is going to be a long trip.

CHAPTER EIGHT
RESPONSIBILITY

Wind howled through the courtyard, whistling across the closed shutters. Faelyn Titansworn stood on the stone floor of the courtyard, watching as the iron covers overhead slowly slid out, blocking the furious winds and violent rains of the Slick-Day. If he listened, Faelyn could hear the soft clinking of Dexteris Crystals in the distance, left out in the Tempest to be refilled.

With a loud clicking noise, the covers were fastened into place by the many attendants of the Summerglass's courtyard, protecting the space from the Slick-Day. Faelyn paced as he waited. The Blood Sorcerer's threat still loomed in his mind, haunting his thoughts. The white stone pillars of the courtyard, while looking a little unsightly under the plain iron covers overhead, still managed to perfectly contrast the bright green plants and colorful flowers that lay around them. The ceiling was two stories overhead, and Faelyn could see through the open passage-ways as Idris approached from the second floor of the Western Wing.

Idris marched firmly down the stairs, already projecting his signature aura of superiority, despite the fact that the training had not even begun yet. He wore robes of a vermillion, lined with dozens of Scorcher Crystals.

"You're late," Faelyn called out, laughing a bit.

"And you're still learning what is and what is *not* appropriate to say to your instructor," Idris said. His solid face was still imposing despite the wrinkles.

Faelyn reached to his side, tapping the Scorcher Crystals that were tied to his waist. He carried several more within the confines of his vermillion vest, but those only served as backups.

Crystals weren't easy to come by for many of Auris's Summoners. Being a member of Arvendon's royal family certainly did have its perks, for Faelyn had never worried about running out of Crystals in his entire life.

"So, today's plans?" Faelyn asked. He unhooked a Crystal and gripped it in his hands.

Idris rolled his eyes, brushing back his dark brown hair—though, if Faelyn was being honest, it was beginning to gray a bit.

"Weapon conjuration? The art of burning? Preserving a blaze that has already begun?" Faelyn asked.

"Today you are going to be working on Azamar's Blast," Idris said, his voice like ice.

Faelyn groaned. "You know that I'm not good at that."

"Which is precisely why we are going to continue working on it," Idris said. "Now, refasten the Crystal, stand on that stone, and get ready." Idris pointed.

Faelyn sighed, tying the Crystal back to his waist, then stepping on the section of stone. Faelyn raised his hands, calling upon the blazing power running through the Crystals at his waist. He closed his eyes, reaching deep within the Crystal's energy reserves.

There.

Faelyn took hold of the spark, dragging it through his skin, pulling it to his fingertips, feeling the heat as it rose through his arms and produced a slight flame at the points of his nails. He smiled, opening his eyes once again. He noticed the slight burn of one of the Crystals at his waist as he used its power.

"You've done this before, you know what to do," Idris said, pacing around Faelyn. Idris raised a hand, a slow string of smoke trailing his fingers as he walked.

The servants understood the signal, wheeling out a stone wall followed by a human-shaped stone figurine clad in steel armor.

"I still don't understand why I'm not allowed to just blast my way through the wall," Faelyn grumbled.

"Because, while this wall is breakable, not every obstacle you encounter will be so easily surmounted," Idris said, coming to a pause by Faelyn's side.

The servants were retreating to the open hallways, though they were behind the railings now. They had set up the stone wall—about ten feet across and six feet tall—in between Faelyn and the target. The target had been wheeled out onto the massive circle at the center of the courtyard where Faelyn stood.

Faelyn narrowed his eyes, growing the flames on his fingers into longer, more defined gusts of fire. He brought his hands together, pushing the ball of flame forward, turning it into a small, steady stream of heat.

The orange flames danced wildly, almost excitedly. Faelyn grinned, feeding off his power's excitement. True, he may dislike practicing spells like Azamar's Blast, but that didn't mean he couldn't enjoy the simple *pleasure* of using his powers.

He exhaled, pushing the thin stream of flame forward. It was no thicker than his thumb, though that was the idea. It drifted across the courtyard, hissing as it collided with the stone wall.

"Good." Idris nodded. "You're getting better at that. Any Master Summoner can destroy a few barriers in a fury of rage, but what truly separates the experts from the apprentices is their control. Now, thread it through the stone."

Faelyn frowned, focusing as he pushed the flame further. "I'm..."

Faelyn grunted. "I'm trying," he said, pushing harder. He lunged slightly, his feet carrying him a few inches.

The dark stone wall began to tremble as a small hole, no more than a few inches in diameter, began to burn through.

Faelyn shifted his hands, directing the flames toward the weak point, threading them through the growing hole.

"Now," Idris said, beginning his pacing again. "I know you've made it this far before. What you've done thus far is easy. How about we make today the day you finally figure this out?"

Faelyn closed his eyes, Idris's words bouncing through his mind. He reached out, feeling the flames as if they were his own fingertips. He pressed against the wall, pushing even more energy through the hole. He could feel the other side, barely. He could feel a faint impression of what was beyond, but nothing specific.

"Feel the flames, Faelyn," Idris whispered, his footsteps echoing softly in the massive courtyard.

The Slick-Day howled outside, causing the iron shutters to shake in the wind. The steady patter of rain caught Faelyn's ear. Faelyn's eyes cracked open at the sound.

"Focus!" Idris snapped.

Faelyn's eyes shut once more, tightly. He reached out again, feeling his way through the flames, nearing the wall and weaving through it just as he did before. He could sense the air currents of the room, licking the tips of his fire, feeding the tendrils ever so slightly. He giggled a bit, enjoying the strange sensation.

"Now," Idris said, his pacing stopping once again. "Start the burn, but carefully. Do not rush it, only bring it to a blaze once you are ready."

Faelyn nodded, gently pushing more energy through his hands, burning the Crystals a bit faster. They were beginning to drain more quickly, but Faelyn would have more than enough to complete the act, assuming he did it correctly. He could feel the cold stone of the target with the flames. He began to feed the energy through the wall, pushing it toward the target, withholding it just before it made contact.

That was the trick with Azamar's Blast; he had to begin with a simple tendril of flame, feed it through an obstacle, and then focus all his energy on the very tip, igniting the target at the end in what was a sort of small explosion.

Sweat dripped from Faelyn's brow, sliding down his face and landing quietly on the stone floor. He kept his eyes closed, his body tensing as he forced more and more energy into the point of the tendril. His hands shook, the heat in his fingers growing with each passing second.

No, Faelyn thought, his body tensing further. He was starting to lose his grip.

He gave one more push, trying to concentrate his energy on the end of the tendril, toward the target. Then, he failed.

Bright orange flames exploded through the stone wall, scattering bits of debris and tearing apart the barrier.

The target, meanwhile, was left perfectly unharmed in the aftermath of the blaze, a visible monument of the failure.

Faelyn cursed, the brilliant heat of the fire washing over him. He severed his connection to the flames, leaving only smoke and ash in their place.

Servants rushed to restack the stones, carefully placing them atop the wheeled dolly that the wall had been pushed out on.

"I was close," Faelyn said after a moment, turning to meet Idris's gray eyes. Thoughts of Breakdown slithered through his mind, gently warning him to take a break. Faelyn reluctantly obeyed.

"It doesn't matter how close you were. What matters is that you didn't do it," Idris said, dismissing the servants. "You are to try again. This time, maybe try thinking about what might happen if you do this in real life and fail. Perhaps that will give you the motivation you need."

"See, that's where I start to wonder why I'm even doing this," Faelyn said. "I extract exponentially more power from each Crystal than the average Summoner." Faelyn tapped the Crystals at his side. He had only burned through one of them, leaving seven more that were still full. "Most Summoners would be through four or five Crystals by now; I've only used one. Why do I need to focus on fancy little maneuvers like this when I can burn my way through any conflict while using as much energy as I want? I'm a Titansworn. The royal bloodline is pure, you know that just as well as I."

Idris sighed, turning to Faelyn. He brushed his dark brown hair back. "I told you to stop questioning me. I understand that, in there, you're the Prince of Arvendon," Idris said, pointing toward the center of the Palace. "But here, when you're with me, I will treat you like one of my students, do you understand?"

Faelyn fell silent, glancing at his hands as they cooled.

"Besides, let's say that someone you care about is standing between you and the people you're trying to hurt. What will you do then?" Idris continued, his icy voice overpowering the violent rains of the Slick-Day beyond the iron shutters. "Everything that I teach you will likely be of value to you at some point. You can have faith in that fact, Faelyn. Now, I—"

"My Prince," a voice called from the edge of the courtyard. "The King requires your presence in the throne room," the servant said.

Faelyn nodded. He turned to Idris after a moment, expecting a response.

Idris sighed. "We'll continue this later."

Faelyn walked the white halls of Summerglass, watching the pillars pass as he stepped forward. A quartet of guards trailed him quietly, their vermillion armor clinking rhythmically with their steps. The marble floor made his footsteps very noticeable as he made his way toward the throne room, and—if he was being honest—he liked that. The noise he brought with him announced his arrival.

He nodded to a passing officer, clad in his vermillion armor ornamented with Arvendon's golden sigil: a blazecrest circling a flame. Faelyn's own vest bore the seal as well, and he wore it with pride. That sigil reminded the world of Arvendon's strength, their power, and their mercy. Faelyn laughed a little to himself at that last part. Merciful wasn't exactly the word he would use to describe Arvendon's policies. Their city maintained their position as the most powerful empire on Auris through threats and surveillance.

Not only that, but they boasted more land than any other country. While unprotected lands themselves weren't of much value to leaders, the Crystals that grew there were; more land meant more Crystals, and more Crystals meant more wealth.

He turned down another one of Summerglass's massive hallways, gorgeous white-marble arches crisscrossing the top of the glass roof. At the moment, there were iron shutters protecting the glass windows above from the Slick-Day.

Faelyn passed by a small group of men wearing voluminous gray robes—Whisperers.

They stopped to bow as he passed.

Faelyn nodded back, his eyes lingering on the men. Faelyn had no reason to dislike the Whisperers. They were among his father's most loyal subjects. Yet, something about them always set Faelyn on edge. The thought of someone being able to alter his thoughts—if only slightly—deeply troubled him.

His father mostly used them to read the intentions of those who surrounded him. It was an effective tactic, for even just the knowledge of a Whisperer's presence had likely staved away countless attempts on the King's life.

Faelyn shivered a bit at the thought. He had never truly worried for his father's life, or his own, but the simple fact that virtually every other nation on Auris would benefit from their deaths was... unnerving.

Hence why Faelyn was trailed by four Scorchers. They were only Lesser Summoners, of course, but a Lesser Summoner was still *more* than capable of defeating half a dozen Stormless—or at least slowing down a Master Summoner. The men were likely distant cousins of Faelyn's, for his family had made a point of genetically tying together nearly all of central Etherus's Scorchers, funneling them into the Titansworn family in an effort to create the purest bloodline possible. It had taken generations, but the program had worked. Faelyn had heard rumors of a similar breeding program having taken place with the Whisperers, though, if that were true, then Faelyn's ancestors had done a very good job of covering it up.

He rounded the last turn, now finding himself in the Entry Hall.

Dozens of golden braziers lined the walls, Incendiary-fueled torches hanging in between each one. Lavish furniture lay pressed up against the marble pillars, where countless nobles chatted with one another. Summerglass was a peaceful place, in truth. Even on days when the Tempests were more pleasant, many people still opted to stay within the warm, welcoming walls of the Palace.

Faelyn nodded to the nobles, who bowed as he passed. He passed by row after row of guards, their shifts now doubled following the ordeal with the Blood Sorcerer.

The guards bowed, opening the massive marble doors to the throne room. The light of the Crystalline chandelier of the Entry Hall slowly vanished as the door closed, replaced by the massive, primal fury of the fires that burned within the throne room. Faelyn had always found the display to be a little bit excessive: the massive pendant bearing an ever-burning flame, the dozens of braziers and hanging torches that lined the extravagant white-marble pillars, row after row of guards lining the floor, and of course the Whisperers lurking in the shadows of said pillars.

His father sat on his throne of gold and orange, the red cushions contrasting the Scorcher Crystals that were lined within the golden frame of the massive chair. The King waved Faelyn forward, leading to a rather awkward stretch of silence as Faelyn crossed the large throne room.

When he finally reached the throne, Faelyn fell to one knee in a ceremonial bow before his father. He made a point of leaning down *extra* low just to show his father how arbitrary this all felt.

"You may rise, son," his father said, nodding his round head. He wore his golden crown, the small orange Crystals shining brightly as they reflected the flames. He had long brown hair, not golden, like Faelyn's; Faelyn got that from his mother. His father brought a hand to his thick beard, stroking it as he beckoned Faelyn forward. Then Faelyn noticed the stone chair beside his father.

"Is that..." Faelyn trailed off. "Is that for me?"

"You said it yourself, Faelyn. I told you that I wanted you to be more involved in the politics of our country, and I am going to hold to that," his father said, smiling deeply. "Go ahead and take a seat. You are going to start sitting in on my meetings from now on."

Faelyn broke into a smile. The stone chair was a little underwhelming, especially compared to the masterpiece of a throne that his father sat in, but it would suffice. He took the few steps up to his chair, settling into the thin cushions with his head held high. He straightened his back, running a hand through his long blond hair and looking ahead. Feeling a hint of pride, Faelyn raised his eyes and stared at the distant doorway.

Looking out over the throne room, he now understood why his father insisted on such a display. The massive golden pendant hanging from the high ceiling made for a rather magnificent centerpiece. The braziers gave the room the extra light it needed, and, as he looked out at the dozens of Scorcher guards and Whisperers, Faelyn couldn't help but smirk. He was surrounded by people who obeyed him, *him!* Nothing could hurt him here, for, even if something were to get past those guards, then Faelyn could call upon the countless sources of fire in the room to burn any possible threats to ashes before they even so much as laid a finger on him.

Which was precisely why Faelyn's face fell so dramatically as his mind drifted to the Blood Sorcerer. Even here, his father had been overpowered. Even here, surrounded by Scorchers, Whisperers, and flames, his father had been outmatched.

His father nodded to the guards across the throne room.

They opened the door, sending in the first person.

As it turned out, the day-to-day duties of a king were incredibly boring. Faelyn had at least assumed that many of the conversations would be somewhat interesting, but they mostly just pertained to things like "ensuring that the signs in the market district are cleaned once a month," or "making sure that the poorer citizens of the city didn't walk too far into the wealthier divisions," or "preventing the new shipments of textiles and shorebeans from being tampered with on the hundred-foot walk from the ship to the warehouse."

Faelyn shook his head, wandering out of the throne room after what felt like an eternity. It had only been a few hours, of course, but had he been told several days had passed, well, Faelyn probably would've believed it.

He could hear his father following him from a distance, speaking with some of the guards as he passed. Faelyn smiled a bit. His father was good at what he did, he would surrender that much. Somehow, his father made each guard and servant in the Palace feel appreciated and understood—though Faelyn wasn't sure how. He turned left, starting down the Eastern Wing once again, seeking out Reluraun.

The Cloudwalker spent much of his time in the dome, a training pit not far from the courtyard. Faelyn preferred the courtyard because he liked to feel more in touch with his surroundings, and the open feel of the area made for a more realistic setting when it came to practicing the application of his powers. The dome was large, yes, but it always seemed a little cramped, for most of the large central arena was sectioned off into private training areas.

He turned another corner, the fires blazing in their braziers as he passed. His guards trailed quietly behind him, the only sound in the massive corridor the soft clinking of their armor. Faelyn glanced at one of the Incendiary-fueled torches as he passed it, feeling its warmth in the air as he neared it. He continued onward, the slight tingle from the flame that had come over him slowly passing.

A chandelier hung from the ceiling of this corridor as well—there was one in nearly every room of the palace, though few rivaled the splendor of the ones in the Grand Ballroom or the Entry Hall.

Faelyn looked up, silently wishing that the Slick-Day could be over quicker so that the iron shutters could be opened once again.

This hallway's ceiling was lined with long glass windows, as were many of the hallways in Summerglass. It made for quite a beautiful scene on Blazedays, when the sun was shining and the skies were clear... Yet, with the iron shutters closed, everything felt dreary. Faelyn supposed he was a little biased when it came to the Tempests, as were all Summoners.

Reluraun, on the other hand, loved Slick-Days almost as much as he did Cyclones. He claimed that there was a certain order to the chaos of the wicked winds of the storm. The Tempests rotated often enough in Arvendon—based on the concentrations of energy in the area—that most Summoners were satisfied with the climate.

He passed through the doorway of the dome, entering the marble arena. The sound of clashing swords reached his ears, as did the *whishes* and the *booms* of Summoners' magic as they trained. Faelyn glanced at the now-covered curved ceiling of the massive room, and slowly let his eyes drift across the chamber.

It was easily several hundred feet in diameter, and the entrances and exits along the sides were raised from the rest of the room, which was lowered so that one could easily see across the arena. Several large stone dividers dotted the central arena, which had a white-marble floor, as did the rest of the chamber. Duelists fought within some of the sections, while Summoners trained alone in others. Faelyn started toward the far side of the dome, seeking out the private rooms where Reluraun often trained.

Faelyn followed the sound of rushing wind—though it was hard to distinguish from the pattering rain outside—and found himself carried down a staircase, leaving the large dome behind and entering the private hallways. He stopped beside a door, listening as air swirled within, then knocked.

The wind did not cease, though a voice called out: "Come in."

Faelyn turned the brass handle and opened the white door slowly. Wind pushed against it, making it several times heavier than it should've been. Faelyn grunted, flinging the door open and stumbling into the room as it slammed shut behind him.

The plain white-marble walls and floors of the small room were empty—as they always were—though Faelyn wasn't focused on that. He was focused on the swirling objects in the center of the room. Faelyn looked up, squinting through the furious gusts of air, trying to meet his friend's eyes.

Reluraun stood in the center of the room, wind-wood daggers levitating around him. He thrust his hand forward, one of the daggers shooting toward the wall at an incredible speed. Reluraun drew his hand back, closing his fist and twisting it. The light gray dagger flipped in midair, turning on its side and hurtling back toward Reluraun. Reluraun twisted his hand again, catching the dagger by the hilt, stopping its flight. He turned to Faelyn, the winds dissipating.

"What's up?" Reluraun asked casually. He sheathed one of the strange daggers, but kept the other in his hand. Mint-green Crystals clinked at his side, contrasting his red vest.

"I've been thinking about everything," Faelyn said, standing a little straighter. "And I wanted to apologize for last night. I didn't realize that Elric had been sent after Velarus."

"Ah," Reluraun said, tossing the dagger into the air. It hovered there, at his command, slowly twisting over his palm, a slight gust of wind brushing through its gaps. Wind-wood daggers were designed specifically for Cloudwalkers, for they possessed several curving holes and openings that allowed air to pass through, which made them very easy for Cloudwalkers to manipulate. "Rest assured,

Faelyn, I took no offense to your behavior. If anything, I'm just surprised at the fact that your father didn't tell you."

"Eh, it's alright," Faelyn said, leaning against the cool marble door frame. "He explained that he was trying to keep me away from all this Blood Sorcerer business, for my safety, you know?" Faelyn explained.

Reluraun's face fell. "So he really thinks it's that much of a threat." Reluraun's emerald eyes darkened. He lowered his head.

Faelyn paused, realizing his mistake; Reluraun's father was out there, right now, following the Blood Sorcerer.

"I don't think that it's necessarily *that,*" Faelyn said quickly. "I just think that he wants me to stay out of more delicate matters until my ascension is closer, if that makes sense."

Reluraun eyed him.

"You do have to admit, even if the Blood Sorcerer is some sort of imposter, it is still a somewhat alarming prospect," Faelyn said.

Stop talking, you idiot! Faelyn thought.

Reluraun let the knife drop into his waiting hand. He sheathed the dagger, pacing the room quietly.

Faelyn lowered his gaze.

Reluraun's auburn hair was tossed casually to the side, creating a friendly—yet messy—look. His face was furrowed into a focused frown, his expression mirroring one that Elric often wore.

"I'm worried about him," Reluraun said quietly. He paused, turning to meet Faelyn's eyes.

"You shouldn't be," Faelyn said. "Your father is one of the most powerful Summoners in Arvendon, right? And, besides, you even said that he was instructed *not* to engage Velarus, but only to follow him."

"I'm still worried," Reluraun said. "I know he's powerful, I know he's experienced, but if this Blood Sorcerer is real…"

"If the Blood Sorcerer is real, then we will figure out some way to defeat him," Faelyn said. He laid a hand on his friend's shoulder. "If anyone can handle a mission like this, it's your father." Faelyn paused. "Trust in your father, and trust in mine. They've been in their positions for decades now, they'll do what's right."

"I know," Reluraun said, turning back to Faelyn. "Maybe that's what I'm worried about." Reluraun retied the satchel of Crystals at his waist and checked the sheaths of his daggers, seemingly wanting to end the conversation there.

"Wait," Faelyn said as Reluraun started toward the door. "What do you mean?"

Reluraun turned slightly, standing with his hand on the brass door handle. He looked at Faelyn for a brief moment. "Nothing," Reluraun said, opening the door. "I always just feel a little more on edge with my father out of the city."

"You and me both," Faelyn said, smiling softly. "Elric's one hell of a Summoner, we're lucky to have him on our side."

"Yeah..." Reluraun trailed off. He opened the door, disappearing past Faelyn's guards and into the hallway beyond.

That was a little strange, Faelyn thought. He ran a hand through his long, curly, golden hair and started out toward the hallway. He needed to get back to his training anyway.

CHAPTER NINE

THE WASTELANDS

Castien Varic eyed the markings on the monolith. It was easily twelve feet tall and at least six feet wide. Triangular Runes were carved into nearly every inch of the rock. The monoliths were among the most important sites on Auris. Without the protective wards they powered, there would be no possibility of life on this harsh continent. Even now, getting caught unprotected in some Tempests would often lead to death. Thankfully, the Ancient Rune-Writers had created these wards to dampen the anticipated effects of the Tempests in certain areas, allowing civilizations to bloom. Of course, this was before the Tempests had descended as a result of the Vanishing.

Those triangular Runes remained still, immortalized in stone, even after the Rune-Writers—and many other Sects—had been wiped out in the Vanishing. It was an unspoken pact among the nations of Auris that kept these rocks standing. Even in the darkest of wars, each nation was strictly forbidden to destroy another's wards. Auris had very little land that one could live on as it was, and reducing that space even further would be catastrophic.

"Be ready, the winds will be picking up soon," Surge said, leading the force past the monolith.

A white, transparent film hung in the air, running through the rock—the ward. It extended out in both directions, connecting with other monoliths placed at intervals around the city and its fields to form a sort of dome over the Arvendon.

"Good," Ilyana muttered.

The winds of the Slick-Day were gentle within the wards, but it was clear even just from looking that they were much stronger outside. The rains were relatively light as well, but that was soon to change. Ilyana didn't seem to mind, for she was a Dexteris; her Sect's Tempest was the Slick-Day.

Castien passed through the film, rain instantly pelting his face. He held up a gloved hand, pulling his leather hood tighter over his eyes. He reached up with his other hand, tying the face-covering closed. All sets of armor, even those of the Stormless, came with the hood and face-covering for the sake of protecting the wearer from the Tempests.

Surge slipped on his helmet, the bright red steel shining despite the heavy rain.

The cobblestones were slick here, so much so that Castien almost fell once or twice. *I guess they call them Slick-Days for a reason,* he thought.

"Gods," Ilyana said, her voice muffled through the blue-gray mask she now wore. There were two slits for her eyes cut in the thick fabric that connected all the way from the top of her hood to her upper collarbone. "Sometimes I forget how barren it all is," she said, looking around.

"Welcome to The Wastelands," Luka said as Castien looked up.

Gray, cracked land extended in all directions. Countless rifts and rises made the ground a fractured mess. The landscape was dull and unmoving, save for the occasional ghost tree blowing in the wind—though, with their empty, crooked branches and black wood, they didn't do much to help the scenery. There were black spots on the ground from the scorching sun of past Blazedays and cracked fissures from the cataclysmic lightning of the Storm Gales.

The last time Castien had left the city he had been with friends, *real* friends. They had been sent to The Highlands to assist Arvendon's troops in the skirmishes that had started between Freyfall and Arvendon. Thanks to the troops' work, the skirmishes had not escalated into all-out war.

The conflict had started over land. True, unprotected land was largely unimportant, but Crystals grew there... meaning that the more land Arvendon had, the more Crystals they would possess.

Looking out at the scorched, corroded wastes, Castien felt very cold—and not from the chilling rain. He was unprotected now. He was *outside* of the wards. Grass couldn't grow out here. Hardly any animals could survive, save for the nrekuma. Life as he knew it seemed to have vanished the second he passed through that ward.

This world... This was Auris in its natural state. This was what the entire continent would be reduced to, if not for the wards.

The Rune-Writers had set to work creating the wards as time itself had begun. At the dawn of Auris, when the Harbingers had first set foot on these violent lands, there had been nothing to protect the people from the looming arrival of the Tempests. Humanity had lived in tiny settlements, hidden deep within the caverns of The Highlands. Yet then the Harbingers had brought the gifts of Summoning to those who they deemed worthy, and those gifts were passed on from generation to generation.

The Vanishing had been a setback, of course. Over half of the Sects on Auris had been wiped out over the course of the war that began due to the arrival of the Tempests.

The Blood Sorcerers were one of the Sects that had supposedly gone extinct, yet now it would appear that they had returned. How, exactly? Well, the fact that there was no easy answer to that question is likely the very reason the King suspected foul play.

"Do we really have to travel in this?" Saevi called out, her voice nearly lost to the winds.

"Elric is still several miles ahead of us, perhaps more," Surge shouted from the front of the group. "If we don't keep moving, we're going to lose him." He turned back to the broken path ahead of them —though Castien supposed it wasn't much of a path at all; it was more of a fragmented trail.

A ghost tree stood to their right, its twisting black branches and cracked body standing in bold defiance to the powerful winds of the Slick-Day. Castien could see the beginnings of the twisting roots that plunged deep into the ground, gathering what water they could from the deep chasms and cracks of The Wastelands.

To think that most of Auris is like this. Castien shook his head.

The ground was dark and devoid of nutrients from the endless cycle of scorching and freezing. Some of the unprotected lands of Auris were capable of sustaining life, at least to some degree. The Highlands experienced mostly Frostfalls due to the high concentration of cold-energy there, making them somewhat livable... And Asari's Dunes of Despair were supposedly the perfect environment for krellins.

"I'm getting tired of this," Saevi announced, raising her hands. The Scorcher drew a tendril of flame from the Crystals at her waist. Rain and fire hissed as they collided, but Saevi didn't care. She held her hand forward, wrapping the tendril around her body, only leaving a little room so that her armor didn't catch alight, and continued walking.

"That seems like a waste of energy, dear." Ilyana laughed. "It's not even like the Slick-Days' rains are cold, am I right?" Ilyana turned to Castien and Luka.

Castien looked up to the gray clouds as Luka grumbled, wondering where among them the sun lingered. Try as it might, only a pale gray glow was able to shine through the heavy rain clouds.

No thunder crashed through the flat Wastelands. Slick-Days never came with thunder. The only time lightning touched the surface of Auris was on the day of a dreaded Storm Gale.

Ilyana wore her dark blue Crystals on the outside of her cloak, allowing them to suck in the energy that floated invisibly through the air.

Summoners could not draw energy directly from the Tempests themselves, but they *were* capable of extracting energy from the Crystals that absorbed and somehow converted the power of the Tempests, granting Summoners their abilities. However, even Summoners had their limitations, for, once one's Crystals were empty, they might as well consider themselves Stormless. Not to mention Breakdown, of course. Though, given his lack of Summoning experience—because he was Stormless—Castien didn't know much about the phenomenon.

"Be on your guard," Surge called, looking up to the sky. "Elric should be leaving markers on the ghost trees by now, so be on the lookout."

"That's not the only thing we need to be on guard for," Ilyana muttered.

"Huh?" Castien turned to the Elosian woman.

She looked at him with unreadable eyes. "Of course, I keep forgetting that you're Stormless." She shook her head. "It must be nice to not have to worry about having to face Summoners in battle."

"I—" Castien restrained himself. He closed his eyes, taking a deep breath. While it was true that most Stormless were never burdened with fighting against Summoners, she wasn't exactly looking at the whole picture.

"Besides," Ilyana continued, "the Nyghtmaere is active again, according to our scouts."

"The what?" Castien asked.

"The Nyghtmaere, it's an Utryan word for 'Monster.'" Ilyana glanced sideways at Castien. "You truly haven't heard of him?"

"Not since I was in The Highlands," Castien said. "Our squadron didn't think he was real."

"Well, tell that to the soldiers who he's murdered over the last two years," Ilyana scoffed. "Some say that he's the reason the skirmishes started in the first place."

"A singular person cannot cause a conflict of that size," Saevi said.

"A Shadow-Swift can," Ilyana said plainly.

Castien turned to her, then back to Ilyana. "The Nyghtmaere is a Shadow-Swift?" Castien gaped. "No one has seen one for centuries."

"Until about two years ago you would've been correct, but they've been popping up all over The Highlands over the past few months," Ilyana said. "Are the Stormless really *that* unaware of the world around them?"

Castien bit his tongue once again, pushing his rising anger deeper into himself. *Not now.*

"Shadow-Swifts haven't been proven to be real." Saevi laughed. "They don't even have a damn Tempest!"

"They don't need one," Ilyana shot back. "Of the few times that Arvendon has been able to get their hands on a Shadow-Swift Crystal, they haven't been able to figure out what fuels them. One day they're empty, and a few nights later they're full again, regardless of the Tempest."

"Bah." Saevi waved a hand through the lightening rain.

Castien looked up. A bit more light peeked through the clouds. It was likely nearing late afternoon; the Tempest should be dissipating soon enough.

"Enough talk about the Shadow-Swifts," Surge said from up ahead.

"They're real, by the way," Luka whispered to Castien.

Castien tilted his head, looking at the Cryostalker. He met his ice-blue eyes and cracked eyelids.

"The Shadow-Swifts," Luka said. "I've seen them before, but only from a distance."

"Well, there's no point in talking about them because they're not going to hurt us," Arthion said, the Whisperer joining the conversation for the first time in several hours.

"And why is that?" Luka challenged. "How do you know that

they won't take an interest in a group that includes almost all of Arvendon's most powerful Summoners?"

"Because they have no reason to," Arthion said. "Just—" He sighed. "Just trust me on this, we'll be safe. If the Blood Sorcerers truly are back, I'm sure the Shadow-Swifts want answers just as badly as we do."

"You talk as if you know these things for certain." Ilyana narrowed her eyes through the slits of her hood.

"And I almost certainly *do* know these things." Arthion shrugged. "Shadow-Swifts do not show themselves unless they have reason to do so. Therefore, I have no fears that we will be ambushed—not by them at least."

"Here," Surge said, slowing to a stop beside the next ghost tree.

Castien stepped toward the front of the group alongside Ilyana. There, through the now lightly falling rain, Castien spotted an etching in the thick black wood of the twisting ghost tree. It was an arrow pointing to the right, with a cursive E carved beneath it. And beneath it there was one word: *"Follow..."*

"Follow what?" Arthion asked.

"I assume the ghost trees," Surge said. "There are few enough of them that he likely marked each one individually." Surge looked off to the right, and Castien spotted the faint impression of a ghost tree in the distance.

A chilling wind blew across the group, causing Castien to shiver. He was reminded of his damp clothing, not that he could expend the energy to worry about it. All soldiers had to get used to being wet at one point or another, for four of the Tempests involved precipitation.

"What is it?" Saevi asked.

"It appears that he's leading us in the direction of The High-lands," Surge answered. "Strange..."

"It would make sense, though," Ilyana said. "The Highlands are massive, and the caverns within those mountains are virtually endless."

"Yes, but many of them are sealed by Runes," Luka said. "I've spent plenty of time in The Highlands. Trust me, even if those caves were easy to find, the Blood Sorcerer would have no way of getting in."

"Which is precisely why, if he somehow *did* find a way in, it would make for the perfect hiding spot," Ilyana suggested.

"I like how we're all ignoring the simple possibility that the Blood Sorcerer is just taking The Highlands as a shortcut to Freyfall." Saevi snorted sarcastically.

"Saevi's right," Surge said. "And don't call him that."

"What?"

"Velarus," Surge said. "Don't call him a Blood Sorcerer, because he's not one."

"We don't know that yet, remember? That's why we were sent after him in the first place: to find out if he truly was one," Saevi countered.

"Which is precisely why we will assume that he is merely a trickster until proven otherwise," Surge said. "Understand?" Surge glared at the group through his steel helmet.

Castien nodded slightly, as did the rest of the group.

"Good. Now let's get going," Surge said.

The expedition crew started walking again, this time diverging from the "trail" and continuing on the cracked rock of The Wastelands. Castien stepped with caution, careful to avoid the occasional chasm that seemed to drop endlessly into the darkness.

"So how do you do it?" a voice suddenly asked.

Castien looked up, a little startled. Arthion walked beside him, his gray mask still covering his face.

"Huh?" Castien asked. Another light wind blew against his covered face, causing Castien to shudder. His feet ached, and his legs shivered. They weren't even to the northern parts of Etherus yet, and the cold was already starting to penetrate his armor.

"How do you resist the influence of my kind?" Arthion asked. "I've never met anyone who was capable of such a thing, and you can imagine my surprise when I heard that you were a Stormless."

"Oh, um..." Castien trailed off, his thoughts a jumbled mess. He straightened his back, then pulled his gloves on a little tighter. His hands were cold and shriveled messes, yet there didn't appear to be anything Castien could do about that. So long as a Blazeday or a Cyclone came soon, his clothes would dry. Hopefully one would come soon, for Castien had heard of men getting diseases from the wet climate of Auris's southeastern lands.

"I hope it's okay that I'm asking," Arthion said after a moment. "I'm merely curious as to what it is that you are capable of. I mean, it is quite impressive that someone of your station was sent along with this crew."

Castien forced his attention back to the Whisperer. "Yeah," Castien said. His anxiety rose once again.

The others were nearing the next ghost tree and talking amongst themselves.

Castien stepped over a particularly large crack as another strong gust of rain-filled wind pelted him from the side.

"My apologies," Arthion said quickly, taking a step away.

"No, it's alright," Castien said, forcing a smile. He realized quickly that Arthion could not see it through the mask. "Sorry, I'm still just a little overwhelmed."

"Understandably so." Arthion's eyes softened. "Believe me, I myself am overwhelmed too," the Whisperer continued. "I mean, just look at who we're traveling with. I may be a servant of the King, but that doesn't mean I don't get a little intimidated sometimes." Arthion laughed.

Castien smiled, letting out a small laugh as well. "To answer your question, sir, I learned a sort of meditation technique from my mother," Castien said, his nerves easing a bit.

"Ah," Arthion mused. "And, please, call me Arthion. No need for this formal nonsense. You may be Stormless, but you're still on this expedition, same as the rest of us." Arthion patted Castien on the back with a wet, gloved hand.

Castien smiled, feeling a sudden warmth within him as his

anxiety subsided. Suddenly, the rain didn't seem so bad. *At least I'm not completely alone.*

"So, tell me more about this technique."

"Well," Castien started, thinking back to that strange place in his mind. "It took months to master, but my mother was insistent that I learn it."

"I assume she wasn't a fan of Whisperers?"

"Something like that." Castien looked down.

"I'm sure it would be quite a surprise to learn that you are now becoming friends with one." Arthion chuckled.

Castien's face fell. "She—" Castien swallowed. "She passed away a few years back, right before I joined the Stormless Corps."

"Oh," Arthion said. A heavy silence fell over them, save for the soft patter of rain and the slight howl of the wind. "My condolences," Arthion said after a moment.

Castien snapped back to reality. "It's alright," Castien said, swallowing once again. "She and I had drifted apart anyway." Castien forced out a laugh.

Arthion remained silent.

"It's pointing us farther north," Surge announced from up ahead. "Keep a good pace and maybe we can reach one of the shelters by nightfall. We don't know what tomorrow's Tempest is, and, if it's one of the deadlier ones, then we're going to have to—" Surge stopped.

"What?" Saevi asked, stepping forward. Castien approached as well. "What is it?" Saevi asked again.

Surge held a finger to his lips and dropped into a crouch. He motioned through the rain for the others to do the same.

Arthion motioned for Castien to follow, and the two of them took cover behind the ghost tree. They squatted beside Surge, who was still looking out into the distance.

Then Castien saw it.

A few hundred yards ahead, something moved through the thick sheet of rain: a large, hulking mass. Castien could tell what it was even from this far away, though he had only ever seen this breed of beast once in his life. The creature was nearly twenty feet in length, and upwards of ten feet tall.

"Niventia's Light," Saevi whispered. "Is that a—"

"Nrekuma," Surge said quietly.

The creature was but a shadow from this far away, though even from here Castien could make out its four clawed legs. If he squinted, he could locate a few stray tendrils dangling from the beast's back.

It raised its head, vaguely looking in their direction. It may have been far away, but the predator's senses were *very* precise. Even from this distance, they were not completely safe.

It turned the other way and bounded off into the distance, a collective sigh of relief running through the group. The ground rumbled slightly, and soon the only sound was the soft patter of the rain.

Surge held up his hand, motioning for them to follow.

Castien stood up, his legs shaking more than he realized. He shuddered. The horrifying beasts were the only things other than krellins that could survive in The Wastelands. They were deadly, easily the deadliest creature on Auris—other than man, of course. He hoped that he would not have to worry about them.

Surely, I won't have to, Castien thought. He was with some of Arvendon's strongest Summoners, and, despite the threat that one of the mighty nrekuma may attack the group, Castien would be safe. *Surely.*

CHAPTER TEN
STRANGE WHISPERS

Faelyn Titansworn once again found himself leaning against the dessert table, Reluraun at his side, as the nobles danced in a mesmerizing circle before him.

Reluraun chewed loudly on a brightly colored dessert, seemingly oblivious to the rest of the world as he focused on the pastry in his hand.

"It puzzles me," Faelyn started, tilting his head slightly, "how you are so frighteningly thin, yet all I see you do at these parties is eat and drink."

Reluraun snorted. "It's called the Knyvet Blessing," Reluraun said between mouthfuls. "No matter what we eat we always stay thin. It's nice, you know?"

"Must be..." Faelyn muttered.

Reluraun seemed to be on his best behavior tonight. He didn't even have a drink in his hand yet. Reluraun's words from the day before echoed in his mind, puzzling him once again. *Maybe that's what I'm worried about.*

Faelyn turned away, frowning to himself as he watched the

dancers. He allowed his ears to drift to the small orchestra on the opposite side of the ballroom, listening to its melodies.

The marble walls and massive size of the room generated a wonderful echo for the music, though Faelyn could barely hear it over the chatter of the crowd. He still didn't fully understand the point of the Gold-White Harvest parties. Why couldn't they simply harvest the warded fields on the outskirts of Arvendon and be done with it? Faelyn didn't know. For some reason, they had to throw parties almost every night for two weeks, host festivals, and have a massive celebration on the Solstice at the end of the two weeks. Faelyn supposed it generated income for the city and his father, given that it attracted people from all across Etherus and even beyond.

The parties were an effective distraction for the citizens as well. The rumors about Velarus's threat were gaining momentum, and the Whisperers confirmed that the nobles were growing suspicious. Word had gotten out among the nobles about the Blood Sorcerer, as Faelyn knew it would. There had simply been too many guards and Whisperers in the throne room that day—one had undoubtedly told their spouse, who had told another, and so on.

It wouldn't be long before the King was confronted, and things would only go downhill from there.

"I will say for once I'm a little glad that we have all of these parties, you know?" Reluraun said suddenly.

"That's never something I thought I'd hear you say," Faelyn said, coming out from his thoughts.

"Well," Reluraun started, licking his fingers as he finished the pastry, "I simply like having something to distract myself right now, I guess."

"Ah," Faelyn said. "Worried about your father again?"

"That, and the fact that many of Arvendon's most powerful Summoners are not currently in the city," Reluraun said.

Faelyn froze. His gaze slowly slid to his father, who sat a few hundred feet away at his table, as he usually did. "Listen, Rel," Faelyn said, lowering his voice. "My father told me that he has no intention of informing me of the details regarding the whole Blood Sorcerer business, so you're going to have to be my informant on this one, okay?"

"*I* get to be your informant?" Reluraun asked.

"Yes," Faelyn said. "Now keep your voice down. What did you say about the Summoners being away from the city?"

Reluraun swallowed, leaning in and speaking more quietly this time, though his gray eyes were still alive with excitement. "Your father put together an expedition and sent them out a few days ago," Reluraun whispered. "They are to rendezvous with my father once they catch up to him, and together they are going to continue following the Blood Sorcerer until they locate his hideout. Once they do that, they have permission to engage if they deem it the easiest way out of this whole ordeal."

"Who exactly did he send?" Faelyn asked, his eyes scanning the room.

"He sent some of our most powerful Summoners," Reluraun said. "Delmorian and Surge are gone."

Faelyn cursed. "Anyone else?"

"He also sent a Whisperer and a Scorcher, though neither are Master Summoners," Reluraun said. "Oh, and I think he also sent a Stormless with them as well: a tracker of some kind, as I understand it."

"Hmm." Faelyn lifted his crystal glass to his lips, taking a sip of water. "This is what you were worried about, right? You were worried that my father would send away all of our most powerful Summoners, leaving us open to attack," Faelyn realized.

"I fear that he is putting all of his sunbird eggs in one basket, yes," Reluraun said. "Even if we are fine here, what if something happens to that expedition? We can't afford to lose Surge and Delmorian—not to mention my father."

"You're right," Faelyn said, his gaze settling on the King. "I think I need to go have a word with my father."

"Faelyn, wait," Reluraun said, laying a hand on his shoulder. "What about me?"

"What about you?" Faelyn asked, turning around.

Reluraun pulled him closer, his light brown hair still looking like a disheveled mess despite his obvious attempts to comb it. "If your father knows that I'm continuing to tell you what I know—especially after he specifically told me not to—then he won't let me sit in on any more discussions," Reluraun said, his eyes darkening.

"Wait!" Faelyn started. "Are there discussions that my father isn't letting me listen to?"

"It would appear that way," Reluraun said. "Namely the ones with the Council."

Faelyn cursed, pulling Reluraun past the dessert table and up against one of the marble pillars that lined the room. The shadowed edges of the room shuffled occasionally with servants, but being overheard by servants was better than being overheard by other nobles, Faelyn figured.

"We're already vulnerable at this time of year... Our gates are open, and we welcome hundreds of people into this palace every single night... not to mention the truth of the Blood Sorcerer spreading... It almost feels like..."

"Like someone was planning for this to happen," Reluraun said, eyes widening. "You think that this might all be a trick?"

"I wouldn't be surprised," Faelyn said. "Celes has been breathing down our spines for decades now, not to mention Freyfall. Hell, even Cyfalion might benefit from something like this."

"Then what is the whole business with the Blood Sorcerer?"

"A trick of some sort as well?" Faelyn guessed. "Maybe some combination of a Whisperer and a Cloudwalker manipulating the surroundings and emotions of those in the throne room that day?"

"Your father suspects something similar," Reluraun said. "I remember him saying something about the Blood Sorcerer possibly being some false memory planted by a Whisperer."

Faelyn nodded, his brow furrowed in thought. "If he thinks that the Blood Sorcerer isn't real, then why would he send our most powerful Summoners after him?"

"I'm not sure." Reluraun scratched his head. "Even if the Blood Sorcerer isn't real, something important still happened in the throne room on that day. This could all be the first stage of an elaborate trap."

"A trap that we are falling right into." Faelyn shook his head, cursing again. "He shouldn't have sent them away."

"He didn't send *everyone* away, you know," Reluraun said. His thin lips broke into a smile.

"What do you mean?" Faelyn tilted his head.

"Think about it, Faelyn," Reluraun grabbed him lightly by the shoulders. "You and I may be Arvendon's best hope. If something is about to happen, it's up to *us* to prevent it."

Faelyn looked away.

Reluraun was shockingly immature despite the fact that he was already almost twenty. His eyes almost reflected anticipation.

"Only you would be excited about the fact that the fate of the city might rest on our shoulders," Faelyn muttered.

"Hey, relax," Reluraun said, lowering his hands. "Your father is still here, as well as Idris. We have nothing to worry about. I'm just saying that we could definitely help if we wanted to."

Faelyn's eyes drifted to the center of the ballroom, where dozens of nobles danced beneath the massive crystal chandelier. He watched as Whisperers and servants moved beneath the shadows of the pillars. He watched as the orchestra began their next piece. He watched as his father laughed once again.

"Okay," Faelyn said. "Here's the plan. You focus on gathering information and keeping an eye out for threats. I'll find a way to convince my father to bring back Surge and Delmorian without letting him know that you have been acting as my informant."

"Sounds good," Reluraun said, turning back to the ballroom. "I'm going to go see if I can find out anything else about this expedition. I'll see you in a bit, okay?"

"Good luck." Faelyn nodded, leaning against the marble pillar as his friend rejoined the masses. Faelyn sighed, his eyes falling to the floor. He hated going against his father like this, but his options were rather limited.

I'm not imagining all of this, am I? he thought, rubbing his head. Arvendon truly was vulnerable right now; that much was a fact. Even if rumors were the only active threat to the city, they still needed to stay vigilant, especially with how lenient the Arvendon's security was at the moment.

Someone moved behind Faelyn.

He jumped, reaching within his Crystals. Flames licked his fingertips as he landed. A Whisperer stood behind the pillar, blank eyes watching lifelessly as Faelyn lowered his hands.

"My apologies," Faelyn said quietly, waving the flames away from his fingers. "You startled me." Faelyn smiled casually.

The Whisperer's ice-blue eyes sparked to life, his withered face remaining strangely still. He did not smile back, his short gray beard dangling from his wrinkled chin.

Have you been listening to my thoughts? Faelyn raised an eyebrow.

The Whisperer did not react. Either he hadn't been listening or he was extraordinarily skilled at masking his emotions as he used his abilities.

Faelyn's eyes drifted to the man's cloak. He tried to peek at the gray Crystals within, seeing if they were being drained, but they were covered by the man's long gray robes.

Without another word, the Whisperer shuffled off into the shadows, moving to a different part of the ballroom.

Faelyn shivered, but shook off his fears. It was probably nothing.

Damn Whisperers. They always unnerved him. Faelyn started off into the center of the ballroom, deciding that, between the news of the Summoners leaving the city, the possibility of a trap being laid for them, and the spook the Whisperer had given him, he deserved to take some time to enjoy himself.

Faelyn stood in the center of the massive ballroom, watching as the servants began sweeping up the mess.

The nobles and courtiers filed out of the room, chatting quietly. Faelyn's father spoke quietly with nobles near the ballroom throne, surrounded by guards. They slowly made their way out of the room, leaving through the back door as they escaped to their chambers.

Reluraun walked over silently, his steps a little uneven.

Faelyn glanced at the empty glass in Reluraun's hand. *Figures.*

"Well?" Faelyn asked, straightening a little. Whisperers shuffled in the shadows of the pillars, following Faelyn's father out the servants' exit.

"As it turns out," Reluraun started, "Saevi Embrore is the Scorcher they sent, and Arthion Aldrich is the Whisperer; both are Lesser Summoners, but I've been told they're rather powerful for their station."

"And the Stormless?"

"Castien Varic." Reluraun leaned back, stretching casually. "Apparently, he's exceptionally skilled at detecting and resisting the influence of a Whisperer, and, given that your father suspects that the 'Blood Sorcerer' may be the result of a powerful Whisperer's tricks, he sounds like a decent addition to the team."

"And you're certain that he's just a Stormless? Not a Summoner?" Faelyn asked, tilting his head.

"That's what I've heard." Reluraun shrugged, brushing his disheveled hair out of his eyes. "Any ideas about your father yet?"

"Not really," Faelyn admitted. "Although I suspect that I may be able to at the very least get some information out of the Council meetings I'm now required to sit in on."

"Information such as?"

"Well, so far most of the conferences have been unimportant, but a few caught my attention," Faelyn said. "It seems as if Celes is preparing for something."

"Oh?" Reluraun leaned forward.

"Yeah," Faelyn sighed. "And, given what we just got out of with Freyfall, I really wouldn't be surprised if Celes made a move against us."

"Nightingale wouldn't be foolish enough to attack us," Reluraun said.

"The King of Celes is a wise man, perhaps wiser than even my father. He might be looking at our skirmishes in The Highlands differently than we are, and if he catches wind of the Blood Sorcerer…"

"Perhaps he already has?" Reluraun suggested. "That would explain why Celes is preparing for something."

"Well, we don't know if they're preparing for something. It just seems that more troops are leaving Celes and going to the Etherus-Elos border to the north," Faelyn said. "Our troops have returned from The Highlands, but they are tired. Even though our conflict in Utrya never escalated into a war, it was certainly more than a mere disagreement."

"A disagreement that we resolved," Reluraun said, narrowing his eyes. "You made sure of that, didn't you?"

Faelyn closed his eyes. "I did what I had to," Faelyn said firmly, his eyes snapping open. "My father wanted me to get experience through actual conflict, and that was what I got."

"I still can't believe you wiped out an entire squadron." Reluraun shook his head. "And that was over a year ago too!" He paused. "If anything, that just proves that you and I are Arvendon's best chance at unraveling this situation.

"I know," Faelyn said quietly. He blinked, forcing the thoughts of battle from his head. He couldn't afford to get caught up in those memories now. Not that they were particularly haunting, it was just that… he didn't like to think about what he had done. He could rationalize the use of his abilities against other Summoners, but the crew that he had fought was almost entirely made up of Stormless—that was what irked him so deeply.

"Well, it's good to know that the conferences might not be entirely useless," Reluraun said.

"Yeah." Faelyn nodded, looking around once again.

The servants maintained a healthy distance away from them so that they didn't intrude on their conversation, and Faelyn's guards stood at the entrance of the room, chatting casually.

"Listen, I'm going to turn in before too long. I'll talk to you tomorrow, okay?" Reluraun patted Faelyn on the shoulder, turning to leave through the servants' exit.

Faelyn lingered for a bit, pacing around the massive dance floor, which was now empty save for his guards in the corner.

The extraordinary crystal chandelier hung overhead, its glorious light refracting the Crystals and flames within, shining its beauty all across the room. The marble pillars stood silently in the dimming light. The chandelier began to fade, the final servant flipping the switch in the corner of the room as she left.

Movement to his right caught Faelyn's eye. He spun, searching for the source.

There. Behind the pillars, a lone figure shuffled through the shadows.

Faelyn squinted, recognizing the dark gray robes of a Whisperer. *Strange, I thought they all left.* Faelyn rubbed his chin, then paced a little closer to the lone Whisperer.

The Whisperer turned, his ice-blue eyes meeting Faelyn's gaze.

The same one from earlier? Faelyn thought with a start, continuing forward.

The Whisperer raised a hand.

Faelyn paused.

Something flickered in the Whisperer's hand. He snapped his fingers, then disappeared behind another pillar.

Faelyn frowned, turning around. Everything seemed the same.

Nothing had changed, no one had responded to what Faelyn had assumed to be a signal of some kind.

The Whisperer reappeared by the front entrance of the room.

Faelyn turned around, seeing that his guards were still standing by the servants' corridor, chatting amongst themselves. Faelyn grumbled, but turned back to the Whisperer.

The Whisperer met his eyes again, his withered and wrinkled face breaking into a slight smile. He shifted slightly, then started off into the corridor beyond the ballroom.

Faelyn sighed, turning back to his guards, who were yet to notice him, and grumbled once again. He started after the Whisperer.

It's time we figure out who you are, "Whisperer," Faelyn thought, forcing a sense of command into his steps.

Faelyn passed through the white-marble doors, entering the huge hallway beyond. He turned to his right. There was nothing. He then turned left.

A flicker of a gray cloak disappeared behind a corner at the end of the hallway.

Faelyn frowned. *Helionn's sun, he walks fast,* Faelyn cursed in his thoughts. He picked up the pace, walking under the grand half-arches that dotted the ceiling. Faelyn's eyes narrowed in focus as he sped up in the empty hallway.

He turned the corner, entering the Eastern Wing. A staircase led down to his left, and the hallway continued on to his right. He rounded the staircase, glancing upwards as well. Still no sign of the Whisperer. He sighed, turning once again.

Someone peeked around the corner at the other end of the hallway, then disappeared again.

Faelyn smiled. *There you are,* he thought, walking again. He passed one of the courtyards of the Palace, the massive windows that made up the wall to his right allowing the glorious starlight to pass through the glass windows. He glanced out, looking across the square courtyard and catching movement in the opposite hallway.

"How are you doing this?" Faelyn muttered, coming to the corner where the man had shown himself a few moments before. Faelyn looked down the next hallway, doors lining the wall to his left, the wall to his right still made up of massive windows. The ceiling was lower here—in order to make room for the floor above.

Faelyn caught another flash of the gray cloak at the end of this hallway. *Wasn't he just in the next hallway over?* Faelyn looked back out the huge glass windows of the second floor down to the first floor.

Something gray flickered there as well.

He looked up, looking through the windows of the third floor and scanning the hallway. Between the flicker of the torches and the glow of the chandelier, he caught more movement. He turned around, hearing a footfall on the staircase he had passed earlier.

What the hell? Faelyn thought, laying a hand against the wall. Maybe there was more than one Whisperer here... *But they had all gone with my father, right?*

A door slammed behind him.

Faelyn jumped. Yet, when he looked, it seemed as if the wooden doors of the wall behind him were undisturbed. Almost... *too* undisturbed. Faelyn stepped forward, staring at the brass door handles.

They sparkled with dust. Cobwebs dotted the corners of the door frames.

Yet... people use these doors all the time. These are conference rooms and storage closets, some are even commonly used servant passages. Faelyn shook his head, taking another cautious step forward.

Cyclone's winds, I should've brought my guards, Faelyn thought.

The guards were always less attentive after the parties, and he had left in such a rush that they must've not seen him exiting. Surely they would've noticed that he was gone by now. *Where are they?* Faelyn brushed the thought aside. He turned back to the doors, which were now spotless.

What? Faelyn started, reaching for one of the door handles. It was clean and crisp, just as it should have been.

He turned the brass handle, feeling resistance as he opened it. He heard *wind* beyond it... He grunted, planting his feet and pushing with all his might.

The door flung open, revealing a dark closet. The room beyond was small, barely big enough for four people, and filled with mops and dustpans.

Faelyn shook his head, still hearing the echo of wind in his ears as he turned from the room. He shut the door quietly, turning back to the hallways.

The Whisperer—or Whisperers—were nowhere to be seen.

CHAPTER ELEVEN

THE CLOUDWALKER

"The shelters," as it turned out, were little more than a few mounds dug into the broken, rocky ground of The Wastelands. It had been sufficient, of course, for when the sun had risen and Castien had awoken from his uncomfortable sleep he had found himself surrounded by Wisps; today, the Wispwinds had descended once again.

The Wispwinds were the only "useless" Tempest, for they refilled no Sect's Crystals. It didn't matter to Castien, of course. He didn't much care about the energy cycle or the Crystals. All that mattered to him was that the Tempests didn't kill him, which was a fair enough concern.

Wisps were small, incorporeal creatures that seemed to be the living embodiment of energy, though of what energy no one was sure. They were headed by an orb no larger than a fist, and each bore a lengthy tail that was easily six or seven feet long. They floated through the landscape, covering the air almost as densely as the fog of a Mistveil, though they remained closer to the ground.

A Wisp passed by Castien, making a slight whistling sound as it moved. "Whistling" wasn't the right word, Castien supposed. It was more of a *hissing* sound—not that it mattered. The white Wisps drifted by Castien, occasionally passing through him with their immaterial bodies.

Castien laughed a little as one flew through him. Here, outside of the wards, the action created a sort of tickling sensation.

"I suppose we got lucky," Surge said, standing up. They were still under the cover of the shelter, and the sun was just beginning to peek out from behind the horizon.

In the distance, to the southwest, Castien could barely make out the silhouette of Summerglass Palace. He shuddered. He was getting farther from Arvendon with every hour.

"We should pack up. We need to keep moving." Luka leaned over to where his small collection of supplies lay. The Cryostalker appeared to be rather suited to living in the wilderness.

"Knyvet seems to be leading us directly into The Highlands," Surge observed.

"Annoying that our little 'Blood Sorcerer' wouldn't take the main highway through The Highlands," Saevi said. "Would've been a little more convenient for us."

"He is likely taking the most direct path back to his hideout, which saves us some time, actually," Ilyana said. "The sooner we find where he came from, the sooner we can all go back home."

"Weren't you the one who was excited to be out here with us?" Luka asked, raising a cracked eyebrow.

"Well, yes, but that was before I remembered how much I hate being outside of the wards," Ilyana snickered.

Luka shook his head, muttering a curse.

Ilyana merely grinned wider.

"We should be catching up to Knyvet soon," Surge said, heaving a pack over his shoulder. "The markers on the ghost trees are becoming more infrequent, likely meaning that his Crystals are running low. He'll only be coming down when absolutely necessary."

"Which is precisely why we should keep moving. Come on," Luka said, picking up his pack as well. "We have no time to waste. If

Commander Knyvet runs out of Crystals before we catch up to him, then we risk losing Velarus."

"He's right," Surge said. "Come along now." He waved the group along, starting toward the mouth of the small cave where they had all spent the night.

They passed through the mouth of the crevice, coming out to the barren wastes once again. Wisps danced through the empty landscape, weaving through the warm air with a sort of ethereal beauty.

Castien squinted through the thick cover of Wisps, the hissing and humming of the immaterial creatures filling his ears. He broke into a light jog, carefully avoiding the small cracks and sharp stones of The Wastelands as he ran.

Arthion lingered behind, but picked up his speed slightly.

"Sorry," Castien said, realizing he was falling behind. He reached Ilyana, who was at the back of the group. Surge and Luka led, as always, followed by Saevi.

"Try to keep up," Ilyana said, frowning.

"I said I was sorry," Castien said, trying to steady himself.

"Sorry doesn't prove to me that you won't slow us down, Stormless," Ilyana said, her sharp features twisting as she spoke.

"My name is *Castien*," Castien hissed, feeling the heat rise once again. His face warmed, but he pushed the feeling down once again. *You're outnumbered*, Castien thought. He was surrounded by Summoners. He was the only one who was powerless among this group of people who could practically be considered demigods.

"Whatever," Ilyana said, shrugging. "I'm just saying, if you're the reason Velarus gets away, you'll be hearing from me." She walked off, joining Saevi toward the front.

Castien's anxiety spiked. He quickly fell back into the folds of his mind, only slightly. He synced his breathing to his heartbeat, finding his inner self and sealing out the external world. *There.* He felt himself falling deeper, to that place where he was truly alone, to that place where there was... nothing. Castien frowned, tensing slightly.

His thoughts were uninfluenced, at the moment.

Castien opened his eyes, glancing at Ilyana up ahead as she walked beside Saevi. Castien released himself, suddenly becoming aware of the world and all its noisy facets, namely his bow and pack clinking against his back.

The Wisps hissed and whistled past him, occasionally passing through him and giving him a slight tickle. The Highlands loomed in the distance, their peaks a massive, hulking shadow on the horizon.

Castien no longer had any doubt that that was where they were headed. It did make perfect sense, after all. There were plenty of places to hide in The Highlands... Plenty of places where one could set up camp and go unnoticed.

"Surge wants me to do inventory on our supplies," a voice said, pulling Castien from his observations.

"Hmm?" Castien turned, finding the cracked-skinned, pale-faced Luka walking beside him.

"Surge would like to know how much food you brought," Luka said, a bit more straightforward this time.

"Oh, right," Castien said, feeling his stomach growl. It was not an urge he could satisfy, of course. He had eaten last night, and he would again before they rested this evening—that would be enough. Rationing out one's supplies was better than going hungry altogether.

"We brought enough for ourselves to last around two weeks," the Cryostalker said, turning back to the silhouettes of The Highlands in the distance.

Castien paused, tilting his head. *Two weeks?* Castien asked, eyeing the small pack on Luka's back.

"Two weeks." Luka nodded.

Castien snorted.

Luka's face remained steady. "We're being serious."

"Wha—" Castien started. He had brought seven days' worth of rations, and even that had been a stretch to fit in his pack while still leaving enough room to comfortably carry his bow and quiver. "How could you possibly be carrying that much?" *Do Summoners not have to eat or something?*

"We're Master Summoners, remember?" Luka said. He patted the ice-blue Crystals that were hidden within his red-brown leather armor. "If one is experienced enough, they can extract energy from the Crystals and use part of it to feed their body."

Of course they can, Castien thought, barely containing a grumble.

"I'll need a refill in four or five days," Castien muttered.

Luka nodded, falling silent.

Castien glanced sideways at the Cryostalker, once again examining his pale and cracked skin. *How do they even get like that?* Castien thought. A Cryostalker's ice manipulation could explain the cracked and dry skin, as they were often in cold environments. *But why would it be like that permanently?* For some reason, Castien couldn't bring himself to ask.

"As I figured," Luka said.

Castien felt a sudden burst of shame. He could almost hear Luka thinking: *This is why we shouldn't have brought one of the Stormless.*

"Well, do not worry, Castien," Luka continued.

Castien found himself smiling—at least someone remembered his name.

"I fear that we will not have access to much in The Highlands... if that is in fact where we are heading," Luka said. "I'll let Surge know that we need to conduct a hunt soon." Luka started off in a jog.

"Wait," Castien called. Luka paused, turning around. Castien glanced down at his newly acquired shortsword that hung on his waist, then back to the barren landscape around him. "What are we hunting? We're in The Wastelands."

Luka smiled, his dry lips parting to reveal bright white teeth. "Why, nrekuma of course."

Commander Elric Knyvet squinted through the pale-white swirls that blanketed the land. He scanned the black-rocked Wastelands from above, his eyes focused intensely behind the glass of his goggles. He looked down to his thick leather jacket and unbuttoned it slightly. Reaching into the top inside pocket of the jacket, he produced a small watch. It was already past noon, and the Blood Sorcerer had yet to depart from his shelter.

Elric grumbled, gently sliding the pocket watch back into the heavy, fur-lined insides of his coat. He tightened the strap on his thick hat—whose insides were also lined with fur—and prepared to move.

A bitter wind blew through the cloud tops. Elric shivered, aghast that, even with a coat this thick, he could not fully escape the cold of the high altitude. Before he began, he unbuttoned his tan jacket once more, checking on the mint-green Crystals within.

Nine empty, two full.

Elric sighed, buttoning the jacket once more and raising the fur collar. It would have to do. He reached deep into his mind, searching for the source of his power.

There.

Elric tugged on it, drawing wind from the Cloudwalker Crystals, slowly giving it a new shape once again. The invisible platform he had materialized for himself began to dissipate, the loose shape lost to the true wind once more as Elric began to fall.

He pulled on the power again, harder this time, drawing even more breeze from his Crystals. Pleasure surged through his body, coming from the usage of his powers. Something about the *rush* of Summoning was just... indescribable. With a wave of his gloved hand, Elric was fully upright and stable once again. It felt as if a sudden force had appeared beneath him, pushing back against his weight and keeping him suspended in the clouds.

Elric pushed one hand forward and began using the other to shape the gusts around himself. With a sudden *lurch*, Elric flew forward—pushed by the invisible hand of his power. He kept his arm extended, propelling himself through the air high above the ground.

Wind ripped at his goggles, his helmet, and his coat, but Elric held strong. There was a certain beauty to Cloudwalking, but... There was more to it than simply floating around like a sunbird. Cloudwalking required constant focus, and the utmost strength of mind. Even the slightest mistake and Elric would be sent spiraling out of trajectory.

But it was worth it. It was all *so* worth it. Cloudwalking filled his veins with a sensation that nothing else could match. Using his abilities sent a rush through his blood and a bolt of joy to his mind. Even going a few days without using his powers left him... wanting. For it was his powers that had pulled him from the shadows of his past. And, by hanging on to the *high* of Summoning, he knew that he would never again fall prey to his former weaknesses.

Keep moving. If you hesitate, your mind will snag once again.

He began to pick up speed, grunting against the freezing winds. The deafening gusts silenced his hearing, and Elric once again found himself thankful that he was wearing goggles. It was a practice that Cloudwalkers had adopted several centuries ago, for it seemed that the eyes did not handle high wind speeds well—at least, not without watering to the point where one couldn't even see.

Elric didn't have much time. The Blood Sorcerer had likely either decided to spend the day resting—which was unlikely—or he had snuck out beneath the cover of the useless Wispwinds. Elric had woken at the crack of dawn. He had risen to the sky to keep watch, but he had seen nothing.

His only hope now was spending the entirety of one Crystal on the journey north, where he suspected Velarus was going, and hope that he found some sort of possible destination. Once the Crystal ran out, Elric would be forced to use his final one to head back south, and safely land. He didn't want to get too far ahead of the expedition that the King had promised to send.

Elric was flying faster than any animal could ever hope to move, and before long he was approaching the start of The Highlands with frightening speed.

The mountains began to rise below him, their peaks growing progressively more jagged. He started to withdraw his hand, slowing the force that pushed him. With his other hand, he began to lower himself, only slightly. He had traveled several miles within a few minutes and was likely nearer to the Blood Sorcerer once again. Not all Cloudwalkers were this fast, though Elric... Elric was not like most Cloudwalkers.

The Wisps shifted upward, climbing the slopes of The Highlands as they rose. To the north and west, mountains ran in endless waves.

Elric shuddered. The Highlands were a dangerous place, especially now. Even if the skirmishes between Freyfall and Arvendon were mostly in the past, the threat of an ambush still lingered.

Flinching, Elric realized that he was dangerously close to the mountain in front of him. He banked upward with a wave of his hand, his body lurching higher into the clouds. His stomach doubled, and Elric released his grip.

Elric found himself thrown through the air. Gasping, Elric twisted and tumbled as he fell, trying to gather himself. He had made a turn too quickly. He reached out with a hand, sensing something beneath him in the gusts. He extracted what felt like the last of the wind from the Crystal he had been draining and summoned a blast of air beneath himself.

With a loud *whoosh,* Elric slowed to a stop on the invisible platform, levitating. He groaned, rolling to look beneath himself. The remaining bits of energy in the Crystal emptied.

Elric fell the last few feet, crashing into the fluffy snow of the mountain. He lay there for a moment, groaning. It had been a fairly soft landing, compared to some of his others. The snow was nice enough, and for the moment not unbearably cold. Elric gave himself this time to catch his breath.

It was only when the snow's cold began to seep through the seams of his cloak that Elric decided it was probably time to get up.

He turned, finding solid footing beneath the snow, and pushed himself to his feet. Elric brushed the snow off his jacket and wiped it from his gloves and goggles.

"Could've been worse," Elric muttered. *It could always be worse.* Elric turned around, reorienting himself.

The Wisps dropped off before him, meaning that he was facing south. He turned around, facing upward. That way was north. Finally, he turned toward what he figured was west. The Wisps were thinner up here in the mountains, but not *that* thin. Elric squinted, trying to make out anything unusual against the shape of the mountains. He took a step back, turning back to where the towering peaks began.

Within a few minutes, he was able to locate the makeshift trail that led through the base of the mountains. He followed this trail with his eyes, tracing it with his finger as he did so. *It seems to be turning this way,* Elric thought. *And then maybe this way... and then...*

"Gah!" A tingle shot through Elric's spine, feeling like a claw to his nerves from Calida herself. He jumped, spinning, drawing his wind-wood daggers as he landed.

A Wisp whistled by, seeming to hiss with laughter. Elric grumbled, slipping the personalized daggers back into their sheaths.

Elric cursed, then turned back to the path. He found it again, tracking it by the slight consistency of Wisps that seemed to gather around it. It went farther north, weaving between the mountain Elric stood on and the one directly opposite him. Elric squinted once again, peeling off his goggles.

Bitter cold slammed into his eyes, and Elric grimaced. He kept the goggles off, however, choosing to value the gift of sight over his own comfort. Convenient as the damn things were for flying, Elric couldn't stand the goggles otherwise.

Another Wisp hissed past Elric, narrowly avoiding him. Elric cursed this one as well, quite colorfully. Reorienting himself yet again, Elric finally found himself making progress in tracking the path.

The Blood Sorcerer would be forced to take it, for it was nearly impossible for someone without the gift of Cloudwalking to diverge from the small trails in The Highlands. Besides, even if one was able to survive the elements, the odds of running into a wandering Shadow-Swift were a little too high for most people's liking.

Elric briefly scanned the skies, ensuring that no shadows were watching from above. Shadow-Swifts were by far the deadliest Sect, in Elric's opinion. They were capable of somehow disappearing into thin air on command, and then reappearing seconds later, only to slit your throat.

Elric only knew such things because of legends. He, of course, had never encountered a Shadow-Swift himself. Though, given that Cloudwalkers and Shadow-Swifts were the only two Sects forced to share the sky with one another, Elric was always ready.

Well, "ready" wasn't exactly the right word. No one was ever "ready" to fight a Shadow-Swift. What Elric meant was he was "ready" to flee the scene as fast as possible at any given moment, should a Shadow-Swift show up. Cowardly? No, Elric didn't think so. It was practical. The only way to survive an encounter with a Shadow-Swift was to run or pray that they showed mercy.

Oh, Elric thought. *I should probably be trying to figure out where the trail leads.* Elric snickered to himself. He always appreciated the fact that he could laugh at himself, for it made his lonely flights across Auris far less... well... lonely.

Wait, Elric squinted.

On the mountain directly to the west, there was a slight depression in the rock. It was low, and only a few hundred feet above the trail. It almost looked *unnatural.*

Elric took a step forward, tracing a line from the trail to the spot on the mountain. He brought his finger back up, scanning the areas around the path he had traced in the distance.

Yes, Elric thought. There was a slight zigzagging to the rocks below what appeared to be a small cavern of some sort. There were plenty of ancient caves in The Highlands, many of which were locked by Runes, but this couldn't be one of them. It was too close to the edge of the region.

"A hideout of some sort?" Elric wondered aloud. Perhaps the cave was already there, and was in fact natural, but the zigzagging rocks indicated a lightly carved path that had been traveled at least a few times—recently too.

That must be where the Blood Sorcerer's camp is. Even if it wasn't, it was still worth investigating. But not now, not when he was so far removed from the others. He would use his final Crystal to go as far south as he could and wait for the expedition.

Then, he would travel with them north, investigate the small cave, and see if his suspicions were correct. And, finally, they would stop at the Arvendi-helmed outpost on the Etherus-Elos border. It always felt nice to have a plan.

He may have lost track of the Blood Sorcerer—for now—but he had a feeling he'd be able to find the Summoner again. The paths within The Highlands were limited, and the Tempests were not kind to those who were careless. And, besides, if the Tempests didn't kill those who strayed from the paths, the Shadow-Swifts would.

CHAPTER TWELVE
HERQEN

Two years ago...

Asteros Silverglade stood beside Shalheira and Lucien in the grand atrium of Erydon.

Shalheira's black hair was bound in a tight braid, concealed by the Shadow-Sand hood that she often wore. Asteros was still yet to tell her where they were going tonight. She did not like it when the truth was kept from her, but in this case Asteros had deemed it better to *show* her where they were going, rather than tell her.

Fortunately, she had not told any of the others about tonight's excursion. Though Asteros hadn't directly told her not to, it seemed she understood that a certain level of secrecy was expected in regard to the situation. She had asked a few questions, though he had not fully answered any of them. It was better if he waited.

Asteros found himself once again marveling at the intricate carvings that covered the massive ceremonial chamber as he walked. He had always been fascinated by them, and, despite Lucien's mockery of him, Asteros enjoyed the time he had spent transcribing them—even if it had already been done by their master many years before.

The small fortress had been built as a gift to the Shadow-Swifts, hence the carvings that told their glorious history. Though for what was supposed to be a retelling of events, the engravings held remarkably little real information. The inscriptions were mostly exaggerated stories of the battles of the Ancient Shadow-Swifts. These were, of course, very impressive. But they were of very little use to Asteros. However, whatever was beyond Herqen's door... *that* would be valuable.

They neared the end of the corridor, coming to the crack in the ceiling. It led to a rather long tunnel that would eventually take them outside. The passageway had been hollowed out by their ancestors to serve as a sort of "backdoor," after they had accepted the gift of Erydon from the Stonemasters and Rune-Writers. The main entrance of the fortress was protected by a Rune-Lock, which was essentially impossible to bypass unless one knew the proper actions required to open it.

It was one of these same locks that protected the door Lucien had found—separately—on the mountain called "Herqen." No two Rune-Locks were alike, and each one was virtually impenetrable.

Erydon's gate required one to utter the phrase "Erydon is our sanctuary, but the Unbound is our home" while displaying the Shadow-Swift power of umbrakinesis. Naturally, this door was foolproof. But this same method was not used for all the doors. Many Rune-Locks did not even require words to be spoken, nor did they require Summoning. That was what made these doors so utterly insurmountable: The secret to entry could be *literally* anything. Ranging from drawing pictures in the ground to moving one's body in a specific way, one could not simply guess what would make the Rune unlock and expect to succeed. The Rune's protective spell also created a barrier, so one could not carve a hole in the mountain and create an alternate way in. Even shifting into the Unbound wouldn't allow one to pass through the ward.

But Asteros's key offered a way inside.

The key was a light weight in his front pocket. It was a small object, and it was more of a rock than anything else. Haldir had given it to him shortly before his death, saying that it was "capable of opening any door in the world."

"Ready?" Asteros asked.

Lucien grunted in affirmation.

Shalheira nodded and shifted.

Asteros did the same, transferring the matter of his body into that strange place between worlds: the Unbound.

Black fog coated the room, oozing from Asteros's form. Though much of his surroundings looked the same from the Unbound, everything was still covered in a slight film of darkness.

Shalheira motioned for the two of them to lead the way, black mists seeping from her body.

Lucien was the first to take flight, aiming for the crack in the ceiling.

With a smile, Asteros leapt into the air and followed suit. Darkness enveloped him. Seconds later he shot from the small opening in the mountain, soaring like a wraith in the night.

Shalheira followed, her hood and cloak flapping furiously in the phantom winds of the Unbound.

Asteros's Crystals clinked together as he continued draining them. He propelled himself through the frozen air with ease. The shift had drained a considerable amount of energy, but he had prepared more than enough Crystals for the journey.

Gusts of frost swirled around him, passing through his body as if it were nothing. Flying was not just a method of travel... No, it was an *artform*. It was something that no land-bound mortal could ever understand. This was *real* power.

Lucien was already shooting across the sky, leading the way for the two of them to follow.

Asteros soared through the open night, stars lighting the mountain-stage for his glorious performance. And, with more grace than any dancer could ever hope to possess, Asteros closed his eyes, and soared.

He whipped through the air, flipping and diving in spellbinding patterns. He spun in massive loops, drawing plumes of dark smoke across the sky. Wind rushed through his short hair, kissing his firm skin before slipping off into the open night. He dashed along the frost-filled gusts, banking on seemingly nothing before leaping back into the sweet, sweet midnight air.

This is what it means to be alive. This is what it means to live.

Half of him in the Unbound, the other half in Auris, Asteros shined. His dark luminosity trailed across the glorious star-scape, leaving his mark on the stunning constellations. The lights above were clear this evening. Sure, it wasn't quite like the view Keries got from his "secret" perch atop Telenaris, but it was stunning none-theless.

Furious winds pushed against him, trying to force him back onto the ground. But the raging currents of air didn't so much as inconve-nience Asteros. He *dominated* them, banking off one and then another, keeping a part of him within the Unbound as if in blatant defiance of nature's will.

There was an intoxicating silence to the evening, despite the howl of the wind as it wove through The Highland's peaks. All this land, untouched by humanity since the dawn of time because the Tempests prevented all but the most powerful of Summoners from being able to survive up here. So much of the world was reduced to bitter wastelands, subject to the tyranny of the Tempests. It was only because of the Rune-Writers that humanity lived on now. For the Rune-Writers had placed protective wards throughout Auris, allowing for a handful of cities to be built without having to fear being destroyed by the looming Tempests. But that had been before the Vanishing, when the Rune-Writers, along with six other Sects, had gone extinct due to the arrival of the Tempests.

He turned his head to see Shalheira twisting in the skies, bending the air to her will. The six Shadow-Swifts of Erydon did not have much in common, but their love of flying... that was perhaps the one thing they shared.

Lucien shot a plume of darkness to the side, his signal to Asteros and Shalheira to begin descending.

Asteros severed the streams of black smoke that had been pushing him forward, and fell. Asteros remained calm as he reoriented himself, aiming his body toward the small indenture on the slope of Herqen. It approached rapidly, and, with one final push, Asteros slowed to a stop just a few feet above the stone landing.

Lucien landed first.

Shalheira landed next to him, shifting out of the Unbound as she did so.

Asteros mirrored her. They looked at one another, the thrill of flight still fresh in their eyes. Shalheira smiled softly, and took a step forward.

"Here we are," Lucien said, shifting back to Auris. Lucien's black hair was tied in a ponytail, and his pointed beard accentuated his sharp, Northeastern features. Lucien wasn't particularly old—at least, not by Shadow-Swift standards.

A Stormless would've been dead for at least a decade or two before they reached Lucien's age, but that was beside the point.

"Shall we?" Lucien asked. He motioned to a cleft in the rock where two colliding slopes met.

"That's it?" Asteros stepped forward.

"Well hidden, isn't it?" Lucien said. He began approaching the cleft, which was still some distance away.

"Where have you taken me?" Shalheira demanded. "I was promised an explanation upon our arrival."

"And you'll get your explanation," Asteros said. "Though, once you see where we are, I doubt you'll need one."

Lucien led them to the cleft. Though, as they neared it, Asteros realized that it was, in fact, an opening. There seemed to be a small cave on the other side of the gap.

"This way," Lucien said. He slipped between the rocks, entering the small cavern.

Asteros followed suit, a horrific odor assaulting his nostrils upon entry. He coughed, covering his nose with his hands. After a few steps he nearly tripped on something.

Right, Asteros remembered. Lucien had killed nine men in this chamber. Of course, he hadn't taken the time to clean the place up before Asteros and Shalheira arrived.

"Calida's Claws," Shalheira cursed, coughing as well. She lowered her eyes, her enhanced vision allowing her to spot the bodies that littered the cave floor. "I guess I shouldn't be surprised."

"Don't be so quick to judge," Lucien cautioned. "These scholars were of great use to me before they passed."

"Before you killed them, you mean," Shalheira said.

Lucien grunted.

Asteros turned his attention to the wall opposite himself. It was there that he found the Rune-Lock.

Thousands of complex lines were carved into the wall, weaving across the wall like waves. Square Runes were inscribed periodically, forming the web of protection that sealed the door.

"By the Six," Shalheira breathed. She took a few steps forward, realizing what she stood before.

The massive Rune-Door loomed over them, lying in wait. This construction was built nearly a thousand years ago and had laid untouched ever since. The Stonemaster Sanctuaries were things of legend: secret hideouts of the late Summoners before they were wiped out by the arrival of the Tempests during the Vanishing. Whatever was inside, it would be from *before* the Vanishing.

The Tempests had destroyed everything on Auris that wasn't protected by the wards, meaning that any information that was vulnerable was lost. Unfortunately, that had ended up being almost *all* of the knowledge that Auris's Summoners and Stormless possessed up until that point. The rooms on the other side of that door, however, would have been preserved.

Shalheira neared it, laying a hand on one of the square Runes in the center of the wall.

It sparked to life, taking on a bright white glow. The light spread, illuminating the rest of the Runes one by one.

It was a beautiful display. Asteros was left breathless, unable to resist marveling at the mastery with which the door had been built. His knowledge regarding doors like this one wasn't terribly extensive, though he knew that the number of Runes on this door seemed... high.

"How did you find this?" Shalheira asked, transfixed on the glowing Runes.

"The Freyfallion scholars," Lucien said. "They led me right to it." Lucien kicked one of the corpses. "Obviously." Lucien added. "Now step aside, my dear, don't spend up your awe just yet. Asteros has something to show us." Lucien nodded to him.

Asteros advanced, reaching into the pocket of his armor and producing the key. The dark stone fit into his hand, though it was slightly larger than his palm. The key itself was covered in Runes, which Haldir had fused together using an unknown method. Only the extinct Rune-Writers could write Runes that held power. Haldir had seemingly carved Runes from somewhere and transferred them onto this stone, making a combination that could unlock doors.

Haldir had been incredibly intelligent, far more intelligent than Asteros could ever hope to be. But he had grown old, as all men eventually do. Hardly even a day after his two-hundredth birthday Haldir had died in his sleep.

Asteros raised the stone, sending a jolt of umbrakinesis through it.

It rumbled as if waking up. Seconds later it began to glow, taking on the same bright white glow as the wall itself.

The stone lifted from Asteros's hand, levitating through the air. It inched toward the door, rattling with unstable energy.

Asteros had used it once on Erydon's lock, but seeing it work on Herqen's was something else entirely.

It drifted toward one of the square Runes. The stone shook slightly, emitting a bright tendril of white light and extending it toward the Rune. The tendril hooked onto the Rune, sapping the light from it.

More tendrils grew from the stone, reaching out and latching onto the other Runes of the door, disabling them as well.

Moments later, the lights of the door were all but gone, leaving only the glow of the stone. It returned to Asteros's hand, still glowing.

"What in Izara's Shadow was that?" Shalheira demanded.

"A key," Asteros whispered. He advanced. Reaching out a hand, he *pushed* on the door.

It moved.

"Help me push it open," Asteros said. He started pushing again, the others joining him. The door was quite heavy, as it was made entirely of stone.

Rock grinded against rock as the door moved backward. It took all of a minute for the three of them to push it open, finally giving them just enough space to enter.

Asteros slipped inside, his feet landing on the stone floor of the interior. His senses were instantly overwhelmed by the stale air of the chamber.

Lucien and Shalheira followed seconds later.

Asteros made for the torch on one of the nearby walls. It was, of course, unlit. But—assuming that they were like Erydon's torches—Asteros knew that these were powered by a combination of Runes and Incendiary.

He softly laid a hand on the metal sconce, dust grazing his fingers as he felt the flames ignite from deep within the bones of the torch. Fire appeared as if out of nowhere, providing some much-needed illumination in the pitch-black darkness of the cavern. He motioned for Lucien and Shalheira to follow him.

Shalheira lowered her hood, exposing her delicate features. There was a strange beauty to the young woman, a sort of ethereal grace that only a being who had lived and fought for decades could acquire.

Asteros pushed aside these thoughts, now was no time for admiration. Now was the time for action. He continued down the hallway, igniting each torch he passed as he did. He could sense their amazement—he felt something like it too. They were within a chamber that had been untouched for nearly a millennium. This place, though... It seemed to have been built like Erydon.

"Wait," Lucien said. "Shouldn't we stop and look for artifacts? Maybe a diary?" Lucien asked.

"Stonemasters built Erydon," Asteros said. "They designated the grand atrium entirely for storytelling in our home," Asteros continued. "And knowing the Stonemasters..." Asteros trailed off.

He slowed to a stop as they entered a large room. Asteros knew this place—he knew what it must be: the grand chamber.

The room was *colossal;* thousands of square feet in size, the ceremonial atrium was incredible. Not only that, but it mirrored Erydon's with its rounded walls, dome-like ceiling, and seemingly endless collections of inscriptions in the ancient tongue.

Asteros laid a hand on one final torch, illuminating the room.

"...This place will be the same," Asteros finished. He spun around, facing an awestruck Lucien and Shalheira. "Take your time, my friends. Information that is over a thousand years old lies all around us."

Shalheira turned her eyes to the wall beside her, examining the text. "And it seems that the Stonemasters wrote in detail as well," Shalheira said. "These writings... They're almost written like a journal."

"A journal of what?" Lucien asked.

"That is what we are here to find out," Asteros said, approaching one of the walls. "Whoever created this place clearly found their knowledge worth recording, meaning that it must have had some significance."

"But..." Shalheira started. "There must be a lifetime worth of information written on these walls. It will take us months to translate it all!"

"If it takes us months, then it will take months," Lucien said, nodding to himself.

Asteros could see the gears turning within Lucien's mind; there was something brewing. There was something to be found on these walls, he could *feel* it. There were secrets here, secrets that would change the world.

"What do you intend to do with all of this?" Shalheira asked. "Information like this will be of little use to us." Shalheira paused. "We should share it, should we not? Share it and come out of hiding for once?"

"No," Lucien said. He spun around, his calculations seemingly complete. "We will be coming out of hiding—eventually—but not to share this information."

"Then why?" Shalheira asked after a moment.

Asteros advanced. Lucien had been clear about wanting complete control over whatever they found, was this what he meant?

"If this information contains what I think it does," Lucien began, "then we may finally discover the truth about the Vanishing. Not only that, but we could uncover the ways that the Ancients lived. All of their insights, knowledge, theories... they would all be ours."

"Ours to do what with, Lucien?" Asteros stepped forward.

"Whatever we wish," Lucien said. He raised his hands. "If we wanted, we could indeed share it with the world." He paused. "Although I was hoping that we would choose a more *ambitious* objective."

"Such as?" Shalheira asked.

"Domination," Lucien said.

Asteros started.

"Before you speak, at least hear me out," Lucien said. "The Shadow-Swifts have been Auris's most powerful Sect for centuries, yet we have nothing to show for it. Our continent is shattered, divided into six countries, split like the members of our Sect. If we use this knowledge correctly, we could bring this land together."

"With us at the top?" Shalheira stepped forward. She turned to Asteros. "You can't seriously be considering this?"

Asteros made no response.

"Think of how it would be, Shalheira," Lucien continued. "Rather than hiding from the world in our fortress, we would be *rulers*. We would have the power to reunite this land under one common force."

"And that force... would be us," Shalheira said. She stared for several moments. "Erydon exists not just to protect *us* but to protect the people of Auris," Shalheira said slowly. "Our power exceeds even *our own* comprehension; to subject the continent to our whims would go against all that we stand for!"

"And what do we stand for, exactly?" Lucien challenged. "Neutrality? Peace? We are instruments of war, it's time we started acting like it."

"So that's it then?" Shalheira snorted. "Just uproot all of Auris's governments? Our continent is thriving, why intervene now?"

"Auris is not thriving. No, it is *barely surviving!*" Lucien snarled. He paused, taking a deep breath. "We cannot sit by and do nothing while our entire society is on the verge of collapse. Tensions are so high that half a dozen wars are mere *minutes* away from starting. The limited fields under Runic protection already struggle to provide for the continent as it is, and our population only keeps growing. This world's problems are not simply going to wash away like disheveled sand in foreign waves. No, they will only get worse. They will get worse, and worse, until humanity reaches its breaking point and order is replaced by *anarchy.*" He paused once again, his voice softening. "I understand that you may be frightened. I am too, believe me. But we cannot allow something like this to happen while we are on the precipice of acquiring the power to prevent it."

A heavy silence fell over the group. The warm, stale air of the cave smothered them, sealing the trio in their moment of quiet. The only sound in the chamber was the soft crackling of the torch, and the gentle burn of the Incendiary within.

"He's right," Asteros said softly. He turned to Shalheira.

She stood silently, staring at the floor. Shalheira was rarely pensive, but this was not a decision that one made hastily.

To Asteros, it was clear: Lucien had a way forward, and it was clear that they needed one. Auris was struggling, as it had been for decades. If Lucien offered a solution to their problems, then they owed it to the continent to at the very least try it. Besides, hesitation was not in Asteros's nature.

"If we do this," Shalheira said softly. "If we use this information in the way that you intend, then you must promise me one thing."

"And what is that, my dear?" Lucien asked. He tilted his head.

"That we do it for the right reasons," Shalheira said.

Lucien blinked.

"If we intend to extend our influence across the entirety of Auris, you must promise that we are doing it for the right reasons," Shalheira said. "I know what you claim, but I don't just want to hear you *say* that you're doing this for humanity's sake." Shalheira paused. "Promise me this, and I will devote myself to your cause."

"That's it?" Lucien asked. He smirked. "Fine then: I promise."

"Good." Shalheira nodded. "Know that if I deem your actions to be of the wrong intent, I will not hesitate to voice my concerns. Test my patience and I leave, is that a deal?"

Lucien's smile persisted. "That is a deal."

Asteros stepped forward, preparing himself. Lucien had laid out a great task for them: finding a way to use this information to save Auris. It would be no easy feat, true, but, if anyone could do it... it would be the Shadow-Swifts. They were the most *powerful* Sect on Auris, and the world knew it. They had spent long enough locked in that mountain, keeping themselves isolated for the sake of common safety. But now, now that was about to change... It was time that the Shadow-Swifts became who they were meant to be.

"Well then," Asteros said. "Let's begin."

CHAPTER THIRTEEN
THE HUNT

"You're insane," Arthion whispered, huddled against one of the boulders of The Wastelands.

"No, I'm hungry," Surge said, gripping his massive greatsword in both hands. "Or I'm not... but *he* will be if we don't do something." Surge nodded to Castien.

Castien felt his face heat up; he kept his eyes forward.

The nrekuma sniffed at something in the ground, plunging its razor-sharp teeth into one of the cracks in the land. It brought its head back up, snarfing down a few krellins that it had uncovered from the ground. The creature's thick mandibles clicked against one another as it swallowed, then turned away.

Castien shuddered.

Click. Click. Click.

He forced himself to keep his eyes on the creature. The massive beast stood at over two or three times Castien's height. Apparently, the one they had seen a few days before had been *small.*

"How long are we going to sit here?" Ilyana hissed. "If we wait too long, it'll just wander off!"

"We wait for Luka's signal," Surge said.

Ilyana grumbled. She fell back against the large boulder and rolled her eyes, holding her butterfly-blades firmly.

"Luka has taken down one of these beasts on his own before. I trust his judgment," Surge grunted.

Castien glanced to the side, staring at the ghost tree where Luka was hidden. Turning back, Castien allowed his gaze to fall on the creature once again. It had to be at least thirty feet long, and its scaled black hide was shining despite the darkness.

The sun would rise soon, and with it another Tempest. Judging by the rising winds, it would be a Cyclone... which meant they needed to hurry. Cyclones were too dangerous to travel in—without the cover of the wards, at least.

"Be careful," Castien muttered, lowering himself once again.

"Don't worry about us, Stormless," Surge grumbled. "Just stay low and stay out of it." Surge kept his gaze fixed on the nrekuma.

Click. Click. Click.

"Kid, calm down," Ilyana said. "You won't even have to do anything."

Castien lowered his gaze, noticing his white-knuckled grip. He released his fists, then took a deep breath. She was right.

"I still don't get why you can't just blast it into smithereens," Arthion whispered to Surge.

"Nrekuma are built to survive in The Wastelands. Their skin photosynthetically absorbs Summoning energies, to an extent," Surge said, the massive silver sword in his hands shimmering in the falling moonlight. "Either way, you won't have to fight it, so why do you care?"

"Good point," Arthion muttered, lowering himself to where Castien sat against the stone.

"It shouldn't be long now," Surge said.

Castien glanced at the bright white Crystals hanging from Surge's armor—Voltarian Crystals. Voltarians commanded lightning, one of the most dangerous elements.

Something whistled through the air. A loud crashing noise

followed, almost like shattering glass... or... *ice.* Castien jumped up, seeing chunks of ice rolling across The Wastelands. They rolled to a stop at the nrekuma's feet.

The nrekuma whirled around, sniffing them.

Click. Click. Click.

The creature's massive razor-sharp mandibles clicked against one another as it prodded at the ice. There was a certain *intelligence* to its eyes, something that Castien had never seen in the eyes of any other animal.

That's what makes them so deadly. They're nearly as smart as we are. Castien watched with both fascination and terror as the nrekuma raised one of its thick, sinewy legs, and brought it down upon the ice, destroying it.

A sudden bolt of fire crashed into its back.

The nrekuma shrieked. The horrific sound pierced Castien's eardrums like an arrow.

Castien dove, his muscles going limp with terror. Chaos ensued. Castien watched as Surge sprinted around the boulder and charged the creature.

Ilyana dashed to the side, tapping her Crystals to give herself a burst of speed.

Castien's heart thundered, pounding through his head and nearly beating out of his chest. He managed to lock eyes with Arthion, who looked equally terrified. *At least I'm not the only one,* Castien thought.

Another blast of light shot through the night, followed by a sizzle of heat.

Castien peeked around the edge of the rock.

Saevi stood at a distance, orbs of flame circling her. She thrust an arm forward, one of the fist-sized fireballs hurling itself toward the nrekuma. It crashed into the thick, dark hide of the beast, agitating it further. Saevi threw out her other arm, another ball of fire launching through the air. Seconds later, more flames appeared around her, slowly manifesting with the power of her Crystals.

Ilyana moved with inhuman speed. She neared the creature within seconds, dropping into a slide and unlatching both of her blades. The butterfly-swords extended, locking into their elongated forms just in time for Ilyana to plunge them into the exposed leg of the nrekuma. She whirled, twisting as she slid and using the impaled blades for leverage to make a turn. With a grunt, Ilyana pushed off the ground, vaulting over the creature and ripping the blades from its black legs, which now gushed dark red blood.

The nrekuma screamed again, throwing back its head and letting out a primordial roar.

Surge charged, his silver greatsword rippling with lightning.

Castien stumbled back at the sight of the glowing blade, his jaw hanging open.

Surge leapt, lightning shooting from his legs and propelling him into the air. He released one hand from the sword, sending a blast of electricity toward the creature. Surge let out a vicious battle cry, landing atop the creature with a loud *thud* and plunging the electrically charged sword into its back.

The nrekuma thrashed, jumping and twisting and turning. It swept its colossal barbed tail toward Ilyana, who dodged it casually. Saevi continued bombarding it with firebolts while Surge held strong to his blade, sending wave after wave of electricity through the beast.

With each flash, the creature shook, crying out with that deafening shriek.

Castien looked out, locking eyes with Arthion once again.

Arthion shook his head in disbelief, horrified.

The nrekuma screeched, tossing Surge from its back with a half-broken claw.

Surge cried out, falling to the ground.

The nrekuma reared, swinging its tail toward Surge. Castien shouted, his hand whipping toward his bow, but it didn't matter.

Ilyana jumped out of nowhere, severing the nrekuma's tail from its body with a blindingly quick slash.

Then, Luka entered the fray.

Luka, Master Cryostalker and Agent of the King, showed why *he* was the one leading this hunt. He charged from behind the ghost tree, raising both hands and letting out a battle cry.

Hundreds of small ice shards flew from his palms, materializing in the air as he ran. They crashed into the nrekuma, piercing its skin in dozens of places.

The beast cried out, turning to face its new attacker, but Luka was ready.

Luka drew his sword with one hand, extending his other arm beneath himself.

Ice coated the ground beneath him, making the rocky Wastelands slick. Luka slid, spraying more ice as he did so, and angled his blade.

The nrekuma hesitated, caught off guard by the slide, and that was all Luka needed. Luka severed the creature's leg, then leapt into the air and cut off its right mandible.

Castien watched in awe as the team worked together.

Ilyana stabbed one of its back legs, sending it crashing to the ground, while Saevi concentrated on a specific spot of the creature's back, slowly burning through the now-glowing skin. Surge blasted the creature again. The lightning reflected off harmlessly, sizzling into nonexistence, but it had been sufficiently distracting.

Luka grabbed onto the creature's other mandible, swinging himself to its back. He reached out with a hand, clinging to one of the creature's spikes. The nrekuma screamed, and Luka sent a pulse of ice through the horn, freezing it.

Surge's sword crackled with energy. He stabbed the creature in the stomach, sending a shock through it.

The nrekuma reared up, Luka still hanging onto the back of its neck. Luka seemed to be trying to pull the creature *upward,* rather than lowering himself.

Then, Castien saw why.

As if in slow motion, Castien watched as Luka planted his blade in the nrekuma's back and raised both hands. While flailing through the air, Luka wove a *gargantuan* ice spike, growing it from the ground and angling it toward the monster's underside.

The ice spike slammed into the nrekuma's jaw.

The creature fell with a crash, the frozen spike impaling its skull and shattering its bones.

Castien stepped forward, shaking.

Surge withdrew his blade, de-electrifying and sheathing it. Ilyana carefully wiped the red blood from her blades, flipped them back into their shorter forms, and sheathed them as well. Saevi lowered her hands, the balls of flame disappearing into nothing. And, finally, Luka stepped down from the nrekuma's back, pulling his sword from its neck as he did so.

Castien found himself walking forward, awestruck.

The creature's mouth hung open at an odd angle, showing just enough for Castien to see the massive ice spike that still impaled it. The spike continued through the nrekuma's forehead, coming to a sharp point at the top, which was crested with red blood.

The remaining mandible dangled, half-attached to its left jaw. Its legs slumped to the ground, sliced beyond recognition. Its deep eyes hung open, that vague sense of intelligence lingering in the empty gaze. A hole had been burned through its back, still smoking from Saevi's flames.

Castien could only watch as Surge and Luka began cutting away at the thick scales around its chest, trying to reach the meat within.

They were just so... perfect, Castien thought, his body going numb. He distantly heard footsteps beside him.

Arthion stepped to his side, arms folded. "Such beautiful, terrible destruction, isn't it?" Arthion said softly.

"I..." Castien trailed off. "It never even stood a chance," Castien said after a moment.

"Did you expect it to?" Arthion asked.

Castien met the Whisperer's amber eyes but didn't respond.

"You haven't seen Master Summoners fight before, have you?" Arthion asked, tilting his head.

Castien shook his head.

"Ah," Arthion mused. "Well, now you have."

"It was so…" Castien trailed off once again, unable to pick the words from his jumbled mind.

"Maybe you didn't realize it before, my friend," Arthion started. "But you're on an expedition with some of the most powerful people on Auris. This isn't like your other assignments." Arthion walked off, approaching the rest of the group.

Castien stood, feeling like a fool. He didn't belong among these people. Arvendon's most powerful Summoners walked alongside him, and here he was, just another Stormless kid who thought he could make a difference. There was nothing he could do.

If they wanted to, these people could kill him in a fraction of a second. Even if the Blood Sorcerer was real, the man couldn't possibly stand a chance against this crew, could he?

Castien stumbled forward, anxiety burning in his chest once again, making it harder and harder to breathe with each passing second.

His heart did not slow, his nausea did not dissipate. Castien did not belong here; he knew that much—maybe he always had. Yet… a part of him had thought that maybe, just *maybe,* he was here for a reason. But no. He was an infant fighting alongside gods, only brought along for the ride because they thought he was "special."

Castien watched in silence as they skinned the creature, extracting the meat from the corpse. *Food,* Castien reminded himself. *Food for me.* He shook his head.

Killing a nrekuma was nothing to them. And in that moment Castien's anxiety began to turn into something else, something different: terror.

No one deserved this kind of power. No one, not a single soul should possess this capability of destruction. If the Summoners could do this to a nrekuma, Castien could only imagine what they could do to a Stormless if they wanted... To an entire *legion* of Stormless.

Castien found himself more afraid than he had ever been in his entire life. The other Stormless... they thought that the Summoners were *like* them; some even viewed them as equals. Never had Castien realized just how wrong they were.

The Summoners were so cognizant of their superiority that they didn't even bother exploiting the Stormless—as many might have. No, they knew that the Stormless were so pitifully weak that they weren't even worth manipulating. Besides, why would the Summoners need to command the Stormless? The Summoners already had *everything*.

Castien's teeth clenched, the weight of the bow on his back becoming apparent to him as the world seemed to cave in. This wasn't right. None of this was right. He had been given the gift of life only for his entire existence to be rendered pointless—and not just him, *every* Stormless on the continent was worthless in this world of Summoners.

This whole place was so twisted and terrible... so impossibly backward it couldn't possibly be reality. And yet it was—and there was nothing Castien could do about it.

CHAPTER FOURTEEN

THE SANCTUARY

Twenty-two months ago...

Asteros Silverglade paced through Herqen's chamber. Shalheira had returned to Erydon, claiming that she needed to rest. Lucien, however, had stayed. Several hours had passed since their last conversation.

"This has been... underwhelming," Lucien grumbled.

"Not necessarily," Asteros said. He paced around the large room, scanning the inscribed walls. "We only hoped to find knowledge that would help us, and that is what we have done."

"And how does all of *this* help us, pray tell?" Lucien motioned to the walls. "All we have found are the pointless ramblings of a frightened Stonemaster."

"Pointless when they were written, yes. But the Stonemaster's writings are not without value to us," Asteros said. "Through his words we have learned that the Vanishing was not exactly what we had once believed."

"Yet we still don't know *what* it was," Lucien countered. "All we know is that it had something to do with The Highlands, and how does that help us?"

"For nearly a thousand years scholars have been trying to discover *where,* exactly, the Tempests came from; now we know that they originated in The Highlands," Asteros said. "The fact that they came from one specific place already contradicts what we thought we knew."

"Two months of reading these damned walls and that's all we know." Lucien cursed. "We were supposed to find information that we could *use.*"

"Don't underestimate the power of this knowledge," Asteros snapped. "Besides, the Stonemaster confirmed that there were other sanctuaries like this one."

"A shame he couldn't tell us where they were," Lucien muttered.

Asteros listened as the Incendiary torches crackled softly, echoing through the stuffy chamber. It was these torches that the Stonemaster who built this chamber had seen by, and now it was these torches that Asteros used to read his words... fascinating.

"This was your idea, Lucien," Asteros said after a moment. "You were the one who wanted to use the information we found as a weapon."

"And you were the one who agreed to do so," Lucien shot back. "Regardless, you can hardly blame me for my aggravation."

Asteros closed his eyes, taking a deep breath. Lucien was right. Their expectations had been high—far too high. The Stonemaster's writings had consisted of repetitive journal entries, simply detailing how terrified he was of what lay ahead for him.

Curiously enough, the Stonemaster hadn't called it "The Vanishing," rather, he used no name at all. He had been strangely unaware of what, exactly, was on the horizon. All that seemed clear was that he was frightened. The sanctuary itself had been built for the sake of shelter, they had discerned... but even that was not said directly. One of the few things that the Stonemaster had said outright was that "The Great War," as he called it, had shifted to The Highlands.

Interestingly enough, there was also no mention of the looming Tempests either—which had always been believed to be the cause of the war. It was slowly becoming clear to Asteros that war may've been caused by something else, and that the Tempests had somehow arrived later.

"There's something I still don't understand," Asteros said, breaking the silence.

"And what might that be?" Lucien asked.

"How could the Stonemasters have built this cavern in the first place?" Asteros asked. "The Tempests are responsible for powering most Crystals, but there were no Tempests before the Vanishing."

"Our Crystals aren't filled by a Tempest," Lucien said.

"But could all of the Ancient Sects have been powered by the moonlight, as our Crystals are?" Asteros asked. "It's possible, yes... But I find it rather unlikely."

"What are you getting at?" Lucien asked. "The Runes are proof that at least some Ancient Summoners had access to magic, there's no debating that."

"I'm not questioning whether magic was present, I'm merely raising the question of *how* such magic came to be."

"You think there might've been a source other than the Tempests?" Lucien asked.

"Our magic comes from the skies—from the weather—as does the magic of all other Sects," Asteros said, pacing. "What I am coming to suspect is that the Ancient Summoners somehow drew magic from a force like the Tempests before the Tempests had even descended."

"Or the Tempests were already there," Lucien suggested. He folded his arms.

Asteros stopped. "Could that be?" Asteros asked, spinning to face Lucien. "It would make sense, but why would the histories have lied about such a thing?"

"Perhaps to cover something up?" Lucien shrugged. "The Vanishing is clearly far more complex than we realized."

"Indeed." Asteros nodded.

"Regardless, we simply do not possess the knowledge to find out," Lucien said.

"What do you mean?" Asteros asked.

"We don't know where the other chambers are," Lucien said. "And we aren't well versed enough in the ancient tongue to know if there were somehow hints in this cavern that we missed."

Asteros blinked. *Wait,* he thought. Lucien was correct that they didn't know enough, but what if there were a way to remedy that?

"I have an idea," Asteros said.

Lucien raised an eyebrow.

"Freyfall," Asteros said simply.

"What of them? Their skirmishes with Arvendon?" Lucien raised an eyebrow.

Asteros shook his head.

The research party that Lucien had killed had not gone unnoticed by Freyfall. They had wrongfully accused Arvendon of the murders, which indirectly drew attention to Freyfall's subtle advances in The Highlands over the last several years. As a result, Arvendon had sent troops to the region to enforce their borders, and Freyfall had retaliated.

"No, not the skirmishes," Asteros said. "Their scholars were the ones who first led you to this chamber. Clearly, they know more about the Ancients than we do."

"What of it?" Lucien asked.

"If anyone would know where to go from here... if anyone would be able to pick up on any clues we might not be smart enough to uncover, it would be them," Asteros said.

"Yes, but unfortunately for us Freyfall's scholars are not up for sale," Lucien said.

"They don't have to be," Asteros said. "Anyone whose true goal is to learn more would be inclined to join us." Asteros paused. "Though, even still, I doubt that any scholars would leave their station without a bit of *convincing.*"

"What do you propose?" Lucien asked.

"We send Shalheira," Asteros said after a moment. "We send Shalheira out into the mountains, or even into Freyfall if we have to, and she will bring us back three scholars."

"We would have to tell the others, then," Lucien said.

Asteros paused.

Keries, Malik, and Lyseria still did not know of their discovery here in Herqen. The Shadow-Swifts did not share much with one another under normal circumstances, but bringing three—presumably Stormless—scholars into their fortress would not be possible without an explanation.

"So, we would tell them," Asteros said. "It's time we reunited our clan either way," Asteros continued. "I will inform Shalheira of her new task, you may do as you wish." Asteros turned to leave.

"Asteros," Lucien said.

Asteros turned.

"You know she will not like it," Lucien said. "Having to threaten the scholars to win them over to our side."

"I know," Asteros said. "But she is the best of us when it comes to interacting with the outside world. If anyone can bring us three scholars *without* anyone dying, it will be her."

"Either way, she will eventually need to shift her perspective," Lucien said. "Surely you can see that, if we continue on this path, we will undoubtedly face conflict."

Asteros sighed. "We all have to do things we don't want to."

Keries Nightbloom woke up cold. Stiffness plagued his bones, fatigue infested his muscles, and a thick blanket of nothingness smothered his thoughts. He woke like this every morning. The sickness would fade throughout the day—most of the time, at least. He rolled out of bed, setting his feet firmly on the floor. He wobbled a bit but soon was oriented well enough to start moving; that tended to help the sickness.

His room in Erydon was bland, the walls mostly blank. Material possessions brought him no joy—not anymore. His thoughts drifted to the glorious star-scape through the ceiling above, and a slight smile spread across his face, beating back the suffocating thickness that slowed his thoughts. The relief was slight, but it was *everything.*

Just make it through the morning, we'll figure out the rest later, Keries thought. He stumbled out into one of the many passageways of Erydon, seeking out one particular room. Few carvings lay in the walls of these corridors. This section of Erydon was mostly used as private quarters for its Shadow-Swifts, and fairy tales held no place here.

"Keries?" a young voice called from inside the room up ahead.

Keries smiled softly. "It is me, young one," he said, struggling to remain steady as he entered the chamber.

Lyseria leapt from her small bed, wrapping her little arms around Keries and squeezing him tight.

Keries frowned. "Another nightmare?"

The child nodded, refusing to let go of him as they stood in the entryway to her room. Keries shuffled toward her bed, trying to set her down while he pulled a chair toward her nightstand.

She reluctantly released her grip on him and settled onto the bed. "It was like last time," she said quietly. Lyseria was the youngest of the Shadow-Swifts, barely even at her eighth year.

"Your parents, again?" Keries asked.

She nodded, her long, stringy black hair still uncombed.

Keries looked sullenly at the stone floor. She had only been with them for a few months and was still far from adjusted to a life without her parents. Keries did his best to fill the void that the girl's parents had left, but some things couldn't be replaced.

"This time, we were back in Freyfall, in the market," Lyseria began. "It was just like that day that we were really there. The Wispwinds were blowing, and the market was crowded," Lyseria continued. "People were shouting things, throwing things, and then—"

Keries grimaced. He knew the story all too well. "It's alright." Keries rose from his chair and pulled her into another embrace. "They're going to be okay, I promise," Keries said, stroking her matted hair.

"You promise?" Lyseria asked, pulling back slightly to meet his eyes.

"Ly, I've been around for almost a hundred years," Keries said. "I know how these things go," he said.

She watched him with those fragile, ice-blue eyes of hers. She was so young… so breakable.

"Okay," she said, sniffling.

Niventia's Light, she doesn't deserve this, Keries thought, pulling her close once again. One so young had no place in a life like this. Malik was one thing, but Lyseria…

"Where is your brother?" Keries asked after a moment.

Lyseria withdrew, rubbing her eyes. "I think he went down to the Sand-Pit," Lyseria said.

Malik spent more time down there than any of them.

Keries held Lyseria's frail form close, allowing her to savor a few more moments of safety, but they weren't just for her. She was his *cure.* When he was around her, he felt normal again. Things felt *real.* It was as if he were actually living his life, rather than just watching it go by… helpless.

"I'm going to go see how he's doing, alright?" Keries said.

Lyseria nodded.

"Don't you worry about a thing," Keries said, standing up and stroking his beard. "You'll come to like it here. Besides, you're safer with us than you were in Freyfall."

Lyseria said nothing, her eyes growing distant.

Keries sighed, he hated leaving her like this. But Malik needed his guidance nearly as badly as she. The boy spent hours upon hours in the Sand-Pit, practicing with his abilities. A part of Keries was glad for this, for Malik had quickly become one of the more powerful Shadow-Swifts of the order. But Keries knew that only tragedy could drive someone to train that hard.

Keries wandered out of her room, making his way through the twisting passages of Erydon. The Sand-Pit was at Erydon's very lowest point, which was still several hundred feet above the base of the mountain. Erydon had not been built with the goal of making it accessible for those who weren't Shadow-Swifts; thus, carving its entry at such a high altitude made certain that only Summoners could enter. And, of course, those who did reach the door would not be able to find a way in, thanks to the Runic Lock.

The warm air of the grand atrium wafted over his dulled senses as he entered the massive chamber. This was among the warmest of rooms in Erydon, for it was kept both lit and heated by the Scorcher Crystals fastened to the walls. There was very little direct airflow from outside into the room—which didn't help Keries's constant congestion. Most of the chambers possessed very long, very small shafts that led outside, allowing for air to flow through.

Keries passed through the main atrium, seeing a few of them dotting the rounded ceiling of the passageway as the floor began to slope downwards. They were no greater than a finger in width. They were built in groups of three, placed with only a few feet separating each cluster. They were crafted by The Stonemasters who had built Erydon to provide ventilation, ensuring that the Shadow-Swifts they gifted it to didn't suffocate in their new fortress. The wind-shafts served their purpose well enough, though some of the corridors were rather chilly, especially on Frostfalls.

Not that Keries cared, for the sickness kept his senses muted enough that he barely even noticed the crisp bite to the air. He only felt emptiness... the slight distance from who he was, and who he wanted to be... A gap he could never fill. Not while he was a Shadow-Swift. Not while he followed Niventia's Path, at least, not like this.

He heard the *whisk* of the Shadow-Sand first as he neared his destination. The Sand-Pit was just a few curves ahead. He continued down the increasingly sharp decline, rounding one final corner and coming to the place where all six of the Shadow-Swifts had honed their skills. The Sand-Pit was a large, circular chamber with a domed roof and a massive pit of black sand in the center of the room. The depression was perhaps forty feet in diameter, and was filled entirely with Shadow-Sand.

Malik, clad in his bulky black armor, danced across the pit, slashing down targets made of sand in all directions. He flipped, cutting down another with his longsword. He was the only one in the clan who preferred a heavier, two-handed weapon, though he wielded it *very* well.

Malik Summoned another target, a humanoid figure rising from the sand and drifting toward him. Malik growled, his light blue eyes burning with focus as he rushed the target. He cut it down with a single strike, severing the mock-human in two. It was then that he noticed Keries.

More figures had begun to rise from the black sand, but they fell instantly as Malik released his control over the substance. He stepped out of the Pit, wiping the sweat from his brow and sheathing his massive sword. He ran a hand through his short black hair, catching his breath.

Keries watched with amusement as the Shadow-Sand settled back into the Pit. It looked as if it were nothing more than what was commonly found on coastal beaches, save for the discoloration.

But Shadow-Sand was far from ordinary. Shadow-Sand was a substance native to the Unbound, and, since the dawn of the Shadow-Swifts, it had obeyed their commands. Unfortunately, it was near impossible to transfer Shadow-Sand from the Unbound to Auris, so they were forced to use it sparingly. It was the same material that made up the Shadow-Swift's weapons and armor... for it could be compressed and welded together when exposed to extreme heat, and then set into a specific shape when exposed to acute cold. They had used it for as long as their Sect had existed, for it was the only substance that would shift with them back and forth between the Unbound and Auris.

"Keries." Malik nodded. He began taking off his armor, showing his impressively muscled body. The boy was only eighteen, but he was beginning to rival even Lucien and Asteros in both strength and skill.

"Malik, wonderful to see you training again," Keries said, watching as the boy unhooked the Crystals that had been wrapped around his torso. He wore them like many Summoners, hooked onto crisscrossing bandoliers that wrapped around both shoulders. Currently, he carried eight Crystals, though he looked to have only expended about two or three of them; Keries must've caught him early in his routine.

"Good to see you down here yourself," Malik said. "Although I don't suppose you've come here to train, have you?" Malik asked.

Keries shook his head. "Lyseria had another nightmare."

A shadow passed over Malik's young, square face. He remained still, his eyes growing hard. "Her parents again?" Malik asked after a moment.

Keries nodded.

Malik showed no reaction.

"They are your parents too, Malik. Don't forget that," Keries said, tucking his hands behind his back.

"They *were* our parents, until they discovered what we were," Malik spat. He took off his sashes of Crystals and replaced them with a loose white shirt.

Keries remained silent. *How in Niventia's Light do I respond to that?*

"Lyseria needs you, Malik," Keries said after an uncomfortably long silence.

Malik picked up his longsword once again, heaving the blade over his head and into the long sheath on his back. He picked up the Crystals next, undoubtedly preparing to place the emptied ones in the Pocket.

"I know," he said. Malik looked back to the Pit, its black sands beginning to churn at his mental command. A slight aura of darkness came over Malik as he called upon one of the Crystals he wore, awakening the sands once again.

"I don't mean down here, Malik," Keries said, advancing. "She needs you *up there,* talking to her."

"There won't be anyone left to talk to if I'm not strong enough to protect her," Malik said bluntly. "She doesn't understand that yet... it seems that you don't either."

Keries held his cold gaze.

The sands stopped moving. Malik looked to the rounded, blank ceiling of the chamber, sighing. The room was mostly empty, with the small perimeter surrounding the pit mostly kept open for the sake of both safety and storage, should one desire to leave their armor down here.

"She needs you more than any of us," Keries said.

Malik did not answer. He simply grumbled, and pushed past Keries, ascending the spiraling corridors back to the main rooms of Erydon.

Keries remained still. The sickness crept in slowly, paralyzing him, forcing him to ponder his failure. *You can do nothing right,* it seemed to whisper. *You are weak, Keries Nightbloom—a small child among mighty warriors. They have lost everything, yet they stand tall. Why can't you do the same?* Keries lowered his head. It was right. And so he stood there—he didn't know for how long—a single sentence echoing through his mind: *Why can't you do the same?*

CHAPTER FIFTEEN

THE HIGHLANDS

Castien Varic sat quietly in the corner of the cave. The Cyclone raged outside, unearthing stones and tossing them into the air as if they were nothing more than feathers.

The winds howled outside of the small indenture. The Cyclone was too dangerous to travel in, so they were stuck in this cave for the rest of the day. This cavern had been carved into the ground naturally. It was composed of an entry hole near the eastern side, and a fairly small open space that made up the rest of the shelter. The cavern's ceiling was only about four feet high, and the entire expedition was huddled against the ground, waiting for the Cyclone to end.

Some were sleeping, but most were just watching the Tempest beyond.

Ilyana was still carefully polishing her blades, ensuring that all of the red nrekuma blood had been wiped off.

Castien's fear had subsided, though traces of his anxiety remained. At least he wasn't hungry anymore. But he *was* still painfully aware that he did not belong here. It had been several hours since the hunt, yet Castien found himself continuously replaying the scene in his head.

It had been a beautiful slaughter. There had only been a single moment in which Castien had thought that the nrekuma might actually harm someone, and, even then, the Summoners had been in control.

Castien looked up to Ilyana. She was sitting nearest to him. On her other side sat Luka, and next to him was Surge. Arthion sat with Saevi on the other side of the small shelter, quietly watching the Tempest rage outside.

"You fought well," Castien said softly.

Ilyana paused, then shifted her gray eyes to Castien. "Excuse me?" She raised a curved eyebrow, her Elosian face shifting.

"When you were hunting the nrekuma," Castien explained. "You fought well."

Ilyana lowered her gaze. She made a grunt that sounded like an affirmation. Ilyana seemed to be about to return to brandishing her blade, but she paused once again. Ilyana set the sword down, then shuffled herself closer to Castien.

Castien's heart instantly beat faster, his muscles tensing.

"Listen, kid," Ilyana started. "I don't know what your game is, and I really don't even know what you're doing here, but—"

"I'm here to see if the King's hypothesis about the Blood Sorcerer being a Whisperer in disguise is true," Castien said quickly.

"Right..." Ilyana nodded. "How exactly are you supposed to do that?"

"I..." Castien started, trailing off. "I, um... It's a sort of meditation, I guess? It's almost like I just listen to my own heartbeat for a while and focus on my breathing, then see if I feel anything strange."

"Ah," Ilyana said, her sharp Elosian features bending into a smirk. "So, you're a Listener then?"

"A..." Castien tilted his head, his brain slowly mulling over the words. "A what?"

"A Listener," Ilyana said. "It's an old Elosian term for someone who can resist Whisperers." Ilyana frowned once again. "You've never heard of that? It's not terribly common, but the term itself is well known."

"I..." Castien fumbled with his words. *There are others like me?* He was only capable of the feat because of what he had gone through. *Have others done the same thing?*

"You're not very good at talking, are you?" Ilyana raised another thin eyebrow.

Castien felt his face heat up, the pit in his stomach seeming to open once again.

"Anyways," Ilyana continued. "What I was trying to say was I don't know why you were put on this expedition, but I hope you don't expect us to hold your hand throughout this whole thing. Hunting the nrekuma for food was one thing, but if it goes further than that..."

"I understand." Castien lowered his head and felt his mind close in on itself. He felt *ashamed.* Ashamed that he was even here. Ashamed that he had burdened the others to "look after" him.

"Listen though," she leaned in closer. "If you're interested, I may have a way for you to gain the favor of a few powerful people," she whispered.

Castien flinched, his ears twitching. He tilted his head, putting his ear closer to her.

"I know a scared Stormless when I see one," Ilyana said. "If you're really looking to get some security back in Arvendon, I can help." Ilyana leaned back. "But I need something in return, alright?"

Castien leaned back as well, turning to look at her.

Her Elosian face was twisted into a smirk, her thin gray eyes alight with a sort of predatory joy.

Castien's apprehension would have stopped him before, but what did he have to lose?

"Alright," Castien said quietly.

Ilyana's smile grew. "Good choice," she said softly. She didn't seem to have any intention of saying what, exactly, she wanted from him.

She looked around, ensuring that no one else was listening. "I normally wouldn't offer something like this to one of your kind, but all things considered you might be one of my better choices here." Ilyana looked around again. "I don't know if you've noticed, but I'm not exactly favored by the others... And, besides, you look honest enough, for a Stormless."

Castien nodded hesitantly, feeling a shiver run down his spine.

"I'll tell you more in a few days. All you need to know now is that you'll come out of this agreement with a few more friends than you have now." Ilyana paused. "In the meantime, just stay out of our way and we won't have any problems." Ilyana shuffled away, winking.

Why would she offer me that? Castien thought. Ilyana was a Master Summoner—a very powerful one, in fact. *Do I really look that pitiful?* Castien instantly felt his face heat up again.

I really need to get myself together, Castien thought. This wasn't who he was. But who was he? He thought that he was a soldier—a Stormless fighting for his country. But he was no Summoner, which meant that his efforts were inconsequential. Were his past accomplishments worth nothing this whole time?

Footsteps yanked Castien from his thoughts. His eyes shot toward the small opening, where the Cyclone raged beyond.

A figure entered the Crystal-lit cavern, hunched over and crawling due to the low ceiling.

It was a man. He seemed to be fairly tall, though Castien couldn't be certain. The man wore a plain leather jacket that went all the way past his knees, and a strange leather hat that seemed to be lined with fur. He was actually wearing *goggles* too.

It clicked.

Castien had heard of Cloudwalkers wearing goggles before, and, judging by the fact that no one instantly attacked this man as he entered, it seemed that his arrival was expected. *Yet he had been out in a Cyclone!* Castien looked at the violent winds beyond. Cyclones were the Tempest of the Cloudwalkers, and if this man truly was a Cloud-walker… then that would explain why he had been able to survive.

"Elric, it's about time you showed up." Surge let out a booming laugh. "How did you find us in here? I had thought for certain that we had hidden ourselves well enough from you."

"Your Crystals are giving off a slight glow," the man—Elric—said. This was the Cloudwalker who the King had sent ahead to follow Velarus. "And forgive me for saying so, but I didn't exactly think that a cave with a glowing mouth was natural."

"Took you long enough to find us," Luka chuckled. "I was starting to think that you'd lost your touch."

Elric laughed, unlatching the buckle on his hat and revealing a head of messy auburn hair. He undid his goggles as well, looking upon the small cave with emerald eyes.

"Luka, my friend, somehow I'm not surprised that the King put you on this crew." Elric's face bore thick lines, though they were not wrinkles. It was merely that he had strangely *firm* features.

"So, I assume that you've run out of Crystals, then?" Surge asked.

Elric nodded. "Yet it seems that I'm in luck, for the Cyclone came just in time." Elric unbuttoned his coat and produced a sack of dull, mint-green Crystals. He crawled closer to the opening of the cavern and fastened the sack to the wall, producing a strange steel and wood dagger to hold it in place.

Castien watched through the small opening in the top of the sack as the Crystals steadily began to glow once again, drinking in the invisible energy that danced through the winds of the Cyclone.

"Where is the Blood Sorcerer?" Luka asked.

"Holed up in some cave to the north, just at the start of The High-lands," Elric said, rubbing his blazecrest-shaped nose. "I know the way. We'll catch up to him once the Cyclone subsides."

"If we're going into The Highlands, we need to send a message to the King," Surge said. "Do you think you can travel to the border for me?"

"Of course." Elric nodded. "I'll head out at nightfall, then find you again on the trail north. The cave is raised above the valley path a bit, but I can show you how to get up there." Elric scanned the group for seemingly the first time, his emerald eyes turning inquisitive. His gaze settled on Castien. "A Stormless is with you... You're not a Summoner?"

"No," Castien said. He felt his face warm once again.

The handsome Cloudwalker's face twisted into a smile. "Wonderful!" Elric exclaimed. "It's about time the King realized that the Stormless are more than just mindless numbers in his forces." Elric grinned widely.

Saevi rolled her eyes.

"Oh, stop it, Saevi," Elric shot. "I'm sure this Stormless is here for a good reason anyway."

"He's a Listener," Ilyana cut in. "The King thinks that the Blood Sorcerer may be a Whisperer in disguise, and he wants Castien here to see if his theory holds any truth."

"Ah," Elric mused.

"I'm sorry, a what?" Saevi tilted her eyes toward Castien.

"It's an Elosian term," Elric said. "Try traveling some, Saevi. Maybe it'll expand your comically dense mind." Elric snickered.

Saevi's tanned face turned a shade of red, and she quieted.

Elric turned to Ilyana. "And what are you doing here? You're someone I didn't expect to see."

"What? You're surprised to see the winner of the King's competition on this journey?" Ilyana asked, feigning shock. "You think that just because I declined to become his Agent I'd decline to go on this mission?"

"I'm just surprised the King trusts you enough to put you on a job this important." Elric shrugged and looked around again. "Although, with a crew like this, there isn't much you could do. One step out of line and I'm sure the Cryostalker will freeze your brain until it bursts." Elric laughed again.

Luka joined him this time. "You're right about that one." Luka grinned, his cracked lips parting to reveal another smile.

"Oh," Elric said, his eyes settling on Arthion, who had been silent thus far. "I thought I recognized you, but I suppose I don't. Who are you?"

"I'm a Whisperer, obviously." Arthion smiled, chuckling a bit. "My name is Arthion Aldrich, and I can now rightfully claim that I am one of the most trusted Whisperers of the King, for he chose me to go on this journey."

"Hats off to you, my friend." Elric grinned. "And, yes, I feel as if I've heard of you... but I always get the Whisperers mixed up."

A light silence fell over the group, the only sound the loud whistling of the Cyclone's winds.

"Well then," Elric said, rubbing his hands together. "I suppose that we will just be waiting this out, then?"

No one responded.

"I'm going to get some rest. It feels like it's been an age since I've slept," Elric said.

"We should probably be resting as well," Surge said. "Once night falls, we set out again." Surge looked around. "All of you: Make sure you're ready by then. But, in the meantime, you should all get some sleep. It may not be very comfortable here, but I assume most of you are used to it." Surge smiled grimly, then turned over on the ground.

Castien frowned, looking at the hard stone floor. He had become accustomed to sleeping in poor conditions during his time in The Highlands, yet having spent so many months in Arvendon had reacclimated him to the luxury of a bed. But... this would have to do.

Castien Varic walked through the cold night air several hours later. Small flakes of snow were beginning to fall from the darkness above. *Frostfall,* Castien thought. *Great.* The Highlands had slowly transformed from distant shadows to all-too-real mountains right before his very eyes as the group continued north.

Elric had traveled north to the border and not yet returned. He had delivered a message for Surge. It could be assumed that the message was for the King, and, given that emissaries regularly passed between the border and Arvendon, it would likely reach him soon.

The winds were picking up, and the bite in the breeze nagged at Castien's vest. Fortunately, his uniform had been built to protect him from the Tempests and the cold, especially due to the fact that his last mission had involved him going to The Highlands.

Mystery still shrouded that strange period of skirmishes in the mountains. The fight had started over land, and no one had ever really ended it. Shadow-Swifts had supposedly popped up randomly from time to time, stealing parties from their patrol paths and leaving little more than a few drops of blood.

Castien supposed it didn't matter, for the skirmishes had never escalated into war. If anything, Castien was surprised that no other nations had thought to ally themselves with Freyfall and try to finally knock Arvendon down a few pegs. But that was in the past, and there was no use thinking about it now.

A shadow dashed across the sky.

Castien froze, his hand snapping to his bow.

Surge led the group through the dark Wastelands, seemingly not noticing. Luka reached up, catching a flake of snow on his cracked hands, savoring the Frostfall with a blissful ignorance of the shadow above.

"Look out!" Castien shouted, nocking an arrow as he yelled.

The group stopped suddenly, looking around.

"In the sky!" Castien cried, raising his bow. The wood felt familiar in his gloved hands... it had been so long since he had actually *fired* the bow. There was shouting around him, words like "Nyghtmaere"—the Shadow-Swift who had terrorized The Highlands for the last few months—ringing through the cold air. Castien barely heard them.

He closed his eyes, the shadow falling from the sky with a beautiful grace, arcing toward the expedition crew with an eerie silence.

Fire bloomed in the night, lightning bolted through the air, dancing around the crew. Ice began Crystalizing in the air, shards forming.

"Wait!" Surge shouted. The fire vanished, as did the ice, and the lightning.

Castien hardly processed the words.

Someone shouted at him, but Castien was falling into the depths of his heartbeat once again, finding that place of focus and peace where he was truly alone.

The wood creaked as Castien drew the bow, his eyes cracking open slightly.

The shadow continued dashing toward them.

Castien aligned his mind with the shot, marking where the attacker would be, letting his instincts calculate the arc and the wind. Castien shut his eyes, and, just as his fingers were beginning to tense, he *released.*

Air whistled around the wooden arrow. Castien kept his eyes closed, feeling the tension flee from the string and bow. Finally, he cracked his eyes open, the shouting around him resuming once again.

The shadow floated down, coming into focus beneath the pale gray moonlight of Lotius.

Castien stumbled back, recognizing the brown coat and the strange goggles of the figure before him.

Elric Knyvet dropped to the ground, holding in his hands a long wooden arrow.

Castien felt his face warm, blood suddenly rushing to his head. He took another step back, the dead silence of the group deafeningly loud. He had just shot an arrow at *Elric.* And here Elric was, standing before Castien, arrow in hand.

Elric lowered his goggles, pulling his coat down to reveal a wide grin. "That was some shot," Elric said, taking a step forward and handing the arrow back to Castien.

Castien took it with weak fingers, his legs feeling shaky.

Elric smiled, clapping Castien on the back. "If I hadn't been able to stop it with the wind, it probably would've hit me!" Elric boomed a laugh.

No one joined in.

"Sor—" Castien started, the words feeling clumsy in his mouth. "Sorry. I thought you were—I, uh…" Castien's face grew even warmer, and the world seemed to spin faster, and—

"Calm down, lad." Elric smiled warmly once again, his emerald eyes sparkling in the night. "I don't blame you for being a little jumpy, not when we're this close to The Highlands." Elric turned away, facing Surge. "I've delivered your letter to the border, they said it will take a little while for it to reach Arvendon, but the King will receive it soon enough."

"Thank you, Elric," Surge said, his dark eyes reflecting his gratitude. He glanced at Castien, but said nothing.

"We're getting close to the cave," Elric said, turning back to the mountains just ahead. "We'll walk until we get close, then I'll scout it out."

"Do you really think that they would set up camp so close to the end of The Highlands?" Saevi asked. "It seems a little foolish to me."

"Indeed it does," Elric said. "But I can't imagine this is their final hideout. It is likely just a place for the Blood Sorcerer to restock his supplies."

"Well, come along then, we have no time to lose," Luka said quickly. "If we aren't careful, we'll be spotted. Hell, I'd be surprised if the Blood Sorcerer hasn't seen us already."

"Luka's right," Surge said. "They have the high ground, which gives them a good vantage point. I'd say that the odds of him still being unaware of our pursuit are very low." Without a word more, Surge walked forward. Luka and Elric joined him at the front, followed by Arthion and Saevi. Castien lingered for a moment, but finally started walking again.

He had just shown that he was somewhat useful, at least. *Only for the arrow to be picked from the sky like a berry from a tree,* Castien thought. True, it was a good shot. However, an arrow could only do so much against a Master Summoner.

"Hey," a voice that Castien instantly recognized called. Ilyana paused, waiting for him to catch up as they walked.

Castien broke into a little jog, though he wished that he hadn't. He recognized that predatory look in the Dexteris's gaze.

"That was a pretty impressive shot," Ilyana said quietly as they started walking again.

"Thanks," Castien mumbled.

"Maybe you'll be more useful than I thought," Ilyana mused.

Castien grimaced, but said nothing. He felt that oppressive, condescending tone wash over him again and again. Summoners were kind to the Stormless—for the most part, at least—but Castien was beginning to tire of this company.

His father's words echoed in his mind... He needed some way to regain power. He needed to be *needed*. Otherwise, he wouldn't survive. Ilyana had offered him a deal, but what did that really mean? What was her goal?

Maybe... Castien thought to himself, his father's words bouncing through his thoughts once again. *Maybe I do have an opportunity here.*

"Why did you pick me?" Castien asked. "Why didn't you make your offer to one of the others?"

"I have my reasons," Ilyana said simply.

"And why don't you tell me what those reasons are?" Castien raised an eyebrow, forcing some conviction into his voice.

"You're hardly in a position to make demands from *me,*" Ilyana snorted.

Castien hesitated. She was right. But he *needed* to try something. He couldn't stay in this vicious trap of self-pity for the rest of the trip.

"I'm just saying it seems a little strange," Castien said. "Maybe even suspicious."

"Sure it does." Ilyana rolled her eyes. "Are you through?"

"Why won't you just tell me what it is you're going to have me do?" Castien asked. He blinked a few times, finding his own tone somewhat shocking.

Ilyana sighed. "Because I first need to make sure that I can trust you," Ilyana said.

"Why would you think you couldn't?"

"Because what I'm about to tell you isn't something the others are meant to hear," Ilyana said firmly.

Castien started. *Yes!* His instincts were correct. There was more to this than she had let on.

Ilyana leaned in. "The King suspects that someone in his high court, perhaps even on his Council, is a Celesian spy," Ilyana whispered.

Castien stared at the ground, walking silently. *A spy?*

"He put me on this expedition at the last minute to ensure that everyone in this group could be cleared," Ilyana said. "He trusts these Summoners more than anyone else, but he can't lead this country if he has to look over his shoulder at every turn."

"The King put you on this crew just to make sure that there wasn't a spy among us?" Castien frowned.

"That's one way to put it," Ilyana said.

"So," Castien started, "what have you determined?"

"What do you mean?"

"Is there a spy among us?" Castien asked, feeling his pulse spike.

"I don't believe so," Ilyana said. "The King was fairly certain that there wasn't, but he wanted to be sure."

"Why does he even think there's a spy in his court in the first place?" Castien asked.

"Because Celes's army has been steadily moving toward the Elos-Etherus border," Ilyana said. "These movements have only begun recently, and the trend seems to have begun around the time we first spotted the Blood Sorcerer."

"You think they're moving to attack because of the weaknesses the Blood Sorcerer exposed? You think that they received word of his actions?"

"I think that Celes is waiting for an opening," Ilyana said. "If Arvendon were to fall under attack, Celes would be the first city to join against them."

Castien thought for a moment. "But wait, why would the King even pick you to uncover the spy? Aren't you from Celes?"

"Because he knew that no one wants to watch Celes fall more than I do," Ilyana said.

Castien tilted his head. *That wasn't something I expected to hear,* he thought.

Ilyana paused. She lowered her eyes, then met his gaze after a moment. "King Brennan Nightingale of Elos," Ilyana said quietly, holding his gaze. "He is a Dexteris, as is his family, and his extended family. I was told that I bore some of his royal blood too, and that, if I tried, I might be able to work my way up to a respectable position in Celes, the capital.

"But the politics... By the Six, I couldn't stand it," Ilyana continued. "I watched noble after noble 'disappear,' after making a poor decision," Ilyana said. "I no longer felt safe in my own city... So I left, and made my way to Arvendon, searching for a life away from the backstabbing nobles of my home," Ilyana said. "Yet, in Arvendon, I couldn't resist showing off my power; I entered the King's competition and won." Ilyana paused again. "But I couldn't become trapped in the politics of yet another throne, so I declined to take my position as the King's Agent." Ilyana stopped for a moment, closing her eyes. "So now here I am... Banned from Celes and hated by Arvendon."

"And the King saw this," Castien finished for her. "He saw that you needed allies, and he chose you to lead this investigation, for you had already proven your competence in the contest," Castien said. "But what does any of this have to do with me?"

"As I've said, I've almost certainly ruled out everyone in this party," Ilyana said. "But, when we get back to Arvendon, I'm going to need your help. I have a contact within the city, but I only know as much as he does. If we don't know who the spy is by then, then I'm going to need you to help us find out."

"And if your contact does know who the spy is?" Castien raised an eyebrow.

"Then I'm going to need you to help me kill them." Ilyana grew cold.

"Would the King not just arrest the traitor?"

"Not if he wishes to keep this whole ordeal a secret," Ilyana said. "An arrest would draw the public's attention, and if the city were to learn that a Celesian spy had been among their leaders... Panic would follow."

"But why must *you* kill him?" Castien asked.

"A crazed Elosian Dexteris inexplicably killing a random noble is far easier to pass off than an arrest," Ilyana said. "Besides, I've already been promised a pardon, and, if you help me, I'm certain he would ensure that you go free as well."

"So..." Castien trailed off. "I help you kill a spy, and that will gain me both the favor of the King and the royal court?"

"That's the idea." Ilyana nodded. "Don't concern yourself with my task for now," Ilyana said. "Focus on staying safe, we'll figure this whole mess out when we get back to Arvendon." She sped up, catching up with the rest of the party.

Castien looked up, noticing that the ground had begun to incline.

Elric walked ahead, and then stopped, holding up a gloved hand. The others paused. Elric pointed with his other hand toward the small slopes which were beginning to rise immediately before them. Snow now lay around them in clumps, and the Frostfall was beginning to pick up.

Castien followed Elric's hand, tracing it up the small hill to their left. Apparently, they had arrived at the camp... and, judging by the subtle disturbances in the snow ahead, someone was home.

CHAPTER SIXTEEN
REKINDLING

Twenty-two months ago...

Asteros Silverglade sat in the grand library of Erydon. "Grand" was a bit of an overstatement, for the library only consisted of a few dozen short rows of wooden book-shelves. Asteros had read nearly all of the books by now.

He was currently reading over Haldir's notes on the Runes, which had become more relevant in times of late. Haldir's knowledge had allowed him to forge the key, but he hadn't recorded everything he knew, unfortunately.

Haldir had taught Asteros and some of the other Shadow-Swifts how to read the ancient tongue, though once he had done so he seemed to have lost interest in teaching his pupils. His own research had clearly taken him far, leaving Asteros to wish that he had recorded more than a few simple journal entries.

The journal entries were not without their value, though. They detailed how Haldir had found part of what appeared to be a small disabled ward of sorts. The ward was powered by Runes that were hidden in the stones, which Haldir had cut out to create the key.

Asteros now recognized that these disabled wards were likely ruins from "The Great War," as Herqen's Stonemaster called it... For it made sense that there would be partial Runes left behind, even after so long.

Footsteps announced the approach of someone—Shalheira, judging by the quick pace.

He turned, watching the entrance to the library as she neared.

She entered, squinting against the stark white light of the library. It was lit by the bright white Voltarian Crystals; they made for better reading light than the standard Scorcher Crystals.

"Shalheira." Asteros nodded, smiling warmly. "I've been hoping to see you."

"Always glad to know that I'm desired." Shalheira winked. "What is it?"

"It's about our..." he trailed off, remembering that he was yet to tell Keries, Malik, and Lyseria what they had found. They were likely somewhere else in Erydon at the moment. "...discovery."

"Herqen?" Shalheira raised an eyebrow. "I thought we had uncovered all that there was to find."

"We translated the words, yes," Asteros said. "But I fear that there is still more work to be done... A simple translation does not always tell the whole story."

Shalheira began pacing. "You think that we may have missed something in the cavern?" Shalheira asked.

"You and I both know that the ancient tongue was riddled with strange accents and variations that only the Rune-Writers and Stonemasters could understand. It was a trademark of their language," Asteros said. "It's been known for centuries that there are slight innuendos and implications hidden within some letters."

"But there are no Rune-Writers or Stonemasters left to fully transcribe them. So, what does it matter?" Shalheira asked. "Even if there are more clues in those writings, there is no way to uncover them."

"Just because there aren't Stonemasters and Rune-Writers

doesn't mean there aren't people who can transcribe their messages." Asteros smirked.

"What do you mean?"

"Do you recall how we first discovered Herqen's cavern?" Asteros asked.

Shalheira frowned. "The..." She blinked a few times. "The Frey-fallion scholars led Lucien to it, no?"

"Exactly," Asteros said. "We have known about those chambers' existence for years, but we have never been able to find one. The scholars, however, were able to uncover one's location after only a few months in The Highlands."

"You think that they're capable of helping us?" Shalheira asked.

"Given enough *encouragement,* I think that they'd be both capable and willing."

Shalheira narrowed her eyes. "Encouragement?"

"Do not fear, Shalheira," Asteros said. "We will not use force." Asteros paused. "In fact, we won't be using anything at all, for it will be you who recruits the scholars."

"What?" Shalheira advanced. "Why me? This is your idea."

"Because I knew that you would have concerns regarding our methods," Asteros said. "So, in order to prevent any disagreements, I opted to simply send you to accomplish the task."

Shalheira looked around, as if searching for an answer. Her gaze steadily returned to him. Her eyes softened, a slow smile creeping across her face.

Asteros stood up, nearing her. He met her gloriously passionate eyes. Gods, even just looking at her he could see the plans forming in her mind. Yet, unlike the times when he saw that look in Lucien, he felt no fear. He trusted her, and she trusted him. It was almost like...

But no. That could never happen. Especially not now, not in the middle of all of this. Yet he saw that look in her eyes. A dying ember of what could've been love, reborn in the souls of two monstrous killers who had been torn apart by the shadows of their pasts. She drew closer to him, and he to her.

He felt her warm breath on his skin and leaned in as he reached out with a slow, firm hand. He basked in Shalheira's cool winter scent.

Her eyes closed, her face melting into a swarm of devilish grins and desires.

He advanced, daring to get closer to this beautiful woman than he ever had before.

Heavy footsteps startled them, causing them both to jump. They were recognizable as Lucien's, for only *he* could walk with such confidence.

Shalheira leapt back a few feet, reaching for her daggers.

Maybe in another life, Asteros thought, turning to the doorway.

Lucien Shade marched in, clad in his black armor. He paused when he noticed the tension in their stances. He looked back and forth between the two of them, then smiled knowingly.

Cursed bastard, Asteros thought. *He's too perceptive for his own good.* Yet Lucien, to his credit, said nothing of the matter.

"I hope I didn't interrupt anything," he said, daring to give one last playful smirk as Asteros and Shalheira looked at each other. "But I have news."

"Your interruption is pardoned," Shalheira said, stepping forward. "I was simply accepting the task Asteros was offering me."

"So you will be recruiting the scholars for us?" Lucien said, raising an eyebrow.

"I'll begin by searching the mountains," Shalheira said. "I know there are still research teams up here, perhaps I would be able to sneak away with some of their scholars." Shalheira flashed a smile at Asteros. "Now tell us, Lucien: What is your news?"

"I believe that the skirmishes are escalating," Lucien said.

Asteros's face fell. "How do you know?"

"Their outposts in The Highlands are growing," Lucien said.

"Growing how? In size or in occupancy?" Shalheira asked.

"Both," Lucien said. "The Arvendi are sending more troops as well."

"Well, so?" Shalheira stepped forward. "What do we care if they continue these petty fights? In the end either Arvendon will reclaim their land or Freyfall will take it for themselves. What does it matter to us?"

"It matters because the soldiers are seeking shelter in clefts and cracks like the one that we found Herqen's cavern in while they are out of camp," Lucien said. "And, if they discover Herqen's Rune-Door, then our lead on the rest of Auris has been lost."

"So, we keep them away from it," Asteros said firmly. "If a party draws too close to Herqen, we eliminate them."

"Kill them?" Shalheira asked. "Is that truly how we wish to resolve this issue?"

"If you have a better idea, I'd love to hear it," Lucien countered. "We have no other options. We cannot risk losing our advantage."

"I told you that I would not stand for cruelty," Shalheira growled. "I suggest you come up with another plan, or you may find yourself without my help."

"Shalheira." Asteros pulled her aside. "These men are marching to their deaths anyway. If Arvendon doesn't kill these soldiers, the cold will. We are killing men who are already dead, in essence. We are merely ensuring that our secret stays secure."

Shalheira looked back to Lucien. Her eyes shifted to Asteros. After a moment, she lowered her head.

"Fine," Shalheira said. "Kill no more than is necessary," she said softly. "I will bring back the scholars as soon as I can, though I fear it may take several weeks to find a willing group."

Asteros turned to Lucien. "You heard her. If we're lucky, we won't even have to kill anyone at all."

"Understood," Lucien said. A devious smile flickered across his face.

"I will continue scouring Herqen's walls to see what I can discover myself. I will also prepare the others for the scholars' arrival," Asteros said. "You both have your assignments, now let's get to work."

CHAPTER SEVENTEEN

THE LOST SECTS

Faelyn Titansworn stood before the swirling colors of the mural. The brilliant crimson of Zephyr's armor clashed beautifully with Calida's forest-green swords. Faelyn's eyes traced the golden energies as they flowed through the painting.

The mural depicted each of Auris's Six Gods in their human form. Niventia, Goddess of light, life, and prosperity, stood on the left, her hand extended. Her white battle armor was covered by a gloriously extravagant opal gown that sparkled with every color. The artist had somehow spun each color of the rainbow into her armor to represent its resplendent glow. White beams extended from her hands, shooting across the painting.

Zephyr stood to the right of her, his twin red swords raised. Zephyr dove toward the other side of the mural, frozen in an eternal lunge. His feet were positioned just above the pale tan stone of a forgotten canyon, where the prophetical battle between the Gods had occurred at the Arrival. Zephyr, God of time, seemed to be twisting in midair due to a trick of the artist, meant to mimic his ability to see things before they happened—and react accordingly.

Tarathiel, God of the stones and mountains, stood closest to the center. He wore ordinary brown robes and had both hands raised; they were wrapped in sand. Rocks were flying behind him in the distance, hurtling towards the three Gods on the other side of the painting... Izara's Gods.

Calida stood at the front, facing Tarathiel, green swords extended. A long black tail grew from her back, lined with wicked spikes. Her hands were tipped with horrific claws, and her knuckles lined with protruding bones. She was the Goddess of deception and change, and was commonly depicted as half-beast in order to convey the shift of animals from their rudimentary state to the eventual birth of mankind.

Helionn stood next to her, facing Niventia's side as well. He too was floating above the ground, clad in golden armor that reflected the light of a thousand suns. A burning radiance surrounded him. Pillars of flames wrapped around his entire body, for he was the God of the sun... fire was his element.

Finally, Izara stood on top of the boulder opposite of Niventia. Her hand was extended as well. Darkness exploded from Izara's outstretched palm, sinking into the land, piercing the rock and draining the life from the world itself.

The Goddess of Death, Faelyn thought, rubbing his stubble. *I need to shave,* he thought, rubbing it again. He turned back to the painting, his eyes shifting to the silver sun behind it all: Dyvnire, as it was called in the ancient tongue. Clouds dotted the black sky in the back, reflecting the icy-silver light of the fallen star. Faelyn squinted, staring with fascination at the strange orb. The painting itself covered the entire entry hall of the Titansworn family chambers, and that was no small feat. The wall was easily two hundred feet long, and at least seventy feet tall.

"Looking for answers in art once again, I see," Idris said.

Faelyn jumped. "You startled me, Idris." Faelyn rubbed his shoulders a bit. He turned to his trainer, watching as the older man's gray eyes fell on the mural.

"I figured that I might find you here," Idris said, looking at the painting. He turned back to Faelyn. "We have work to do, come on."

Faelyn lingered, his eyes settling on Dyvnire once again. "What was it?" Faelyn asked. "Dyvnire. What was Dyvnire?"

"That is a question for your religion teachers, not for me."

"Which is exactly why I'm asking you," Faelyn said. "My teachers always say that Dyvnire was the will of Izara personified into a celestial body, but they never give me an answer that actually makes sense."

"That is because there is no sensible answer," Idris said, turning away once again. He passed by another torch in the large hallway, his eyes glowing as he glanced at it.

"What do you think?"

"What do I think about what?" Idris asked, a hint of annoyance bleeding through his tone.

"What do you think about the Gods, the Goddesses, Dyvnire?" Faelyn asked. "What do you think about the rumors that the return of the Blood Sorcerers marks the beginning of the Resurgence... the implication that, if the Ancient Sects are returning, the Gods could eventually return to Auris as well?"

Idris sighed, taking a few paces back toward Faelyn. "My dear boy," Idris began. "How can the Gods return if they were never here in the first place?"

Faelyn tilted his head.

"I've studied magic long enough to understand that the things that supposedly happened in these legends and fables are impossible," Idris said.

"Impossible for a normal human, yes, but not for a God," Faelyn countered.

Idris sighed. "I am not here to debate you on religion, Faelyn. I am here to teach you how to shape your power into a weapon that you can use to protect your kingdom from *real* threats," Idris said. "Now come along."

"Why are we down here?" Faelyn asked as Idris closed the door of one of the private rooms of the Dome.

Idris locked the door, his red robes swishing as he turned. He reached inside them, producing a large book.

"We are here, rather than the courtyard, because we need more privacy for today's lesson," Idris explained. "Besides, you know that I hate being anywhere near the exterior walls when it's a Storm Gale."

As if on cue, thunder sounded above. Idris rolled his eyes, he had always said that he found the theatrics of Storm Gales to be a bit excessive—and a bit terrifying, Faelyn suspected.

"So," Faelyn said, straightening his red vest. "What is it that we are working on today that is so top secret?"

"Actually." Idris opened the large tome. "Not that I want to fuel the rumors about the Blood Sorcerer, but I have decided that I should teach you of the Ancient Sects."

Faelyn started. *The Ancient Sects?* "What do you mean?"

"The Lost Sects were real, Faelyn," Idris said. "The Gods? Well, those are up for debate. But there were fifteen Sects at one point... and, given that the Blood Sorcerers may in fact be returning, I would not rule out the possibility of *all* of the Sects returning."

"So you are thinking about the Resurgence," Faelyn said.

Idris paused. "Please don't use that silly term." Idris walked toward the corner of the marble room, where a pile of equipment lay. He picked up a large bullseye and carried it over to the far wall of the chamber.

Faelyn tilted his head as Idris fixed it to the wall. "What are you doing?"

"The Lost Sects were all very powerful," Idris said, ignoring the question. "Far more powerful than the surviving Sects, it seems. But they were not without their weaknesses." Idris stepped out of the way. "I figured that a good place to start would be the Blood Sorcerers, given that they pose the highest threat of returning."

"They were masters of controlling the bodies of others, as well as of manipulating blood," Faelyn said, glancing at the open tome. Sure enough, he saw splotches of red ink on the wrinkled pages.

"Indeed." Idris nodded. "Yet, they had one thing that they could never overcome: distance."

"You're saying that they couldn't reach those who were far away from them?"

"Precisely," Idris continued. "Blood Sorcerers were said to have been able to take complete control of those close to them, and even summon blood-storms that could affect large groups of people within a single room—which is what I suspect Velarus did on that day in your father's throne room... if he is a Blood Sorcerer, that is."

"So how can we stop them?" Faelyn asked, his eyes narrowing.

"Attack a Blood Sorcerer before he can reach you with his abilities, and he is no harder to fell than a common soldier," Idris said. "Which is why we shall begin by working on Madavaro's Arrows, a spell named after the fourth-century mage who created it."

"You're teaching me a new spell?"

"Times are changing, Faelyn." Idris turned to him, his gray eyes cold. "Things in this world are not as they used to be, and I promised your father that I would prepare you for anything that you may face, and so I shall prepare you to fight a Blood Sorcerer."

Faelyn remained silent, stepping aside as Idris approached.

Idris turned to the bullseye, which was covered with an iron chestplate. Idris raised his hands, closed his eyes, and the Crystals within his robes sparked to life. Fire danced at his fingertips, drifting from his hands to the air around them. Faelyn *felt* the heat as Idris shaped the flames into small lines—almost resembling...

"Arrows..." Faelyn realized.

Idris remained silent, focusing. The slivers of fire grew pointed, continuing to multiply in number as Idris waved his hands in *very* specific patterns. Soon, nearly a dozen bolts of flame burned in the air, their light casting shadows on the white walls of the room.

Idris's eyes snapped open. He thrust his hands forward, the bolts of flame shooting forward with blinding speed, burning through the iron and scorching the target beyond. Idris waved a hand, and the flames snuffed out, leaving eleven small holes in the chestplate.

"Armor piercing, long range, and easily controllable. Not to mention that the power output is low enough that you will remain far from Breakdown," Idris said. "You are to learn this spell before you leave this room, understood?"

"How come you've never taught me this before?" Faelyn asked, raising an eyebrow. "I would think that armor-piercing attacks are something you would've shown me earlier."

"You were not ready for this spell before." Idris turned to the book.

"And I'm ready now?"

"No," Idris said, flipping his eyes back to Faelyn. "But the world won't wait for you to be ready, Faelyn. You must be prepared for anything and everything. Your father was given six weeks, and one of those weeks has already nearly passed. I do not know if there is an army of Blood Sorcerers marching to our gates, but, *if* there is, you need to be ready to *defend your home.*"

Faelyn paled, but nodded. He stepped over to the book, where it lay open on a stone table.

"This will teach you the hand motions, as well as the mental commands that you must use so that you are able to cast the spell. Though I must warn you: It requires a tremendous amount of focus. Azamar's Blast is a difficult spell, but this is even a step above that... this spell is only used by the most powerful of Summoners."

Faelyn leaned over the book, scanning the faded text.

"I will teach you one spell for each of the Lost Sects," Idris continued. "None of them will be easy to learn, but *all* of them may soon be necessary to know. Your enemies will know your weaknesses; it's only fair that I teach you theirs as well."

"Do you think that the other Sects are returning?" Faelyn raised an eyebrow.

Idris paused, looking away. Idris's lip quivered, as if he wanted to speak but couldn't find the words.

"Begin," Idris snapped, ignoring the question. He began pacing. "We have another ball tonight, Faelyn. Neither of us have the luxury of time, so I suggest that you get started, understand?"

Faelyn nodded, brushing the thought aside. Now was no time for sentiments. His kingdom was in danger, and he needed to be able to protect it.

Faelyn flipped the pages of the book while sitting on one of the soft couches lining the opposite side of the massive mural. He skimmed the details of the Skin-Shapers: shapeshifters who could alter their physical form. He had taken the book from Idris—with permission of course—and had been reading it in his spare time. Thankfully, tonight's party was over, which meant that the palace was empty once again.

His parents were likely asleep, and the only ones who seemed to be awake in the palace were the guards and servants, hence why he was reading in the entry hall to the Titansworn quarters.

He turned to the next page, but not before looking up at the painting once again. The room was surprisingly large, given that it was on the fourth floor of the palace. It was part of the tallest of Summerglass's six main spires—one for each God.

This page spoke of the Illusomancers: masters of illusion and deception. Faelyn had always been fascinated by their ability to create hallucinations. Their manipulations reminded him of a Whisperer's. However, Illusomancers could manipulate the eyes and ears of their targets, whereas Whisperers targeted the mind. Yet, unlike Whisperers, Illusomancers could—according to the ancient stories

—wrap entire *battlefields* in their illusions, twisting the eyes of soldiers to see whatever the Illusomancers willed them to.

Faelyn turned the page again, listening to the dull chatter of his guards as they leaned up against one of the pillars. Footsteps sounded above as more servants and guards walked past on the balcony that overlooked the entirety of the chamber. That section of the castle was only used for the covert movement of servants and guards, placed above the large hallway so that servants were able to move between the rooms of the royal family without disturbing them. Faelyn, however, knew about the false wall behind him that led to the staircase. Every once in a while, when he was younger, he had snuck up there for some peace and quiet during his father's parties.

He turned back to the book, reading the page about the Starburners. Starburners seemed very similar to Scorchers, though it was said that Starburners harnessed the light itself, rather than heat. Faelyn skipped to the part where it named their weaknesses.

Close quarters, Faelyn read. Starburners could project energy across unbelievably long distances and apparently could conjure weapons as well. But, if you were able to get around those weapons and get a hand on a Starburner, you could disable them with ease.

Every Summoner and soldier alike had memorized the weaknesses and strengths of the Sects from a young age. Scorchers, like Faelyn, typically had very little control, and were easy to defeat in tight spaces or when surrounded by allies. Voltarians took a long time to charge up their attacks, meaning that, once you dodged or blocked one, they were vulnerable. Cryostalkers had a great deal of control, but their longer-range attacks were far weaker than their other spells. Cloudwalkers were fast, but easy to knock off balance. Whisperers were fairly useless in duels, and Dexterises—while quick—were essentially just Stormless fighters who moved a little faster.

It struck Faelyn as odd that someone had bothered to write a book about the weaknesses of the *Ancient* Sects, though the book itself did seem very old. The knowledge would be useless to more or less *everybody* in today's world. Yet scholars were as they always had been... obsessed with the past, even when it could very well have nothing to do with the future. Though, in this case, their work was paying off.

He turned to the next page, starting to read about the Revenants and their necromancy when movement overhead caught his eye. Turning, Faelyn looked up. He eyed the balcony overhead and saw one of his father's Whisperers, catching a flash of the whites of the man's eyes.

Was he watching me? Faelyn thought, slowly shutting the book. He stood up, staring at the gray robes of the Whisperer as the man turned away. Faelyn remained still, his gaze fixed on the man's hood.

The Whisperer turned slightly, catching Faelyn's eyes once again.

Busted. Faelyn smiled, taking a step forward.

The Whisperer sprang into action, nearly breaking into a run.

Faelyn cursed. He turned around and charged the white-marble wall behind him. His guards jumped to their feet, cursing as well. Faelyn whirled, pulling against the mounted torchstone on the back of the nearest pillar.

It shifted, stone grinding against stone as the false door in the wall opened.

Faelyn slipped inside, charging up the circular stairwell.

Most of the light faded as the door slid shut, closing automatically—locking his guards out. Faelyn heard them pull against the torch again, waiting for the door to reset.

Why would one of the Whisperers be watching me? Faelyn wondered, dashing up the stairs in the dim torchlight. He busted through the wooden door at the top of the stairs, coming out to the stone catwalk that overlooked the massive room below. He dodged a servant and looked across the room. He spotted a flash of a gray cloak as the Whisperer disappeared behind a door on the opposite side of the chamber.

"Helionn's Sun!" Faelyn cursed, sprinting down the side of the room, making for the bridge on the far end. He reached it, fire dancing at his fingertips as he called upon the flames in his Crystals.

A familiar warmth flooded his veins, the fire burning bright as he crossed the bridge that connected the two sides of the balcony from their gap over the center of the hallway. A massive chandelier hung in the center of the room, its Crystal light shining brightly despite the late hour. Faelyn wheezed, his lungs burning as he sprinted across the balcony. He tore open the door that the Whisperer had disappeared into. He froze, nearly falling down the stone stairs to his left as he crashed into something—or someone.

A pair of ice-blue eyes glowed in the darkness. Someone snapped their fingers, a strange hum settling over the darkening stairwell.

Faelyn blinked. The Incendiary torches suddenly faded. *What?*

The figure disappeared, dashing upwards.

Faelyn blinked again, the light in the chamber now significantly reduced. Faelyn couldn't make heads or tails of what had happened, all he knew was that he needed to catch this Whisperer.

He sprang to his feet, following the stairwell upwards. They were on the sixth floor now, and the top of the spire was only a few flights above. The Whisperer seemed to be cornering himself.

Faelyn slowed, realizing that he had no reason to hurry. There was nowhere for the Whisperer to run. Once he reached the top, he would be stuck, and the only way back down was past Faelyn.

"You were there the night I was talking to Reluraun, weren't you?" Faelyn called out into the fading light. He heard wind; he must be nearing the top. He panted, his lungs still burning from his sprint. "You're the same Whisperer I caught spying on me then, aren't you?" Faelyn paused. "What do you want with me? Did my father command you to spy on me?"

Footsteps shuffled, then stopped.

Faelyn frowned. He continued following the spiraling staircase, his hands alive with fire in the darkness. Faelyn felt a coolness come over him, despite the heat. It was partly his focus, yet it was also... a breeze.

"You've cornered yourself." Faelyn took another step forward. "Now all that's left to do is…" Faelyn trailed off.

The hatch to the roof of the spire was still closed. He would have heard it open had someone pulled the latch. *Did I miss the sound?* Faelyn wondered. He took a step forward, reaching the base of the four-rung ladder below the hatch. Faelyn extinguished the flames, pushing open the hatch, the hinges squealing.

He climbed up the small ladder, pulling himself to his feet on the small circular balcony at the top of the spire, just under the cone-shaped roof. The landing was no greater than five feet in diameter—barely big enough for two people. Faelyn looked around. Lights burned in the night, the Crystals and torches of Arvendon lighting people's homes as the moons rose overhead.

Waves crashed in the distance, the Salarin Sea refusing to rest despite the late hour. Faelyn looked around, the palace and its spires stretching out below him. Arvendon slanted toward the sea. Beyond the line of torches that marked the wall, Faelyn could see a few lights that marked the farmhouses of Arvendon's fields. And, beyond it all, he could see the faint, white, transparent glow of the ward that protected Arvendon and its fields.

One thing he did not see, however, was the Whisperer.

Faelyn turned, taking a deep breath of fresh air as a gust of crisp evening wind blew past him. Looking out at the city that would one day be his, the Whisperer still haunted the corners of his vision, slivers of gray cloak slipping past his eyes.

Something strange was happening, both out in the scorched world beyond and within these very walls. Faelyn frowned, staring at the city's lights once again. He needed answers. The Whisperer spying on him… one of his father's *own servants…* it didn't add up. Faelyn turned, climbing back through the latched trapdoor, and locking it once again.

The torches now burned brightly, as if they always had been. The rushing wind was gone, replaced by the quiet crackle of the flames.

Something occurred to him.

Faelyn turned, his pulse quickening. *If I'm right...* He needed answers, and he needed to get them as *soon* as possible.

Faelyn knocked, the heavy iron clacking loudly against the wooden door.

Someone grumbled on the other side of the door, and Faelyn heard a bed creak.

He backed slightly, settling on his feet. Faelyn looked around the dimly lit corridor, waiting for Reluraun to open the door. It was late, true, but Faelyn needed to talk to him *now*.

"Who's there?" Reluraun rumbled, his voice low.

"It's me," Faelyn said. He heard the footsteps quicken and approach the door.

Reluraun opened the door, his even-messier-than-usual hair nearly covering his eyes. "What are you doing here?" Reluraun asked, straightening. His eyes fell, examining Faelyn's sweat-stained vest. "What happened?"

"Nothing happened," Faelyn said, pushing the door open and slipping past Reluraun. "Which is exactly the problem."

Reluraun shut the door, turning on the lamp fixed on the wall beside the door frame. "Yeah, just come right in I guess..." Reluraun mumbled, stalking back to his bed, where his robe lay. The lanky boy threw the robe over his undergarments and turned back to Faelyn, who found himself standing in the small bedroom.

Faelyn had only been in Reluraun's room a few times and was always shocked by how small it was. It couldn't have been more than fifteen feet across. A small wooden table with two chairs sat on the other side of the room, against the wall.

Reluraun pulled a chair out for Faelyn, and then one for himself.

"I know that it's late, but I needed to talk to someone," Faelyn said, sliding into his seat.

Reluraun settled into his own, brushing his hair out of his eyes. "I already heard: My father is alive and well, yes, I know," Reluraun said. "I heard about the message Surge delivered too: The Expedition has gone well thus far, and has run into no conflicts. However, Velarus is heading into The Highlands, and they are going to lose contact with our emissaries soon."

"That's not why I'm here," Faelyn started, trailing off. He looked around the room, his eyes settling on the large tapestry that hung behind Reluraun's beige bed. It depicted the Knyvet family tree. Faelyn's eyes slid to Elric's portrait. "I think that someone has been spying on us."

"Who?" Reluraun asked, sitting up. His emerald eyes flickered, suddenly alert.

"It sounds strange, I know," Faelyn said, turning back to Reluraun. "But I think that it's one of my father's Whisperers."

Reluraun furrowed his brow, resting his arms on his knees. "Why would one of your father's own servants be spying on us?"

"Likely because they began to suspect that we are doing a bit of spying of our own," Faelyn said quietly.

"But they would have no way of knowing that."

"Right, but I think that the Whisperer overheard us that first night in the ballroom."

"How?"

"He was standing right behind the very pillar that we were leaning against," Faelyn said. "I don't know for how long, but, even if he didn't hear our entire conversation, he could've used his abilities to pick up on what we were talking about."

Reluraun frowned, his eyes distant. He rubbed his chin. "Has your father said anything to you about this?" Reluraun asked, raising an eyebrow.

"No," Faelyn admitted. "Which is why I'm a little confused." He paused, his mind drifting to the first chase and then to the events of this evening. "There's something else," Faelyn said. "I know that it's likely that the Whisperer was sent by my father, but what if... what if he wasn't?"

"What do you mean?" Reluraun leaned forward.

"What if the Whisperer is working for someone else? What if he isn't even..."

"What if he isn't even a Whisperer at all?" Reluraun finished. "Celes has spies all throughout Auris, I wouldn't be surprised if one of them was within this very palace."

"But a Whisperer?" Faelyn asked, second-guessing himself. "That isn't exactly the easiest position to infiltrate, most of those men have been with my father for decades."

"Precisely why that would be the perfect position *to* infiltrate, Faelyn." Reluraun paused. "Think about it, it makes sense."

Faelyn's brow furrowed, his eyes growing distant. It just couldn't be possible. Infiltrating his father's Whisperers would be *incredibly* challenging, and, if that had truly happened, why would the Whisperer be more focused on Faelyn than his father?

"He almost seems to be... a Scorcher," Faelyn said, looking up again.

"How so?"

"Tonight, I followed him," Faelyn explained. "I followed him through the servant staircases above the Titansworn Atrium, and when I finally caught up to him it was almost like..."

"Almost like what, Faelyn?" Reluraun asked, leaning forward.

"It was like the torches were dimmed," Faelyn said, shaking his head. "It was practically pitch black in there when I followed him, yet, on the way back, it was completely normal."

"Could the Whisperer have altered your mind to make things seem that way?"

"Not unless he was able to manipulate my thoughts while he was still running, which most Whisperers can't do." Faelyn frowned.

"Well, what happened?" Reluraun asked. "I assume he got away?"

"Yes," Faelyn said. "But something was strange about that. He climbed the staircase to the tallest spire of Summerglass."

"Wait, wouldn't he have cornered himself then?"

"Exactly," Faelyn nodded. "Yet, when I reached the top of the staircase and climbed out to the landing, he was nowhere to be found."

"And that's where you lost him, I assume?" Reluraun asked, tilting his head.

Faelyn nodded once again. "I've followed him once before," Faelyn said. "The night that I first caught him eavesdropping on us."

"And what happened then?" Reluraun asked, leaning forward even more.

"I followed him through the hallways until he lost me once again."

"He lost you, just like that?" Reluraun asked, confused.

"Well..." Faelyn trailed off, remembering the strange shadows across the courtyard, and the flickers of the cloak through the windows. "I'm not sure. It was almost like... like he was in two places at once. It was like he was moving faster than he should've been."

"Hmm..." Reluraun stood up, his white robe floating around him. He paced, rubbing his chin. "So you've found evidence of him being a Scorcher, because of the torches. You've found evidence of him being a Cloudwalker—assuming that he reached the top of the spire and flew away. And, finally, you've found evidence of him being a Dexteris due to his strangely quick movements... All of this, of course, on top of the fact that he is playing the part of one of your father's Whisperers."

"Now do you see why I wanted to talk to you about this?" Faelyn asked, standing up as well in the dim light.

Reluraun nodded, continuing to pace.

Faelyn turned to the small burning lamp by the door. He drew upon his Crystals, strengthening the blaze a bit so that there was more light in the room.

"I'm glad that you came here tonight," Reluraun finally said. "I think that your suspicions about this Whisperer are well backed. I still think that the most likely answer is that your father is trying to keep an eye on you, and this Whisperer is messing with your head. That being said, it is worth investigating."

Faelyn nodded.

"I'll see if I can pick up anything else in the meetings that I'm allowed to sit in on, you keep investigating this Whisperer of yours, sound good?" Reluraun rose to his feet.

"Yeah." Faelyn approached the door, opening it softly. The hallway light poured into Reluraun's dim room.

"Good luck, Faelyn," Reluraun called. "And be cautious: If your father truly is spying on us, then we must tread *very* carefully."

CHAPTER EIGHTEEN

THE CAVE

Elric Knyvet ascended, pushing the ground beneath him with a careful focus. He had told the others to wait below, and they had obeyed. They knew how he operated. He worked best alone, and on the fly. Besides, if the Blood Sorcerer was in the cave, then Elric would simply retrieve the others before advancing.

His anxieties started to creep in, the endless rivers of doubt beginning to trickle into his thoughts.

Elric silenced his thoughts, moving forward. He was not that person anymore. If one did not give themselves time to hesitate, then their fears would never take control.

He reached to his sides, unsheathing the wind-wood daggers and twisting them in his hands. Their gentle, carefully carved holes funneled the wind, making them easily maneuverable for Elric. He had a feeling that he may need these tonight.

He drifted closer to the cave, passing over the zigzagging path made in the snow by the many sets of footsteps of those who had come and gone from the outpost.

The snow was growing thicker and the Frostfall stronger. It had been several hours since they had first arrived at the cave, and Surge had decided that it would be wise to wait and see if anyone came out; no one had.

And so Elric approached. He twisted his hands, shaping the wind beneath him with his mind and slowly tilting forward.

As he got closer to the small peak, Elric noted that the mouth of the cave was unlit, and almost unnoticeable in the night. He neared the cave, the frozen air biting at his thick coat. He dropped to the snow as quietly as he could, landing a few yards to the side of the cave.

While the supposed Blood Sorcerers likely knew that they were being pursued, it was unlikely that he had spotted Elric tonight. There didn't appear to be anyone posted outside.

Probably wise, Elric thought. *A guard would make this secret hideout not so secret, after all.* They had done all they could to hide their presence, but Elric's experienced eyes had helped him pick out their footprints. Elric took a few crouched steps forward, gripping the daggers tightly in his gloved hands. He tapped his Crystals, sending a slight breeze forward.

Elric pushed the breeze a little farther, feeling the cave. *Yes... this is bigger than I thought,* Elric thought to himself, feeling the feedback from the gentle push. He pulled back, releasing his Crystals and continuing forward.

The mouth of the cave was small—barely large enough to fit a single person—though the depression around it was what gave it away.

Elric approached the small opening.

Darkness surrounded him, and even deeper darkness seemed to await him within. Yet... there was something in there. He could feel it. Elric approached, pulling off his goggles and freeing his vision.

He entered the cave.

Instantly he found relief from the cold winds. The stagnant air of the cave was warm and welcoming. He was now in total darkness, navigating his steps solely based on the patterns of wind that he gently pushed through what appeared to be some sort of corridor.

There seemed to be a fork up ahead.

His footsteps whispered against the cold stones of the cave, and Elric found himself listening for an echo. There was a slight one—enough of one that, if someone were truly listening, they would hear him coming.

Elric considered retrieving the others. But did he even need to? His younger self would have. His younger self would've rushed out of the cave terrified. But he was not that person anymore.

He could do this. If there were Blood Sorcerers ahead, he would go back for help. But, until he confirmed that there were, he would continue alone. Overcoming his former self was a fight that never ceased, but this could be a step in the right direction.

Elric pushed another gust through the corridor, finding his winds met with a dead end to the right, and a continuing passage to the left.

He took the left hall, nearly bumping into the jagged rocks that poked out from the strange cavern. The Highlands were filled with caves like these—carved by Ancient Stonemasters—and almost all of them were left unused and abandoned, though many of them were guarded by Rune-Locks.

As he continued, he began to hear voices.

Ah. Elric grinned in the darkness. *Someone is here after all.* He tilted his head, quieting the winds and listening as he crept through the narrow corridor. *Now to determine if there is a Blood Sorcerer among them.* He kept to his promise—he would not call the others until he knew for sure.

"...I wouldn't think that they'd be able to find us here, last I saw they were several miles back—still in The Wastelands," a voice said.

A light became apparent in the distance, refracting off the dark rocks of the cave.

"You underestimate them," another voice said. "Many have made that mistake, very few have lived to tell the tale."

"And fewer still have faced one like us and survived," the first voice snapped. "He has already left anyways. Even if we are discovered, it will be too late. He will reach the rendezvous point within a day or two."

"Yet we are still here," the second one said. "Why were we ordered to stay?"

"The Empress is wise; she would not have us here if not for good reason."

"I am growing tired of this inaction," one said. "The longer we leave Celes and Freyfall hanging in uncertainty, the greater the chances are of them betraying us."

What? Elric thought with a start. *Celes and Freyfall... they've already aligned with the Blood Sorcerers?* Elric paused, resolving to listen before continuing.

"Trust our Empress," the first said. "We will soon hear from the other three cities, and our Empress will move forward with her plan."

Cyfalion... Suchara... Elric furrowed his brow. *And Arvendon.* He felt a vengeful calm settle over his thoughts. The Blood Sorcerers were delivering the same message to every city on the continent: Join us, or die.

Suchara and Cyfalion are the only two that don't seem to be completely under their control. Cyfalion had never trusted Arvendon, but Suchara... there might be the possibility of an alliance there.

"We have time," the first continued. "So far as we're concerned the Shadow-Swifts don't even know what we're doing."

"And we're trying to keep it that way."

"Well, then it's a good thing that he's already left, isn't it?" The first seemed to walk away from the conversation—closer to Elric.

Elric's heart jumped. If he moved now, he would likely be heard. He would have called the others earlier, but he didn't want to risk missing the Blood Sorcerers' conversation. His curiosity had gotten him into this predicament, he could only hope that he wouldn't have to use his combat skills to get out.

The Blood Sorcerer continued growing closer to Elric's corridor, judging by the sound of footsteps.

"Where are you going?" the farther one asked.

"To keep watch for the pursuers," the first said.

Izara's Shadow. Elric crouched, tightening his grip on his knives. Unless there was another exit, the Blood Sorcerer would likely have to walk right into Elric.

There was no avoiding this. Elric had waited too long to retrieve the others, and now he was paying the price. Fortunately, he was one of the deadliest Cloudwalkers in the world.

A shadow appeared at the end of the corridor, approaching him.

Elric sprang into action, sprinting to the corner and dashing into the Blood Sorcerer. Elric slammed him with a blast of wind, flinging the Blood Sorcerer into the chamber beyond.

Elric turned the corner, taking a fraction of a second to note the small fireplace in the center of the circular room. Dark *red* Crystals were scattered across the room. Finally, his eyes settled on the pair of dark-robed men, one standing in the center of the room... the other rolling to his feet beside him.

So they truly are Blood Sorcerers, Elric thought with a shock.

They turned in an instant.

Elric dropped the knives, throwing out both hands and sending another brick of wind toward the pair. The condensed air flew across the round, low-ceilinged room and crashed into the one on the left, throwing him against the curved wall beyond.

The one on the right rolled out of the way, flinging back his robes to reveal a set of filled blood-red Crystals.

Elric's eyes widened, and he opened his hands. His daggers flew back into his palms.

The Blood Sorcerer extended his hands. A beam of red energy materialized between his outstretched hands, rippling with power. The Blood Sorcerer grinned.

Elric threw his daggers forward, propelling them carefully with wind.

The Blood Sorcerer jumped, spinning in midair and wrapping the liquidated energy around itself before *hurling* it at Elric.

Elric dove out of the way as the wave of blood magic shot through the air.

It crashed into the cavern wall, sizzling into nothing.

Elric hit the hard ground with a roll. His thrown daggers clattered uselessly against the far wall as the second man stood up. Elric twisted, pushing off the ground with a gust and launching himself to his feet.

The second man grinned, a flicker of red dashing across his hand.

Another Blood Sorcerer. Elric cursed, whipping his hands forward once again. He began shaping the air before him, twisting it into another boulder-like shape as the first Blood Sorcerer began summoning another torrent of energy.

The second Blood Sorcerer, to Elric's dismay, charged.

Elric tensed, throwing the block of wind toward the Summoner.

He dodged it with a low duck, and slid toward Elric.

Elric cried out, opening his hands to call his daggers back. He felt them rise from the ground, flying through the air.

A sudden, crushing weight slammed into Elric's body. He instantly released his Crystals, falling to his knees as an oppressive fog crashed into his mind, clogging his thoughts.

Seconds later he was on the ground. His arms were no longer his. His mind was held in a tight headlock, and his body was locked in a rigid statue. Elric pushed, straining to move his arms against the invisible weights. The world grew hazy as a figure stood over him.

The Blood Sorcerer held out his hands, red orbs glowing brightly in his palms. He laughed.

Elric tried to scream, only to find that his throat was constricted. His muscles *cramped* with a terrible intensity, straining against the phantom restraints as the Blood Sorcerer took control of his body.

Elric's legs bent mechanically. His arms twisted, and he found himself sitting up, almost fixed into a kneel before the man who controlled him. The final bit of control over his body slowly faded away.

"The Empress is going to be *very* happy to meet you." The Blood Sorcerer laughed.

Elric groaned, twitching his fingers. His body ached. Fatigue surged from each and every muscle as he continued struggling.

"Don't even bother trying to move," the Blood Sorcerer said, his dark face twisting into a wicked grin.

Elric shifted his eyes to the bright-red orbs in the Sorcerer's hands.

"You're ours now," the Blood Sorcerer rumbled.

A tendril of red energy flashed before Elric, then winked out.

Elric started, trying to move.

Another tendril flashed, replacing the one that had vanished.

He's just drained one of his Crystals, Elric thought.

"Velarus, help me hold him down," the Blood Sorcerer barked.

Velarus, Elric thought, his eyes widening. He finally ceased, letting his muscles crumple in on themselves as he fully succumbed to the Sorcerer.

Another tendril winked in and out of sight, but this time Elric was ready.

He used the brief lapse in control to grab on to one of his own Crystals, extracting a slight pull of wind from it. Elric pulled, and felt resistance.

The Blood Sorcerer was somehow pushing against Elric's summoning.

Elric groaned as distant footsteps approached. The second Blood Sorcerer—Velarus—stopped behind him. Elric felt a cold hand on the back of his head, and became aware of his own heartbeat.

Thump. Thump. Thump.

It was slowing down, as if it were being depressed by... *Oh no,* Elric thought with panic. Now was not the time to lose focus. Despite the Sorcerer's control, he was able to thread a slight bit of power through his body, if only he could...

Thump... Thump... Thump...

Elric screamed, and, with every bit of energy left in his exhausted body, he forced his hand open.

The Blood Sorcerer in front of him glanced at the open hand in shock, and then moved to close it.

Elric roared, bringing a vicious grin to his face, and then... he *PULLED.*

One of his daggers flew through the air just as the Blood Sorcerer's hand was reaching Elric's.

With a tilt of his head, Elric angled the dagger to the side, and watched as it sliced the Blood Sorcerer's hand clean off. Elric snapped his eyes shut. Blood splattered across his face.

The Blood Sorcerer screamed, releasing Elric.

Thump... Thump. Thump.

Elric opened his eyes and threw a hand forward, sending a blast of wind into Velarus.

Velarus flew to the cave wall, the air knocked from his lungs.

Elric whirled, opening both hands and calling his daggers back to his palms.

The Blood Sorcerer rolled over, screaming while clutching his stump of a hand. Blood squirted from it, pooling on the floor beside him.

Elric looked him in the eyes—the same eyes that had been alive with delight while Elric had been under his control—and Elric smiled. He swung the daggers with blinding speed, stabbing the man through the heart and throat simultaneously.

The man's wicked eyes drifted to emptiness as the seconds ticked by, and the life faded from his face.

Elric turned around, finding Velarus rising to his feet and gasping for air. The man's hood had fallen, revealing long black hair.

Elric took a step forward, his daggers whistling back into his hands in an instant.

Velarus cowered, raising his hands to the side, his cloak laying open.

Elric hesitated. *Hadn't Avenos said...* Elric made his decision.

He thrust his hands forward, sending the daggers flying. The daggers crashed into the Crystals hanging from Velarus's cloak, shattering them.

Red energy exploded into the air, drifting into the stones right before Elric's eyes as Velarus collapsed.

Elric held out his hands, the daggers slipping back into them with nothing more than a thought. Elric stomped his foot on the remaining Crystals that lay beside the dead Blood Sorcerer, sending another flurry of liquidized energy into the air.

"Please," Velarus begged, crawling across the floor. "You've taken my power from me, there is nothing I can do to you now... There's no reason to torture me."

"So I suppose you want me to just kill you, then?" Elric tilted his head, kneeling beside the man.

He looked up, his black hair and blue eyes shining in the firelight. "Please," Velarus repeated. "I know your kind. I only ask that you give me the sweet mercy of death... *Please.*"

"Oh, my friend," Elric reached out, running a hand through the long black hair. "I would, but... I need you to tell me where *the real* Velarus is."

"Wha—" the man started,

Elric tightened his grip, holding the man by his hair.

He cried out, his head thrown back by Elric's pull.

"I may not have seen Velarus with my own eyes," Elric whispered, his fingers tingling as he held a dagger to the imposter's throat. "But the King was wise enough to tell me that he was *bald.*" Elric reared back.

The man tensed, holding his hands to protect his face. But Elric wasn't planning on killing the man... no. Elric merely needed to ensure that he would not go anywhere while he fetched the expedition crew.

Elric slammed the wind-wood blades into both of the Blood Sorcerer's feet, feeling the crunch of a bone beneath the hilt.

The Blood Sorcerer screamed, writhing on the floor.

Elric grimaced, but held strong. *This is for your city,* Elric reminded himself. *It needed to be done.* He rose to his feet, leaving the imposter struggling on the ground.

"When I return, it would be in your best interest to tell me the truth," Elric whispered. "Some of my friends may not be so *gentle.*"

Castien Varic stepped into the circular room, falling silent as he took in the scene around him.

Elric stood in the center of the room, kneeling over a bleeding man in dark robes. Surge and Luka were positioned around him, with Saevi, Ilyana, and Arthion just behind. They were watching the man intently, yet no one spoke.

Blood was splattered on the floor next to where Castien stood, along with a detached hand. Castien stepped over a dark-robed corpse, trying to avert his eyes from the deep hole in the man's throat.

"You're right," Surge grumbled. "This isn't him." Surge stood up, turning away from the whimpering man on the ground. "But you still should've waited and returned with us."

"By the time I thought I had a chance to leave, they had discovered me," Elric said.

"Then you should have fled," Luka growled. "They would've either followed you and ran right into us, or stayed in here while you gathered our help."

"What does it matter now? I handled it," Elric countered.

"Barely, judging by the way you seem to stumble a little when you walk. What happened to you, anyway?" Surge asked.

"It's not important, I'm fine." Elric brushed off his shoulder. "What is important is that the King was wrong; the Blood Sorcerers are real."

A heavy silence fell over the room. Someone shuffled their feet. Castien looked down. He knew what this meant for him. If there were no Whisperers involved, then he had no reason to be here. He never should've been here in the first place.

"What happened?" Luka asked.

"I charged in and attacked them," Elric explained. "They knocked me to the ground, proving that their powers were real... Yet I overtook them anyway."

"And somehow the very same breed of Summoner held an entire throne room hostage." Surge rubbed his chin.

"Ah." Elric took a step toward the man on the ground. "Now you see why I have arrived at a certain... conclusion. These men were Lesser Summoners, and the real Velarus is a Master Summoner."

"Why do you say the 'real' Velarus?" Saevi asked, raising an eyebrow.

"Because this man was pretending to be him," Elric said. "Once they saw me, the other called this one 'Velarus' likely to trick me into thinking that we had caught him. I don't think they counted on any of us having seen Velarus before."

"And none of us have," Surge mumbled. "Luckily, King Avenos is thorough in his debriefs."

"But why would they have one of their own pretend to be Velarus?" Arthion asked.

"Because then we would have no reason to push onward," Elric said. "The real Velarus is somewhere out there, farther along the trail... and they don't want us to find him."

"So then what is *he* doing here if Velarus is already gone?" Saevi asked.

All eyes turned to the Blood Sorcerer.

Surge took a step forward. "You can tell us," Surge whispered. "Or we can *make* you tell us."

The man whimpered, sliding himself up against one of the walls.

Arthion stepped forward. "Listen here, dear boy," Arthion said, kneeling beside the wounded man. "I am a Whisperer, and, even if you try to resist our interrogations, I will still be able to extract the information directly from your mind. So let us expedite this whole endeavor, and simply cut straight to the part where you tell us everything you know."

"I—" the Blood Sorcerer started. He trailed off, coughing.

"Let's start with something simple," Arthion said, hovering on the balls of his feet.

Castien watched with fascination as the Whisperer worked, yet, when he checked for the pull on the room, Castien felt nothing. *Tarathiel's Stones!* He was doing this without his powers.

"What is your name, your *real* name?" Arthion asked.

"Kels, sir," the Blood Sorcerer said quietly.

"Where are you from?"

"I was raised in Freyfall," Kels responded, his voice pained.

"And how did you become a Blood Sorcerer?" Arthion prodded.

"I... didn't," Kels stuttered. "I was working as a cobbler in Freyfall, and then one day a man came in and said that he was looking for me—because I was a cousin of Velarus. Before I was able to respond, he put me in a headlock with his powers and forced me to listen to him."

"You're Velarus's cousin?" Surge asked.

"Estranged, yes," Kels said. "I don't understand what they wanted with me, but apparently they assumed that, since we were related, I would possess the same powers as him."

"And these Crystals, Kels..." Arthion reached down, picking up one of the broken Crystals. "Where did you get these?"

"They were—" Kels started. "They were given to me by our Empress."

"And your Empress is..." Arthion raised an eyebrow.

"I don't know," Kels said quickly, his breathing increasing. He moved his leg, grimacing. "I swear by Calida's Claws that I don't know. All I know is that her fortress is somewhere in the northern Highlands."

"And what do you know about the Vanishing, or the Resurgence?" Luka stepped forward. "Your kind was supposed to be wiped out, yet here you are."

"I don't know anything," Kels rasped. "I swear to you they've kept me in the dark."

"You were talking about Celes and Freyfall. What have you done there?" Elric asked forcefully.

"We..." Kels stuttered once again, taking a deep breath. "We sent other operatives into the cities, and we gave them the same threat that we gave Arvendon... That's why we didn't just take your city by force: Our forces are spread too thin. We thought that sending emissaries first—and then soldiers if necessary—would be the quickest way to gain control."

"Why?" Surge growled. "Why are you doing any of this?"

"I don't know," Kels whispered. "I didn't ask any questions. I don't know why any of this happened, I just... When I learned that I had these..."

"When you realized what you were, you couldn't resist," Castien found himself saying. "You didn't want to risk having your powers taken away for your curiosity. I understand." He stepped forward, feeling a sudden conviction. "Ease off, he's telling the truth."

The group looked to Arthion, who closed his eyes briefly, and then nodded.

Kels sagged, his black hair matted and tangled across his blood-stained face.

Castien understood the man's motivations, though he couldn't say that he would've done the same thing in his situation. *But if I were to learn of powers that I never knew I had...* Castien's thoughts trailed off. It wasn't worth pondering.

"It just doesn't make any sense," Surge said, rubbing his stubble of a beard once again.

"What?" Ilyana asked, stepping beside him.

"The Blood Sorcerers returning," Surge answered. "Why here? Why now? And why in *Calida's Claws* are they trying to bully the cities of Auris into subjugation?" Surge shook his head, shutting his dark eyes.

Castien stared at the ground.

"I guess no one really knows what happened during the Vanishing." Ilyana shrugged. "All we know is that one day a war began, and when it ended half of the Sects had disappeared, and violent Tempests suddenly ravaged the lands."

"We don't even know where their power comes from," Luka said. "The Blood Sorcerers... we never knew where the power of the Ancient Sects came from, because the Tempests didn't exist until after the Vanishing. Yet even now, with these Crystals right before us, we still have no idea what powers them."

"Which is why we need to find the *real* Velarus," Surge said. "If anyone knows what's really going on here, it's him."

"Or, at the very least, he'll lead us to his hideout," Elric added.

"Our little informant thinks that the hideout is somewhere to the north," Arthion interjected, rejoining the main group.

Kels nodded. "Velarus headed straight that way, there is a rendezvous point a few days' walk up ahead."

"Do you know what's at the point?" Surge asked.

"I don't know, I suspect Cloudwalkers, or some other means of transportation. But, if he's already there, then you'll never catch him," Kels said, his voice shallow.

"So we need to go," Luka resolved, standing up.

"Like, right now, right?" Saevi said. She rose to her feet as well.

Castien turned to Arthion, who turned to Surge.

Surge nodded. "We have no time to lose," Surge said, addressing the whole group. "We're closer to Velarus than ever before. Now is not the time to let up, my friends. Pack your things."

"What are we going to do about him?" Saevi asked.

The others turned to where Kels sat on the floor, still rubbing his wounded leg. Elric turned to Luka. Luka turned to Surge.

"Isn't it obvious?" Surge asked.

"Wait," Kels whimpered. "Wait, what's going on?"

"We have to kill him," Surge said, drawing his massive greatsword.

"No!" Kels shouted, scrambling back against the wall behind him. "No, please! I thought that, if I told you everything I knew, then you would—"

"Surge," Arthion said, stepping between the general and the Blood Sorcerer. "He's right. We have no reason to kill him. He told us everything we wanted to know."

"And his kind had no reason to threaten our kingdom," Surge said coldly, pushing past Arthion. "I've made up my mind. I was put in charge of this expedition, and I am telling you that this man must pay for his crimes against our city."

"And *I* was appointed to this position by the King himself, specifically so that I could stop any of you from acting irrationally!" Arthion put himself between Surge and Kels again.

Kels shuffled back farther.

Castien took a step forward, seeing the terror in the powerless Summoner's eyes.

"Surge, he's right," Elric said from behind. "Let him go."

"No," Luka countered, stepping forward. "Any Blood Sorcerer who we leave behind, powerless or not, is a loose end."

"And let me guess: No loose ends, right?" Ilyana taunted. "Is that why you don't like me? Because I'm a loose end?"

"Now is not the time for—" Luka started.

"Oh, I think now is a *perfect* time." Ilyana advanced. "You've been holding this against me for years now... whispering in the King's ear that I couldn't be trusted... spreading rumors around the city, saying that I disgraced the Crown!"

"And what would you say you did?" Luka challenged. "You refused to take a job that *hundreds* would've killed for!"

"Why do you even care? You got what you wanted!" Ilyana shouted, drawing her blades.

"I don't even care about my position anymore!" Luka's Crystals flared .

Ilyana took another step forward, raising her blades. "Then why are you even here?"

"I'm here in hopes that I'll one day be able to get my revenge on you for dishonoring me." Luka raised his hands, frost coalescing in his cracked palms. "You're a monster," Luka spat. "No better than any other criminal. If I had it my way, you'd be in a cell beneath the palace rather than here, getting in the way." The air grew cold. Luka's eyes flashed, the air chilling further.

Ilyana took a step back, sliding into a defensive stance.

Castien knew her reasons for doing what she did. He wanted to say something. He wanted to speak up, to stand up for her. But he did not. He didn't do anything.

"We are wasting time," Surge rumbled, his sword sparking. "Let's kill the Blood Sorcerer and be on with it!"

"You are *not* killing an innocent man!" Arthion shouted, standing firmly between Surge and Kels.

Shouting followed, chaos filling the chilled room as Luka and Ilyana resumed their argument.

Surge pushed against Arthion, trying to move him out of the way without harming him.

Saevi just laughed, soaking in the horror of it all.

Castien's heart raced. It was too loud. Everything was *too loud*. The lights were too bright. The fire moved too quickly, everything was *wrong*. Castien stumbled back, the shouting seeming to grow louder as his legs began to shake. His heartbeat thumped in his chest.

His breathing grew shallow, as if the air were growing thin. Despite the chilling cold, Castien felt hot, too hot. Everything was wrong. He shouldn't be here, he shouldn't even—

He gasped for air, feeling as if his chest were closing in on itself. He stumbled over, grabbing onto the wall of the cave for support as the arguing continued. *It was just like... It was just like...* Castien gasped again, his heart thundering in his ears. The world seemed to spin, the loudness growing and growing and growing until it was—

Someone thumped to the ground. Castien's head shot to the side, his eyes darting frantically around the room. The pit in his stomach opened, and Castien's insides plummeted.

Arthion rolled to a stop, laying on the floor, dusting himself off and rubbing his shoulder, having been knocked over by Surge.

Surge advanced. Ilyana shouted. Luka moved, the air freezing over again. Finally, the cold became too much, and Castien shut his eyes, blocking out all sounds except for that of his own heart.

The fire snuffed out, plunging the room into darkness.

Castien cracked his eyes open, hearing the soft *cut* of a sword meeting flesh.

His head grew heavy, and Castien surrendered himself fully to the floor.

Loud footsteps shuffled, and people whispered.

It was too late.

A small flame bloomed in the darkness, wandering and twisting around Saevi's outstretched hand.

Surge wiped the blood from his blade, turning away from the Blood Sorcerer's corpse on the floor. He had done it. Kels was dead.

Arthion said nothing as he rose to his feet in the near darkness.

Ilyana stared at the fallen figure; Luka did as well.

Saevi shook her head, sending the small tendril of flame toward the corridor from which they had entered.

Elric sighed, looking over at Surge with something like disappointment flickering in his eyes. Elric's eyes settled on Castien, and he quickly made his way over to help him up.

Castien shook his head, feeling distant. It was almost as if he were watching a Tempest from his barrack window, when in reality he was standing in the middle of the storm, barely surviving the vicious winds.

Elric pulled Castien to his feet, his kind eyes solid yet cold.

Surge led the group out of the cave, guided by Saevi's light.

Castien walked on his own after a few moments, though Elric and Ilyana stayed close by him.

Castien's mind was blank. His thoughts had fled him, abandoning him to the empty loneliness of his own brain. He didn't belong here. He never did. It was too much; it had *always* been too much. He shouldn't have even made himself stand out, back before he had saved his former crew in The Highlands. He shouldn't even be among Arvendon's ranks. He wasn't a soldier—he never would be. He was a boy, running away from a past that he couldn't even bring himself to *think* about.

It was wrong. All of it was wrong. And there, as they passed through the mouth of the cave and reentered the barren wastes beyond, Castien realized that things may never be right again.

CHAPTER NINETEEN
THE SCHOLARS

Sixteen months ago...

Asteros Silverglade stood quietly on the other side of Erydon's Rune-Locked Door. The Crystals fixed upon the walls seemed brighter than usual this morning. He turned back to the door, awaiting Shalheira's return. His eyes traced the back of the door, configured of several sliding stone bars and arm-like curves of Runed rock that moved in response to the lock.

Life had been unbearably boring for the last few months, especially given that all Asteros could do was wait for Shalheira to return with Freyfall's scholars. Lucien, who was currently out of the fortress, had only been forced to raise his blade once—though he did kill far more than necessary—for most of the skirmishes between Arvendon's troops and Freyfall's had taken place far from Herqen.

A loud clicking sound signaled the opening of the lock.

Asteros stepped back.

The massive arms on the inside of the stone door swept across one another, rearranging themselves so that the doors could open. The bars slid to the right and left, then moved downwards, out of the way of the entrance. Another arm inched slowly along the wall, stone scraping against stone. Nearly a minute passed, filled with the sharp, unpleasant screeching of the stones as they obeyed the commands of the lock. With one final sweep, the Runes along the doorframe illuminated with an almost white glow, and the doors opened.

Asteros squinted against the bright sunlight of The Highlands that managed to pierce through the Frostfall.

Four figures stood before him with Shalheira at the front of the group.

Asteros blinked several times, the silhouettes before him slowly melding into faces.

"Asteros," Shalheira said coldly, stepping forward.

His breath caught at the sight of her. It was almost as if he had forgotten her beauty. *Not now,* he thought.

Shalheira's dark, hard eyes burned into his.

Asteros lowered his head. *She knows that Lucien has killed more than he needed to.*

"Welcome home," Asteros said, pulling her into a tight embrace before she could react. He breathed in the cold scent of the northern air that lingered on her black cloak.

Reluctantly, Shalheira closed her arms around him. She pulled away quickly, recollecting herself.

"You—" Shalheira started.

"Later," Asteros said quietly, nodding to the three figures standing in the entryway.

She nodded slightly and turned back to the three scholars who were too busy marveling at the grand entry hall to even notice their brief discussion.

"Eithor!" Shalheira snapped.

The oldest of the three scholars turned to face her, his withered figure shuddering a bit at the harshness of her voice.

"Introduce yourself," Shalheira commanded.

The figure nodded slowly, lowering the simple hood of his gray robes to reveal a messy, wiry head of hair. "My name is Eithor Vassel-let," the man said. "I am one of the most knowledgeable experts on Rune-Reading, and I am rather capable when it comes to under-standing the ancient tongue." Eithor paused. "I am honored to have this opportunity to see the Sanctuaries with my own eyes... and, for the time being, I swear my services to you, Master Silverglade." He bowed, his frail form refusing to dip more than a few inches.

Asteros turned to the other two scholars, each of whom wore the same plain robes as Eithor. He motioned for them to introduce themselves.

"I am Soran Mallum," a younger, bald man said, stepping forward. "My knowledge of the Rune-Writers and Stonemasters is rather extensive. Though many can say the same, few know the mechanics of their language better than I."

Asteros smiled slightly. He knew all too well the complexity of the ancient tongue when it came to the order and shape of the letters. While some languages simply held one symbol to represent each letter, the ancient tongue possessed several different forms for each sound.

"Tsarra...?" Shalheira said.

The last of the scholars locked eyes with Asteros—something that neither of the other two had done. A fire burned beneath the red-brown pupils that stared at him.

Shalheira has not broken this one yet. Asteros looked back to Soran and Eithor, noting their discomfort at simply bearing Shalheira's gaze.

"I am Tsarra Selic," she said, lowering her hood to reveal long, flowing black hair, a bit like Shalheira's. "I dabble more in the styl-istic preferences of certain Rune-Writers and Stonemasters."

She was going to be useful. The language of the Ancients had evolved as time went on, and many of the direct records came from a time long *after* the Vanishing, not before.

A loud clicking noise sounded as the door began to close.

The three scholars turned to watch as the complex arms and bars slid across one another, sealing the thick stone door that resurfaced from the floor of the chamber. The slab slid to a stop as it collided with the top of the doorframe. The arms continued grinding along the stone, nearing their places.

"Fascinating," Eithor breathed, his willowy voice sounding quiet against the screeching stone.

The door sealed once again, its Runes flickering slightly as their wards were reactivated.

"I have seen hundreds of sketches... but I never thought I would see one of these with my own eyes." Eithor stepped back.

Asteros smiled. *He has no idea what is in store for him.*

"I will show you to your quarters, Freyfallions," Asteros said, raising a hand and turning around.

"Erydonians," Shalheira corrected. "You serve us now."

Asteros bristled, grinding his teeth slightly.

Shalheira met his eyes with a sharp gaze.

Yes. She knew all too well what Lucien had been up to while she was away.

"She speaks the truth," Asteros said, still facing the empty end of the grand entry hall. "We will not ask you to act against Freyfall, though we must forbid you from assisting them in any way while you are within this mountain."

"Understood," Eithor said, almost sounding eager.

Asteros smiled once again. Shalheira had gathered quite a... *strange* collection of scholars. Though he trusted her. She would settle for nothing less than the greatest minds of Auris to tackle this task.

Asteros waved his hand slightly, signaling for them to follow. He started down the rectangular chamber, turning off into one of the stairwells that lined the edges of the room. This one led to a mostly abandoned wing that had once served as servants' quarters. Erydon had once been far more prosperous than it was now. Asteros supposed that six people were hardly enough for one to call their organization a clan.

"You are free to roam about the fortress as you please, though you are not to enter the Southern Wing. Those are the private quarters of our Shadow-Swifts." Asteros didn't need to turn around to confirm that they had heard him. He was certain that Shalheira had made it clear that one wrong step was all it took to earn one of these scholars a strict punishment.

"How do you gather food at this high of an altitude?" Tsarra asked, tracing a hand along the inscribed walls.

Asteros continued walking, keeping his eyes level as he passed through the narrow, curved passageway, continuing up the incline.

"Our ancestors stockpiled dry foods of all sorts, filling much of the interior of the mountain," Asteros said. "Through a method of Transcendence, they were able to ensure that our food source was always replenished by the energies of the Unbound." Asteros himself wasn't even sure how they had managed such a trick, though they hadn't dared tamper with the complex contraption responsible for their food production, for he didn't want to unintentionally disable it.

"Water?" Soran asked, his accent dragging across the syllables. His accent was the thickest of the three, as if he'd been raised in the Ice Fields.

"The mountain's snow filters through small pipes on the exterior of Erydon; it flows into our fortress and keeps our wells full," Asteros explained as they finally reached the top of the incline.

The small passage opened up into a large common area here, with several doors branching off into the smaller private rooms for each individual servant. An abandoned hearth sat in the center of the far wall, and dusty, unused chairs lay clattered about in the common area.

Asteros had suggested that they clean the area up, if only to save the scholars a bit of time, but Lucien had insisted on keeping it the way it was.

Lucien wanted to make their message to the scholars clear: You do not belong here, you are our guests, and you will obey us.

Asteros supposed that it was an effective way to deliver such a message, though forcing them to live in an abandoned area filled with krellins seemed a bit... excessive. Asteros noticed the critters' webs littering the corners of the room and painting the backs of the fallen chairs.

A krellin scurried across the floor, its twelve legs clattering against the stone.

Asteros reached out lazily and blasted the tiny creature with a spear of umbrakinesis, instantly killing the pitiful thing.

Eithor jumped a bit, and Soran gaped. Tsarra only watched, seemingly amused.

Asteros eyed the woman once again, though she kept her eyes fixed on the twitching corpse of the fallen krellin.

"I do hope you find your rooms... suitable," Asteros said. "We will give you some time to get settled and find your way to the banquet hall. I would recommend eating something before night falls. We have work to do."

"What have you done?" Shalheira hissed, pulling Asteros into one of the side passages. Her eyes seethed with rage.

"Lucien ensured that Herqen's secrets were not discovered. We had no choice," Asteros said softly.

"And the dozens of innocent soldiers who died by his hand?"

"I'd hardly say they were innocent; soldiers know that they are risking their lives when they enter the legions. Many of them have even killed others," Asteros retorted.

"And the Arvendi?"

Asteros smiled sharply. "The Arvendi-Freyfallion Skirmishes were inevitable. Let us just be thankful that they didn't escalate into a war."

"A war that wouldn't have even come into question had we not intervened!" Shalheira glowered. "I cannot believe that you would allow Lucien to do this! You know that all he cares about is this idea of *domination.*"

"Do not insult the nature of the man who ensured that we remained undiscovered," Asteros said calmly, taking her hand. "He may be brash, he may be violent, but Haldir trained him that way for a reason."

Shalheira's eyes softened slightly, her slender fingers relaxing beneath his touch. "He didn't have to do it," she whispered. "They wouldn't have even found the door, regardless of our intervention."

"Logically speaking, you're probably correct, though can we really place our faith in the simple fact that the door was hidden in plain view?" Asteros asked, meeting her gaze. "Look, forget about the door for a moment and think about what this has done for our order."

A long pause settled over the pair as Shalheira looked away. Asteros rested his eyes on her delicate face, her flawless skin, her warm features. Her amber eyes drifted back to him. "The world has forgotten who we are, Shalheira. And we have given them a reminder."

"I—" Shalheira started, her eyes weak.

"Why do you think that the scholars came with you?" Asteros prodded, pulling her close once again, breathing in the cool scent of The Highland snow on her cloak. "They knew of our work in these mountains. In our era of observation, we lost our grip on Auris. Now, Lucien has gotten it back," Asteros said.

Shalheira's face wavered, as if she were stuck in her thoughts. After a moment, her thin lips parted into a slight smile. "You're a genius, Asteros," she whispered, wrapping her arms around him.

Asteros pulled down her hood, running his hands through her tangled black hair.

She ran her fingers along his back, sliding them down to his waist as she melted into his touch. The cavern faded away, leaving only Asteros and Shalheira standing in the mystifying light of the Crystals.

Her scent enveloped him, his thoughts washing away like lines in sand. A cool breeze whipped through the air, slithering down Asteros's spine.

Shalheira tilted her face toward his, her eyes opening slightly.

His hands drifted lower, and he leaned down. Warmth tingled his head, pooling in his stomach as the cold shield of his heart thawed to a puddle of untamed fire in his soul.

"Asteros—"

"Shh," Asteros whispered, bringing a finger to her lips. She closed her eyes once again, a strange sadness coming over her face. He delicately raised a hand, lifting her chin ever so slightly.

She gasped, flinching slightly.

Asteros released his hand, only for her to reach for it seconds later. *Gods, she is beautiful.* Something changed in her composure, her strong form dissolving into the gentle shell of a woman broken by years of killing.

"You have no idea how much I've missed you," Asteros breathed, her ear right beneath his mouth.

She pulled back, letting him see her face once again. Her eyes were watering.

Something awakened inside of Asteros, a primitive, protective side of him that had been dormant for so long. Someone had hurt this woman. Someone had cut her as deeply as one had once cut him. Years of cold indifference, drilled into his mind by Haldir and Lucien, evaporated like water beneath the blazing sun. He had been told not to care. *Commanded* not to care—about anything. For one could not kill while one cared. But, in a moment, it all changed. The woman before him burned away the monster within him, giving way to the man who had been chained by guilt for so long.

He brought his lips to hers, her grip tightening around his waist.

The kiss destroyed him, tearing apart his soul and putting it back together again in all of a second. Her warm skin grazed his lightly, a brief moment of passion that neither had ever dreamed of, but that both deserved.

She pulled away but slid back into his arms once again. They both knew they shouldn't. They both knew they *couldn't.* Yet some things were beyond their control.

"Shalheira," Asteros whispered, bringing his lips to hers once again.

"We can't."

"I know," Asteros said, kissing her again. "But one cannot hide from destiny."

Shalheira pressed her lips against his, her warmth filling his cold soul.

Asteros pushed her against the wall, his hands still wrapped around her in an eternal embrace.

She gasped again, trembling under his touch. "Asteros," she whispered, tilting her head away from another kiss.

Asteros receded.

She closed her eyes, shrinking into her cloak. She lowered her gaze.

"Shalheira..." Asteros started, stepping toward her. She stepped away, backing farther down the cramped hallway, brushing against a Scorcher Crystal and knocking it from its pedestal on the stone wall.

It crashed to the floor, shattering. Tendrils of orange light billowed from the broken Crystal, washing across the floor. Heat licked Asteros's booted feet.

Shalheira lowered herself to the ground, her trembling hands reaching for the fragments of the shattered Crystal. She held a few fragments in her palm, and then let them tumble away. Shalheira knelt, keeping her head low. Something was troubling her, something that she had been hiding from him... something that their rising love seemed to have brought out.

Asteros wished he could protect her from whatever it was that was harming her mind. Yet he could not, not right now. He could only hold her. His past flashed before his eyes, nearly summoning tears of his own. It faded like a snowprowler in a Frostfall, vanishing into the void of memories that he tried to forget.

"They have arrived?" a voice asked from behind.

The pair whipped around.

Keries stood in the frame of the passage, his face cast in an ominous shadow from the lack of light in the hall.

"Keries?" Asteros stood, Shalheira at his side.

"The scholars," Keries said. "They have arrived?"

"They have," Asteros said. "And soon you will see what it is that we have discovered."

"Nearly a half-year after you found it," Keries grumbled. "Why is it that you didn't show us earlier? You claimed you had only found more details of the Vanishing, but, if you brought in these *outsiders*... there is clearly more to it than you say."

"Be ready tonight," Asteros said, "and all will be explained. Our conquest begins this evening."

"Conquest?" Keries's gaze darkened.

"We are not conquerors," Shalheira interjected. "We are going to be something *so* much more: We are going to be saviors."

Keries frowned, meeting Asteros's gaze. "So you have been keeping secrets," he said, narrowing his eyes.

"Haldir kept many from us as well. You and I both know that," Asteros said. "Sometimes it is merely better for us all if things are left unsaid." He paused. "Yet tonight... Tonight the unspoken will finally be told. Shalheira has brought us the necessary resources to begin our revolution, and, tonight, what we learn will change Auris forever."

Lucien Shade thrust his blade through the Utryan's throat. Warm blood poured from the wound as Lucien tore the sword away, ripping at the skin of the poor man's neck.

He collapsed, choking on his own blood. Lucien smiled grimly, turning to the soldiers beside him.

They stared at their fallen comrade, none of them daring to draw their weapons.

Lucien shifted, vanishing into a shadow of darkness as the Unbound enveloped him. The men jumped, this time reaching for their axes as Lucien moved between them.

The Wispwinds raged through The Highlands. Tendrils of white, insubstantial energy rolled along the mountain side. A Wisp passed through Lucien, leaving behind a trail of pearl-colored essence that followed the Wisp like a shadow.

Lucien phased back to Auris, plunging his blades into yet another pair of soldiers. Freyfall had ordered an Utryan retreat a few days prior, and, while many had listened, some had not. These men had not listened; they had instead opted to take shelter on one of the lower parts of Herqen.

Lucien had allowed Arvendon and Freyfall to tire each other out and stayed out of most conflicts. Yet, if a stray squadron happened to set foot on Herqen... Lucien would do what he needed to.

"Nyghtmaere! Nyghtmaere!" one of the soldiers shouted in his thick accent.

Lucien laughed at the nickname they had given him—or, he supposed, that he had earned himself. It was an ancient Utryan word for "Monster," which Lucien supposed was fitting—given his growing reputation.

Utryan folklore was rich and very well developed for a culture that was so advanced. Typically, Lucien found the most religious of peoples to be the least developed, for they spent so much time poring over their prophetic books of nonsense that no one ever bothered to actually take a look at the world around them and try to solve their problems—rather than trying to pray them away.

Yet Utryan technology had rivaled that of Arvendon for centuries, the capitals somehow always managing to keep up with each other.

Whispers in the wind... A Silver Sun... Screams... Flashes of white...

Lucien severed the arm of another man, cutting through bone like butter as he continued pondering the various beliefs of humanity. Strange how killing had come back to him so easily, despite decades of stagnation in Erydon. After a childhood of vicious training and survival, one should think he wouldn't be shocked at all, though a part of him was still pleasantly surprised.

The others knew nothing of his past, and that was the way he wanted to keep it. It was fair, given that he knew nothing of theirs. That was the way it should be, when one became a Shadow-Swift, they swore to leave behind all that they were—and would've been— so that they could become something more. Or, more accurately, something less.

Haldir's teachings had long since worn off on Lucien. Erydon only existed to serve as a sort of prison for the Shadow-Swifts, not as a fortress for the strongest Sect in the world. Not that he could blame his ancestors for agreeing to such terms. He knew firsthand how dangerous their powers were if allowed to flourish and grow—as did Keries, apparently. Though the older man never spoke of his past, Lucien knew that it involved an accidental usage of his powers, prior to Keries's discovery of his own heritage.

Yet it was not his place to ask, nor was it his place to care. Keries was Utryan, and his devotion to Niventia far surpassed that of the other Shadow-Swifts. He would be alright, if only because his faith provided the answers to whatever knowledge he sought.

Lucien phased back to the Unbound, rushing the final soldier— who was the captain, judging by the stripe on his uniform—on the mountainside path. The captain wore the typical Utryan steel-fur armor that was supposed to both protect and warm its wearer. Unfortunately, nothing could protect him from what Lucien was about to do.

Lucien tackled the man, burning through several of his Crystals to transport the man into the Unbound. Putting a non-Shadow-Swift through Transcendence required a great deal of energy and was a feat that not even Asteros or Haldir had ever been able to accomplish with much accuracy. It was for this reason that Shadow-Swifts used Shadow-Sand: It required far less energy to Transcend.

Lucien pulled the man with him as they dove between Realms.

The soldier's dark eyes widened in terror. The world turned black, coated with the shadow of the Unbound. Darkness cascaded from the pair, tumbling from them like water from the Sucharan Falls.

The man grunted, clinging to Lucien in the foreign land.

Yet Lucien was far stronger than the poor soul.

Lucien reached into the captain's armor, feeling for something specific. He found it. Grabbing hold of it and ripping it from the man's armor, Lucien took hold of the list.

He sent out a flash of umbrakinesis, the wave of darkness throwing the man from Lucien into the endless valleys of darkness in The Highland's rifts. Lucien phased back to Auris, the soldier inevitably phasing back with him. That was the apparent catch of Transcending another: They would return when you did, making it impossible for one to trap another in the Realm-between-Realms.

The lessened gravity lingered on the man's body for a few precious seconds, giving him time to rise unbelievably high into the Wisp-filled sky. Not even a moment later, the man dropped, his scream drowned out by the gentle hum of the Wisps and the howling mountain wind.

Looking down to the list in his hand, Lucien smiled. He knew that there would be a captain roaming these mountains, and he was all but certain that he would have *this* very list. Lucien produced the stone tablet, his eyes scanning row after row of names.

There had to be a few hundred soldiers on this list. Utryan captains were trusted with master lists like this, which contained the names of every soldier in their area as well as their squadrons. It allowed for captains to easily keep track of who needed to be positioned where, though Lucien had very different reasons for acquiring it.

It was a longshot, but, if one of the scholars Shalheira brought back had a child in the Utryan forces, then this trip would be *more* than worth the trouble.

Lucien sidestepped another Wisp as the mass of ghastly white energy floated by him. He had no reason to dodge such a thing; it would simply pass through him as if he were nothing. Yet instincts often overrode logic in Lucien's mind. He reached into a compartment of his black armor, checking his Crystals. The Transcendence of the soldier had required a considerable amount of energy, though Lucien found it to be a worthy sacrifice. The others would disagree, but something about the glorious rush of the wind and the horrified cry of the victim pleased Lucien's soul itself.

He would have enough to get back to Erydon without having to walk—barely. Yet that was all he needed. Tonight was likely to have clear skies, as many evenings did in Auris. Occasionally, two of The Tempests would descend on the same day, resulting in one of them occurring at night, rather than during the day. Such evenings were rare, however. The sister moons of Auris often overpowered whatever obstacles dared obscure their blinding glare.

Lucien turned back toward Erydon, breathing in what little he could see of the terrible beauty of The Highlands. Wisps covered much of the mountainscape, though he knew what lay beneath: jagged, ugly cliffs and ridges of the endless, treacherous mountains that made up their home. A fitting place for a "Nyghtmaere" like him to live, a fitting place for them all... A snowprowler's den nestled within the very drifts that people knew to avoid, yet ventured through all the same. And, when one entered a predator's hunting grounds, the predator always killed.

He felt no remorse for the men he just killed. No guilt shrouded his conscious as he phased into the Unbound, separating his body from the terrible chains of mundane existence. The soldiers knew what they were up against. They had thought that a monster awaited them in these mountains.

And Lucien had just proven them correct.

CHAPTER TWENTY

SECRETS UNTOLD

Sixteen months ago...

Asteros Silverglade paced before the three scholars as they slowly ate the "Rebound" food in their bowls from the endlessly replenishing stores of Erydon. Asteros had always found the stuff to be a bit bland, though years of eating it had numbed his sense of taste to the point that he didn't much care anymore. He could tell that the scholars, however, did care, for their noses crinkled ever so slightly before every bite, and it seemed as though they had to force each spoonful down their throats to avoid spitting it back up.

"Where are the others?" Shalheira asked, dragging a hand across Asteros's back in that beautifully gentle way of hers.

Lucien groaned at the show of affection from his spot against the far wall. Lucien's pale Elosian face even flushed.

Asteros turned slightly as she stepped behind him, a smirk creeping across his face as her scent once again smothered his senses.

Asteros had introduced Lucien to the scholars, thinking that it was the formal thing to do. However, Lucien seemed to take note of each of their surnames, as if remembering them was important somehow.

Asteros shook his head; Lucien was always up to something, but he truly had no idea why Lucien would care about the last names of a few random Utryans.

"They will be here," Asteros said, turning back to the scholars.

They ate silently, sitting at the stone tables of the main dining hall—which was a fairly grand title for a room that simply consisted of a long stone table and mostly blank stone walls. Crystals dotted the walls—mostly Scorcher—as were many of the Crystals in Erydon. They provided the most "natural" light, allowing the Shadow-Swifts to have a faint reminder of the fires that they used to live beside, prior to their induction into the clan.

Something about the Crystals was different, though. It had an effect on them, one that even spread to the scholars. The Crystals seemed to show that the Shadow-Swifts had no need for such a barbaric thing as traditional flames, for Crystals were as easy to obtain for them as wood was for the common man.

"With all due respect, you live off of this filth?" Soran asked through a bite of Rebound grain.

Asteros eyed the bald man, who had been by far the most impolite with them since his arrival. Asteros didn't mind, though. It was nice, in a sense, to have a different type of person among them, almost making it feel as though he was among regular people once again.

"You'll have to learn to live off of it too," Asteros said, nodding slightly and meeting the man's gaze.

Soran grunted, eyeing his next spoonful with extra disgust.

"You won't have to live off of it for too long if you keep up that attitude," Tsarra snorted.

Eithor chuckled softly, the older man seeming to wither away with each movement of his body.

Soran shot Tsarra a look, but said nothing.

Asteros didn't miss the subservience in his gaze. Tsarra clearly led the group—or at least she used to. And, if Asteros knew anything about leadership, it was that the one who held the power did not like to give it up. He eyed Lucien, who had apparently noticed as well. The two shared a brief look, then turned to the doorway at the sound of footsteps.

"You've been keeping secrets from us?" Malik marched into the chamber, his shoulders pulled back aggressively as he watched.

Shalheira laughed into Asteros's ear, trying to hide her amusement.

"You're surprised?" Asteros asked.

Malik stopped before him.

Asteros held the boy's dark gaze with no effort at all. Malik was a child, one who was barely even a third of Asteros's age. Asteros was not intimidated by him.

"Surprised? No," Malik spat. "Try annoyed."

Asteros pursed his lips. He turned his head slightly, noting Keries and Lyseria's arrival.

"Our secrets will soon be yours as well, Malik," Asteros said. "We only withheld the information from you earlier because we lacked the resources to pursue our new interests," Asteros said, tilting his head toward the scholars.

Malik grunted at this, stepping back a bit, though the frown remained pasted on his face.

"And let's not forget that Malik here can be a bit... impatient sometimes," Shalheira added, throwing in a devilish grin.

Asteros smiled, turning his head and nestling his nose in her hair.

Malik scowled, but said nothing, turning to the scholars. "And what about you three?" Malik asked. "What made you stupid enough to follow a Shadow-Swift all the way here?"

"Pursuing the secrets of the past is my life's work," Tsarra said. "My friends are the same, and, by following this wonderful woman here, we are raising the chances of discovering the knowledge that we have pursued for *years*," Tsarra said for the trio.

"Not to mention that your lady friend here said she'd string our guts out like laundry on a Blazeday if we didn't go with her," Soran muttered.

Asteros snorted a laugh, rubbing Shalheira's back.

Lyseria giggled as she approached alongside Keries.

Keries rubbed his beard, examining the scholars, who grew increasingly uncomfortable beneath the inscrutable stares of the six Shadow-Swifts. All save for Tsarra, who seemed to take on the attention as if it were some sort of elaborate challenge.

"When are we leaving?" Keries asked softly, leaning close to Asteros.

Lyseria moved with him, clinging to her father figure like a shadow.

Asteros moved down to pat the little girl on the head. He saw her so rarely. She was so young that she rarely ventured out into the curving passages of Erydon on her own. Asteros wasn't even certain if she knew her way around the fortress yet.

"As soon as they are finished eating," Asteros answered, nodding to the scholars.

Eithor looked up, lowering his spoon as he did so. "You're waiting on us?" Eithor asked.

"Who else would we be waiting for?" Shalheira asked.

Eithor turned to the others, who quickly lowered their bowls as well. "Well, come on then!" Eithor said, standing up from the stone bench. His body shook slightly.

Gods, how old is he? Asteros wondered. Though he supposed it was a bit unfair to think of the man in such a way, especially considering that Asteros himself was likely only a few years his junior.

Tsarra and Soran stood as well, staring expectantly at the Shadow-Swifts.

"Shall we, then?" Lucien said, standing up a little straighter.

Asteros looked to each of the Shadow-Swifts, and then the scholars. He nodded. "Follow us," Asteros said, leading the group of nine away from the long stone table.

Keries stumbled slightly as he began walking, then rubbed his head. The poor man was afflicted with something that none of them could understand. It was a disease not of the body, but of the mind, something that could not be fixed by the targeted power of umbrakinesis.

Keries described it as a sort of haze that simply settled over his vision and rarely departed. He claimed that it smothered his senses and fogged his thoughts, and, though Asteros believed him, he still found it strange that Keries was such a talented swordsman, despite his apparent affliction.

"How are we going to get them to Herqen?" Shalheira whispered, falling in step with Asteros.

"Combined, we possess more than enough power to carry the three of them with us through the Unbound," Lucien answered from behind, his pointed ears picking up their conversation.

Asteros nodded slightly, before tilting his head back to address the whole group. "Tonight, we will show you that which will change the course of history," Asteros announced, quickening his pace. "We have found something that was once believed to have been lost: a record of the time before the Vanishing, coming directly from one of the Ancient Stonemasters themselves."

"And what has the record told you?" Tsarra asked, pushing her way toward the front of the group.

"Something worth pursuing," Asteros answered, turning down another of the narrow, curving passages. The slight incline awakened his muscles, preparing him for the flight ahead.

"If what you found is so important, then why wait until the scholars were here to continue?" Malik asked.

Asteros sighed. They needed the scholars, but keeping said scholars from knowing how vital they were would ensure that Asteros remained in control.

"This discovery puts us centuries ahead of any who have

researched the Ancient Times," Asteros said. "For once, my boy, time is a luxury that we have."

"For now, at least," Soran muttered.

"What do you mean?" Lucien growled.

Soran cowered slightly beneath Lucien's venomous tone. He stumbled over his words a bit, trying to find a proper explanation for his outburst. And, though it took him a few tries, he answered nonetheless: "Freyfall is considering a full-scale assault on The Highlands," Soran said, fumbling with his words a bit.

Lucien eyed Asteros, the pair sharing a look of grave concern.

"When did you hear this?" Shalheira asked, turning slightly to Soran.

"I overheard some of the King's advisors discussing the possibility of such an attack a few days prior to our departure."

They quieted, falling into step beside him and continuing through the doorway to the grand atrium. This was unwelcome news, yet one quick glance at Lucien confirmed what needed to be done about it.

Lucien would continue watching over Herqen, eliminating any who set foot on it. It was a cruel plan, but it was perhaps the only way to ensure that the cavern remained hidden.

Asteros couldn't help but notice the scholars marveling at the inscriptions once again. Though the carvings held no important information, they were likely impressive to the scholars' academic eyes nonetheless.

Thoughts swirled in his head like rain clouds before a Storm Gale. If the Freyfallions were truly planning an extended expedition into The Highlands, the Shadow-Swifts would have to be ready for anything. Freyfall's advances in Summoning and technology were not things to be ignored.

Curses, Asteros thought. *Not even a year after we begin rising again, a new foe threatens to send us crashing down once more.* But no. That would not happen. If Asteros discovered the truth behind the Vanishing, he would have all that he needed. Control would not even be a question anymore. The Shadow-Swifts would rule, Asteros's new, *revised* plan had ensured that much.

The others assumed he had simply whittled the last six months away, waiting for Shalheira to return so that they could continue their quest. But that could not be further from the truth. Asteros had been reading, and observing. Auris balanced on the edge of a blade; all it would take was a *slight* push for the whole continent to come crashing down upon itself.

And the Shadow-Swifts were going to be that push.

The group slowed to a stop before the small depression of Herqen's slopes. Dropping from the sky like divebrisks into the sea, they lowered themselves to the rocky surface below.

Eithor and Soran teetered as Asteros, Lucien, Shalheira, and Keries released their hands, freeing them from the binding curse of Transcendence. Tsarra stood firmly, doing her best to look unimpressed at the whole show of being literally *flown* across the stellar night sky.

Stars littered the darkness above, looking like white sand spread across dark stone. The aurora glowed a strange purple-blue tonight. It was beautiful, perhaps one of the most beautiful nights Asteros had ever seen. He felt as if he could almost see the City in the Stars that Keries always spoke of. Asteros sometimes found himself unsure what to believe. He had once considered himself to be a devoted Navesian, considering that he was raised in Arvendon. Yet now... Now he wasn't sure what to think.

Shalheira stood near him, a slight breeze pushing her scent through his nostrils and into his heart. Something about the way his stomach fluttered whenever she was near made him believe again. It made him believe in all the strange things that Keries said... Something like how love could be nothing less than a gift from divinity; at least, that was how Asteros now saw it.

Haldir had told them that love only distracted one from their true goals, and perhaps he was right, though at this point Asteros didn't much care. Haldir had been a bitter man, and, though Asteros had valued his leadership, he couldn't say he missed him. Haldir had only trained Asteros for a few short decades, whereas Lucien had spent the better part of a century under his influence.

Perhaps that was where the Elosian's bloodlust came from... Asteros recalled Haldir saying several times that one of the Shadow-Swifts needed to be a brutal, ruthless killer so that the others could focus on the more delicate matters of maintaining order while the "knife" of the organization ensured that peace held strong.

Lucien rarely spoke of those days. In fact, he practically never did. He only said that Haldir made him into what he was now, and by now Asteros had realized that was the only answer he would ever get when he asked about the man's past.

Tsarra nudged Asteros, as if in boredom.

He glared at her, and she rolled her eyes. *Gods, that woman truly is insufferable,* he thought. Asteros pushed past her, ignoring whatever game she was trying to play. She knew that the scholars were more important to the plan than the others did—that much he was certain of. The indenture lay ahead just as they had left it, undisturbed by the near-endless Frostfalls of The Highlands.

"Is this it?" Eithor asked, hesitantly following Asteros.

"Quiet," Lucien commanded, marching past the man.

The group neared the strange cleft that disguised the Rune-Door up ahead.

Asteros took the lead, passing through the cleft first. The others followed, only noticing its existence once they were practically near enough to touch the surface of the mountain.

"Calida's Claws," Soran whispered as he entered the cave. The warm air of the shelter was a welcome change from the bitter cold of the night winds.

Asteros turned to the scholars, who were squinting in the darkness, trying to make out what was before them.

Lucien, Shalheira, and Asteros reached into their armor and produced one Scorcher Crystal each. The scholars did not possess the enhanced night vision of a Shadow-Swift; they would need the Crystals to see.

Eithor took the Crystal from Lucien's hand, the Shadow-Swift baring his teeth just to scare the poor old soul as he did so.

Soran absently took hold of Shalheira's Crystal, still too entranced by the Runes before them to be intimidated by the woman.

Asteros, Shalheira, and Lucien already knew what lay within the safehouse, of course.

"Thank you," Tsarra said, taking Asteros's Crystal as he offered it to her. Her red-brown eyes burned with an intensity that rivaled that of the Crystal she held.

"Is this what I think it is?" Soran breathed. "A Fourth Century Rune-Door? Created with the purpose of keeping out all but those who created it?"

The man had stared at the thing for hardly even twenty seconds and had deduced that much already? Asteros thought.

Lucien's mouth hung open, and he shot Asteros a glance. Asteros returned it, shrugging slightly. Shalheira had said that these were the best Rune-Readers in all of Auris, it seemed that she was right.

"How do you know this?" Lucien asked.

"And how long have you known about this?" Malik bristled, turning to Asteros.

Asteros ignored him, instead allowing Soran to answer Lucien's question.

"The carvings resemble the structures of the late Stonemasters and Rune-Writers, not those of early times," Soran said, holding up the Crystal and squinting at the cavern's walls.

Asteros found himself marveling at them once again as well. The chamber was no larger than thirty feet across, yet every inch of the wall was covered with ancient inscriptions. A massive pair of stone doors that resembled those of Erydon stood at the heart of it all, the intricate carvings wrapping themselves all throughout and around them.

"Ah, yes," Eithor said, stepping closer to the wall. "I can see what you mean, Soran. It is indeed intended to be a safehouse of some sort." Eithor pointed to one of the swirls that looked almost like a wave curling around a mountain of sand. "Right here: the end of the identification access curse."

"Or lack thereof, it seems," Soran added. Asteros understood a little of what they said, for he too was well versed in the ancient tongue.

"Ah, but the Runes appear to have been placed with a grip on the inner cavern that is tighter than most," Eithor said, tracing a line on another part of the wall. Circles and swirls surrounded it.

"This level of protection is simply unnecessary," Soran said. "One can only infer that they were…"

"Afraid," Tsarra said from her spot beside Asteros. She strode forward, following the line with her eyes across the wall. "They were afraid of something… something out here in The Highlands."

"For something to scare a Stonemaster this powerful…" Eithor started, the old man suddenly seeming shockingly alert. "Could it have been directly related to the Vanishing?"

Asteros watched the man carefully, his slight limp gone. *An act, then, Asteros* thought. *Why would he pretend to be weaker than he is? He already knows that we would be able to defeat even the strongest of men.* Perhaps the scholars were more dangerous than they seemed, for they appeared to be playing some sort of game that even Asteros didn't understand.

"Even a Lock like this one is not insurmountable," Soran said. His accent seemed to have faded slightly. "But we would need something strong enough to puncture the Runes."

"And something strong enough to pierce the Ward," Eithor added. "Something like—"

"Shadow-Sand," Tsarra said. "Shadow-Sand should be strong enough. All we would have to do is find the right pressure points."

The scholars set to work immediately, running their hands along the grooved lines of the Rune-Lock.

Asteros watched in awe, he couldn't help himself. These scholars were far wiser than he had ever imagined. In mere minutes they had already determined a way to break through the door, whereas Asteros needed Haldir's Key to get inside.

"This is a test, isn't it?" Soran asked, stopping for a moment. "You always knew how to open this door, yet you simply want to see if we can figure it out, right?"

"We have a way inside, but it is... unconventional," Asteros said. "It would be in your best interest to continue with your preferred method, for you have my attention."

Soran turned to the other scholars, who stepped away from the wall. Soran exchanged a glance with Tsarra—who nodded.

"I suspect that you have a few weapons made from Shadow-Sand, correct?" Tsarra asked Asteros, stepping forward.

All but Lyseria produced their weapons, for she had yet to complete the initiation.

"How many do you need?" Asteros asked, producing his sword from his sheath.

"Just this should suffice—for me, at least," Tsarra said, taking the weapon and turning it a bit, weighing it in her hands. Asteros noted the way she held the sword: Her grip was comfortable, almost familiar. She was no stranger to weapons.

"Your dagger, if I may, sir." Eithor bowed before Lucien, who sneered, but surrendered his dagger to the older man.

Soran silently claimed Keries's sword, and the trio quietly approached the center of the door.

They muttered to themselves, resuming their tracing of different swirls with their fingers. The lines turned jagged in places, running into strange, foreign shapes and unusual inscriptions of Ancient Runes.

"Found one," Tsarra announced, pausing at the far corner of the cave and holding the point of her sword up against a small circular indention in the wall. There were hundreds of them across the cavern, yet apparently she found something different about this one.

"Me too," Soran called, readying his sword and placing it near a similar-looking hole.

"Let me see..." Eithor trailed off, shakily holding the dagger in his right hand as he scanned the wall, holding the Crystal with his left. "Ah, here we are!" he exclaimed. He set his Crystal down, as did Tsarra and Soran.

Eithor placed the tip of his dagger in the small cleft formed by one of the many jagged lines that wove across the wall, angling it so that the blade covered part of the minute pathway in the stone. Soran performed a similar motion, positioning the point of the blade in the small circle, and stepping back, gaining firmer footing. Tsarra matched his stance, doing the same with her blade.

"On the count of three," Tsarra said, preparing herself.

Lyseria grabbed Keries's hand. Lucien watched nonchalantly, Shalheira's face shimmered with fascination, and Malik somehow still managed to look annoyed at the fact that he hadn't been told about this cavern sooner.

"Three... Two... *One!*" Tsarra shouted, slamming her weight into her sword.

Soran did the same, and Eithor dug his dagger into the slit, almost seeming to carve out a bit of the stone.

Metal grinded against stone. And then: silence.

A few seconds later, a loud clicking noise sounded through the small cavern, the curved walls cast in an enigmatic light from the Scorcher Crystals that lay scattered on the ground. Asteros recognized the clicking. *It's the same sound that Erydon's door makes when it opens.* He turned to Lucien, whose sharp eyes were wider than Asteros had ever seen before.

"It's... opening," Shalheira whispered. This time, stone ran against stone, and the inner mechanisms of the door began shifting.

Asteros could practically see the massive black arms of rock that were undoubtedly twisting and turning on the other side of the door.

The scholars handed back the weapons to the Shadow-Swifts, who sheathed them as they watched the grand door open with awe.

The Runes illuminated, a pale white light igniting within the rocks. The door slowly creaked open, revealing a pool of darkness within.

"How did you do that?" Asteros managed to ask, shaking off his amazement.

"We located the three Primary Stone-Readers and tripped all three of them at once," Tsarra said. "Easy trick if you know how to find them, yet apparently something that the Ancients never thought to do."

Tsarra was the first to step forward, cautiously treading on the first few feet of the interior of the cavern. Tsarra's foot hit a stone, causing a clicking sound to ring through the chamber. She gasped, leaping back with a quickness that rivaled that of a Dexteris.

A gentle fire ignited in the hanging torches, previously hidden by the darkness. A collective sigh of relief ran through the group. It seemed that properly opening the Lock had triggered the torch.

Asteros still found himself trembling with anticipation as they passed through the magnificent door. It swung to a close behind them after a few moments, effectively sealing them inside the comfortable warmth of the cave.

"What is this place?" Malik breathed, scanning the inscribed walls around them. The main entryway paled in comparison to Erydon's, with only two passageways leading out from a small circular room. The right led to the living quarters of the Stonemaster and Rune-Writers who had lived here, whereas the left led to the inscription chamber.

"It's... like Erydon," Lyseria whispered, clinging to Keries even still.

"No," Soran said. "Erydon was a fortress, meant to be defensible and capable of granting its residents a victorious outcome, should they be attacked."

"This is a bunker," Tsarra finished for him. "Just look at the Runes along these walls. They are all continuations of the protective wards around Herqen."

"Wards that we just bypassed," Eithor added, offering a grin full of brittle teeth.

"Look here!" Tsarra pointed, her eyes fixed on a large circular epicenter that sat in the middle of the curved wall before them.

Asteros squinted against the firelight, trying to read what she had pointed out.

"This is a sealing curse," Tsarra said, paling.

Asteros frowned, he had missed that on his earlier journeys to this cavern.

"Intended to lock the cavern permanently, even if those who tried to enter possessed the correct keys... yet it was never activated," Eithor continued. The trio of scholars turned to Asteros.

"Where have you brought us?" Soran asked, leaning in. "I've read about fortresses like yours. This is not one of them. Stonemasters are among the strongest of the Ancient Sects, what in the name of Niventia could've possibly led to one creating such a place as this?"

"Follow me," Asteros said quietly, starting down the left passage.

The other eight followed without a word, obeying his command. Even Malik didn't dare voice another complaint. The fires ignited as they passed, triggering automatically. They passed through another door frame, entering the massive domed chamber that held the records that Asteros had shown to Lucien and Shalheira so many months ago. A collective gasp whispered through the group as a ring of torches ignited on the outside of the room.

"Niventia's Light..." Keries breathed, staring in awe at the gloriously complex inscriptions that blanketed the walls. "This rivals even Erydon's story wall."

Tsarra and the others started scanning the walls. She quickly skimmed one of the Stonemaster's entries.

"The Great War…" Tsarra whispered, already beside a section of the wall, dragging her fingers along one of the inscriptions in the ancient tongue. "That was what they called the war leading up to the Vanishing before it happened, right?"

"From what I can gather, yes," Asteros answered, folding his hands behind his back.

"Yet something's missing…" Tsarra finally said after a few moments. "It's almost as if the Stonemaster purposefully omitted certain—key—details from his record."

"That he did," Asteros confirmed. "I looked a bit in his personal chambers, and found that he was greatly concerned that this cave would be found by people in the future who wished to follow in his perpetrator's footsteps."

"People like us," Keries said. He paused, stopping in the center of the room. The older man appeared deep in thought, and Asteros knew what he was going to say before his mouth even opened. "We should not be here."

"Keries, what are you going on about?" Lucien asked. "You want to know what's in here so badly and, now that you know the truth, you want to leave? This knowledge is *powerful*… Far too powerful to leave behind."

"Lucien," Keries said, closing his eyes, his voice growing distant. "This chamber only holds knowledge that will tear this order apart. It was locked away for a reason, even the Stonemaster who built it says so, Asteros alluded to it as well."

"I did not say that this was locked away for a *good* reason, though," Asteros corrected. "The Stonemaster was likely only trying to preserve his own Sect from certain destruction by hiding such information—something that he failed to do regardless."

"So then why did you bring us here?" Keries challenged, raising his head. "So that we could revive the Ancient Sects? So that we could restore Auris to the ways of old? So that we could reimburse our libraries with knowledge of powers long forgotten? You only want this knowledge so that you can transform our gentle, watchful grip on Auris into something far more sinister."

"Hey!" Shalheira shouted. She turned to Asteros. "Are you really going to let him talk to you like that?"

Asteros remained silent, flicking his eyes toward the scholars.

"You know nothing of what you speak," Shalheira said. Her beautiful, sand-colored Sucharan skin shimmered in the firelight.

"Oh?" Keries tilted his head. Lyseria backed away from him slightly.

"Asteros brought Lucien and me here months ago. He told me that his goal was to use this knowledge to restore order to Auris, and save the people of this continent from themselves," Shalheira hissed. "Our cities are on the brink of collapse. Population overflow is an issue that we currently have no way to solve... And here we are, perhaps able to use the secrets of the past to guide our race into the future."

Keries recoiled, seeming to fade back into the gentle man who they all knew so well.

"Our aspirations were never akin to what you assume them to be, right, Asteros?" Shalheira asked. "Asteros?"

Lucien smiled sharply in the shadows of the circular chamber, remaining silent. His Elosian features were accented by the raging fires around him, making his smirk all the more unsettling.

"I have spent the last several months thinking over what was *originally* our plan," Asteros said, cocking his head slightly.

The scholars turned to him, suddenly interested in his words.

"Yet I realized something: We were underestimating ourselves," Asteros said. "I have reason to believe that we will learn all that there is to know about the Vanishing soon enough," Asteros continued. "But how could we use that? We could revive the ways of old, perhaps use them to take control... build a slightly better world... but why stop there? Think about it: The Vanishing removed the Ancient Sects, right? Which means that the energies of the Ancient Sects are no longer on Auris. Tempests are made up of Summoning energy, so why wouldn't the same thing be possible with them?"

"What are you talking about?" Shalheira asked.

"The Tempests were brought by the Vanishing, so couldn't *another* Vanishing take them away?" Asteros began. "If we learn enough about the Vanishing... what caused it, where it was done, how it began... we could *recreate* it." Asteros paused. "We could create *another* Vanishing, one that wipes out the Tempests themselves." Asteros trailed off. "We could conquer Auris so easily—without spilling a drop of blood. The Summoners of Auris would no longer have their powers, rendering them Stormless."

"No..." Shalheira whispered. "You said—"

"I said that we were going to change the world," Asteros snapped. "We are."

"Asteros," Shalheira hissed, grabbing him by the collar of his cloaked armor. "You told me that we were going to save the world, not tear it all down."

"Shalheira, trust me," he said softly. "We are not destroying Auris. We are uniting it."

"How?" Keries asked, his placidity returning like sunbirds in the summer.

"By removing the Tempests, we would be the only Summoners that still had access to their powers," Asteros said. "Our rule would be unchallenged."

"And unchallenged rule is simply *tyranny*," Shalheira growled.

"Exactly." Asteros nodded. "So, we don't rule; we briefly take control of the continent and find the greatest leaders among the people," Asteros said. "We gather Auris's greatest minds and put them in charge, thus uniting the continent and preventing corruption, and then we step down."

"And what about when they die?" Shalheira challenged. "How would succession work?"

"We would choose new leaders, and, when they pass, we would choose new ones," Asteros said.

"And when we die?" Lucien asked.

"Our children would carry on our legacy," Asteros said. "Just—" Asteros paused, taking a deep breath. "Perhaps it would be better if I showed you." Asteros raised his hands, drawing upon the power within his Crystals.

"What is he doing?" Lyseria whispered, the young girl once again clinging to Keries.

Asteros guided his hands through the well-practiced motions that he had learned over the last six months—an old technique, created by the Ancient Shadow-Swifts, then forgotten due to the fact that many found it to be useless. But to Asteros... it was everything.

Calling upon the power stowed within the Crystals in his armor, Asteros prepared his plan. With one movement of his hand, he summoned a swirling ball of darkness between his palms. It hissed and whirled within his grasp, responding to his movements as he shaped it into the patterns that he had burned into his mind weeks before.

In an instant, darkness exploded into the room, expanding and reshaping itself. The group watched in awe, the terrible power swirling in a violent Tempest of darkness and shadow. Slowly, the tendrils of umbrakinesis settled into place, forming letters and drawings that he had created himself, answering his summons.

"What are these?" Eithor asked, drifting forward. He stared at the three-dimensional collection of letters, numbers, maps, and images. Umbrakinetic Inscribing was a power that had not been used for centuries.

"They're... plans," Tsarra realized, reading them slowly. Perhaps three or four thousand words filled the room now, each one made of translucent rings of darkness.

"Plans for what?" Shalheira asked, marveling at the feat as well.

"Unity," Tsarra breathed. "He wasn't lying. His plan is detailed... foolproof, even."

"There's just one problem," Lucien interrupted. "We still don't have any clue where the other caverns are."

Asteros released his grip on the room, allowing the floating inscriptions to dissipate.

"Other caverns?" Soran asked, turning back to the inscriptions.

"Yes, there were said to be multiple other caves like this one, and we are hoping that they might yield the information that this Stonemaster failed to provide," Shalheira answered.

"Where did you read such things?" Eithor asked.

Asteros thought for a moment, then pointed them toward a section of the wall. The ancient tongue grew a bit muddled here, as it only vaguely hinted at the fact that there were other caverns, he had simply assumed that The Stonemaster meant "other caverns like this one," though he was not sure.

"Unfortunately, we have no idea as to where the other chambers are. All we know is simply that they exist, which does not exactly help us," Lucien rumbled.

"No," Tsarra said, tracing one of the square-like markings. "It tells us far more than that," she continued, moving her finger to what appeared to be the tail line of the word "location."

"What are you getting at?" Asteros asked, moving closer. "It says that there are others, in different locations, what's so important about that?"

"Look," Tsarra said, glancing back at him. "The tail of the letter points to this part of the wall, which is a stylistic line meant to separate paragraphs, but, if you follow the marking, it leads to this section here."

Asteros followed her finger, realizing that what he had assumed to be nothing more than a simple divider was, in fact, the key part of the puzzle that he had been missing.

"How did you—" Lucien started.

"The word 'location' can be drawn with hints as to *where* the subject is," Tsarra explained. "Oftentimes, especially in the Fourth Century, Stonemasters would disguise such clues in the form of dividers, or other mechanical functionalities."

"So what does it tell us?" Shalheira asked.

"Well…" Tsarra followed the line, and then traced it to yet another paragraph of words. "It appears that this section is explaining the tactical advantages of stationing one's battlements on the northeastern side of Bareholde. Which, if my memory serves me correctly, is only a few miles northwest of here, correct?" Tsarra glanced back. Asteros nodded.

"But it doesn't say anything about the actual cavern, it only mentions the proposed battlements, which are then said to never have been built," Lucien challenged, reading the lines as he said the words.

"Right, but the fact that the tail of the word from the cavern section points to this implies that another chamber was built there, likely in place of the failed battlements," Tsarra explained.

"If that's the case, then why not just tell us directly?" Malik asked, clearly annoyed that he was incapable of fluently reading the wall at which he stared.

"If the Ancients had been clear in their wording, my field of study would not exist," Tsarra said, smiling softly. "Although they did not generate such confusion without purpose, I assure you. This Stone-master likely did so simply because he wanted to make certain that only another like him would be able to discern the location of the next cavern."

Silence settled over the group, yet it was a silence of victory, a silence that told that there was nothing left to be said. A silence that meant their work here was done. A silence that meant that there was only one thing to do now: go to Bareholde, and begin the first part of Asteros's plan.

Asteros's plan was far more than just a simple outline. It detailed exactly what each of their steps was to be. It started with the young prince in Arvendon, then the lost princess of Celes, and it ended with the erratic princess of Suchara. They were the future of Auris, and Asteros was well aware of that fact. He had spent the last several months carefully researching each of them, as well as several others. He needed to know *exactly* who he was dealing with, and how he was going to get them to agree to an alliance without directly threatening them.

It was a genius plan. Yet it was also incomplete. Not only did he still not possess the necessary knowledge—nor the techniques—to cleanse Auris of the Tempests, he had no idea what would happen to his own Sect when he tried to keep the state of the moons as they were. There were many variables that were yet to even be determined, although Asteros had no doubts that the next cavern would provide slightly more information, if nothing else. Yet there was no way he could know that for sure. All they could do was go to Bareholde, and find out for themselves.

CHAPTER TWENTY-ONE

INTERCEPTION

Thunder rumbled through the mountains. Castien kept his eyes low, focusing on his breathing as he trudged through the knee-deep snow of The Highlands. Snow fell violently around him, so dense that the sun's light could barely be seen beneath the brunt of the frozen Storm Gale.

Surge led them through the Tempest, claiming that there was no time to lose.

Castien couldn't bother caring at this point. So what if he got killed in the Tempest? It wasn't like anyone actually cared about his safety anyway.

The mountains stretched to the sky in every direction, and the small valley in which the group walked was steadily inclining. Bitter wind snapped at Castien's face despite the protective mask he now wore. Snow pelted his exposed eyes with an undeserved ferocity, and the cold air itself seemed to be relentlessly piercing his armor.

A sudden break in the wind offered some much-needed relief. Castien looked up, seeing a strange bend in the air right in front of him. He looked to the side.

Elric walked to his right with a hand raised. Castien looked to the bend, then back to the Cloudwalker. Elric smiled from behind his thick coat, continuing to use his powers as a windbreak for Castien. Castien shook his head, looking down.

Even the Tempests could be foiled by a Summoner's power. Was there anything Summoners could not do? Even now, Castien was certain that Elric was annoyed at the prospect of actually having to *walk* somewhere, rather than flying.

Movement to his left caught his eye. Instinctually, he glanced in that direction, meeting Ilyana's gaze. He looked away quickly. Ilyana said nothing, but instead moved a little closer to Castien so that she too could be protected by Elric's windbreak.

More thunder rumbled above, lightning illuminating the dark afternoon sky. Somewhere in the distance, a bright light flashed, leaving an imprint in Castien's vision for several seconds afterward.

The lightning struck again somewhere through the howling wind, then retreated to the electrified sky in a fraction of a second as if it had never even left to begin with.

"It shouldn't be too much farther," Surge yelled from the front of the group.

Wind, thankfully, carried the sound back to Castien's ears, but he was only half listening. Why should he care? Once they did find Velarus, it wasn't like he would actually be able to do anything, right?

"We're getting close, Castien," Elric said. "Soon we'll be on our way back to Arvendon."

Castien shivered, the frozen air biting through the shield and chilling his skin.

"We'll get you home safely," Ilyana added.

Castien rubbed his arms, the fatigue in his legs rivaled only by the frigid sense of cold within them. *Since when did they start treating me like this?* Castien thought. It was almost like they were pretending to care for him.

"Once we confront Velarus, once and for all, this will all be over,"

Elric continued. "You'll be celebrated upon your return, and who knows? Maybe you'll even receive a promotion or two."

"I'm leaving the Stormless Corps," Castien said. He blinked a few times, his mind slowly reeling itself back in. The words echoed in his mind. *Leaving...* He hadn't meant to say that. Yet, even now, Castien knew that he had spoken true. There was no reason for him to stay—not anymore.

"Oh," Elric said, his voice sounding quiet against the howling wind. There was more thunder up above.

"Castien, you can't leave the Corps," Ilyana said. "Have you forgotten that shot at Elric? That was *incredible,* if I didn't know any better, I—"

"I haven't forgotten about that," Castien said, cutting her off. "How could I forget about when I shot at my Commander?" Castien felt cold, but not from the frigid air. His mind was distant once again, and the pain he felt was all but inconsequential.

"But—" Ilyana started.

"Ilyana, leave the boy alone," Elric interrupted, strengthening the windbreak slightly.

Despite himself, Castien rubbed his arms gratefully at the relief from the Tempest's winds.

"Please, just go walk with the rest of the group, if you wouldn't mind," Elric said.

Ilyana turned to Elric, shooting him a look. Elric simply nodded, and Ilyana left.

Castien glanced up as the Dexteris sped up slightly and found a new spot alongside Saevi just behind the three leaders of the group.

The Storm Gale raged around Castien, the winds ripping at the break nearly as unsettling as the frequent bolts of lightning that rained down from above in the distance.

"I'm sorry," Elric said after a moment.

Castien turned to him, trying to find his way back into his own mind.

"About the whole situation in the cave." Elric turned his soft emerald eyes to Castien. He had taken his goggles off, sacrificing a bit of comfort in the storm... why?

"It wasn't your fault," Castien said quietly, his voice weak against the strong winds. More thunder sounded up above.

"No, but I didn't exactly do anything to help," Elric said, grunting as he twisted his raised hand slightly.

Castien found himself watching Elric's fingers, wondering what it felt like to have such power, such *control* coursing through his veins.

"It doesn't matter anyway," Castien said, his gaze shifting back to his feet. "Even if we would've let that Sorcerer live, he probably would've been killed by his own Sect for telling us what he did." Castien felt his face shift into a cold frown beneath his leather mask, though he wasn't sure why.

"That's... not what I'm sorry for," Elric said. "I do wish that we would've let that man live, but that's not what I'm talking about."

"Then what are you talking about?" Castien turned to meet Elric's emerald eyes once again.

Elric stared back. "It used to happen to me too," Elric said, turning his head forward once again. "When we were fighting, and you got that look in your eyes... and when you fell to the ground." Elric looked back to Castien. "It was getting hard to breathe, wasn't it? And everything was just a little too loud for your comfort, right?"

"Yes—" Castien started, fumbling with his words. "Yeah," Castien said after a moment, threading his thoughts through his diluted mind. "That was exactly what it was like. Doesn't everyone have to deal with that?"

"Castien, if everyone had to deal with that, then most of society wouldn't even be able to function," Elric said. "The fact that you are afflicted with the same condition I was, coupled with the fact that you are on *this* expedition, is nothing short of incredible," Elric said, laughing a little. "I mean, by Niventia's Light, Castien, it took me a few years of private sessions with a Whisperer before I could even handle going out to the battlefield on my own," Elric said.

Castien found himself smiling slightly. "Really?" Castien looked back to Elric.

Elric nodded.

Castien felt his heartbeat increasing, but not like it had in the cave. This was a sort of *excited* feeling. "I had always just thought that I was... I don't know. Maybe just that I wasn't as good at dealing with nervousness as everyone else," Castien said.

"Castien, look at me," Elric said firmly, a sudden seriousness overtaking his voice.

Castien did so, feeling himself lock into Elric's gaze.

"Castien, you are not weaker than everybody else. You are much, *much* stronger," Elric said. It wasn't reassurance. No, it was almost like Elric was speaking purely in facts. There was a certain conviction to his voice, and Castien almost believed him. "If what I saw in the cave has happened before, then I suspect that you have the same disorder that I did when I was younger... I still have it, I've just been trained to keep it under control."

"What?" Castien tilted his head. *Disorder?* "What are you talking about?"

"Your mind is overly sensitive to threats, through no fault of your own," Elric said. "For whatever reason, your mind looks at any common thing as a possible threat, and triggers a part of your brain that is meant to protect you in a case of true danger. Yet, for you, that part of your mind is triggered accidentally, and at random times."

"Oh," Castien said, his gaze falling again. He started to process the information, letting his mind wander once again.

"Does it happen often during arguments?" Elric asked.

Castien turned back to him. He thought for a moment. "I suppose, yeah," Castien said.

Elric nodded. He looked at Castien with a mix of something like curiosity and pity, but masked the look quickly.

Castien frowned, his thoughts involuntarily drifting back to... to... *yelling. Angry voices in the next room... Night after night of screaming matches while he hid in his room...*

"You'll get through this, Castien," Elric said. "I went through a new type of treatment for the condition—the treatment that involved private time with a Whisperer, as I said earlier—and I'm willing to bet that I could set you up with the same thing, once we get back to Arvendon, if you'd like."

"Oh," Castien took a deep breath. *What do I have to lose?* "Sure," Castien said, trying to sound almost casual about it. "I guess it's worth a try."

"Good," Elric said, nodding to himself. "In the meantime, I suppose it wouldn't do any harm to start trying to figure out what it is that's causing your anxiety. I still remember a lot of what the Whisperer asked me when—"

A sudden crash of thunder interrupted Elric, the deafening sound startling the group.

Someone shouted up ahead.

Castien squinted through the falling snow, trying to make out what was going on. The valley walls closed in up ahead as the incline continued. It seemed that the mountain was getting steeper. Someone shouted again, and more lightning flashed—but not from the sky.

Elric's covered face became a mask of determination. He scanned the area behind Castien, looking to the steeper, rockier part of the incline around them.

Castien turned around, then back to the rest of the group.

Fire bloomed in the frozen winds, followed by the sound of shattering ice.

More shouting.

"Up there," Elric said, pointing behind Castien.

Castien spun, laying eyes on a large boulder a few dozen yards up the slope.

"Get behind that rock, and stay there," Elric commanded. He released the wind break, prompting a sudden onslaught of violent snow.

More color exploded up above, followed by a river of red in the air.

Blood Sorcerer... Castien thought, his muscles tensing. The pit in his stomach opened, and his breathing quickened. His eyes darted rapidly.

"Wait," Castien gasped, his limbs shaking. "Elric, wait, I—"

Elric gripped him by the shoulders. "Castien, you have to trust me," Elric said. "Get behind that rock. Once this is over, I'll come get you, but, until then, you must stay safe." Elric tightened his grip, giving Castien a slight squeeze.

Castien met those firm emerald eyes, and found himself nodding. His breathing still came in shallow waves, and his heart thundered even more loudly than the storm beyond, but Castien still nodded. This man knew what was happening to him. This man knew what it *felt* like. And so Castien trusted him.

Elric released Castien, and lifted into the air with a wave of his hand. The Cloudwalker dashed off into the snow, charging into the battle without hesitation.

Castien watched the Commander in awe, though he quickly pulled himself from his thoughts. Castien turned around, laying eyes on the boulder once again. He bolted through the knee-deep snow. He became painfully aware of the freezing-cold snow that had somehow slipped into his insulated boots, and he grimaced. But Castien pushed onward, his aching muscles screaming at him to stop. There was no time. His breathing increased again, his heart racing. *There is no time for this.*

Castien reached the sharp incline, falling to all fours and grabbing onto the jagged rocks that rose from the peak before him. He pulled himself up with gloved hands, hearing another distant crash as lightning exploded beyond. His mind didn't even stop. It didn't matter. Nothing mattered. All he was able to pick out from his jumbled thoughts was that Elric wanted to protect him—and that Elric had commanded him to hide behind this rock.

Castien pulled himself up one final time, his feet slipping against the slick stone. He stumbled, but made it to the small ridge anyway. Castien panted, breathing heavily and dropping into a crawl. He rounded the large stone, and curled up against it as another explosion of fire illuminated the near-dark mountainscape.

He heard more shouting and more explosions. More thunder... Castien's eyes snapped shut, and he tried to attune his breathing to his heartbeat, as he often did.

In... thump, thump, thump, thump, thump... out. Thump, thump, thump, thump, thump, thump... hold... thump, thump, thump... in...

Another crash, this one sounding closer. Castien's eyes shut even tighter, and he found himself uttering a prayer to Niventia. It wouldn't matter. Nothing mattered anymore.

Someone shouted—a voice he recognized. Castien's eyes snapped open. Elric.

Another voice called out—a female voice. Thunder followed.

A strange sound that Castien could only describe as pure *energy* tore through the air, followed by a faint glow of red behind him.

Castien sat up, peeking out from behind the boulder. Around fifty yards away, through the dense snow, Castien saw movement. His gaze cleared, suddenly and without warning. He was able to make out one side of the fight—his own. Opposite that side, higher up on the mountain, was a group that Castien didn't recognize.

Red light shot from one of the strangers—a Blood Sorcerer.

Have you forgotten about that shot at Elric? It was incredible! Ilyana's words echoed through his mind. Castien's bow felt heavy on his back, almost as if it were... calling to him.

Castien, you are not weaker than everybody else. You are much, much stronger... Elric's words sounded through his mind as well, bringing clarity. Castien knew what he needed to do. There was no use in hiding any longer. There was no reason to stay behind this rock while his friends were in danger. Summoner or not... a few well-placed arrows couldn't hurt.

Castien jumped into action, sliding down the incline he had just climbed as he reached for his bow. The wood was warm in his gloved hands, despite the bitter cold.

But he was too far. Shooting in a snowfall this thick would be next to impossible, unless... unless he was down there too.

More lightning exploded through the air, crashing against one of the assailants.

He reached the bottom of the incline and broke into a sprint. He charged into the falling snow, ignoring the freezing pain in every part of his body.

Saevi came into view first, launching bolts of flame from a distance as the group fought ahead. Another blast of fire left her fingers, and she twisted her arms as the next one formed.

Castien charged past her.

Arthion stood somewhere to the side and yelled something at Castien.

Saevi called out as well, but Castien ignored both of them.

He passed Luka next, who was sliding across the thick snow, hands extended as he iced the ground beneath himself. Luka banked off a large stone in the valley and slid back toward the fight, barely sparing Castien a glance. The Cryostalker leapt into the air, leaving a pillar of ice behind him as he raised his sword, letting out a battle cry.

Castien passed Surge, who reached out with one hand, lightning arcing from his fingers toward the attackers. He charged as well, his other hand bearing the oversized greatsword which now sizzled with electricity. He shouted something at Castien, but Castien didn't hear.

Castien could now plainly see the assailants.

Ilyana dashed through the jagged ridges, butterfly-swords extended. Then she froze, her muscles locking as a red mist came over her. She fell to the ground, tumbling down the icy slopes.

Elric dashed through the air, a pair of knives following him, guided by phantom hands. A bolt of red light crashed into him.

Castien cried out as Elric fell into the snow, rolling to a stop.

Castien nocked an arrow, searching for that place within his mind once again. He pulled at his thoughts, tugging away at the fear and anxiety until he could find... *There.* His eyes snapped open, his instincts calculating the wind, snow, and chaos of the battle in seconds. He could see it in his mind's eye as his vision settled on one of the dark figures. He was perhaps ten or twenty yards ahead, up a sharp incline, and moving quickly. Castien knew the shot. He had hit several like this before. He closed his eyes, trusting perhaps the only instincts he had, and released.

The arrow whistled through the air.

Castien's breath caught, the falling snow seeming to slow as the arrow moved. The seconds passed, and the arrow soared toward the unassuming assailant. The cloaked figure twitched his head, then turned.

The arrow whizzed by the attacker, missing by a few inches.

Castien froze as he locked eyes with the Blood Sorcerer.

Surge cried out behind him, charging at another one of the attackers.

Elric rose to his feet once again, hurling a blade at Castien's target.

The Blood Sorcerer tossed a bolt of crimson energy at Elric, knocking him to the ground once again. The Blood Sorcerer turned back to Castien... Then the Blood Sorcerer charged.

Castien cried out, turning around and sprinting toward Saevi and Arthion, toward safety. Castien's breathing grew shallow, and the snow seemed to push back with every step he took, yet he kept running. He couldn't stop.

Every muscle in Castien's body lurched to a halt.

Castien opened his mouth, but no words came out as he collapsed face first into the snow.

Icy cold slammed into his face, but Castien couldn't even so much as flinch. His arms and legs tensed, twitching violently as he tried to move them—and failed.

He uttered a groan as his body moved involuntarily. His arm

moved by a phantom command, twisting and planting itself in the snow beneath him. He pushed against it, propping himself up. Castien took in a gasp of air, trying to shout once again.

Footsteps sounded behind him. Thunder rumbled above, and the sounds of battle slowly faded. Castien found himself turning around. He closed his eyes, wincing at the bite of the snow against his legs.

His eyes snapped open, bringing him face to face with the hooded man. *The Blood Sorcerer.*

"A Stormless," the Blood Sorcerer whispered. A bright red orb hovered in his palm, energy radiating violently from it.

Castien felt his body shake.

The Blood Sorcerer twisted his hand, forcing Castien to turn. "Velarus!" the Blood Sorcerer shouted, his light eyes seeming to sparkle in the red light.

Castien felt his legs twisting once again, his body seeming to lose its senses. Castien grimaced as he was forced to face the Summoner. Castien felt another pulse in his body, sending a wicked twitch through his bones. Castien snapped his eyes shut, screaming against the phantom restraints. His breathing increased, his heart pounded faster, and faster, until... it slowed.

"Easy there," the Blood Sorcerer whispered, twisting his other hand as a matching red orb materialized. "Can't have you passing out on us." The Blood Sorcerer smiled sharply, tightening his grip on Castien.

Castien's stomach plummeted as another figure came into view through the thick snowfall. Lightning scattered through the clouds, briefly illuminating the mountainscape.

Blood-red robes trudged through the snow. The hood was lowered by delicate hands, revealing a bald head. Black eyes rose in the falling snow, meeting Castien's gaze. At last, they had found Velarus... and here he was, seconds away from killing Castien.

"Thank you, Edhyr," Velarus said softly, stopping before Castien.

"Where's Imri?" the Blood Sorcerer holding Castien—Edhyr —asked.

"Holding down the others," Velarus said, lowering the bright red orbs in his hands. They dissipated. "They'll be incapacitated for several minutes."

"Then we should kill them before they wake. Who cares what the Empress says?"

"I care," Velarus snapped. "They are far too valuable... We cannot let them go to waste. With the proper training, they could easily have overpowered us, do not forget that." Velarus glared, then turned his black eyes back to Castien.

Castien grunted, resisting once again.

"Find out what he is," Velarus said coldly, opening the flaps of his thick robes.

Castien felt something prick at his skin. Castien gasped, feeling a strange sensation ripple through his body, making his insides tingle and twist. Castien's eyes snapped shut and then opened once again.

"He's..." Edhyr started after a moment. "That's impossible."

"What?" Velarus advanced. "What is it?"

"He... He's a *Starburner.*"

Velarus paused, his hand half frozen inside his cloak. He looked back to Edhyr. "You're sure?" Velarus looked to Castien, then back to Edhyr.

Edhyr seemed to nod.

Castien's mind went blank. *Starburner.*

"At the very least maybe this'll set things in motion," Velarus whispered, pulling a multicolored Crystal from his robes.

Castien's eyes widened.

Hues of purple, orange, red, and gold danced within the Crystal, beautifully colliding yet never truly mixing.

A Starburner Crystal, right before his very eyes—one of the Lost Sects somehow brought back in the essence of this Crystal. It was... impossible.

Castien snapped to attention. His eyes locked on the Crystal. *Pulling...* He blinked, tensing. His body was—*Pulling...* Castien gasped, crying out as his body twitched again. *Pulling...* Castien fought the urge to reach out, to grab hold of that Crystal and absorb the energy inside.

What is happening to me? Castien furrowed his brow, focusing on the Crystal as it hissed and pulled at him. *No... It was... impossible...*

Castien felt his eyes slip shut, and felt his mind reach out toward the Crystal. Castien gasped, feeling the power in hands that did not exist. He was *there*. He had *power*. He had—

Castien's thoughts exploded.

His eyes snapped open as a dagger crashed into the multicolored Crystal, shattering it.

Castien screamed, collapsing to the ground as the Blood Sorcerers sprang into action. Castien fell, finally free of the Sorcerer's control, yet still unable to move.

Someone shouted, more blades soared through the air, singing in the snow as they flew. He heard Velarus shout... then Edhyr... something about a Cloudwalker. Everything was very *hazy*. Castien felt tired—tired like he had never felt before. He rolled over, taking in a breath of fresh air as he leaned his head back into the snow. It felt as though it had been centuries since he had rested.

Gold-purple energy danced through the snow, orange and red glows lacing through the fallen shards of the Crystal, barely a hand's length away from Castien's fingers. Castien felt the energy again—that *power*.

Yet, it was gone: Shattered.

"No, no, no, no, please don't do this," someone said. The snow seemed to shake, and someone fell to the ground beside Castien.

Castien blinked, struggling to keep his eyes open as a familiar face appeared over his own.

Ilyana.

Castien managed a slight smile.

Ilyana let out a gasp, then wiped her brow, lowering her mask. She smiled too, her sharp features twisting into a wide grin.

"Thank the Six, you're alive," Ilyana whispered, extending a hand.

Castien shook his head, the strange fog lingering. Yet, he took the hand. Castien rose to his feet, stumbling a bit until Ilyana steadied him.

"Come on," Ilyana said, dragging Castien away. "We have to find the others."

"But—" Castien trailed off, spinning around as Ilyana dragged him. His eyes settled once again on the Starburner Crystal. He reached out with a numb hand, trying with one last desperate attempt to reclaim that power.

The Crystal's fragments shook in the snow, the last bit of color draining from their once-vibrant shards.

Castien felt his eyes growing heavy once again. He tripped, falling to his knees. The world grew dark, and his eyes slowly began to shut. He reached out toward the Crystal, his arm growing leaden.

Castien's eyes closed as the last bit of light sparkled within the shattered Crystal... and winked out.

CHAPTER TWENTY-TWO
THE ILLUSION OF INNOCENCE

Faelyn Titansworn sat beside Idris, in the back of the ballroom. People danced before them, spinning and twirling through their routines with ease while others ate and drank on the periphery of the room. Idris wasn't dressed in his robes, for once. Tonight, he wore a vest of gold and red, though his hands were still gloved.

Faelyn looked down at his own gold and red vest with a white interior. The colors of his clothing were slowly shifting to the white and gold of the Harvest, and by the time they reached the Solstice the whole Council would be clad in exclusively gold and white.

"You do realize that you could be out there socializing, right?" Idris asked, turning his head ever so slightly. "Though you never were one for politics, were you?"

"Ironic considering I'm poised to inherit the kingdom," Faelyn muttered. "Yet I suppose I don't really have much of a choice in that."

"No," Idris said. "No, you don't. Though I wish that you did."

"Meaning?" Faelyn tilted his head, though he kept his eyes fixed on the spinning couples in the center of the ballroom.

The small orchestra played beautifully off to the side, and the massive chandelier hung resplendently in the center of the room. On the opposite side of the orchestra, Faelyn sighted Reluraun taking another plateful of meat from the long table that held the buffet. Of course, Reluraun would be eating again, despite their mission. Although, above it all, Faelyn kept his eyes toward the pillars that lined the walls, searching for the Whisperer. There were dozens of Whisperers lurking in the shadows, yet none seemed to be the one who had been spying on Faelyn.

"Meaning that I wish we didn't have to put all of this on you," Idris finally said. He took a sip of the light purple wine in his crystal glass, turning back to the tables before him. He sat separated from the tables—per his request—for he had wanted a night off from the relentless prying of the nobles who were lucky enough to sit with the King's Council.

"You and my father always said that I have to become King so that others do not," Faelyn said, running a hand through his golden hair, which he *had* actually taken time to comb tonight. "Besides, I'll have you and the rest of the Council to help me."

Idris took another sip of his drink, and the heavy smell filled Faelyn's nostrils.

Faelyn wrinkled his nose. Idris drank a rare Sucharan variety of wine, one that Faelyn did not particularly care for.

"We still stand by you," he said, lowering his glass and glancing at Faelyn. "But with all of..." He trailed off. "With all of this going on, it's beginning to feel much more... real."

Faelyn shifted uncomfortably in his seat. "You're telling me," Faelyn muttered.

"I must confess, Faelyn, as the weeks have passed, I have grown increasingly worried." Idris turned to him.

"Worried about?"

"About the Blood Sorcerer," Idris said. "The people of this city are growing more restless. I fear that many have already heard the truth."

Faelyn didn't respond.

"Don't think me a fool, I know that you have been trying to learn everything you can about the situation," Idris said.

Faelyn narrowed his eyes. "You're the one who sent the Whisperer to watch me, aren't you?"

Idris tilted his head, eyes narrowing in confusion. "What are you talking about?"

Faelyn too tilted his head, reading his eyes. He had seen Idris lie to countless courtiers and nobles, Faelyn knew him well enough to know when he was being dishonest; now was not one of those times.

"Was it Father?" Faelyn asked, glancing to where the King made his way around the lower landing, greeting the guests.

"Faelyn, what are you talking about?"

Faelyn turned back to him, meeting his gray eyes once again. He looked to Reluraun, who was now speaking with some of the officers who had found the time to attend the ball this evening. *Good, at least he's doing something useful now.*

"Nothing," Faelyn said, turning his gaze to the shadows of the pillars once again. "It's nothing. Forget I said anything." Faelyn rose, the odor of the wine slowly fading, replaced by the roasted blazecrest that sat at many of the ball's tables.

Faelyn started away, and Idris did not stop him. Faelyn passed by a table, nodding to the well-dressed nobles who sat at it. He neared yet another long table, and another, acknowledging those seated and dodging the chair legs with mastery. He needed to check in with Reluraun. More importantly, he needed to find the Whisperer. The state of the city was too fragile to have a rogue Whisperer running about.

Thankfully, the expedition crew would be returning soon, and with Arvendon's strongest Summoners home once again Faelyn would feel much safer. With any luck, the expedition would return just in time for the Solstice, which was now only one week away.

Faelyn scanned for Reluraun, slipping between dresses and vests of white, gold, and red, to honor the Titansworn family, as well as every other color imaginable for those who chose to represent their own house. Faelyn glanced at the side of the room once again for good measure before turning back.

There, lurking behind one of the pillars, was a pair of ice-blue eyes.

Faelyn paused and stared at the eyes for a moment. He took a step forward, shrugging off a couple as they bumped into him.

The Whisperer's shadow straightened.

Faelyn searched his mind for any alterations, but found none.

The Whisperer spun, then dashed through the shadows.

"Calida's Claws!" Faelyn cursed, breaking into a sprint across the dancefloor.

The Whisperer slipped past the guards at the massive doorway without any trouble; Whisperers had free reign to go anywhere in Arvendon.

Faelyn burst past the guards, pushing past the four guards clad in Titansworn-red armor. He found himself in the massive hallway beyond, just as he had the first night when he had chased the Whisperer. Faelyn broke into a run, passing dozens of nobles dressed in every color of the rainbow as they wandered the public areas of the palace.

The Whisperer whipped around another corner, disappearing down the staircase.

Faelyn cursed once again, taking the stairs two at a time. He paused at the bottom, hearing shouting. He looked around at the twin hallways that extended in either direction.

"Where did he go?" Faelyn shouted.

One of the men standing near him—a noble wearing white and red—pointed behind Faelyn.

Faelyn spun, catching a flash of the gray cloak as it flapped behind the running Whisperer. Faelyn broke into another sprint, his lungs burning, his feet catching fire at his command.

The Whisperer was heading for the exit.

Faelyn didn't stop to look, turning to the left, then down the corridor and to the right as he found himself in the grand entry hall.

More nobles and servants milled about, doing double takes as they realized *who* exactly was sprinting by them.

Faelyn tore through the crowd, bursting through the massive marble doors that lay open in the night. Faelyn's feet hissed against the stones as the warm evening air greeted him. Scents of today's Wispwinds—almost like the clean smell of rain, but slightly different—swarmed his nostrils.

Faelyn scanned the stone path that led down from the hill where Summerglass was, leading to the rest of Arvendon. The ocean crashed in the distance, ships' bells ringing in the night as Faelyn took off into another run.

The Whisperer was ahead of him—by about a hundred yards—but not out of reach.

Faelyn took the curved path down with ease, for he had made this route countless times throughout his life.

Gods... he's fast for someone his age, Faelyn thought, remembering the withered face that he had seen each time he had nearly caught this man. *Nearly* stuck out in his mind. He sprinted down the path, rounding another turn in the darkness and passing a torch that stood on a post. Guards shouted, and nobles cried out as Faelyn ripped past them, but he didn't care. Tonight, he was going to catch the Whisperer.

Faelyn charged into the warehouse, smashing through the wooden door. He had followed the Whisperer through the wealthier districts of the city and into the Sea District. The Salarin Sea crashed just outside the walls of the warehouse that Faelyn had seen the Whisperer vanish into just a few moments before. Faelyn had looped around, searching for an alternate way in, just in case this was a trap of some sort. But he had found only locked doors and broken windows. This warehouse was abandoned, and seemingly empty... which was why it didn't make sense that the Whisperer would lead him here.

Darkness greeted him. He could make out the slight impression of a ramp to his right, and presumed the deepened darkness before him to be a depression in the center of the large room.

A processing tank, then—an abandoned one, Faelyn thought. He considered using fire to light the room, though he didn't want to harm the man... not yet. He needed to learn who had sent the Whisperer first, and what he wanted.

Moonlight poured through the small door frame, illuminating the wooden shards on the ground. Faelyn turned, facing the small, empty depression in the center of the room. It appeared to be abandoned.

Something snapped—or, more accurately, someone.

The moonlight behind Faelyn faded as he spun. He found himself enveloped in total darkness. Searching his mind, Faelyn searched for the Whisperer's tampering. He could find no evidence of any changes. Faelyn steeled himself, ignoring the strange phenomenon and readying his powers, preparing to draw upon the Crystals stored within his vest.

"There's nowhere left to run," Faelyn spat, raising his hands slightly. "I have finally caught you."

Something moved behind him, wind whooshing past him ever so slightly.

Faelyn whirled, but once again was met only by darkness. His footsteps were the only sound in the pitch-black chamber.

"You have mistaken my intentions, prince," a voice called out, behind Faelyn once again.

He spun, facing the empty depression before him. Yet he could make out nothing in the unnaturally dark room. "I have made no mistake," Faelyn said. "I know what you are... spy."

It laughed, a wicked, horrible laugh that echoed around him in every direction.

Faelyn turned in circles as he tried to find the source of the impossible, ever-moving voice.

"Oh... my boy..." the voice laughed. "You have no idea what I am, Faelyn Titansworn, son of Avenos Titansworn."

Faelyn turned once again as the voice floated through the room. *Where is he?* Faelyn thought. The darkness seemed to grow more overpowering with each passing second. Faelyn considered sparking a few flames, if only to set his eyes on the man, but decided against it. This man was only a Whisperer, and Faelyn was in no danger so long as he had his Crystals.

"I think that you have radically misjudged me, young prince," the voice called. It was old, wise, yet also astonishingly firm given the withered look that Faelyn had caught on the man's face in his past encounters.

"Where are you?" Faelyn demanded, nearly drawing upon his flames this time.

The voice laughed slightly. "My boy, if there is one thing that I wish for you to learn first, let it be that you should not waste time asking questions whose answers are irrelevant."

"Fine," Faelyn sighed. "*Who* are you?"

"Ah," the voice said, behind him this time.

Faelyn turned. A faint outline stood before him in the darkness, just defined enough for Faelyn to make out the man before him.

"Now that is a question to which I can provide an answer," the voice said, coming from the figure before him.

How did he do that? Faelyn tilted his head. *I didn't even hear him approach.* Cautiously, Faelyn raised his left hand, calling upon the power within him. He burned the Crystals slightly, drawing a thin tendril of flame from his vest. His chest heated, the warmth spreading down his left arm as the subtle fire climbed his limbs, wrapping itself around his arm slowly.

Orange light blossomed in the darkness. The slight tendril wavered, beating back the night.

The figure before him slowly came into view.

Faelyn squinted, trying to see past the now-bright flames that covered his left sleeve. The fire shaped itself into an orb, collecting in his hand at his mental command.

A face became visible to him. An old, weathered face of a man who was at least twenty years Faelyn's father's senior. His ice-blue eyes seemed to glow in the darkness, and Faelyn began to hear something whispering in the night. If he had any suspicions, they were confirmed now. The roaming voice... The extreme darkness... The strange disappearance and the way he seemed to be in many places at once... This man had been whispering into Faelyn's mind ever since their first encounter, manipulating his surroundings.

Faelyn shuddered, and tightened his stance; this Whisperer was *very powerful.*

"Niventia's Light... So you are a Whisperer, aren't you?" Faelyn asked, raising the ball of flame to stare into the man's hollow blue eyes.

His face broke into a slight smile. "No," the man said softly, his body sagging with age. "Yet, with my situation as it is, it is best if all but you and I think that. I am Eithor Vassellet," the man said, extending his wrinkled hand. "Not many know me by that name here, but I do not mind if you do."

Faelyn reached forward with his right hand, maintaining the flame in his left. Yet, as he made to close his fingers, he was met with... *nothing.* Faelyn stumbled, passing through Eithor's hand as if it were nothing. Something like frost fuzzed where the man's hand lay waiting. Faelyn gathered himself, staring at the man, eyes wide.

"Hmm..." Eithor mused. "How quaint." And then, without a single word more, he vanished.

Faelyn gasped, flaring the flame in his left hand. In an instant, brilliant tendrils of fire exploded from Faelyn's chest, shooting upward, casting the warehouse in their incredible light.

"Easy there, my boy," a voice said from behind.

Faelyn whirled, finding himself face to face with Eithor once again.

Faelyn jumped back, startled to find himself standing on the marble floors of a *mansion*, rather than the wooden floors of an old warehouse. He turned, scanning the room, which was now lit by the magnificent swaths of flame that swam overhead. A chandelier hung in the center of the room, complete with Crystals, though they were unfilled.

Marble pillars lined the slight depression in the center of the room, which Faelyn now recognized to be a sort of dance floor. Stained-glass skylights lined the ceiling, guiding the ethereal grace of the twin moons into the chamber.

Where am I? Faelyn thought. He turned around, looking at where he had smashed through the door. Yet he found no empty door frame, only another pink-marble wall.

What? Faelyn turned back to face Eithor.

The old man smiled slightly and raised a withered hand.

Faelyn's flames vanished in an instant, plunging the ballroom into darkness once more. When Faelyn mentally felt his Crystals, they were still being drained as if they were maintaining the fires above. Faelyn extinguished the flames, turning back to Eithor, whose scarred face was now lit only by the pale gray light of Lotius.

"What... What are you?" Faelyn breathed.

"I told you: You have *no idea* what I am." Eithor vanished once again, disappearing into thin air.

Faelyn cursed, turning back to the marble floor before him. *This is not the same building that I entered.* Faelyn's mind swirled with questions. *And what happened to the door?* It all seemed impossible. It had to be because of the Whispering, it had to be.

Blue-green light winked before him, the light of the moons fading as if they were candles snuffed of their light.

A thought struck Faelyn. It was impossible, true, but... Faelyn took a small step to the left, reaching out toward the marble pillar. He moved his hand forward, pressing against the stone, only to find that there was nothing there.

His hand fuzzed with blue-green frost and vanished inside the pillar.

"Izara's Shadow," Faelyn whispered, turning back to the rest of the large room. "You're an *Illusomancer*," Faelyn breathed.

The voice laughed, as if in confirmation. "I was told you were a quick learner, dear Faelyn," Eithor whispered from nowhere.

Faelyn frowned, stepping forward. He raised his hands, the tendrils of flame now wrapping around both arms as heat sprouted from his chest. "And I was told that your Sect was extinct," Faelyn growled.

"Ah," Eithor said, materializing before him once again. "And that was true, I suppose, until a short time ago."

The man before Faelyn should not exist. He was not real. Someone was trying to trap Faelyn in some sort of trick, and he was playing right into it.

Not anymore.

Before Eithor could react, Faelyn charged, willing the heat within the Crystals forward. Their flames weaved through his soul, wrapping his bones in their glorious power, pushing through his chest, then his arms, then his fingers. And then torrents of flame exploded from Faelyn's hands, burning with the heat of a thousand blazecrests.

Eithor screamed, a horrible, blood-curdling scream. The inferno raged, burning through the man's bones.

Faelyn roared, unleashing the full force of his might on the spy until there was nothing left to burn.

Minutes passed like seconds, and, slowly, Faelyn felt the heat fade. His Crystal burned out, the fires dying at his fingers, the warmth receding through his body and disappearing, leaving only a warm afterimage in his soul. Faelyn stopped, standing up straight. The screaming had stopped. The man was dead. Moonlight poured in once again, this time free from the strange creature's control.

Breakdown once again drifted through Faelyn's bones, weakening them ever so slightly. He had come close this evening, but he was still safe. The power that he had expended was not enough to trigger the reaction.

Ash floated in the center of the room. Swirling in a phantom wind as it fell. *Curious.*

Faelyn took a moment to bask in the overpowering heat of the room—heat that he had created... The heat that he had used to kill Arvendon's spy. He made to turn around, once again finding a shattered wooden door behind him, when he heard the wind pick up—wind that should not exist *inside* of a warehouse.

Faelyn spun, burning his backup Crystal and Summoning the flames once again. The ash danced in the phantom breeze, guided by unseen hands in the dark chamber. To Faelyn's horror, the ash turned and twisted, forming something that almost looked... human.

Eithor Vassellet stepped forward, his body of ash reforged in the moonlight, his skin melting into form as ash faded to flesh.

"I'm disappointed, Faelyn," Eithor whispered, his voice not coming from before him, but behind, as if he were speaking directly into Faelyn's ear. "I offer you my assistance, and you repay me with fire. Yet, as you can see, I am not so easily killed." The voice passed overhead, drifting to the center of the room. Another figure appeared to the right, and one to the left as well, each mirroring the man who stood before him.

The trio of Eithors floated together, levitating in the dark air, drawn to the voice.

Faelyn's jaw hung open as he stared, watching the three men melt into one.

Blue-green frost flashed once again, and the three were gone, replaced by a lone Eithor, levitating in the pale moonlight.

Projections. An Illusomancer indeed.

"How?" Faelyn demanded. "How are you doing this?"

Eithor smiled, his features shadowed by his mysterious hood. "Continue to seek out the spy within the palace, young prince," Eithor said, floating upwards slightly. "There is one in Summerglass who does not belong, though it is not me."

"I—" Faelyn started.

"I will find you again soon, young Titansworn," Eithor said, turning away as he continued to ascend. "I'm afraid I must go. But there is much that you do not know... Much that I am going to show you." And, with that, the Illusomancer floated through the stained-glass ceiling, disappearing into the night.

CHAPTER TWENTY-THREE
DISCOVERY

Asteros Silverglade stood quietly in the corner of his room, staring at the Crystal in his palm. It was loosely cylindrical, though its lateral sides possessed many faces and jagged edges. It looked just like any other Crystal. It radiated with the strange dark energy of umbrakinesis, rumbling with ancient tones that Asteros could never hope to understand.

He turned it over in his hand, gazing into the depthless darkness within the ethereal Crystal. No one knew where they came from—though it was well known to all that occasionally Crystals would grow from accumulated energy in random caves and crevices. No one understood their nature, for, when broken with force, they released all of the energy that they held.

Somehow, these Crystals absorbed energy from the atmosphere —from the Tempests—and converted it into a form that was usable by mankind's Summoners. No technology had ever been able to replicate such a phenomenon. No scholar had ever been able to explain such a thing naturally. Not even the Ancients seemed to understand it.

"Asteros?" Shalheira slipped into his quarters. "What are you doing?" she asked upon noticing the Crystal in his hand.

He held it up to the Scorcher-Crystal lamp on the wall, watching the undulating waves of darkness within the Crystal he held. "All the scientific knowledge we have gained in the last thousand years, and we still know nothing about these Crystals," Asteros mused. "Doesn't that strike you as odd?"

"I suppose I never really thought about it," Shalheira said, sitting down on the corner of his bed.

Asteros turned to her, lowering the Crystal slightly. "Is it something within the Crystal that changes the energy?" Asteros asked, knowing that Shalheira would have no answer. "Or is it something in the Tempests themselves that is captured?"

"Is now really the time for philosophical questions such as these?" Shalheira shook her head, smiling slightly—her lips curling in that beautiful way they did.

"Perhaps the Tempests are drawn to it by some force we have not yet discovered, and what we assumed to be a property of conversion within the Crystals is merely a concept of concentration, instead." Asteros turned back to the Crystal, pacing.

Shalheira absently began turning one of her daggers in her hand. "Why didn't you tell me that you changed the plans?" she asked, looking up from the blade in her hands.

Asteros paused, lowering his head. "I knew you would not approve."

"You thought that I would not approve of a plan that aimed to unite our continent?"

"I thought that you wouldn't approve of the methods by which I mean to do it," Asteros said, meeting her gaze. A slight breeze passed through the chamber, sending a chill down Asteros's spine. Yet he felt warm nonetheless, trapped in her intoxicating eyes.

Shalheira rose from the bed, laying her dagger on the night table as she approached him.

He slipped the Crystal back into the pouch near his waist, raising his hands to Shalheira's gentle face.

She closed her eyes, melting into his touch, her sharp lips curving into that devilish smile that Asteros loved so much. She pulled him into a kiss.

He leaned in farther, pushing her back slightly.

"Asteros," she warned, pulling back for a second.

"What is it, darling?" Asteros asked.

"We shouldn't be doing this," Shalheira said, retreating.

Asteros sighed, but did not move. He had been so close last time, he hated to see her pull away again. "And why shouldn't we?" he whispered. "You've been gone for *months,* and I was counting the days to your return since the second you left. Letting you leave, letting us be paused for all of this, was the greatest mistake of my life. I know now, after nearly a year of waiting, exactly what I want." Asteros took a deep breath.

Shalheira bit her lip, her smile fading slightly.

"It's you, Shalheira," Asteros whispered. "It's you. It's always been you. You're all I want, you're all I've ever wanted."

"Asteros—"

"A life without you is no life that I want to live, even these last few months, just sitting here—knowing that you were away—was enough to drive me mad." Asteros pulled her into another kiss, letting her warmth bleed into his soul. Her glorious scent uncaged his wildest instincts.

"Asteros, you said it yourself. We are going to change the world. Now is no time for us to begin whatever... whatever *this* is!" Shalheira said, putting her delicate hands against his chest.

"What better reason for us to fall in love than this?" Asteros growled. "Society is on the brink of collapsing. Each day more and more people are forced out of cities to make room for those deemed important enough to be protected from the Tempests. The world has practically set itself afire, Shalheira. What better reason to let this spark of love catch alight too?"

Shalheira pulled him in this time, taking him from his feet and into her arms. They fell backwards onto his bed, nestling themselves in the soft fur sheets. She pulled off her cloak, revealing her skin-tight black underclothing as she kissed him harder.

Asteros unhooked his cloak, taking off his coat and diving into Shalheira's beauty.

"Asteros," Shalheira breathed, pulling his tongue to hers.

Asteros fell into her kiss, jumping from the final cliffs of judgment and plunging into the endless depths of passion.

"Tomorrow we save the world," Asteros promised. "But tonight... Tonight, we can be *together.*"

Shalheira blinked a few times at the words, seemingly caught off guard by them.

"What? What is it, what's wrong?" Asteros asked as Shalheira slithered out of his grip.

"I'm sorry," she whispered, picking her cloak from the cold stone floor. "But I can't."

"Can't do what?" Asteros asked, standing beside her.

She turned away from his touch, pulling her cloak on tightly. "I can't be with you, Asteros," Shalheira said. "I just can't..." Shalheira trailed off.

Asteros quieted, lucidity returning to him as his passion faded. "Shalheira—"

"*No,*" Shalheira rasped, curling out of his touch. "You don't understand," she whispered. She stood up, making for the hallway beyond.

"Don't understand what?" Asteros growled, taking her hand. "What aren't you telling me?"

Shalheira looked at him. Yet she did not answer.

Asteros did not know what had made her this way, but he vowed —in that moment—that he was going to fix it. Whatever it was, whatever had scarred this beautiful woman so deeply, was going to pay the price.

He was going to rebuild her heart, one piece at a time. He had told himself for *decades* that he would never take responsibility for the life of another person again, not after... But Shalheira had left him no choice. His vow had been one of ignorance and selfishness. One failure, no matter how terrible, could not dictate the rest of his life—of that, he was certain.

"Please," Shalheira said. "Don't make this any harder than it has to be."

"Tell me," Asteros said. "Tell me what it was. Tell me what happened so that I can help you. Please."

Shalheira looked away, her gaze settling on the stone ground beneath her. "I..." Shalheira started. "I can't, Asteros, I just can't."

"Shalheira," Asteros said. "Look me in the eyes right now," he whispered. "My parents died," he whispered. "If I can tell you about my past, then you can tell me about yours."

Shalheira flinched slightly, and this time it was Asteros who looked away.

"My parents were killed in a Storm Gale, running from our home after my powers were revealed," Asteros said.

"What?" Shalheira whispered. Asteros sat down, pulling her beside him on his bed.

"My parents believed that the Shadow-Swifts were the children of Izara, and, curses, maybe we are," Asteros began. "But my parents were devoted Soltarans—a subgroup of the Navesians so extreme in their faith that they thought that, if anyone possessed the powers of a Shadow-Swift, they should be exorcized and burned."

"Asteros, I—"

"Long ago, Haldir assassinated a Cyfali Ambassador within Arvendon's walls," Asteros continued. "He dropped a Crystal during the fight, a Crystal that was found by the Paladin my parents followed. Being the most devoted of his followers, the Paladin brought the

Crystal to my parents, hoping that they would help him in the purification ritual that he intended for it to undergo. I was in bed when he arrived, barely past the age of fifteen," he whispered. "I awoke to him chanting alongside my parents, standing in a circle around that *godforsaken* Crystal. I leapt from my bed, fearing that one of my parents had been cursed, and when I neared the Crystal..." Asteros trailed off.

The memory burned as if it had happened not one day before. Yet it had been decades, and he still remembered it, clear as it was when he had lived through that evening.

"I was startled, and I instinctually drew power from the Crystal, not even knowing what I was doing," Asteros said. "They called me a monster... A demon. The Paladin attacked me, and I killed him—somehow. The power within the Crystal flowed into my body like a stream into an ocean, and it protected me."

"And your parents?" Shalheira asked quietly.

He closed his eyes, bringing out the memory that he had tried so hard to forget. "The next thing I remember is them running from the house, yelling that I was possessed, and that they were doomed. They sought shelter in the storm, running from me," Asteros whispered. "I found them the next night, lying collapsed on the shores of Arvendon—just beyond the ward—struck down by the Tempest. I knew it wouldn't be long before the city discovered them," Asteros continued. "I knew that I would have no choice but to leave, and that... that was when Haldir found me."

Shalheira took a deep breath, pulling him into a tight embrace.

But the love he felt was gone.

"He came back for the Crystal, and the next thing I knew he had figured out what I was... and then I ended up here," Asteros said softly, trying to regain his composure.

"And he made you one of us," Shalheira finished for him. "One of them."

Asteros nodded. He had been with the Shadow-Swifts for several years before Shalheira had been inducted, though he had already completed the initiation by the time she even came of age.

Fueled by the embers of his parents' death, he had trained rigorously—even more so than Malik did now—trying to gain the strength to protect those he could. Trying to gain the *control* to prove that he was not a monster. Yet it didn't matter. Twenty years after their death he finally grasped the term "acceptance" and realized that, no matter what he did, there was no way for him to bring them back. There was no way for them to look upon him one last time, with love—not terror—in their soft, black eyes.

They were gone.

He was responsible for their deaths. And, though he had reached a state of acceptance, he was far from healed.

He had caused them to run out into the Tempests. They knew the danger of what they did, but they had deemed him an even greater threat than the eternal fury of the Gods. They had fled into a Storm Gale seeking refuge from their own child.

"I'm sorry about your parents, Asteros," Shalheira said softly. "It wasn't your fault. I hope you understand that."

Asteros turned to her.

"They acted out of fear and panic, and accidentally set in motion a series of events that they would've never wished upon you," Shalheira said.

"Shalheira, they knew what they were doing. They knew what I was, they had told me for my entire life that Shadow-Swifts were the foulest of the Death-Queen's Creations. I am one of them."

"They were wrong." Shalheira stroked his back gently. "They assumed the Shadow-Swifts to be evil, but they were wrong," she said. "They thought that you—the sweetest, most gifted person in all of Auris—were a monster. If that isn't proof enough that they were wrong, then I don't know what is." She kissed him lightly, rising from the bed as she did so.

Asteros's lips cracked into a smile. "Where are you going?" he asked.

Shalheira rested a hand on the door frame. Her other hand drifted to the Scorcher Crystal on the wall, extinguishing the light.

Asteros's room plunged into darkness, the only light in the chamber coming from the faint glow of the hallway beyond. Shalheira's long shadow accentuated the delicate curves of her body as she turned to face him.

"I'm sorry, Asteros," she said. "But at least yours was an accident," she whispered. She vanished without another word, disappearing into the corridor beyond, leaving Asteros alone in the dark.

Her final words washed over him like water on glass. *At least yours was an accident.* He had nothing left to give. He had told her that which no one—not even Haldir—knew. His soul had been torn apart that night so many years ago—cut so deeply that he feared it could never be repaired—until he fell in love with her.

At least yours was an accident. Asteros lay in bed, watching the churning light of the Crystals beyond his cracked door as if it would somehow bring her back. But no. She was gone. She was beyond his reach. He loved her, and she seemed to love him, so why couldn't they just... *love* each other?

He may never come to peace with what had happened. He may never forget what had happened to his parents; what he had *done* to them. But with her in his life... maybe, just maybe... he could fully move past this. He could toss aside the person he was and become who he was meant to be: a hero. Being told that he was a monster for the entirety of his childhood had drilled into his brain that all these powers would ever be good for was killing. Haldir had helped him rationalize it, claiming that he was keeping Auris balanced, keeping it safe. That had been enough for a little while. But now... now he needed something more. He was the leader of this clan. He had the power to change not just Erydon, but the entire world. And that was exactly what he was going to do. The Tempests had killed his parents. They had killed countless others throughout history, and he was going to stop them. Tomorrow, they were going to travel to Bareholde and uncover the secrets of old.

Tomorrow, he was going to learn how the Ancients had vanquished half of Auris's Sects. And, armed with that knowledge, he was going to follow in their faded footsteps, and he was going to finish what they started.

Asteros Silverglade squinted through the falling snow, staring into the darkness of Bareholde.

The scholars stepped back from their positions on the Rune-Wall, where they had bested yet another lock with their tricks. The nine stepped back, allowing the door to finish its elaborate opening process.

This chamber was not so hidden as Herqen's, though it would likely have been near impossible to find without the hint from the Ancient Stonemaster's writings. Something else awaited them here, hopefully. While the other Stonemaster had all but confirmed that Bareholde was simply another safehouse, Asteros was certain that this cavern would be more useful than the last.

Not that the information in Herqen hadn't helped them, for it had been what set them on this course initially. It was simply that Herqen's walls omitted several vital pieces of information intentionally. Asteros couldn't blame the Stonemaster for doing such things, for it seemed that the information held a great deal of knowledge that was considered secret.

Yet not all were so wise. Asteros had no doubts that one of the Stonemasters who created these caverns would eventually reveal the information that they needed, which was how the Ancient Summoners managed to destroy half of the Ancient Sects.

"Shall we, then?" Eithor rasped, his aging voice straining to be heard through the Frostfall.

Asteros looked around, locking eyes with each of the Shadow-Swifts standing on the small indenture in the mountain. They were ready.

"After you," Tsarra said.

Asteros smiled slightly at the sharpness of her voice.

"Keep in mind that this cavern could very well be a waste of our time, your greatnesses," Soran muttered, falling into line behind the six Shadow-Swifts. "The odds of this cave possessing any additional information is..." He trailed off as the first of the torches ignited. The entry hall of this cavern was far grander than Herqen's. Rather than the small, cramped passageway of the other safehouse, before them lay a *massive* hallway filled with row upon row of torches.

In the very center of the room, there sat a slab of stone perhaps twice the size of a man. It looked jagged, uneven, accidental even. Yet Asteros could see, even from a distance, the faint indentures in it. It was inscribed.

"What is that?" Malik asked, taking the lead.

Asteros bristled a bit, but let it slide. The boy had been growing restless, and, during the evening that they had taken to refill their Crystals, he had hardly even slept. Of course, Asteros really hadn't rested much either.

"It appears to be an inscription of some sort," Eithor said, hobbling forward.

"An important one as well, judging by the presentation," Soran added, joining Eithor as they approached the stone. It was made of the same black rock as the rest of the cavern and appeared to have simply been left alone while the rest of the bunker had been carved out.

Asteros flicked his eyes to the darkened hallway at the end of the room. There was *much* more to be discovered in this place, yes. But this seemed like as good a place as any to start.

The three scholars crowded around the slab, eagerly holding up their Scorcher Crystals as they began translating it in their minds.

Asteros waited calmly as they chatted quietly.

Lyseria whispered something to Keries, but Asteros missed it.

Gods, what are we going to do with her? he asked himself. A girl that young had no place in this quest, let alone in Erydon. Yet Lucien had insisted that they induct her into the clan upon their discovery; Asteros had caved.

"What does it say?" Lucien asked, his patience finally running out. He brought a hand to his pointed Elosian beard, stroking it as they turned to face him.

"It doesn't seem to say anything that makes much sense at all, I'm afraid," Eithor pronounced. Tsarra, however, was kneeling near the base of the stone. Only a portion of the front side was inscribed; the rest was left empty for some reason.

"Which is precisely the point of it, old friend," Tsarra said as she read. She stood up, turning around. "These are the ramblings of an Ancient Wayfinder," she said. "While I do respect the fallen Sect of fortune-tellers, I find their stories to often be of little use to practical thinkers like us."

"Let me see," Keries said, stepping forward. It was no surprise that he was interested in the predictions of the Ancient Sect. Keries stood before the stone for a few moments, bushy eyebrows furrowed in deep thought. "Ahem," he coughed, motioning to Eithor.

Lucien snorted a laugh: Keries couldn't read the ancient tongue.

"It seems to be in the form of a poem, sir," Eithor started. "It begins "Daybreaks at the dawn of Genesis. Fourteen Harbingers descended from beyond, each bearing the anomalous powers of Summoning. The world they called 'Auris' hiding between the planes of life through Synthesis. The earth was shaped and built by powers still running. Crystals grow, born of the strength of storms. The Harbingers retreat, leaving sepulchers of divinity. Unlocked only by the blood of the dead and the stars, leaving only the sacred to transform. The planes are closed now, locking our world in the depths of infinity,'" Eithor finished. "I'm sorry, my lord, I can't seem to make heads or tails of any of this."

Crystals... Asteros thought, the word catching his ear. *Perhaps they are involved in this in some way...*

"Oftentimes the words of the Wayfinders confused all but the ones who wrote them," Tsarra pointed out.

"Yes, but not to this degree," Keries said, leaning closer to the slab. "There is something curious about this stone, there is no doubt in my mind about that much."

A silence fell over the group.

"Alright, if we've all had enough of *this*, I suggest we see if there's actually anything useful in this cavern," Malik said loudly.

Asteros closed his eyes once again, but held his tongue. The boy possessed an arrogance that rivaled Lucien's when the man was young. Of course, that arrogance was still there, Lucien had simply internalized it.

"Now tell me again, was that a prediction or a story of the past?" Keries asked Tsarra as they began walking.

"There's no way to know," Tsarra said, turning away and picking up her pace. "I already said that I find the Wayfinders to be of very little use to us. Malik is right, we should not dwell on this any longer. If it's that important to you, we can go back and study the entire thing when we have time. Just not now," Tsarra said sharply.

Malik smiled triumphantly.

They're a mess, Asteros thought. *Decades of living within the same walls and we hardly know one another.*

They neared the end of the chamber, entering the narrowing hallway ahead. Asteros let the scholars take the lead. They had figured out not only the location of this cave but a way inside as well —saving Asteros the usage of his key. They appeared to have used a similar method to the one they had used to open Herqen's lock, though this one was slightly different. Rather than having all three of the scholars overriding a lock-point, Eithor had been tasked with drawing a very specific Rune in the snow below the door. Tsarra had said that it had something to do with the type of key the lock required, but that such things were irrelevant when the scholars knew over two dozen techniques for bypassing Rune-Locks.

Asteros was surprised at how easy it was to do such a thing. For, even before the Vanishing, the locks had been considered unbreakable.

Eithor had reasoned that many of the techniques required multiple people and had only been discovered due to extensive testing of ancient lockboxes in Freyfall. He had explained that, once they understood how the Rune-Locks worked, the weaknesses were quite easy to find.

Even the most powerful of magic had its weaknesses.

"Ah, this appears to be it," Eithor said after a few moments of walking. The thick air of the cavern warmed as they entered the grand atrium. Brilliant flames illuminated the massive chamber upon their entry, the ancient Incendiary-fueled torches that lined the circular room coming to life all at once, triggered by the stone they stood on.

"I'm beginning to notice a pattern here," Lucien mused, rubbing his pointed beard once again. The room was nearly identical to Herqen's grand chamber, which also happened to be nearly identical to the main cavern in Erydon.

"Yes, indeed," Eithor said, his ice-blue eyes wide with excitement as he scanned the sheer vastness of the room.

"Stonemasters of this century all seem to have followed the same template in terms of architecture," Soran commented. "Not that I'm surprised... If anything, I'd be surprised if they didn't."

"And why would they build chambers like these, Soran?" Shal-heira asked, stepping closer to the bald younger man. "What purpose was there in recording such knowledge in stone when you already possessed it in your own mind?"

"I presume they found their purpose in doing so to be the same in ours for recording our knowledge in books: so that our words can be remembered long after we have been forgotten," Soran said, drawing nearer to the walls. "For, if one's knowledge died with their body, society would've never moved beyond the age of sticks and stones."

"If that were the case, then why would Herqen's Stonemaster leave out some information?" Lucien challenged. "And, if he intended to keep such things a secret, why record it at all?"

"These are questions whose answers are far beyond our grasp, my boy," Eithor said, raising a hand to settle Lucien's harsh tone.

"I've walked this land longer than you have, I would watch who you are calling 'boy,'" Lucien snarled.

Eithor stepped back, his soft smile falling.

Less intimidated than he usually is, Asteros noted.

"To answer your question: I suspect that the knowledge in Herqen was meant to set us on this path, Master Lucien," Tsarra answered, holding her Crystal up to the wall.

"What do you mean?" Asteros asked.

"The Stonemaster who spent his final days in Herqen knew of what was coming. He also, presumably, knew that there would be people in the future—people like us—who would try to unravel the events of his time. I fear that his concern was likely that the *wrong* people would start looking around in such areas," Tsarra said, brushing her black hair out of her eyes and turning back to the wall.

"And what people would he consider to be the *wrong* ones?" Shalheira asked, raising an eyebrow.

"That, my lady, remains to be seen," Tsarra said simply.

Asteros nodded, turning to face the massive task at hand. It had taken him several days to translate all of Herqen's wall. Granted, with three scholars at his disposal, it would likely be a much quicker process, but tedious nonetheless.

"What are you finding?" Malik asked the scholars.

"Calm down, young master," Eithor said softly as he read. "These things take time," he continued absently. "Although... so far the Revenants have been mentioned far more times than I would have thought—"

"Revenants?" Lyseria whispered curiously.

Asteros shook his head. *Gods, the girl doesn't even recognize the name of one of the Ancient Sects.*

"One of the Lost Sects, my dear," Eithor said, turning to face the young girl.

Her soft face broke into a smile as the old man beckoned her forward. She reluctantly released Keries's hand and approached the wall.

"Look here, child," Eithor said softly, guiding her finger toward one of the words on the wall. "That right there says 'Revenant.'"

"What did they do?" Lyseria asked, her innocent eyes wide with curiosity.

Keries smiled like a proud father at the little girl.

Asteros eyed the older Shadow-Swift curiously. He would never understand why Keries had such an attachment to the girl.

"Why, they were actually quite fascinating," Eithor said, feigning excitement.

He's had children of his own, Asteros realized. He recognized the softness of Eithor's smile, the warmth in his voice. This was a man who had raised a child himself, a man who had led a family. A *father*... And they had taken him away from that life.

"The Revenants were one of the most powerful of the Ancient Sects," Eithor continued. "They possessed a similar ability to that of Transcendence, you see." Eithor paused, smiling. "They were capable of something known as 'Unbinding,' which was like what you do, only, rather than sending one's victims to the Unbound, the Revenants sent them somewhere else entirely."

"And let's not forget about Necromancy," Soran added from the other side of the circular chamber.

Lyseria's head whipped to face the bald man. "Necromancy?" she asked, eyes wide.

"Ah yes." Eithor smiled warmly, laying a hand on her shoulder and pointing at the wall with the other. "The Revenants knew of ways to bring back the dead, reanimating the bodies of those who had passed on to the Afterworld."

"That's enough," Keries said, stepping forward and grabbing Lyseria's hand. "No need to frighten the girl."

"My apologies, my lord," Eithor gasped. "I assure you, I had no intention of scaring the child."

"I'm sure you didn't, but let's move on now," Keries said sharply.

Lucien went back to brooding in the darkness while stroking his beard—like always. Asteros locked eyes with Shalheira, though he quickly regretted it.

He once again found himself trapped in those warm amber eyes of hers, drowning in their beauty. Yet at their core he saw nothing but misery. After what had happened last night, he could only imagine what sort of things she was feeling. Whatever she had been through was traumatic enough that, even after his own sharing, she still hadn't revealed her past. *Izara's Shadow... What have you been through, my love?* Asteros thought, finally pulling himself from her gaze.

"It seems that the Revenants were also umbrakinetics," Tsarra said, breaking the silence.

"What?" Lucien whirled, stepping from the shadow that he had somehow found in the circular room.

"Yes, right here," Tsarra said, pointing with her Crystal. "It claims that, in an encounter with the Revenants, they were met primarily with umbrakinetic attacks, though they seem a bit... different."

"It says something similar here as well," Eithor added. "Unbinding was said to have required a tremendous amount of energy to accomplish, so it would only make sense that the Revenants fought with more efficient abilities."

"But how could the Revenants have had umbrakinesis?" Asteros asked, stepping toward the center of the room. "The manipulation of darkness is central to the abilities of the Shadow-Swifts, and there are no records of two Sects ever *sharing* an ability."

No one spoke, the only sound in the large chamber the soft crackling of the torches.

"Asteros does have a point," Shalheira added.

"I never said he didn't," Tsarra said. "We simply haven't been here long enough to come across a logical explanation for such things. As we've said before: these things take time," Tsarra said, annoyance bleeding into her tone.

"Although all this talk of Revenants does allude to an interesting theory…" Eithor said absently, still reading as he spoke. "By the Six." Eithor paused. "Fourteen—well that's simply impossible."

"What?" Lucien turned his head.

Eithor looked at Lucien, then at Asteros. "My lords, we've been wondering how the Ancients' Crystals were powered… but they were powered the same way as ours all along."

"What do you mean?" Asteros advanced.

"The Ancients' Crystals drew power from the Tempests, just not *our* Tempests," Eithor said. "It says here that there used to be not seven Tempests, but *fourteen*." Eithor fell silent.

Asteros took a step forward. It was impossible. Fourteen Tempests would mean that… there used to be *twice* as many. This challenged everything that they thought they knew.

"Well, if that's the case, then the method by which the Ancients removed half of Auris's Sects is quite simple," Eithor continued.

"Wait," Lucien started. "You're implying that the Tempests were here *before* the Vanishing then?"

"It would certainly seem that way," Eithor said.

"That's *impossible*," Shalheira started. "That changes everything!"

"I urge you to remain calm, for I suspect this is only the beginning of what we will learn from this cavern," Eithor said. "As I was saying, given that the Stonemaster who created this cavern has mentioned several violent encounters with the Revenants, it seems clear that the Revenants and the Stonemasters were enemies, correct?"

They nodded slightly.

Asteros leaned in; the scholar may be old, but his years did not come without wisdom.

Eithor continued. "It seems natural to assume that, given the nature of the Vanishing, The Tempests were simply Unbound."

"What?" Asteros breathed. "You think that the Revenants *Unbound* the Tempests?"

"There's no need to raise your voice, Master Silverglade," Eithor said. "I am simply stating that it seems like a likely explanation, given the nature of the Tempests' disappearance. Look," Eithor continued, motioning with his hands. "Unbinding was the simple act of casting something out into nonexistence. From what we can gather from the Ancient Texts, Unbinding was actually quite similar to Transcendence, for both involve detaching one's body from Auris. Unbinding, however, was permanent. When one Transcends, they still maintain a connection to Auris."

"The difference lies in the fact that Unbinding permanently removes the person," Tsarra elaborated, "whereas Transcendence is characterized by a partial tether to Auris all throughout the act. Eithor is correct," Tsarra insisted. "It would make sense that the Tempests were Unbound, though the Tempests are not people so... how that happened, I still have no idea."

"This cavern will take several days, perhaps, for us to fully translate," Soran said, rejoining the group. "Given more time, we can likely uncover more clues related to the matter."

"Then time you shall have," Asteros said. "Lucien, Shalheira, Keries, and myself can stay here with you, bringing supplies as well as food back and forth between here and Erydon while you work."

The group of nine was on the cusp of a massive discovery, Asteros didn't have to be a scholar to realize that. They were learning things that had been forgotten for over a thousand years, and this was only the beginning.

CHAPTER TWENTY-FOUR
DIVISION

Familiar voices spoke in the distance.

"It doesn't make any sense."

"Who said it has to? We have the proof that they have returned, and, now that they've escaped, we have no reason to drag out this expedition any longer."

"Did you see where they could've gone?"

"Of course I didn't, they were flown out by a pair of Cloudwalkers—besides, the storm was too dense anyway. Tarathiel's Stones, you're not very bright, are you?"

"At least I was brave enough to actually stay in the fight, rather than running and hiding!"

"And at least I was smart enough to avoid getting knocked unconscious by a Blood Sorcerer. Who knows where we would be now if they would have gotten all of us?"

Castien groaned, shifting his legs. A strange heat nipped at his toes. He turned over, recognizing the soft, frozen substance beneath him to be snow. He grunted, trying to find his hands beneath him.

"He's awake," the second voice said.

Castien blinked a few times, realizing that Ilyana was speaking. Castien opened his eyes slowly, the gentle glow of Auris's moons greeting his tired eyes.

"It took him long enough…" Surge said.

"Give him a break, he's probably more shaken than the rest of us," Elric said.

Castien shook his head, snow falling off the sides of his hood. He blinked a few times, the heavy cover still blanketing his mind like a Mistveil's fog.

"Are you alright, Castien?" Ilyana asked, her face appearing over him.

Castien breathed, finding his heartbeat. "Yeah—I…" he mumbled, his voice sounding far away. "I think I'm alright. What happened?"

"The Blood Sorcerers knocked us out," Surge said.

Castien looked to the Voltarian, who was standing a short distance away. Ilyana pulled Castien to his feet, though Castien felt a little unsteady.

"They temporarily shut down our circulatory systems," Luka said from somewhere else. "Not long enough to do any damage, but for more than enough time to knock us unconscious."

"And then they got away," Surge added.

"But, thanks to me, we are all fine," Ilyana said, her voice even.

"Yeah, for once your cowardice actually saved us," Luka grumbled.

To Ilyana's credit, she held her tongue.

"So that's it then?" Arthion asked, pacing in the snow. "We found them, only to lose them again? What are we supposed to tell the King?"

"The truth," Elric said. "Arvendon is vulnerable right now. With all of us out of the city at the same time, there are very few powerful Summoners still within those walls. We need to return before something happens."

"Something is *already* happening," Luka growled. "The Blood

Sorcerers will return to Arvendon in what... five weeks? We need to keep pursuing them, even if it means leaving Arvendon vulnerable for a few more days."

"And how do you propose we follow them? The Cloudwalkers flew them off without leaving a trace," Ilyana said.

"I've tracked down targets before," Luka said. "Trust me, if you give me enough time, I'll find them. We know that they were heading north, and we know that they have operatives in Freyfall and Celes. I can start there."

"Someone still needs to return to Arvendon," Elric said.

"I suggest you go," Surge said. "And someone needs to warn Suchara about what's to come. Perhaps, if we get there quickly enough, we could find ourselves an ally against this rising coalition."

"I'm going with you," Saevi said to Surge. "I was raised there. I know my way around the city and the Dunes of Despair. I could help ensure that you get in and out safely."

"Why not just send Saevi alone?" Arthion asked.

"They won't take us seriously unless I'm there too," Surge said. "If they see that Arvendon's highest-ranking general was sent for this mission, then maybe they'll actually believe this insanity," Surge said.

Castien rubbed his head, looking up at the endless stars in the night sky above.

"It's settled then," Elric said. "Me, Arthion, Ilyana, and Castien return to Arvendon. Saevi and Surge warn Suchara, and Luka continues north." Elric looked around. "We have no time to waste."

Castien turned around, a sudden memory striking him. Castien blinked a few times, his head pounding. *Something about... a Crystal? Wait... did that happen?* Castien whirled, searching the area around him. A few yards ahead, toward one of the inclines, lay a depression in the snow.

"Ilyana," Castien called out. He took a few steps toward the small indenture, feeling the shroud of the mental fog lift.

"What? What is it?" Ilyana asked, approaching Castien from behind.

Castien spun. "What did you see?"

"Huh?" Ilyana's Elosian features tilted into a confused frown.

"Right before I was knocked unconscious, what did you see?" Castien asked again. Ilyana tilted her head, the confusion lifting slightly.

"You were being held by the Blood Sorcerers," Ilyana said. "Though I think they didn't realize that you were Stormless because they seemed to be trying to expose you to a Crystal or something," Ilyana said.

Castien cursed. He turned around, crouching near the snow's depression. "So it was real..." Castien muttered.

"What are you talking about?" Ilyana laid a hand on his shoulder.

Castien whirled around, feeling a sudden wave of aggression. "Did you shatter that Crystal?" Castien asked suddenly. Ilyana blinked a few times.

"I threw a dagger, yes," Ilyana said after a moment. "It crashed into the Crystal, but, by the time I reached you, the Blood Sorcerers were already on the run."

"*Izara's Shadow*," Castien whispered, plunging his hands into the freezing-cold snow.

The watery ice crunched against his gloved hands.

"Castien, what in Helionn's Sun are you doing?" Ilyana cried, pulling Castien back.

"Ilyana!" Castien grunted. He took a deep breath, continuing in a lower voice. "That wasn't a normal Crystal."

"It..." Ilyana trailed off. "Wait, what? What was it then?"

"It was a Starburner Crystal," Castien whispered. "And it was..." *Calling me. I could feel its power... I held it,* Castien almost said, but he stopped himself. What he was saying was impossible. It was utterly impossible that this had happened, and Castien knew that. Yet...

It didn't matter. Either way, he couldn't tell Ilyana—not yet, at least. Not until he had some sort of confirmation. Just as he reached this thought, his right hand collided with a sleek, solid form in the snow. Castien's fingers closed around the shard of the Crystal.

Ilyana grabbed his shoulders.

Castien spun, keeping his hand closed.

"Explain," Ilyana commanded.

Castien forced his mind blank by instinct. He stared at Ilyana, carefully keeping the finger-sized shard concealed. "I don't know," he said. It wasn't a lie—technically. "I don't know what happened. I think... I think that it might've been a trick of some sort." As Castien said this, the likelihood of it being the truth occurred to him. He had been completely under the control of the Blood Sorcerers, and he was barely conscious. And yet...

Ilyana scanned his eyes.

Castien kept his face empty, sorting through the possibility in his mind. *It couldn't have been real... could it?* Ilyana released him. Castien turned around, slipping the shard into his pocket.

"Come on," Ilyana said. She paused, turning back to Castien. "When we get back to Arvendon, I'm meeting with my contact. After that, you're going to help me find the spy, remember?" Ilyana slowly leaned away.

Castien nodded slightly, feeling his stomach turn.

Ilyana walked away without another word.

He turned around, watching as Luka started up the trail north. Surge and Saevi conversed quietly, likely discussing how to reach Suchara as quickly as possible. Arthion and Elric talked quietly as well.

Castien lowered his gaze. It was over. He was returning to Arvendon, and it would be like none of this had ever happened. He reached into his pocket, gripping the small, jagged Crystal. It was drained, the ethereal power within escaping upon its fracture. Yet a part of Castien could still feel it. A part of Castien still felt that rush of energy, that *pull*... that *power*...

He needed answers. He had been born Stormless—cursed to never possess the powers of Summoning. Yet here he was, memories of an unclaimed power fresh in his hazy mind. Castien slipped his hand out of his pocket, leaving the shard inside.

It hardly mattered now, even if it did leave him with questions. The Blood Sorcerer's existence was no longer just a possibility, but a proven fact. Castien's role in this journey was nullified, and the expedition was over. It was all over.

CHAPTER TWENTY-FIVE
THE CYFALI

Faelyn Titansworn stomped through the palace gates, sweat and dirt staining his once-perfect vest.

The guards stiffened at his approach.

Someone would have to be either dead or asleep to not notice his anger. And annoyance. And shock. He had just had an encounter with an *Illusomancer*. He shook his head, running a hand through his tangled golden hair. Faelyn continued forward, ignoring the nobles who gawked at his passage.

He passed through the massive marble doors, the guards nodding as he did so. Faelyn didn't bother nodding back. He strode through the hallways with as much dignity as he could muster.

When Faelyn finally reached the ballroom, he heard his father's voice. "... I told you that you were to..." His father trailed off as Faelyn stepped loudly onto the floor. With a wave, the King dismissed the guards he had been talking to—Faelyn's guards. "We'll discuss this later," he said. His father turned to the guards, who looked at Faelyn. "You've already let him escape your watch once tonight, and it seems he survived. I reckon that he will live if you retire to your chambers," his father said coldly, his amber eyes still on Faelyn.

The lead guard nodded, and turned back to his group, motioning for them to follow as they exited through the servants' door, leaving Faelyn alone in the chamber with his father.

"Father, I—" Faelyn started, stepping forward.

"Don't," his father growled.

Faelyn froze. His body trembled slightly, his face heating up. He looked down as his father approached. He knew this was coming. This was what he got for disobeying his father.

"Do you realize how worried I was about you?" his father whispered, taking Faelyn by the shoulders.

Faelyn remained silent.

"You know that you are *required*, not *requested*, to attend these parties, yet you decided that—despite knowing this—you couldn't be bothered to dedicate your whole night to this event, could you?" his father hissed.

"Father, I swear on Izara's Shadow that I—"

"You could have been killed!" his father roared. His father took a step back, turning around.

Faelyn frowned. Killed? That seemed a little extreme.

"I stayed within the city," Faelyn said, tilting his head. "And, even if I hadn't, it's not like I could've gotten far without you getting word from one of the guard posts."

His father stayed silent, rubbing his eyes. His red cloak dragged slightly as he turned, pacing.

"Listen, I get that you were worried but I don't think that I was in that much dang—" Faelyn started.

"You should know better," his father said quietly. "It would be one thing if you had left on any normal night, but to leave after what's happened…"

"And what has happened?" Faelyn asked, his voice rising. "What has happened? You've been keeping me in the dark since the very beginning of this whole affair with the Blood Sorcerer. Why should I be bothered with the risks if I don't even know what they are?"

"Because I said so!" His father spun.

"This is *exactly* why mother left you!" Faelyn shouted.

His father froze.

The words died as they left Faelyn's lips. Faelyn started, but closed his mouth. What he had said was true, his mother had left the King because of his stubborn arrogance... Because of the way he always believed that he, and he alone, was right *every single time* a conflict arose.

Faelyn stumbled back a bit, his heart racing.

His father lingered, half-lunging toward Faelyn. He recoiled, shaking his head and pacing once again, rubbing his beard with one hand.

"I only did it because I was trying to help," Faelyn said quietly. "I thought that I had found a spy among our ranks, and I thought to—"

"You don't have to be looking for spies, Faelyn," his father said, turning back to him. "You shouldn't have even gotten involved in this situation to begin with; I have it under control."

"Which is why you sent away our strongest Summoners to follow the Blood Sorcerer, leaving our city virtually defenseless solely because you were so terrified of that damned Sorcerer that you wanted to ensure that he didn't come back, right?" Faelyn snapped, his temper getting the better of him once again.

His father stilled, his eyes lowering. Faelyn felt his stomach drop, his muscles feeling shaky as his father took another step forward, once again resting a hand on Faelyn's shoulder.

"Faelyn, my boy," his father began, his eyes suddenly soft. "I know that you don't understand, because to you these stories about Blood Sorcerers and Lost Sects are all *just* stories, but, to me, they are far too real. Yes, I was frightened by what the Blood Sorcerer was able to do," his father admitted. "But not because I was frightened for what may become of myself, but for what may happen to my city... to my family... to *you*."

"So you thought that the best way to protect me was to keep me out of this?" Faelyn asked, meeting his father's gaze once again.

His father sighed, his eyes sagging.

But Faelyn didn't stop. "You can't keep me out of things forever, especially when they're this big. I'm a Scorcher, one of the most powerful in the city, right? So why would you try to keep me away from this?"

"Because you're my son." His father turned away once again. "I know how powerful you are, and I am very proud of you. But I already lost your mother, and that man..."

"The Lost Sects are dangerous, believe me. I understand," Faelyn finished.

His father glanced back, his amber eyes squinting in confusion. "Please explain."

Faelyn's face broke into a slight smile. "You didn't think that I was unsuccessful in pursuing the spy within the palace, did you? Would you like me to tell you where I've been?"

"Please," his father said.

Faelyn grinned, a strange warmth blossoming in his chest.

His father was looking at him differently. Not with shame, but instead something like... *pride*.

Faelyn lingered for a moment, savoring the feeling. "For a few days now I've suspected that one of your Whisperers was watching me," Faelyn started.

"Well, of course they've been watching you. I have instructed them to protect you."

"Right," Faelyn nodded. "But not like that. It was almost like he was *spying* on me, or something. So I started following him. Yet every time that I got close to him... strange things started happening. I would see him in two places at once, or I would watch him go in one direction only to find out that he had gone the opposite way. Yet, when I followed him tonight, he finally revealed himself."

"You're lucky you weren't hurt."

"I don't think that he has any intention of harming me, or this family," Faelyn said. "I think that he might be trying to help us. But there's something else." Faelyn spoke quickly. "I think that the reason he might've not gone directly to you is because he knew you wouldn't trust one of his kind."

"And what exactly is his *kind?*"

"He's an Illusomancer," Faelyn said.

His father stepped back, stunned. "Impossible."

"He knows what happened with you and the Blood Sorcerer and likely didn't want to overwhelm you by revealing that he too is a part of one of the Lost Sects."

"One of my own Whisperers... isn't a Whisperer at all," his father muttered, rubbing his beard once again. He took another step back, and started pacing.

"What? What is it?"

"That shouldn't be possible," his father said, continuing to pace. "Of my forty-four Whisperers, each one of them has been with us since childhood. They have trained with us and been raised within this very city."

"So?"

"So..." his father continued, turning back to Faelyn. "It's impossible for a person to be a part of two Sects, meaning that this person who is impersonating one of my Whisperers was never a Whisperer in the first place. Faelyn, you need to stay away from this Illusomancer."

"What?" Faelyn gaped. "You don't want me to find out what else he knows?"

"Faelyn, we have reason to believe that this Illusomancer has killed *and replaced* one of my Whisperers, either that or he has found a way into our ranks without anybody questioning him. He is *very* dangerous, even if we look past the fact that he is an Illusomancer."

"We can't just forget about—"

"I'm not forgetting about it," his father growled. "I will be on high alert, and I will be watching each of my Whisperers very carefully. If the imposter truly is an Illusomancer, there will be no use in trying to look for him, as he will simply continue to disguise himself with his abilities—which we know frighteningly little about."

Faelyn took a step back, looking to the side as he heard a group of servants shuffle in to clean up the ballroom.

His father turned, nodding as they passed. "You are to go to your room, and stay there for the rest of the night. Tomorrow, I will have you escorted to morning training with Idris, and then to the ballroom, for the party tomorrow evening," his father said, his voice solid. "You will not stray from this schedule, and you are to stay under the careful supervision of your guards. Tomorrow evening the Cyfali Ambassador arrives, as well as a member of the Jaskyan Council. You are instructed to ornament your vest with green to welcome their arrival."

"Father, you can't honestly expect me to—" Faelyn started but stopped.

There was no debating this. His father had made up his mind. "Never let the guards out of your sight. And, if you see this Illusomancer again, shout for help immediately, do you understand?"

"Yes, Father." Faelyn bowed his head, and his father stalked away. Faelyn turned, looking at the mostly empty room, watching absently as the servants swept and cleaned. That empty feeling in his stomach returned, along with the strange weakness in his muscles.

For one *brief* moment, his father had been proud of him. Yet that emotion had faded as quickly as it had come... There was no pride left for Faelyn. He had uncovered something that he had thought to be a *monumental* discovery, and his father had simply taken the information and sidelined him once again. This was *Faelyn's* project, and his father was taking it from him.

Faelyn looked up, feeling a red-hot rage building in his bones. It rose through his chest, and up into his throat, burning his lungs. He stormed out of the ballroom.

His father always underestimated him. He never got a say in what happened. And, despite his best efforts, all he ever did was disappoint. Even when thinking that he was saving the city, all he had done was bring his father a bit of news, and then get banished to his room.

Faelyn's guards followed him through the halls as he exited the chamber. He reached the door to his quarters before long, and pushed his way inside, barely even finding the stability to slip his key into the lock. He collapsed on his bed, slamming the iron door shut with a blast of flame, and allowed himself to drift off into the cold comfort of sleep.

"Focus!" Idris seethed.

Faelyn cursed, the arrow of flame dissipating as he dropped his hand, trembling.

"You want to help your kingdom?" Idris asked, pacing, his gloved hands folded behind his back. "Then focus."

"I'm trying!" Faelyn snapped, still kneeling on the ground. He panted, sweat beading on his brow.

"Then try harder," Idris said. He looked down on Faelyn with something like disappointment, then resumed pacing.

Faelyn grunted, jumping to his feet. Twisting his hands once again, Faelyn drew upon his Crystals, narrowing his eyes on the bullseye hung on the opposite wall of the training room. He closed his eyes, listening to the hum of the fire within his Crystals, pulling it, shaping it. He raised his fingers, feeling the flames creep through his arms and out to his wrists.

Images of the Illusomancer—Eithor—flashed in his mind. Ash swiveled in the shadows, twisting in his thoughts, bending and morphing until they formed that ghostly blue gaze once again.

Faelyn's eyes tore open, his fingers tensing as he snapped the rising flames into the shape of an arrow.

The small bolt of fire trembled, quivering in a phantom wind. Faelyn grunted, sweat dripping down his face.

Idris continued pacing.

The arrow began to drop.

"Focus!" Idris commanded.

Faelyn groaned, closing his eyes once again and tensing his fingers. He felt the flame. He *was* the flame. His hands shook, his body rattling with exhaustion as he pushed the arrow forward, slowly, reshaping it yet again. In order to propel it forward, he first had to shift its energy so that it would maintain its shape through the air.

His eyes cracked open, the bolt of flame in the air slowly drifting from his extended hand. He grunted again, his body burning, his mind threatening to break.

The arrow burst through the air, scorching through the target with pinpoint accuracy, nearly knocking the bullseye off the wall. Faelyn collapsed, his head throbbing, his body aching.

"Finally," Idris said, walking back over to the open tome that lay on the table in the corner of the room. "It's far from mastery, *Zephyr's Watch*, you hardly even managed it. But we're running out of time. Keep working on that in your spare time. But, for now, it's time we begin on the next Sect: Skin-Shapers."

"Helionn's Sun, give me a break," Faelyn cursed. "I've been here for nearly two hours now."

"And some battles continue for several days," Idris countered. "There is no time for rest. To become as powerful as you need to be, you must stretch your mind and push your body to its very limits."

"We have time," Faelyn said, rubbing his eyes as he sat up. "The Blood Sorcerer will not arrive for a little over four weeks, and, even then, that's assuming that he *will* arrive."

"If the Blood Sorcerers have returned, the Skin-Shapers could have done so as well." Idris strolled back to Faelyn.

And the Illusomancers, Faelyn thought.

"They are masters of deception, capable of reshaping their skin and bones to impersonate other humans or even make themselves into monsters. There could already be a Skin-Shaper within our very ranks, hiding in disguise, for all we know. We need to be ready for anything, and, if you listen to me, you will be." Idris extended a gloved hand.

Faelyn looked at it hesitantly, but took it. "Just don't expect much, I'm exhausted," Faelyn muttered, rising to his feet.

Idris flipped through a part of the book, ignoring Faelyn's comment. "Lorkah's Hand," Idris began, holding up the book to the light that hung in the center of the room. "It's a spell as old as Summoning itself. One that you should already be able to do—to some extent." Idris handed the book to Faelyn.

Faelyn took it, skimming the page.

It seemed simple: igniting one's hand on fire, then guiding the flames through the skin and bones of the person you touched.

"Gods, Idris... this is a horrific spell," Faelyn breathed.

"Indeed it is," Idris said. "It was created for the purpose of torturing informants and spies to get information out of them. It was only later that the Scorchers of Hirane discovered how effective it was against Skin-Shapers, so long as you were able to get close enough without getting killed." Idris fished around the supplies in the corner of the room, producing a straw mannequin. He walked over, replacing the bullseye with the mannequin, and then waved Faelyn over.

"Well, aren't you going to demonstrate?" Faelyn asked.

Idris only stared at him.

Faelyn sighed, raising his hand palm up. "Right. You wouldn't want to ruin your pretty gloves." Closing his eyes, Faelyn shoved aside the exhaustion that plagued his bones, reaching deep within his Crystals and drawing out a tendril of power, pushing it through his skin. He felt the heat rising. He pointed it toward his hand, conducting the simplest of spells and igniting the heat into a ball of flame in his palm.

"Very good," Idris said. "Now, condense it."

Faelyn tilted his head, cracking open his eyes. The fire burned steadily, casting dancing shadows of the mannequin on the wall behind it. Faelyn forced the ball of flame into something smaller, pushing it lower into his palm, but being careful to keep the energy consistent.

"Now..." Faelyn grunted, his teeth gritted. "Now what?" he managed to ask, trembling with fatigue.

"Place your hand on the mannequin and guide the fire through the skin and into the figure's body," Idris said, his pale eyes empty.

Raising his hand, Faelyn touched the mannequin, feeling the *hiss* of the straw as it burned. He would only have a few seconds before the whole thing burned, so he needed to be quick.

Faelyn roared, his head pounding. His heart beat with a deafening loudness, thundering through his ears and into his soul. His hand shook violently, and the fire exploded from it, coursing through the mannequin.

"Faelyn!" Idris shouted over the roar of the flame.

Faelyn didn't listen. He continued burning, pushing the flames back into the mannequin as they tried to escape, trapping them in an endless cycle as he burned the very fabric of the mannequin away, bit by bit. His power sung to him, the exhaustion fading from his bones, replaced by ecstasy. A feeling rose in his chest, spreading through his arms and legs and neck until...

Someone tackled him to the ground, and his fires were snuffed out.

Faelyn grunted, rolling beneath the weight of his attacker. He shouted, jumping out from the grip and bringing himself to his feet.

The room around him looked unfamiliar, though it appeared to be the same one that he was in not moments before.

Was that only... minutes ago? Faelyn thought.

Glancing to the pile of ash against the wall, Faelyn had his question answered, for the ash was still falling.

Idris coughed from his spot on the floor, pushing himself to his feet.

"What did you do that for?" Faelyn asked, throwing his hands up in frustration. "I was getting it!"

"You were losing yourself in your power." Idris coughed, brushing himself off.

"I felt... in control," Faelyn said, looking back to the ash. "I was doing it."

"You were on the verge of causing irreparable damage to yourself!" Idris shouted.

"I was not," Faelyn snapped.

"You were. I know." Idris's wrinkled face twisted in disgust. Idris slowly peeled off his gloves, revealing not the ashen-gray skin beneath. The skin was cracked and dead, almost looking inhuman.

Faelyn stumbled back. Niventia's Light... "What—" Faelyn trailed off. "Is that from *Breakdown*?"

Idris then pulled back his sleeves, revealing gray, flaky skin that trailed all the way up his forearms and to his elbows, where it slowly faded. "I lost myself in my power once," Idris said, his eyes dark. "I wasn't pulled out until too much time had already passed." Idris glanced at his ashen hands. "My hands began to burn away, turned to ash."

"But how..."

"Breakdown is not something to be ignored," Idris said, his voice like ice. "I know you've heard of it before, and I know that you've likely ignored it. You are a powerful Summoner, Faelyn, but your body can only take so much, and when you try to feed too much energy through it too quickly... your body itself begins to deteriorate."

"How come that sort of thing has never happened to me, then?" Faelyn asked, taking a step forward as Idris slipped his red gloves back on. "I've felt tired while Summoning before, and I've always assumed that that was just the onset of Breakdown."

"I know you have seen Luka—the Cryostalker—and others like him. Breakdown has damaged the bodies of countless Summoners, and even killed some," Idris said. "Advanced spells require more *mental* focus. Your mind gets more tired, which makes you more susceptible to losing control of yourself." Idris looked down, shaking his head. "I knew you weren't ready. This is my fault."

"What?" Faelyn gaped, his jaw dropping. "No, I can do it, watch."

"No," Idris snapped, grabbing Faelyn's hand as he raised it. "That's enough for today. We can pick up again tomorrow."

"Only if you tell me why I've never come that close to Breakdown before."

Idris's eyes flickered, then dropped. "You've likely never come so close to Breakdown because your powers are simply so strong that you have never neared your true limits. But I saw that look in your eye... You were determined—more determined than I've ever seen you. And, when a Summoner is using their powers on the basis of emotion, it is frighteningly easy to lose oneself in the heat of their power, and things get very dangerous, *very* fast." Idris looked away. "Now, you need to get ready to greet the Jaskyan Council Member soon. As I said, we will continue this later."

Faelyn shifted uncomfortably in his green and red vest. The color felt unnatural, and the fashion of it was borderline hideous. Though his servants had insisted that it looked good on him, Faelyn doubted such things. But he had no say in the matter, he was required to wear the vest, and so he did.

He sat beside his father in the smaller chair at the royal table. He had found himself in this position so many times... overlooking the ballroom, watching the nobles talk and gossip below while others danced to the infectious tunes of the small orchestra.

Servants milled about, serving drinks and food to anyone who was too lazy to make their way to one of the many tables that lined the corner of the room.

Whisperers lurked in the shadows, monitoring the thoughts of the guests.

Faelyn squinted, searching for Eithor, but they were too far away for him to make out any faces.

"I assembled all of my Whisperers in the throne room today," his father said quietly, cupping his hand around Faelyn's ear and leaning down from his luxurious throne. "I checked each one of them to their papers, and I fear that my theory about the Illusomancer using his powers to disguise himself may be true. Each of them matched their papers. So, unless he happened to get his hands on a set of Whisperer's robes, then one of them has been replaced by this Illusomancer."

Faelyn cursed. "What should we do?"

"The same thing we have been doing," his father whispered. "If you are correct about the Illusomancer being on our side, then we have no reason to be afraid. However, if you are incorrect, then the best we can do is simply remain vigilant. I have informed my officers of the incident between you and this man, as well as my most trusted guards. They will be watching the Whisperers to see if any stand out, though I worry that, if we have not caught this man already, then we may never do so."

Faelyn settled into his chair and took a sip of his water. He absently set the glass down on the long table before him.

The Illusomancer was likely here tonight as well. The question remained: What did he want?

"I must say, your majesty, the divebrisk is absolutely divine this evening. Where did you catch it?" the Jaskyan Council Member said, taking another bite of the roasted fish. The dark-skinned man hummed as he ate, signaling his satisfaction. He wore ceremonial forest-green robes, after the color of Cyfalion's flag.

"I'm glad you like it, Etenae Hallan." His father smiled, using the Council Member's official title and last name. "We caught the divebrisk in our very own bay, right here. Only the freshest for you and your people on this night of celebration!"

"I must say, I am pleasantly surprised," Hallan said, his accent thick. "We had been told that cooking is not one of your people's strengths, though you have proven those naysayers wrong."

"I'm glad to hear so." His father smiled, raising his glass.

Hallan's shaved head shimmered brightly in the radiant reflection of the massive chandelier.

His companions also wore green robes, though they were far less elaborate. They ate quietly, only occasionally making conversation with the nobles around them.

It was odd to see these men in Arvendon. It wasn't unusual for other nations to send ambassadors to reinforce their ties with Arvendon, as well as covertly gather information, yet it had been several years since Cyfali had been at the royal table.

Faelyn's gaze drifted to the dance floor once again. He scanned the spinning nobles, but couldn't find one particular tall, lanky young man. *Where is he?* Faelyn stood up, excusing himself and slipping behind the royal table, steadily walking toward the center of the ballroom. His muscles ached, and his head throbbed from the training earlier today, but he pushed the tiredness aside. He hadn't seen Reluraun since his encounter with Eithor, which was somewhat troubling.

He's always here, Faelyn thought, the music slowly fading as he focused on his vision. He looked to the Whisperers once again, watching as they lurked in the shadows.

Eithor was among them no doubt.

Could he have anything to do with Reluraun's absence? Faelyn thought with a start. But it was no use.

Eithor would undoubtedly be in disguise, and there would be no way of finding him—unless, of course, he wanted to be found.

Faelyn dodged a pair of dancers, making for the dessert table. He picked up a berry-flavored pastry, and leaned against one of the massive marble pillars. He took a bite, looking up at the grand chandelier and thinking about the power that hummed within. There had been a Wispwinds today—the only useless Tempest, for it fueled no Sect's Crystals.

Footsteps shuffled behind him.

Faelyn smiled sharply. *You're not as clever as I thought*, Faelyn thought to himself. He finished the pastry, and dusted his hands against each other before lowering them. Subtly, he started burning a Crystal. He tilted his head ever so slightly.

"I was wondering when you'd come," Faelyn whispered.

"What?" Reluraun asked, stepping out from behind the pillar.

Faelyn started, spinning around and looking his friend up and down. His eyes narrowed. "Where have you been?" Faelyn asked, stepping back a bit.

"I was late, I'm sorry," Reluraun said, rubbing his auburn hair and stepping forward. "Listen, I know it's been a few days since we've run into each other, but you don't have to act so surprised to see me." Reluraun paused, his thin lips twisting into a smile.

Faelyn fell forward, wrapping his friend in an embrace. He hadn't even realized that his emotions had been building for the past few days. Faelyn inhaled, holding his friend tight, breathing in his scent of pine and snow.

Reluraun hesitantly set his hands on his back, loosely returning the hug. "Okay, this is new," he muttered, continuing to let Faelyn hug him.

Faelyn pulled back after a moment, his face warm. He rubbed at his eyes, then smiled. "I'm sorry, I just—" Faelyn met those emerald eyes again. "I hadn't realized how worried I was about this."

"About what?" Reluraun asked, leaning casually against the pillar.

"You, our city, my family... everything," Faelyn said, shaking his head. "Sorry," he repeated. "A lot has happened since we last talked."

"You're telling me," Reluraun said, stepping away from the pillar and reaching for one of the pastries on the table. "I have news as well, but I haven't been able to catch you for the past few days."

Faelyn frowned. "What are you talking about? You know my schedule."

"I thought I did," Reluraun said, shrugging. "But every time I went to where you were supposed to be I couldn't find you."

Faelyn frowned once again. *Odd.* He hadn't changed his routine over the last few days.

"Anyway, I learned something very troubling," Reluraun said.

"Me too," Faelyn said. "Well, kind of. It's hard to explain."

"Well, mine isn't, so let me go first," Reluraun said. "Our officers think that there might be an imposter among our ranks, someone who replaced one of our soldiers, or even one of the Whisperers. More so, they think that he might be a Skin-Shaper."

"There is a spy, but he's not a Skin-Shaper," Faelyn said. "He's a Whisperer—or he's pretending to be one at least. I'm fairly certain that he's an Illusomancer."

This time it was Reluraun's turn to frown. "If he's not a Skin-Shaper, then how do you explain the green Crystal fragment that we found in the Whisperer's quarters?"

"The *what*?"

"Last night, in the Whisperers quarters," Reluraun explained. "Your father ordered an investigation into the Whisperers, and the only thing they came up with was a fragment of a broken Crystal. The Crystal was bright green."

"You're sure that it was green?"

"Positive, we can go look at it if you want. I know where it's being kept."

"Perhaps he is trying to mislead us?" Faelyn said. "Because, trust me, he's an Illusomancer."

"Are you sure?" Reluraun asked. "It wouldn't be that hard to make someone *think* that, especially if you were a Skin-Shaper." He paused. "Unless... unless there are *two* imposters."

"Rel, I was—"

Someone shouted across the room.

Faelyn spun, searching for the source of the commotion. He spotted a crowd gathering around the royal table on the upper landing.

"...He's been lying to us all along!" one of the nobles was shouting. "They've known for weeks and they still haven't told us a *damn thing*!"

"He's right." Another noble stood up.

"Our city is in danger, and he hasn't even thought to warn us!" another one shouted.

Faelyn rushed to the crowd, pushing his way through the cramped gathering. *What is going on?* he thought. *Is this something about the Cyfali?*

"The Ambassador must be in on it!" the first shouted. "The King is planning to flee to Cyfalion!"

A roar of shouts ensued. The crowd grew even more chaotic.

Faelyn grunted, shoving his way past another enraged noble. Countless odors assaulted his nose, no doubt a result of dozens of only somewhat clean men jostling against one another. The air started to feel thick.

Reluraun had gotten lost somewhere in the crowd behind him, but Faelyn couldn't turn back now. He needed to get to the center of this.

"My people, I assure you there is no deception at play here," the King said, seemingly trying to quell the anger. "Etenae Hallan and I are merely meeting to strengthen the bond between our nations."

More shouting followed as Faelyn continued pushing his way through the crowd. He was almost to the front, where a small collection of nobles was standing opposite the King's seat at the table.

Finally, Faelyn broke free of the crowd, stumbling out into the small opening ahead.

"What is the meaning of this?" Faelyn shouted, a sudden *command* flooding his veins.

One of the nobles turned to him—a man in blue with a bushy gray beard. "Your father has been lying to us," the man said. "Something happened in that throne room almost two weeks ago, and yet there has been no public address."

"I've heard rumors of a Blood Sorcerer," another noble announced.

Cries of panic sounded from the crowd.

"Me too," another one said.

"Is it true?" The bearded man turned around, facing the King. "Did you have an encounter with a Blood Sorcerer?"

"Please, calm yourselves," the King said. "As I have said, I have been entirely truthful with all of you."

"Then why are there rumors spreading about?" someone shouted.

"Rumors… are just *rumors*," the King said. "Everything is under control. I assure you there is—"

"Where is the General?" the bearded man shouted. "Where is the Cloudwalker? You have sent away our greatest Summoners to face this threat, yet you haven't even told your citizens of the danger we may face?"

"There is *no danger*!" the King roared.

Faelyn watched as his father seethed. He knew that look.

Smoke began to rise from the King's fingertips. "Everyone out!" the King boomed. "Leave Summerglass at once! Return to your homes and *stay there*!"

A heavy silence fell over the room. It lasted only a moment, for the shuffling of feet soon followed.

Faelyn was left standing at the front of the crowd, dumbfounded.

"You," the King said, pointing at the bearded man who had spoken to Faelyn. "You are coming with me," the King growled.

The man started. "Wait!" He looked around.

Guards began closing in around him.

"No! This isn't right! I'm trying to protect the people!" the man cried. "You can't do this!"

"Take him to the dungeons," the King growled. "And escort Etenae Hallan to his quarters." He turned away, starting for the back exit of the ballroom. "Faelyn, follow me."

Faelyn didn't move. This was wrong. All of this was *wrong*. The public was beginning to learn the truth, and his father's solution was to put any disruptors in the *dungeon*. Faelyn was unsure of how this should've been handled, but he knew that his father had made a mistake.

"Faelyn," his father started. *"With me."*

"No," Faelyn said.

The guards dragged the noble away, forcing him out of the room. They did their best to suppress his shouts, but Faelyn still heard.

A separate force of guards walked Hallan out, hurrying him out of the ballroom despite his protests.

"You can't do this," Faelyn said, now alone with his father save for the guards. "They know the truth now. You can't punish someone for accusing you of lying."

"I can," his father said. "And I must."

"But you did lie!" Faelyn exclaimed. "You've been lying this whole time!"

His father lowered his head and began walking toward Faelyn.

Faelyn recoiled a bit as his father approached.

His father stopped before him. "You still have so much to learn, Faelyn," the King said. He raised his eyes, meeting Faelyn's gaze. "You will be king one day, but until then you are to assume that my commands are *orders.*"

"I—" Faelyn started.

"I have told you to follow me and stay silent," his father interrupted. "Are you going to do so?"

Faelyn's breath caught. "Yes, sir." Faelyn lowered his head.

"Good," his father said. He turned away, starting toward the back exit once again.

Faelyn walked silently, following his father like a shadow. He had no choice but to obey, even if what his father was doing was *beyond* wrong. The people were going to find out the truth one way or another; arresting the man who brought it forward only worsened the King's image.

But it didn't matter. What was done was done. There would no doubt be a number of explanations due to Etenae Hallan, and even more to the people of Arvendon. It was all falling apart, and the expedition crew still hadn't even returned.

Faelyn needed to find Eithor again and figure out what he knew. For all Faelyn knew, Eithor could've been behind today's outbursts. For now, though, he had no choice but to follow his father, no matter how *wrong* it felt.

CHAPTER TWENTY-SIX
AMBITION

Asteros Silverglade looked up from his reading at the sound of footsteps.

Keries approached from the hallway beyond Erydon's library. "I've acquired the inscriptions you asked for, sir," Keries said, holding up a few yellowing papers.

"Thank you, Keries," Asteros said, taking the three sheets and looking through them quickly. Yes, it was all there.

Keries lingered.

"What is it?" Asteros asked, raising his eyes to meet the older Shadow-Swift's gaze.

"It's just that..." Keries trailed off, looking away. "Why did you ask for an inscription of the slab? I thought that we had agreed that it was of no use to us."

"And do you believe that, Keries?" Asteros asked.

Keries furrowed his brow, running a hand through his graying hair. "I suppose I don't, sir," Keries said after a moment. "Forgive me for intruding, I had no intention of keeping you." Keries turned away and made for the doorway, but Asteros spoke.

"It's quite alright, my friend," Asteros said, lowering the papers. "To answer your question, I simply wanted to see if there was anything significant hidden between the lines of this poem."

Keries turned back, eyeing the pair of Scorcher Crystals on the table before Asteros.

The bright Voltarian Crystals of the library hummed softly as they locked eyes.

"It's because of the mention of the Crystals, isn't it?" Keries asked. He once again scrunched his eyebrows in thought for a few moments. "What is it that you find so fascinating about them?"

Asteros paused. "I don't know," he sighed. "Something about them seems... strange."

"Well, forgive me for saying so, but I believe that that is simply the nature of them," Keries said hesitantly.

Asteros raised his eyes to the man once again, examining him. *How could a man so experienced, so powerful, be so submissive?*

"I suppose you are right," Asteros said. "Though I still feel the need to investigate them." A silence settled over the pair, the hum of the Voltarian Crystals once again dominating the small chamber. "Thank you for aiding the scholars as they conduct their work, Keries."

"Of course, it's my pleasure, sir," Keries said quickly, bowing slightly. "I am happy to assist in any way I can."

"Although there was something I wanted to talk to you about."

"Yes, sir?"

"It's about Lyseria," Asteros said. "I wanted to bring to your attention that I think she is a bit... out of place, in this whole situation."

"I couldn't agree more, sir," Keries said. "I think it's best that we keep her in Erydon for the next few months. She has no business being involved in matters such as this."

Asteros closed his eyes, taking a deep breath. "That's not quite what I meant, Keries," Asteros said. "If the rumors we heard about Freyfall's assault are true, and if my plan is eventually put into action, we will need all the help we can get."

"I—" Keries started, raising his eyes. "What are you saying, then?"

"I think that you need to prepare Lyseria for the Initiation."

"Absolutely not!" Keries roared.

Asteros jumped from his chair, instinctively slipping into a defensive stance and infusing his body with umbrakinetic energy.

Keries fell still, slipping from his half-lunge back into his standard, docile stance. "I apologize, sir," Keries said, lowering his eyes once again. "I had no intention of reacting as I did, I simply..." Keries sighed. "I do not think that she is ready."

"You do not need to put her through the process now, just some time in the near future," Asteros said. "I suggest that you start testing her in the Sand-Pit, and perhaps in a few months we can begin searching for the necessary targets."

"And I suggest that you let the poor girl be," Keries growled.

"Keries," Asteros said. "I was put in charge of this clan after Haldir's Descent, I suggest that you listen to my orders." The implication was clear—Asteros hoped—obey, or suffer the consequences.

Keries thought for a moment, holding Asteros's gaze.

"Fine," Keries said, turning away. "She will be ready. But I must be allowed to accompany her on the Initiation."

"Of course." Asteros nodded. "Provided that you interfere only if she is in true danger of being harmed. We need her to become independent. Do you understand?"

Keries turned back, his hollow eyes wavering. "I understand."

The wind was Lucien's. The sky was Lucien's. *Everything* was Lucien's. He soared through the air, diving between the raging clouds of the Storm Gale, basking in the eternal glory of flight, *searching...*

Thunder cracked to his left, foreshadowed by the blinding flash of lightning. Sleet pounded the mountainside, though Lucien's Transcendence protected him from even the slightest resistance.

And so he found himself trapped between two worlds. An observer of the terrible beauty of the Tempests of Auris, and a ghost in the dark planes of the Unbound—a feeling that no one other than the Six Shadow-Swifts of Auris would understand.

Lightning arced across his side, passing through his insubstantial form. Thunder clapped through the darkness. It was day, though within the clouds of the Storm Gale it may as well have been midnight.

The Shadow-Sand flasks of water clanged against his black armor—the water that he was carrying to Bareholde. Not that there was any shortage of water in the mountains, given the abundance of snow, but the water of Erydon was infused with strange minerals from the Unbound that seemed to better fuel the human body. What those minerals were, Lucien had no idea. That was just another of the many mysteries of their Ancestors.

Lucien dipped below the clouds, falling into the raging Tempest below. Chaos awaited him beneath the storm. Sleet fell endlessly, blinding Lucien though it could not touch him. Lightning pillaged the mounds of snow, shattering any boulders that dared be even the slightest bit detached from their mountains of origin.

This is what it feels like to be alive, Lucien thought. *This is the natural state of the world... the world that we are disrupting,* Lucien thought with a start. But no, this was about more than that. This was not about eliminating the Tempests; this was about restoring the Shadow-Swifts to their rightful place in the world. Lucien had been subtly whispering into Asteros's ear for the past several months, planting the seeds that had effectively grown into massive tapestries of greed. Shalheira had no idea, of course. He doubted that she would ever find out the details of Asteros's plan, save for the ones that were necessary for her to fulfill her role.

A Silver Sun... Violet wings...

Faelyn Titansworn was the key to everything, and Lucien's plan was likely already working. The young prince of Arvendon was said to be the most powerful Scorcher in generations—perhaps the most powerful Summoner on the continent—and manipulating him was at the very center of Asteros's plan.

Zestari Thala, the princess of Suchara, was his next target; finding a way into the heart of the Southern Empire of Asari seemed to begin with finding a way into her inner circle. Which, fortunately, didn't seem to be a terribly challenging thing to do. Zestari was quick to trust, according to their recent investigations, and she seemed to be *very* trusting in Helionn—the God of the Sun. Helionn was worshiped in almost all of the countries of Auris, though Asari prioritized his worship above all others. That was expected—given the large number of Blazedays in the region—but Lucien found it a bit strange nevertheless.

Whispers in the wind...

His mind drifted further, when something caught his eye. A shadow.

Ah, Lucien thought. *So it has been done.* Lucien slowed, bringing himself toward the large section of darkness on the ground far below. Growing closer, Lucien confirmed that it was what he had expected it to be.

It was precisely what he had been searching for, in fact. The closer he got, the wider his smile became.

It hadn't taken much to arrange for Faelyn Titansworn to be put in this part of The Highlands. A few forged letters had done the trick, which Lucien had taken care of personally. With little more than a few days of planning and a few weeks of waiting, he had ensured that Faelyn would come face to face with a squadron of Utryans. And the small area of scorched rock, void of all snow, was proof that Lucien had succeeded.

Lucien lowered himself to the ground, finding the singed corpses scattered all around the blackened ground.

The captain would be bearing a small stone tablet with the names of the soldiers in the squadron that Faelyn had presumably wiped out. But, truthfully, it didn't matter if it was Faelyn who had done this. The remains were ruined enough that no one could tell who was who.

Picking through the burned bodies, Lucien found the small tablet of stone. There appeared to have been almost two dozen soldiers in this squadron, but there was still enough room at the bottom of the stone; stone was used in place of paper to ensure that the list wasn't destroyed by the Tempests.

He readied his shortsword, and prepared his hands, recalling the names that he had memorized from the master list that he had acquired a few days before. One might consider him lucky that one of the scholars did end up having children in the army. But sending one's sons off to war was a common practice in Freyfallion culture, and Lucien was simply using that to his advantage.

Eithor's children were not truly a part of this squadron, but, once Lucien was through, it would appear as though they had been. Lucien would simply bring the tablet to Eithor—who had no way of communicating with his sons while he was with the Shadow-Swifts —and let grief take care of the rest. Eithor was a wise scholar, and his passion would be a valuable tool.

He had thought about simply exposing Eithor to the Stone, and thus allowing *her* to take almost complete control of his mind, but it seemed to be more trouble than it was worth.

Lucien looked back to the slab, and began.

Keries Nightbloom stood in the Sand-Pit, Lyseria at his side.

"What are we doing down here?" Lyseria asked. Keries closed his eyes, taking a deep breath. *Alvaerelle...*

"We are here to hone your skills, young master," Keries said softly, kneeling beside the girl. "You are to complete your Initiation as soon as we are able to find a squadron with both a Scorcher and a Cryostalker, and I need you to be ready."

Lyseria fell silent, her bright blue eyes growing distant as she stared into the sand.

"What do you know of the Initiation?" Keries asked.

"I know that Malik has done it," Lyseria said. "And all of you. I know that it has something to do with Shadow-Sand, and forging a weapon."

"Very good," Keries said, patting the young girl on the back. "The Initiation is a tradition that has been carried on by each generation of Shadow-Swifts since before even the Vanishing. It is how you will earn your very own weapons." The sickness grumbled, the void calling him. He pulled himself back to Auris, ignoring the distance he couldn't help but feel.

"How does it work?" she asked.

"Well," Keries started, sitting down at the edge of the pit. "First, we locate an Utryan patrol unit with the necessary Summoners: a Scorcher and a Cryostalker; in most cases, they will be only lesser Summoners... Master Summoners are far too valuable to send on everyday patrols."

Lyseria nodded softly as they sat, staring into the strange sands.

"Then," Keries continued, "you will ambush the team—while I watch, well within helping distance—and you will kill them."

Lyseria flinched slightly at this. "Kill them?" she asked.

Lyseria had never killed a man, Keries was all but certain of that.

"Yes, I'm afraid so," Keries said. "But fear not, young one, for it is in our nature to kill." His heart ached as he spoke, but he pushed on. Asteros had commanded him to prepare Lyseria, and, though she was far from ready, Keries had no choice but to obey. "Once you kill both Summoners, you will gather their Crystals and bring them back to Erydon. When you arrive, the others will have the molds prepared, and you will be given your choice of weapons.

"You will use a large amount of Shadow-Sand, and will expose it to the Scorcher Crystals. By breaking the Crystals, you will release energy into the air, which will be absorbed by the sand, melting it," Keries explained. "You will then pour the Shadow-Sand into the molds of your choice, and, by shattering Cryostalker Crystals, you will freeze them into shape, turning them into a substance comparable to steel."

"Is that what your sword is made from?" Lyseria asked, pointing to the sheath that lay across Keries's back.

Keries nodded and drew the black blade, holding it out for Lyseria.

She nearly dropped it, startled by its apparent weight. But soon Keries could see the spark of fascination as she traced her hands along the smooth surface.

Keries stood, striding toward the wall of the cavern. Two daggers, among a half dozen other weapons, lined the nearest wall. Keries selected these daggers and turned back to Lyseria.

"You are small, young one," Keries said. "I would advise you use that to your advantage. You are quicker than most, and smaller, lighter weapons will benefit you."

Lyseria nodded, setting down Keries's blade with a loud clunk.

Keries handed her the daggers, which she slowly pulled out of their leather sheaths. They were made of Shadow-Sand, and would be hers temporarily, until she could forge her own.

"Now," Keries started, "step into the pit, let us begin."

Lyseria took a step downward, placing a foot in the black sand.

Keries drew upon the power within the Crystals hidden within his armor, awakening the sands.

Lyseria stepped back, startled as the sand began to rise.

"It's alright, it is only me," Keries said.

Lyseria nodded, her black hair shaking a bit as she moved her head.

The Shadow-Sand swirled, dancing around Lyseria as Keries shaped it to his will. He would create a simple target at first, one that moved slowly and predictably. The figure came into shape, its form becoming apparent as the sands settled. Keries waved a hand, a blade of sand materializing in the figure's hand.

"Go ahead," Keries nodded.

Lyseria turned back. Her innocent eyes flickered with hesitation. She was not ready.

She attacked anyway. She hurled herself at the sand-man, daggers stretched outward as she flew through the air. Lyseria crashed into the figure, daggers first, destroying it as she fell on top of it. She stabbed furiously, digging her blades into the sand in a rabid frenzy, even as the form that Keries had created melted into nothing.

"That's enough," Keries said.

Lyseria didn't hear him.

"That's enough!" Keries roared.

Lyseria froze, stumbling back a bit.

Keries stepped back, startled by his own voice. The sickness basked in ecstasy, writhing from its brief release. Keries lowered his head, furrowing his brow. Over one hundred years on this Gods-damned planet and he hadn't even learned to control his outbursts. Not entirely, at least.

"I apologize," Keries said. He raised his hands, summoning forth two sand-figures this time. "Try again." Keries focused, watching every step Lyseria took.

She led with her right foot, then brought her left forward. She dove for the closer target, though with a wave of his hand Keries had the mindless figure sidestep the attack.

Lyseria tumbled into the sand, daggers falling from her hand as she missed her target.

"Do not throw so much weight into your strikes," Keries instructed, allowing himself to slip into the proper mindset of a trainer. "If you are off balance, all it will take is one missed attack for the enemy to gain the upper hand."

Lyseria nodded slightly. She grunted and stood up. She tried again, this time more cautiously. Raising her right hand first, she dashed for the figure, bringing her left hand around in a sweeping motion as she did so.

At Keries's mental command, the figure sidestepped the attack once again, though this time Lyseria did not fall.

She turned, lunging for the figure. She made contact, only to collide with the other sand-man as she did so, for Keries had commanded it forward. She fell to the ground, grumbling.

"It's alright, Alvaerelle." Keries froze. *Lyseria. This is Lyseria. Alvaerelle is gone.* "Lyseria," Keries corrected. "It took me several years to gain the control I have now, and decades more to harness my emotions while I fought. It is alright."

Lyseria grumbled once again, turning to the targets. She swung, missing the one on the left as the one on the right hit her with a soft, sandy fist. She gasped, leaping back.

Niventia's Light, Keries thought. *She hardly even knows how to swing a blade.* He shouldn't have been surprised, given how young the poor girl was, yet even still... They would have a lot of work to do.

Lucien Shade stood before Eithor Vassellet, who drank quietly. He had yet to tell Eithor the lie. Lucien would tell him that his sons were dead, though they were in fact very much alive, but not yet. Instead, he opted to let Eithor tell him what *he* had found on the walls of Bareholde. It seemed that the Revenants had entered into a war with the other Sects, somehow trying to gain control of Auris, and starting the war as a result.

The Starburners had led the resistance, the majority of their army made up of Scorchers and Stonemasters. The Revenants had nearly taken control of Auris, it seemed. They had the Skin-Shapers, the Illusomancers, and the Whisperers on their side. The other Sects had been divided fairly evenly, though the Rune-Writers seemed to be scattered across both sides.

What struck him as curious was the fact that there was no mention of the Shadow-Swifts. Not even once was his own Sect mentioned. All of the others—even the forgotten Sects—were brought up at one time or another.

"Strange, isn't it?" Eithor asked.

Lucien blinked a few times. "Huh?" he asked, drawing his attention back to the elderly man.

Eithor sighed. "I said that it was strange how the Revenants were able to gain such control over Auris in such a short time, is it not?"

Lucien thought for a moment, stroking his sharp Elosian beard. "I suppose it is," he said after a moment. "Though with enough preparation, and proper timing, I suspect that taking control of Auris would not be so hard as one might think."

"What do you mean, my lord?" Eithor asked, raising a wrinkled eyebrow.

Lucien held the man's gaze. He would have to do this correctly, and carefully.

"Asteros and I have been planning something, as you know," Lucien said quietly. He raised his eyes to the other two scholars, who were quietly transcribing the writings at the far end of the room. The warm, stagnant air of the chamber muted Lucien's senses as he spoke.

"I suspected as much, given what our master said in Herqen a little while back," Eithor said, lowering his eyes. "Though the fact that you are reminding me now is intriguing."

"Ah," Lucien mused. "And you have every right to be intrigued. Our plan directly involves you, in fact."

Black clouds... Violet wings... Haze...

"Oh?" Eithor said, leaning back slightly.

"I suppose that to say 'directly' is a bit misleading," Lucien explained. "However, we have been looking for someone to fill a certain role for us, if you would be interested."

Eithor took another sip of water, glancing at the other scholars.

"Oh, you needn't worry, my friend. All three of you may play a part in this plan, should you wish. And, unlike what our friend Shalheira has done to maneuver you into aiding us here, I will not force you to help us."

"First, you had my attention," Eithor said. "Now you have my intrigue. What is it that you wish for me to do, my lord?"

"Well, I suppose I should start by saying..." Lucien feigned a pause. "Oh, I had almost forgotten to ask. Do you happen to have any relatives in the Freyfallion Army? I came across a young squadron the other day, and I only just now remembered to ask you."

"My two sons, Camden and Teryth, both are currently fighting for Freyfall," Eithor said. "Though neither has ever left the capital. I suspect that, due to their young age, they will not be faced with any real combat for at least another few years. Why do you ask? Have you received any news from them? I don't know how they would've been able to contact you... But they have always been very resourceful. Bright young fellows, they are. I like to think that they inherited their wisdom from me," Eithor rambled on.

Yet Lucien did not listen any longer. He heard no words, instead focusing on the love in Eithor's ice-blue eyes as he spoke. Pure, untainted love. This was a man who had raised his sons by hand. A man who had allowed them to follow their hearts and fight for their country, rather than becoming scholars like their father. This was a man who had loved his sons very much. And Lucien was about to tell him that they were dead, even though it was a lie.

"Eithor," Lucien interrupted. "I'm afraid I am going to have to stop you there."

Eithor looked up. The warmth in his eyes faded slowly as he brought himself back to reality. "I apologize, my lord," Eithor said, chuckling a bit. "It seems that I got carried away. I do hope that you can understand, for I have not seen my sons since they were put on duty over three years ago. I miss them terribly, and I—"

"Eithor," Lucien said firmly.

"I'm sorry, my lord," Eithor said, lowering his eyes.

"There's something that I want to show you," Lucien said, pulling back the chestplate of his armor. He reached in, producing the stone tablet within. Every captain in Utrya carried one. He had seen the Cyfali using small metal chips they called "Prowler-tags" that each soldier carried for identification. They were far more efficient than the stone tablets of the North, though it was simply the nature of Freyfall to be a few years behind its rivals in the field of warfare.

"What is this?" Eithor asked, gently taking the tablet from Lucien's outstretched hand. His eyes scanned it slowly. "This is a manifest, isn't it, for an Utryan patrol?"

"I found this among the remains of what appeared to be a small skirmish," Lucien said, his voice like gravel. "It seems that this particular patrol was paid a visit by Prince Faelyn Titansworn himself."

Eithor paled. "But—" he rasped. "But I—" His eyes lowered. Eithor paused, almost as if he were frozen. He raked his fingers over the stone, seeming to reach the final names.

Lucien waited.

And then Eithor screamed.

Tsarra and Soran hurried over, trying to comfort him. But he was too far gone. Lucien's plan had worked.

Even as Eithor crumbled to the ground, Lucien couldn't help but smile. Eithor's children were alive and well, but Eithor would have no way of learning that, at least not until it was too late.

Eithor would overcome the grief with time, and then... then all Lucien would have to do was give him a window to Faelyn.

And vengeance would do the rest.

Asteros Silverglade entered Shalheira's rooms quietly. He could sense her presence in the bed; awake, but only barely, it seemed. Asteros rounded the corner, laying eyes on the beautiful woman before him. She fell still, sensing his arrival.

"I know you're awake, Shal," Asteros said, closing his eyes. The darkness of his own eyelids nearly matched that of the room. The Crystals had been extinguished by Shalheira so that she could rest, and, though Asteros hadn't turned them back on, his enhanced vision allowed him to see her well enough. Maps lined the walls of the dark chamber, yet it was mostly empty other than that. Save for the twin daggers on her nightstand; she never let those out of her sight, even while she slept.

She had forged those daggers with her own two hands, just as Asteros had forged his swords. Yet there was something different about her attachment to the weapons... something unusual.

"I'm in no mood to talk, Asteros," Shalheira whispered.

Asteros nodded to himself, but did not move. "I know," he said, closing his eyes once again. "Which is exactly why I'm here." He took a step toward her bed, quietly shutting the door behind him.

"Asteros," Shalheira said, a bit more firmly this time.

Asteros did not stop. He took another step forward, blinking as he did so. Before he could open his eyes, he felt a cold glimmer of steel against his neck. *Zephyr's Watch, she is fast.*

He slowly opened his eyes, finding Shalheira standing before him, dagger raised to his throat. "I mean you no harm," Asteros said, raising his hands.

"Yet you ignore my wishes for you to leave," Shalheira said. Asteros stared into her amber eyes, drowning in their cold beauty. Even in her anger, she was beautiful.

"I only want to talk, darling," Asteros said, raising a hand to the dagger. He slowly turned it away from his throat, pushing it lightly with his finger.

Shalheira let him, her eyes following the blade.

"You need to tell me what happened," Asteros said. "You need to tell me what circumstances led to your arrival here, so that I can find a way to help you. Maybe...maybe after that we can finally focus on *us*."

Shalheira looked at him uncertainly, but he kept his eyes steady. He breathed in her intoxicating scent—that of the cold mountain air. It drove him wild.

His heart fluttered, his stomach plummeting, his head spinning.

Finally, her lips curved into that gorgeous smile of hers. He knew that he was grinning like a fool, though he couldn't stop.

He pulled her close, his hands searching her back hungrily as he brought his lips to hers. Once again, he found himself surprised at the softness of her touch.

Her lips grazed his, locking for only a moment. It was so brief that Asteros found himself wondering if it had even really happened.

He kissed her again as she brought her hands to his face. His hands trembled as his thoughts melted away. He dove into the kiss, leaving behind all fear, apprehension, and anxiety as he lost himself in her touch.

Lightning seemed to explode from his lips, radiating through his soul, shocking his heart back to life. The spark of love reignited once again, burning brightly in his heart. He wrapped his arms around her, pulling her toward the bed. She did not resist.

His stomach felt as if it had fallen from the stars. Her eyes looked like endless pools of warm honey, brewing in the toils of a stream of chocolate. Her skin softer than snow, her touch lighter than a feather, he found himself arriving at a very distinctive realization: He loved this woman.

He had known it before. He had always known. Yet he had not *understood*. Shalheira was not someone he wanted in his life, no. She was someone he wanted to *be* his life. He would give her everything.

No. He would give her *more*. He would not stop until there was nothing left to give.

Something should've been bothering him. Something about his past... Something that he had finally forgotten. A shadow that had been chasing him all his life, only to be burned away by the light of Shalheira's love. It was gone. His fears, his hopes, his dreams, his nightmares. Everything. Everything was gone. There was only her.

And that was enough. No... that was more than enough. It was all he would ever need. It was all anyone would ever need. Nothing would matter, not like this. Nothing would ever be the same.

She pulled back, taking a breath. In the second that his lips were apart from hers, he felt an eternity pass.

He felt the world turn time and time again. He felt the Tempests come and go. He felt the trees turn into stone.

And then she was back. She was back in all her eternal glory, wrapping her tongue around his as they collapsed on her bed. She was back.

Asteros wouldn't just love her. That wouldn't be enough. He would vanquish the Tempests, he would save the world. He would *change* the world. And he wouldn't stop until it was perfect. Until *she* thought it was perfect.

His heart burned like a star in the night, Helionn's own divine light sparkling within his soul. Niventia's path prodded him forward, Izara's shadow pushing him onward through Zephyr's circuit of existence. The six Gods of Auris watched as Asteros and Shalheira became one in the night. Time itself seemed to pause, the Earth holding its breath as their kiss dragged out, outliving the second, and then the moment, and then the hour. Asteros's soul burned brightly as he felt her finally give herself over to him. He kissed her, more passionately than he ever had before.

And, this time, she did not pull away.

Asteros Silverglade listened to the steady heartbeat of Shalheira atop his chest, watching the steady rise and fall of her breasts. His black eyes remained open, refusing to close, though he begged them to time and time again. Yet a part of him was thankful for the moment of clarity. It was rare that one found themselves in such a position as he was in at this very moment... Lying beneath the woman of his dreams, her heartbeat echoing his own, her breathing the silent rhythm of the night's love.

If he could freeze time, he would. If he could stay here forever, he would. And, for the moment, it almost felt as if he *could*. No one would miss him if he stayed in this bed forever. The scholars, the other Shadow-Swifts... they may wonder. But no one else. No one beyond these mountains knew a damn thing about what they had been doing for the last several months. No one would ever know. He and Shalheira had no responsibilities, nor did any of them. No reason to leave Erydon... no reason to leave this room. No reason to leave this bed. He could just stay. He could stay, and stay, and stay until hunger claimed his last breath.

And maybe he would. Maybe he would stay here until the end of his days. Maybe that was what he should have done. Maybe that was what he was meant to do.

But, alas, that was not what he did. He shifted under the covers, carefully moving her head so that it was laid to rest gently against the luxuriously soft pillows on which they slept. He did not know what pushed him from the bed. He did not know why he stood up. He didn't even know why he was walking toward the door, even now, as he did so.

Perhaps he would never know. Perhaps he never should.

Something forced him from the bed. Something beyond even the Shadow-Swifts. Something that he would never understand, something that he would never even think to question. Something that was beyond both reason and rhyme. Something beyond words. A simple... feeling. A feeling that drove him to do what he did next as well. A feeling that forced him to open the door quietly and slip into the hall beyond. A feeling that nudged him to overlook the steadily draining Crystal on the end table of Shalheira's room.

He closed the door and walked down the stone hallway and did not look back. He found himself in his rooms in an instant, slipping into his armor with nothing more than a thought.

The scholars would still be at Bareholde. They would still be awake, even at this hour of the night. They were determined; he liked that.

He would pay them a visit, learn what they had to teach. And he would never look back again.

He did not turn around as he made for the long corridor that led to Erydon's back entrance. He did not look back as he picked up his satchel of Crystals, stuffing them into the cracks of his armor in preparation for his flight.

He did not look back as he shot into the midnight sky moments later. Mists wrapped around him in the coldness of the night. The twin moons of Auris burned everlastingly above the horizon, forever out of reach, but well within sight.

He did not look back as he dove through the clouds, feeling the cold mountain air tear at his skin. He did not look back as he soared through the air, breathing in the very same scent that Shalheira bore. He never looked back.

Something drew him toward Bareholde, that much he knew. That was the singular detail that could've guided him to the truth, though it pervaded his consciousness like a Wisp in the wind. Something pulled him to Bareholde, which would push him further down the path that had been laid for him.

Had he remained in that bed, lying beneath the woman he loved, perhaps none of what lay ahead would ever come to be. Perhaps they would have married, perhaps they would have borne the most powerful children the world had ever seen, and perhaps they would have finally brought peace to the troubled shores of Auris.

But none would ever know. For, even now, none knew of his silent battle. None knew of the forces he fought, the forces he tried to resist as he was propelled through the night by a power that was not his own.

But they would know his name.

And then it became plain to him what had caused him to leave that bed. It was what had been driving him since the very beginning of this endeavor... It was the fuel to his fire: ambition.

Love was one thing, true. But *ambition*... Ambition was the greatest of life's passions.

His ambition surpassed even the strongest feelings of love. One could not both rule this cruel world and find love. A choice had to be made, and Asteros knew what he must choose. His plans called for a future in which romance had no place.

He could not afford distractions, and, somehow, he had always known this.

The world would know who it was who forever altered the Tempests, when he finally did that which he was meant to. They would know his name; of that he was certain. Love carried one's memory for a generation, perhaps two. But *ambition*... his ambition would immortalize him like nothing else.

What was done would forever and always be done. Even the powers of Revenants and Wayfinders could not alter that which had already passed. Even the Harbingers, in all their divine glory, would be unable to alter what he planned to do.

And so Asteros Silverglade flew. He flew toward Bareholde, where destiny called him like a whisper on the wind. He already knew that the Shadow-Swifts were far more closely related to the Revenants than they had previously believed, he could *feel* it. And, if the Revenants were truly responsible for the Vanishing—as Eithor had guessed—then it wasn't just ambition that drove Asteros, it was *fate*.

No matter the cost, he would vanquish the Tempests. He had vowed to learn the secrets of the Vanishing, and, armed with such knowledge, he vowed to change Auris forever.

CHAPTER TWENTY-SEVEN

INVESTIGATION

Faelyn was sitting in a chair in his father's royal chambers. A massive hearth burned before him, nearly blinding him. He drank in the fire's warmth, letting it fuel him. It had been several hours since the brief confrontation between a handful of nobles and the King.

The noble who had started it was still being held in the dungeon, though Faelyn's father was yet to pay him a visit.

"I just don't understand how it could've happened," his father said. "The Council has been careful."

"Even caution cannot prevent the inevitable," Idris said.

There were several officers in the room, and even some commanders of a higher rank. This issue was one that needed to be handled *now*, before it got worse. Etenae Hallan's presence at the dinner had been an unfortunate coincidence, for now the Cyfali Ambassador would likely have questions that he wanted answered.

Faelyn turned to the group. They watched silently, their expressions grave.

The extravagant room spread out around them. The carpet was a deep, royal red, and the walls were a beautiful white marble. Gold ornamented every corner and crevice of the room, and an intricate chandelier hung poised overhead. Behind him was the door to his parents' bedroom, and to the left was the door to their living quarters.

"You're going to need to give Hallan an explanation," Faelyn said.

"I agree with the Prince. The longer we wait to visit him, the stronger his suspicion will grow," one of the commanders said— General Falx was his name. Faelyn recognized him to be on the King's Council. A long scar ran down the left side of his tanned face, starting at his graying hair and trailing all the way to his crooked lips.

"I know," his father growled. "But now there is the matter of deciding what to tell him." His hair was disheveled, his face red.

Faelyn knew that look. "We might as well tell him the truth," Faelyn said. "Lying will only worsen the situation."

"Pallus said far too much," Idris said, naming the noble they had arrested. "Everyone knows the truth, Your Grace."

"No, they don't," the King said. "All they have right now is specu-lation, and until we confirm what happened they will never be certain."

"You can't keep hiding from your own people, Father," Faelyn said. "Free Pallus, make an official announcement, and clear the air with Hallan." Faelyn paused. "Some of what Pallus said was false, we need to ensure that the truth—and only the truth—is being spread."

A spark ignited within his father's eyes. "Unless..." his father started. "Unless we take inspiration from Pallus's accusations."

"What do you mean?" Falx asked, raising a crooked eyebrow.

"Pallus thought that Hallan was aware of the Blood Sorcerer," the King said. "And he thought that I was planning to flee to Cyfalion."

"You're not actually considering it, are you?" Faelyn started.

"No," his father said. "But what if Hallan stayed here, rather than returning home after the Solstice?"

"But why would he do that? Even if we told him about the Blood Sorcerer, it's unlikely that he would opt to stay in the city," Idris said.

"So we keep him here," his father said. "He came with only a dozen guards," his father continued. "If they try to resist, we move them to the dungeons, and lock Hallan in his rooms."

"But why?" Faelyn stood up. "What is the point of *imprisoning* a Jaskyan Council Member?"

"Because if Hallan doesn't return to Cyfalion, then Cyfalion will send a portion of their army to Arvendon," Falx explained, catching on. "They will rightfully assume Hallan has been captured and attempt to rescue him by force."

"And, if we time this correctly, the Blood Sorcerers will arrive at around the same time," Idris continued.

"And, with any luck, they would fight each other," the King finished. "The Blood Sorcerers sent an operative to our city to threaten us, who's to say that they didn't do the same with Cyfalion?"

Faelyn looked to Falx, then to Idris, and then to his father. "You aren't seriously considering this, are you?" Faelyn's voice rose. "This is outrageous! This is a *crime!*"

"If the Blood Sorcerers are real, we will not be able to stand their assault alone," his father said. "If we are correct in guessing that the Cyfali have been threatened as well, then the two forces will fight one another when they meet beyond our walls."

"And, if we're wrong, then they will unite forces and obliterate our city effortlessly!" Faelyn countered. "It's too risky, Father. It's not worth it."

"There is no harm in at least stalling Hallan for a few more days," Falx said. "Perhaps we try to keep him here for as long as we can, and, if the expedition crew affirms Velarus's authenticity upon their return, then we do what we must to force Hallan to stay."

"This is *wrong*," Faelyn said. "We cannot use an ambassador as a pawn in our own troubles." Faelyn could tell by looking at the other officers—who had been staying silent—that he was not alone in this sentiment.

"Oftentimes one must do something wrong for the sake of a

greater right," his father said. He looked around, nodding to himself. "Now, let us go visit Pallus."

Pallus grunted as he was thrown to the ground.

Faelyn stood quietly, arms folded behind his back. This man should've been freed, but he was being interrogated instead.

His father stepped forward, opening his hand. He pulled Pallus to his feet, holding him by his cloak.

"You have no idea what you've done, do you?" his father asked quietly.

Pallus stumbled to his feet, straightening his bushy beard. "You cannot keep the truth from your people, Your Majesty... Not as long as there is breath in my lungs."

"On your knees," a guard spat, knocking Pallus to the ground with the butt of his spear.

The King stepped forward, lowering himself to look in Pallus's eyes as the guards restrained the noble. "I welcome you into my home, allow you to dine at my table, and you repay me by calling me a *liar*?" the King roared.

Pallus stilled, scanning the King's face. "You think I would take this risk without reason? *Everyone* knows that you have been lying for almost two weeks now! It was only a matter of time before someone like me came forward and brought the truth to light."

The King slapped Pallus across the face.

Faelyn took a step forward, his hands flaring.

Strong arms held him back.

Faelyn spun, meeting Idris's cold eyes. Faelyn grunted, shrugging off Idris's grip, but remaining in his place. Faelyn tried to distract himself by looking at the darkened walls of the palace basement where they interrogated and imprisoned those that they captured; Arvendon's dark secret, these chambers were often referred to as.

Hidden from the rest of the city, only accessible through one hidden door... If one ever found themselves in this place, they were unlikely to ever leave.

"I don't know why you did this, but I will find out," the King whispered, lowering himself to Pallus's level once again.

Pallus leaned back, howling with laughter. "I didn't do anything," Pallus cackled. "But you... You've just assaulted one of your own people for *no reason*. And, besides, the Cyfali Ambassador heard what I said. Your secret is out, it's too late."

"You would be wise to stop concerning yourself with me," the King said, pacing around the man. "You will not be leaving this dungeon, I hope you know that."

Pallus looked up, his eyes widening. His face fell for the first time. "Zephyr's Watch, you're going to kill me, aren't you?"

"No," the King said. "We will keep you alive for now. You must live with the weight of your crimes—for a short time, at least."

"This is *murder*," Pallus cried. "You can't kill me for telling everyone what they already know!"

"Even if you are telling the truth, and you truly do know nothing of what you have caused," Falx started, stepping forward, "you and your friends might have just endangered our alliance with Cyfalion; that alone is enough to justify your imprisonment."

"Please," Pallus begged. "I have a family. I'll publicly take back what I said, just please don't kill me."

"Your fate is sealed, you might as well save your pride," Falx spat.

It was then that Faelyn realized something: They were serious about all of this. His father was truly going to have this man killed. His father was going to keep him imprisoned, and then kill him— and it was unlikely to be a quick death. Faelyn had to do something.

"Lord Pallus," Faelyn started. "It's time someone told you the truth: You are righ—"

Someone grabbed the back of Faelyn's neck. He flinched, something pricking his spine.

Before he knew what was happening, Faelyn was on the ground, frozen in place. He groaned, his muscles tingling. He looked up to see Falx stepping back, a glimmer of electricity vanishing in his hand as he closed it. *Voltarian*, Faelyn thought, his mind feeling suddenly empty.

"He'll be alright," Falx said, his voice like gravel. "I only stunned him. He'll be back to normal in a few minutes."

Faelyn tried to move, but his body didn't respond.

"Helionn's Sun, Falx, you could've hurt the boy!" Idris shouted.

"And, if I had not, the Prince would've only further spread this man's *lies*," Falx seethed. "Besides, sparking the spinal nerve only puts him out of commission for a bit, I've done it countless times."

"Yet you have assaulted a member of the royal family, Falx," Idris growled.

"And, if he hadn't, I would've done it myself," the King said.

Faelyn shifted his eyes, watching from his spot on the ground.

"We don't have time for your bickering," the King said. He waved his hand, kneeling beside Pallus.

"I swear to you," Pallus started, his voice shaking violently now. "I didn't mean to—"

"Not one more word," the King commanded. "You will remain in this cellar until I either have you released or executed."

Pallus opened his mouth to speak, but nothing came out.

Faelyn shifted again, slowly regaining control of his muscles.

"Someone help my son up," the King said, holding up his hand.

Idris knelt beside Faelyn, offering a gloved hand to help him up.

Faelyn took it, brushing the dirt off his soft vest as he stood. He knew that Pallus would be killed; there was no other option. If Faelyn's father wanted to keep pretending that he had been telling the truth, it would only be logical that Pallus would be executed for accusing the King of lying.

But perhaps there was something Faelyn could do. The cells were heavily guarded, and breaking one out of the dungeon was not easy... Unless, of course, one had the help of an Illusomancer.

Faelyn closed the door to his rooms, taking a deep breath.

Eithor would be able to help Faelyn break Pallus out of his cell. But could Eithor be trusted? True, he hadn't harmed Faelyn, but what if it was all a ruse? What if Eithor was building his trust just to betray him in the end?

Faelyn turned, his bare chest showing as he scanned his rooms. He had once found comfort here, and he still did. But it wasn't the same. Nothing was the same. Everything felt *wrong*.

A Blood Sorcerer threatening the city, an Illusomancer spying on Faelyn, a Skin-Shaper Crystal found in the palace, and now an innocent man was being held prisoner. The Solstice was frighteningly soon, and Faelyn knew that the ball would go on regardless.

He had to do something. He needed to change *something* about this cursed situation... And, if that meant he needed to trust Eithor for the time being, then he would do so.

Turning, something caught Faelyn's eye. He spun, his eyes settling on his small table up against the marble wall of the room. Faelyn took a step forward, cautiously. *Someone has been in my rooms,* Faelyn thought with a chill, his eyes slowly scanning the yellowing slip of paper on the table. He didn't have to look at the signature to know who it was from.

Fire King...

I'll see you soon.

-E

Faelyn Titansworn's eyes snapped open in cold darkness. His head ached; his body shivered. The slow dripping of an unseen water source returned his mind to some state of lucidity.

He was not in his bed.

This was not the same place he had fallen asleep.

He groaned, rubbing his head and sitting up in the damp chamber. He felt his chest, noting with some relief that his hands were not tied, and he was still in his night-wear. He prodded his sternum, searching for the Crystals that he normally kept hidden there while he slept.

"If you're looking for your Crystals, they are gone," a voice called out.

Faelyn squinted into the darkness, instinctively reaching for powers that were not there to lighten the room.

Footsteps sounded around him. The foreign paces thumped slowly, circling his head. Breathing followed soon thereafter, slow and controlled. Focused.

A lone snap sounded through the dark chamber.

Teal frost flickered. *The Illusomancer*, Faelyn thought with a curse. Yet he felt... something else. Almost a sense of fascination. He was in the presence of a myth, and, though this man was incredibly dangerous, Faelyn couldn't help but feel a bit awestruck.

The dripping continued, though the darkness deepened. Something moved to his right.

Faelyn's hand flashed out, and he once again instinctively called upon his powers—though he bore no Crystals.

Yet, shockingly, orange flames exploded from his outstretched hand, vaporizing the unseen assailant. Smoke chased the fading flames like shadows in sunlight, and darkness enveloped Faelyn once again.

"Go ahead," Eithor said, his voice seeming to speak directly into Faelyn's mind. "Try it."

Faelyn turned, though it had no effect, for he could see nothing in the pitch-black darkness. Yet he obeyed.

At his mental command, a small tendril of flame snaked down Faelyn's arm, manifesting into a bright orb in his palm.

"That's... impossible," Faelyn breathed, staring at the unexplainable fire in his hand. "Without Crystals I—"

"Power is not about the strength that one possesses, nor the resources they wield," Eithor said, stepping forward. His figure materialized as if from nothing, standing just inches away from Faelyn's flaming hand. "No... Power is simply an *illusion*. And control, authority, domination... These are all simply the ways by which we can measure how well one wields that illusion." Eithor's sagging face broke into a slight smile. His blue eyes reflected the fire in Faelyn's hand in an almost divine way.

"You're just making it look like I can use my powers, aren't you?" Faelyn asked.

Eithor winked.

"I need your help," Faelyn said, shifting out of his defensive stance.

"I assure you, Faelyn, we have much more important things to worry about than Pallus," Eithor said, tilting his head.

"More important than a falsely imprisoned noble?" Faelyn asked. He took a step forward, but Eithor remained still. Faelyn glanced down, noting that the floors appeared to be made of stone.

"I have come to you this evening bearing a warning and a bit of advice," Eithor said, pacing in the darkness.

In an instant, Faelyn's flame vanished, plunging the room into darkness once again. Slowly, things began to *change*.

Wood creaked, stones squealed as the room shifted. The wall behind him, one that he hadn't noticed, moved backward, as if sliding on unseen hinges. The shadow of a ceiling overhead stretched, its supporting pillars lengthening. And, finally, light appeared in the center of the chamber. A grand crystal chandelier ignited, its ever-lengthening chain continuing to grow as the ceiling rose. Pillars and supports creaked, struggling to maintain their form.

The room appeared to be a square—a small one—at first, though it was growing larger by the second.

The stone beneath Faelyn began to move, or it seemed to, for Faelyn remained perfectly in place. He stumbled a bit at the illusion, watching with awe as the stone changed to wood, and the floors of the room opened up in the center to form a marvelous fireplace. Windows lined the center of each of the four walls, moonlight shining through each one, creating an impossible sight.

Eithor materialized once again, blue-green frost sparkling in the air above the fireplace, forming the loose figure of a man. The elderly sorcerer floated to the ground, standing beside the fireplace. He waved his hand, a set of chairs appearing beside him. He sat down, beckoning Faelyn to do the same.

"That's… incredible," Faelyn gasped. The room finally settled, forming an unusually tall rectangular chamber that closed in on itself to form a pyramidal roof. The elongated supports looked sturdy as ever, and the two moons of Auris—now multiplied to eight— shined brightly on all sides.

"I thought you might appreciate the display," Eithor said softly, straightening his plain, dark gray robes. "Now, I would like to ask you something." Eithor waved his wrinkled hands once again. A table appeared beside Faelyn, looking almost more real than reality.

He turned his attention to the fire. Eithor watched with interest, his wrinkled face sparkling with delight in the dancing flames. Faelyn reached for the firepit and felt no heat.

"You are a wise one…" Eithor noted.

"How much of this is real?" Faelyn asked, looking upward toward the massive chandelier—a chandelier that looked strangely famil- iar… The grand entry hall, he realized.

"You are asking the wrong questions once again, my boy," Eithor rasped.

Faelyn frowned, turning back to the withered old man. "Power isn't about what you are capable of, it's about what others *think* you are capable of," Faelyn said, rephrasing Eithor's earlier words as understanding clicked into place.

"Illusions work the same way," Eithor affirmed. "It does not matter whether or not what I show you is real. What matters is whether you *believe* it is real."

"And do I?" Faelyn asked. "Do you think that I believe this is real?"

"I think that you don't know what to believe."

"I..." Faelyn trailed off. He was right. Faelyn tipped back his head, examining the impossibly tall ceiling once again. He then turned to each of the massive windows, staring out at the twin moons in each one. Lotius and Oria shone brightly, overlooking matching views of Arvendon's city-scape on each side. *One had to be real, didn't it?* Which would make the other three reflections...

"Do you think that the people of Arvendon fear your family?" Eithor asked.

Faelyn turned back. "If they didn't, they would have ripped control from our bloodline already," Faelyn said coldly.

"And, if they did, they wouldn't be breathing down your necks, threatening to do so." Eithor smiled. "And, of course... they wouldn't have publicly accused your father of lying."

Faelyn started. "So you were there that night," Faelyn whispered.

"Of course I was; not that it would've mattered. The whole city knows what happened." Eithor smiled once again. "Although I seem to be the only one who knows that it is unimportant."

"Unimportant?" Faelyn asked. "Our alliance with Cyfalion is jeopardized. Many would consider that to be something of interest, even if we have stayed out of conflict with the rest of Auris recently."

"Save for the skirmishes in The Highlands, might I add," Eithor said. Something flickered in the man's eyes. Something... strange. Something dangerous. "I heard that you aided in one of those fights yourself, is that correct?"

Faelyn flinched slightly at the razor-sharp tone. "I did," he said hesitantly. "My father wished to expose me to some low-risk combat. Combat in which I could kill a few irrelevant foreign Stormless soldiers while furthering my own confidence."

"Irrelevant," Eithor whispered, chewing on the word. His eyes grew distant. He spoke the word again, saying it as though it were the vilest of curses. "Interesting."

Faelyn recoiled, glancing back to the cup beside him. "You never told me why you brought me here," Faelyn said after a moment, running a hand through his long golden hair, which he now realized was damp.

"I do not plan to, young master," Eithor said, his composure returning. "I plan to *show* you. You need only to rise from your seat."

Faelyn hesitated.

"If I wanted to kill you, my prince, I would've already done so," Eithor said, narrowing his eyes. "I moved you from your bed, tucked away in the most secure quarters of the palace, and brought you here, where you would be subject to my whims until I deemed you worthy of release. Trust me, you needn't worry about assassination at this point."

Faelyn tilted his head, then nodded to himself. *Sound reasoning,* he thought. "Why do you take such an interest in me?" Faelyn asked, pausing.

"Because you are one of the few people in all of Etherus who dares question your father's handling of the Blood Sorcerer's arrival," Eithor said bluntly.

Faelyn flinched slightly. *That was unexpected.*

"You criticize my father for sending away our most powerful Summoners to chase a ghost of the past, when you may be called one yourself," Faelyn said. "I doubted that the Blood Sorcerers had truly returned, yet upon our meeting I cannot help but be drawn toward my father's reasoning."

"I never said that the Blood Sorcerer was not real," Eithor said. "My reasoning for disagreeing with your father is the same as yours. Regardless of the threat we face, it is *never* a good idea to send away as many powerful Summoners as he did."

"Because we now leave ourselves vulnerable to invasion, whether the threat they pursue is real or not," Faelyn continued for him. "Yes, I understand. Now are you going to help me or not?"

"You wish for me to rescue Pallus. I aim to show you that he is unimportant," Eithor said. "Which is exactly the point of this little charade."

"Pallus's words may have harmed my father's image, but Pallus only spoke the truth," Faelyn said. "They are going to kill him; you need to help me rescue him."

"You are not listening to me, Faelyn. You do not know what is coming," Eithor said.

"Then why don't you *tell me*?" Faelyn growled. "Enough of these games. If my city is in danger, then I deserve to know."

"I have been waiting on your action, Faelyn," Eithor reminded him. "You want to know the truth, all you need to do is take a stand."

Faelyn grumbled and stood up. What good did waiting any longer do? Eithor was going to get his way eventually.

Turquoise frost flashed, covering the room, smothering the illusory fireplace and blocking out the impossible windows.

The chair beneath Faelyn was swept away by unseen hands, and he found himself pushed face down in the cold stone once again. Yet, this time, something was different.

Rain fell violently beyond the chamber, accompanied by the ever-present dripping of the loose pipe. Thunder flashed above.

A Storm Gale, Faelyn thought, pushing himself to his knees. Light flared around him, or *below* him. He appeared to be on a balcony of some sort, a very small one.

No... not a balcony. *A spire*, he realized, noting the coned roof overhead. He was standing atop one of the spires of Summerglass Palace. Something was happening below. Smoke rose around the spire, choking the air, smothering even the ceaseless rain.

Darkness undulated beyond, thunder and lightning rolling through the midnight clouds overhead. Storm Gales at night were uncommon, but not unheard of. Faelyn pushed himself to his feet, checking for his Crystals once again. Still gone. It was then that he raised his eyes.

Arvendon burned. Thousands of soldiers poured through the Western Gate, which had been smashed to pieces by violent lightning strikes. Runes lay broken beside the fallen wall, subjecting any who were unfortunate enough to stand in their vicinity to the full brunt of the Storm Gale.

Soldiers of red and orange swarmed the invading force, pushing back with blasts of fire and steel. Crystals shattered in massive numbers, releasing massive explosions across the battlefield. No, not a battlefield. *My home.*

Lightning arced through the invading force, shattering bones, dividing squadrons, and incinerating captains. White energy exploded from the same figure—lightning once again. Faelyn squinted, recognizing the burly figure. *Surge.*

His eyes drifted back to the crippled wall, where soldiers of purple, black, blue, and green hungrily climbed over the fallen rubble. Faelyn counted the colors once again. *Four colors... Suchara, Freyfall, Celes, Cyfalion.* It seemed that all five armies of Auris were involved in this singular assault, counting Arvendon's own. Five nations, five armies... one battle.

Helionn's Sun, Faelyn cursed. *What had happened here?*

And yet despite it all, *all of it*, he found his eyes drawn to one specific detail. Arvendon was burning. Rain was pouring down in otherworldly amounts, no longer dampened by the Runes. Yet still Arvendon burned.

Golden flames exploded from the Northern Wall, incinerating legions of invading soldiers, igniting even more of the city.

Houses burned, and those that did not had already been reduced to ashes.

Cannons boomed in the east, firing from distant shapes in the sea. *Ships*, Faelyn realized. Death reigned supreme, soldiers dying in every corner of Faelyn's vision as he choked on the phantom smoke. Faelyn felt his eyes guide themselves back to the Northern

Wall, where the golden flames exploded once again. It occurred to him now that they were coming from a person. Someone... familiar.

He squinted through the rain, through the smoke, through the darkness. A figure in gold and white stood alone on the wall. He shaped the massive inferno before him, guiding the fires toward the endless stream of invaders. It was a technique he recognized, a technique that Faelyn himself had used many times: unleashing a blast of flame so powerful that it was all but uncontrollable, then subtly nudging it toward one's opponents, rather than using smaller, more calculated strikes.

It was a technique that he had learned from his father. *Father...* he thought, glancing at the figure once again. He incinerated another squadron, shattering the ranks of a Celesian legion.

Shards of ice exploded through the wall of flame, crashing into the palace, beating back the fire. But Faelyn's father held strong. King Avenos rallied his powers, pushing back against the Cryostalkers.

"What... What is this place?" Faelyn asked, stepping back. Wind howled in the stormy night; the sea crashed against the distant cliffs below. And, suddenly, it muted. Sound vanished from the scene, leaving only an eerie silence coupled with the soft dripping of the invisible pipe. The battle continued in silence as Faelyn felt a sudden presence come over him.

"This is the future, Faelyn Titansworn," Eithor said, a shadow materializing behind him. Eithor raised a hand, and the scene froze.

Swords halted in midair, flames stilled, their eternal, primal fury contained by one motion of Eithor's hand. Surge's lightning hung in the air like stars in the night, burning through the ranks of Freyfallion soldiers who had frozen as well. Even the rain itself had ceased, its droplets stuck between the land and the sky.

"This... is *your* future," Eithor said.

"What?" Faelyn breathed, stepping back once again. He brought a hand to his chest, the air becoming heavy.

"This—or something like it—is what will happen, in no more

than a few months' time," Eithor said, his shadow lowering before Faelyn.

Breathing suddenly became very, very hard. Faelyn's limbs felt weak, the gravity of the situation finally crashing down upon him. Arvendon. His home... under attack.

"It's just an illusion," Faelyn whispered, closing his eyes.

Eithor floated closer to him. "An illusion indeed," Eithor said, setting a foot on the ground. "But one without truth? Not at all..."

"You're an Illusomancer, not a Wayfinder!" Faelyn challenged, his eyes snapping open. Anger, red-hot rage, boiled beneath Faelyn's skin. *How dare he show me such a thing? How dare he say such things about Arvendon?*

"About that you are correct," Eithor said, raising his hands as if to surrender himself. "Though just because one does not possess the divine power of foresight does not mean that one is incapable of accurately predicting that which has not yet come to pass."

Faelyn grunted.

"Faelyn, I wish only to help you. Though it is rather challenging to provide guidance when you are so hesitant to my teachings."

"And do you only want to help?" Faelyn growled, advancing. "If you truly wanted to help me, then you would accompany me to my father's chambers and show him what you are showing me!" Faelyn breathed.

"Ah," Eithor smiled softly, his crinkled features pressing together. "You have mistaken the future that I have shown you, dear boy. For, while this is what will happen if your father is swayed to our beliefs, what will happen if he does not change his mind is much, *much* worse."

Faelyn paused, scanning the man's withered face, then laughed. "I don't even know why I listen to you," Faelyn snorted. "If you actually did trust me, then you would be here right now!" Faelyn charged at the Illusomancer.

Eithor did not flinch.

Just as Faelyn suspected, he passed through the man's body with nothing more than a flicker of blue-green frost. Faelyn spun, realizing that he was now standing on what appeared to be nothing, for he had run off of the spire. Yet, of course it wasn't real. He found himself levitating on solid ground.

Eithor turned slowly, a shadow passing over his face. "You will listen," Eithor mumbled to himself. "They will always listen... You need only show them the truth, and they will listen."

"What do you mean?" Faelyn stepped forward, standing on the invisible stones.

Eithor's eyes snapped to Faelyn's, their hollowed, ice-blue forms glowering with rage. "You will listen," Eithor repeated. "I have shown you the truth, yet you have ignored me. You have called my statements lies, and you have deemed my powers to be false. Yet you will believe."

Faelyn advanced once again, instinctively reaching for powers that were not there.

"You are far more powerful than your parents believe you to be, Faelyn."

"What are you talking about?" Faelyn asked, raising a hand against the frozen smoke between them.

"On the night of the Solstice, the palace bells will ring," Eithor said quietly. "You have been warned."

Bells? As in the emergency bells of the palace? Faelyn frowned, running a hand through his wet hair once again. The palace bells were reserved only for dire emergencies. One ring meant that the palace was to be evacuated. Two meant that the palace would be locked down, while third and fourth chimes signified that someone in the Royal Family had been harmed.

"When you believe... find me," Eithor said. "Until then, I shall step back... and observe."

And then the world fell.

Faelyn slipped to the ground as the palace rose around him, the illusory battlefield below rapidly approaching. He crashed to the ground, landing far harder than he should have, though he managed to dodge the other spires. *Illusory spires*, Faelyn reminded himself. He opened his eyes slowly, hearing only the periodic dripping of the pipe as he was greeted by darkness once again.

The illusion was gone. Eithor had vanished once again... and what had he said about the Solstice? Faelyn shook his head, cursing the strange sorcerer. That entire pointless conversation, and he was no closer to aiding Pallus. Though, if Eithor was to be believed, then he had much bigger things to worry about.

He pushed himself to his feet, feeling around in the darkness for the wall that he knew was behind him. Faelyn shivered in the cold, wet chamber, feeling for a door along the wall. He found it.

Pushing it open, he found himself standing in the stark light of the twin moons overhead, the pale gray of Lotius and the turquoise of Oria casting Arvendon in the ethereal hue that Faelyn had come to know.

He was near the docks. Waves crashed in the distance, and ships creaked nearby. Yes... this was real. Everything was real now. The illusion was gone, stolen from the night like stars at dawn, leaving Faelyn with only the cold, bitter reality that lay ahead.

CHAPTER TWENTY-EIGHT

INITIATION

Ten months ago...

Keries Nightbloom stood silently on the mountain ridge.

Lyseria crouched beside him. The snow fell gently—a rare occasion for a Highland Frostfall. It seemed almost as if the Tempests themselves were pausing to witness this very moment.

The Utryan patrol would be arriving soon, passing through this small gulley, following the forged orders of their superiors, who Lucien had impersonated as he gave out the team's instructions. Lucien was a damn good spy and an even better killer. Keries still found himself reluctant to trust someone with so much power, though he supposed that Asteros wasn't too far behind Lucien. Keries had no qualms with trusting Asteros, though perhaps his loyalty blinded him.

One of Niventia's Ideals preached that any who led did so because they were meant to, meaning that Asteros was meant to be the leader of Erydon. Something had changed within him—something important. Ever since uncovering the secrets of the Vanishing, he had not been the same, and Keries had yet to decide if the changes he observed were for the better or for the worse.

Asteros had been growing increasingly close with Shalheira in the past few months... The others knew what was going on between the pair, though they pretended as if they did not. All save for Lucien, of course, who thrived on the little jabs and jokes he shot toward them any chance he got. Keries even recalled a time when Shalheira and Asteros had spent nearly two days alone in Asteros's chambers, pouring over the strange poem they had found in the cavern of Bareholde.

Bareholde had proven to be far more useful to their cause than Herqen, for it had not only drawn the link between the Revenants and the Shadow-Swifts, but it had unscrupulously pointed them toward Epirac—another mountain which evidently held the missing pieces to the mystery of the Vanishing.

The Stonemaster who had created Bareholde had claimed that Epirac was the headquarters of the Revenants, and the Revenants— along with a few rogue Rune-Writers—had done whatever it was that stole the Tempests from the skies within that cavern.

Unfortunately, Epirac had proven to be far more challenging to break into than Bareholde and Herqen. Tsarra had explained that the Runes had been made with three or four times the Crystal-power that had been used to make the other locks. She even went so far as to claim that it was possible that the Harbinger of the Rune-Writers forged the lock himself.

Soran had simplified her explanation by simply saying that they would not be able to get in by tripping the Stone-Readers, as there was no telling how many of them there were.

Hence why Asteros and Shalheira had begun trying to unravel the secrets hidden within the Wayfinder's words.

Lucien held strong to the theory that there was nothing to be found in the lost Sect's predictions, but Asteros felt otherwise. It simply seemed to stand out a *little* too much from the rest of Bareholde's information, almost as if the Stonemasters who had forged the cavern knew that the Wayfinder's predictions were significant somehow.

"It won't be long now," Lyseria whispered, pulling Keries from his thoughts.

The sickness yanked back, reeling him into a state of only half lucidity, as it always did. His face hung naturally in a frown. He shook his head, trying to force the mind-fog to dissipate, but it did not. It never did.

Niventia's Trials, he thought, his eyebrows knitting together as he rubbed his face. *This is all part of her plan for us... for me.* Keries sighed, squinting through the falling snow as he continued watching for the patrol. *One day I will wake up, and the sickness will be gone. One day it will all make sense.*

The bitter wind nipped at his exposed nose. He remained partially shrouded in the Unbound, though Keries kept more of his physical self on Auris than he usually did. If anything happened to Lyseria, he needed to be ready.

She watched quietly beside him, bright blue eyes focused.

Keries had made a warrior out of her—against his wishes. Over the last six months, she had developed a speed and accuracy that even Malik seemed to envy. *But would it be enough?* Keries shook his head. It wasn't that she lacked skill, but simply experience, for she had not killed a single man.

Another innocent young girl who they were turning into a killer. Keries shook his head. Another pure child of Niventia being tainted by Izara's hand.

Life and death. Light and dark. Ebb and flow. Rhyme and reason. Everything had its opposite, everything was necessary. Except for the sickness—that was one thing he could not explain. He knew that others existed on Auris with his condition: the unexplainable, stubborn sense of despair that dominated the minds of a few troubled souls; yet it seemed that none could find either a source or a cure.

"Remember your training, Ly," Keries said, his snow-crested beard blowing in the wind. "Your speed is your greatest weapon, second only to the element of surprise." Keries paused, then spoke again after a moment. "Do you remember the places to strike a man?"

Lyseria turned her borrowed daggers in her small hands. "The throat, the eyes, and between the legs," she said. "Target those to disable the target... or move on to the tendons in the wrist and ankles if those areas are covered."

"And the Summoners?" Keries asked, tilting his head.

"Kill them first," Lyseria said. "If, by some chance, they survive, separate them from their Crystals with umbrakinesis."

Keries nodded, though he felt no pride as she perfectly recited the killing techniques that he himself had taught her. *It's for her safety*, he told himself, though he knew it was only partially true.

"Very good," Keries mumbled halfheartedly.

Something moved in the snow down below.

Lyseria tensed, her grip on the daggers tightening.

"Easy," Keries said softly. "Nervousness will do you no good against Summoners. You are a Shadow-Swift. *They* fear *you*. When they see your armor, they will be terrified. Use that to your advantage. Don't let them intimidate you. Show them weakness and they will exploit it."

Lyseria nodded, but her posture did not soften. Her young body tightened with anticipation. "Is it them?"

Keries squinted through the Frostfall. He spotted at least a dozen figures walking through the passage, following Lucien's forged orders. He glanced to the sky, noting the approximate position of the sun. It would make sense. The time was right. The location was right. It was them.

He closed his eyes. "Yes."

Day breaks at the dawn of Genesis.

Fifteen Harbingers descended from beyond, each bearing the anomalous powers of Summoning.

The world they called "Auris" hiding between the planes of life through Synthesis.

The earth was shaped and built by powers still running.

Crystals grow, born of the strength of storms.

The Harbingers retreat, leaving sepulchers of divinity.

Unlocked only by the blood of the dead and the stars, leaving only the sacred to transform.

The planes are closed now, locking our world in the depths of infinity.

Asteros Silverglade looked up from the collection of papers before him. Something about it still didn't make sense. Asteros's workspace was a mess of paper scraps and fragmented stanzas. He had ordered the Wayfinder's words transcribed several months ago, and was still yet to make any progress in piecing together whatever mysteries were held within.

Epirac: the epicenter of the Vanishing. Whatever had happened to the Tempests had started—and ended—there. And they could not get inside.

It seemed that a rogue band of Rune-Writers along with the Revenants helped them forge a Rune-Lock that even the Freyfallion scholars could not penetrate. Even Haldir's key had failed to open it, for the small device apparently had a limit to the number of Runes it could disable simultaneously.

The Stone-Readers were not only too hard to find, but they were apparently forged of an entirely *different* base Rune system from those of the other caverns. Eithor suspected that it may be possible to open the lock without finding the true "key" to fit the lock. Yet to do so would require some part of said key, meaning that they would at the very least have to narrow down what the lock was seeking in terms of a response. Asteros found himself running over the words once again.

"Perhaps..." Asteros whispered to himself as he moved to another line. Despite months of being stumped, he found himself with shockingly little time to put toward these writings. The Utryans had stopped pushing back against the Shadow-Swifts, but that hadn't stopped the Arvendi from moving against Freyfall. Asteros had been forced to spend several months away from Erydon, trying to quell the tensions of Auris by carefully *removing* a particularly aggressive commander or legislator in either of the rival nations' ranks.

"Blood," Asteros said softly, reading the end of the first line aloud. His eyes shifted down the paper. *Unlocked.* His eyes jumped back to the second line. *Synthesis?* He looked back to the second-to-last line. It seemed to be important, somehow... More important than the others. "Transform." Asteros closed his eyes. *Could it be: the power of the Harbingers?* What was all this about blood though? They had theorized that Blood Sorcerers or Starburners were the key, yet neither existed anymore.

"Izara's Shadow!" Asteros cursed. They weren't talking about Blood Sorcerers... They were just talking about *blood*. "Blood of the dead..." Asteros whispered. *Not the blood of dead Summoners, but the blood of those who raised the dead!* Revenants. Asteros stood up. Shadow-Swifts were distant relatives of the Revenants... but they might be close enough.

Could that be our way in? Asteros had reached several "revelations" over the past few months that felt eerily similar to this one, yet all of them had resulted in failure.

Asteros looked back to the line again. *Stars...* Starburners? So Starburners and Revenants could unlock the doors.

He was so deep in his focus that he hardly noticed when Lucien slipped into the room. Lucien cleared his throat after a moment, causing Asteros to look up.

"Yes?" Asteros said impatiently.

Lucien smirked, then paced over to the table where Asteros worked. "I take it you found something in the writings?" Lucien asked. He leaned over Asteros's shoulder, reading his work. His dark eyes flashed alight with wonder.

"Why did you come here, Lucien?" Asteros asked, turning to face the man once again.

The Voltarian Crystals glowed brightly from their fixtures on the wall, illuminating the small library with their white light.

"I came here because I thought that you might want to know something," Lucien said, his Elosian features twisting into a smirk. "It seems that Eithor is growing impatient."

Asteros closed his eyes once again, turning away in his wooden chair. "I know," Asteros said softly.

"He doesn't care about Epirac or the Vanishing," Lucien said. "He only wants Faelyn." Lucien grinned, causing Asteros to grimace once again. Faelyn Titansworn had killed some Stormless soldiers a few months back. And Lucien, being as he was, had decided to make it seem as if Eithor's sons were among the dead, hoping to use it as a sort of twisted fuel that would motivate Eithor to play a part in their revised plans.

Eithor had taken the bait and developed quite a powerful disliking toward Faelyn.

Lucien had even hinted to Eithor that there may be a way for him to get revenge on the Prince. Unfortunately, they hadn't realized how long it would take them to get through Epirac's wards, and Eithor was growing impatient due to Lucien's continued manipulation.

The old man mostly read now. He read of the Runes, yes, but he read mostly of Arvendon—of the Titansworn family. He would be tasked with infiltrating the Titansworn's Whisperers and manipulating Faelyn, and he wanted to be prepared to tear the entire family apart.

Granted, that entire part of their plan would be of little importance once Asteros was able to replicate the Vanishing, though they had decided that it would be easiest to assume control of Auris if they were able to keep the royal bloodlines largely intact—even if they did have to remove the current monarchs from their positions. Yet Asteros had been insistent that Eithor was to wait until Epirac was unlocked before he was allowed to depart for Arvendon. Yes, it would take many weeks and a lot of very careful planning to infiltrate the Whisperers, but they needed his help to open the Rune-Locks.

"When are you going to tell Shalheira the truth about our plan?" Lucien asked, stroking his pointed black beard. His long, midnight hair was tied back in a ponytail.

Asteros didn't answer.

"Given that she's wrapped around your waist more often than not, I would assume that she loves you enough to see past the methods we have selected."

"It is not that she would be opposed to our methods, Lucien," Asteros said. "She would simply try to *improve* them, and that is what I wish to avoid."

"You wish to avoid progress?"

"I wish to avoid *interference*," Asteros snapped. "Shalheira will only agree to the plans if her voice is heard, and she will attempt to go about this more peacefully, which is a risk that we cannot afford to take." Asteros took a deep breath.

Lucien smiled faintly, his curved features sharp enough to cut stone. "You truly have changed," Lucien mused.

"What is that supposed to mean?" Asteros challenged.

Lucien raised his hands defensively, feigning surrender. "I meant no insult, dear friend. I simply observed a change in your composure from the person you were several years ago, that is all," Lucien said softly. "The old Asteros would never have agreed to this plan."

"The old Asteros would never have had the will to do this."

"Ah! Precisely why I view this change as something of a miracle, rather than a tragedy," Lucien exclaimed.

Asteros eyed him carefully. "I evolved," Asteros said. "I proved that I can do what is necessary to ensure the survival of our order. That is why Haldir chose me. You never did understand that, did you? You never did understand why he chose me over you?"

Lucien's gaze flickered, then turned from soft to... something deeper. "No," Lucien grumbled, looking away. "You were but a boy when you were chosen, nothing more than an infant among immortals."

"Yet he chose me nonetheless; this is why," Asteros said, his dark gaze smoldering. "He saw that you were as you always would be: a killer. He knew that Erydon needed a more dynamic leader than that. We needed someone who was flexible, resilient, yet pliable."

"I agree," Lucien said, turning back to face him. "We needed someone like you, but that's not to say that we *don't* need someone like me either. Just because we needed someone like you doesn't mean that you have a right to lead."

"Yet killing Faelyn Titansworn was something I was wise enough to pick out as a mistake," Asteros said. "That is what separates you and I, Lucien. You would have killed every last Titansworn, every last Nightingale, Thala, Jastira, and Wickenhardt until there was not a drop of royal blood on Auris."

"My plan has simplicity, something that your plan lacks!" Lucien growled.

"My plan is *genius*," Asteros said. "Avenos Titansworn must die, Siraye and Sariah Thala must die as well, and so must the Council of Jaskye and King Brennan Nightingale of Elos. Only Theurgi Wickenhardt of Freyfall is selfish enough to be allowed to remain in power. I was wise enough to see that killing the heirs of Auris's thrones would be a foolish mistake."

"I am on your side, Asteros," Lucien growled, grabbing the table. "I support this plan, I helped create it! Why are you turning on me now?"

"You claim that I should tell Shalheira... Why?" Asteros asked coldly.

"Because we *need* her," Lucien said. "You already forced Lyseria to prepare for the Initiation—which I believe she is attempting at this very moment—and you have encouraged Malik to train tirelessly day and night, yet you refuse to even bring your own lover into our plan." Lucien's eyes burned into him.

"She has no place in it," Asteros said after a moment. "Someone needs to watch over Erydon. And besides, with the scholars on our side, we will have more than enough numbers to accomplish our goals, even if we don't find a way to replicate the Vanishing."

"She is one of our strongest numbers and one of our greatest assets. Surely you can see that, Asteros."

"And surely you can see that we have no need for her to endanger herself when we can do this without her!" Asteros shouted. He froze, a strange, trembling sensation coming over his body. His muscles tensed, his heart pounding. He forced himself to relax, reminding himself that he was in the presence of a friend, not a foe. The tingling sensation faded reluctantly.

Lucien smirked in that infuriating way of his. "So that's what this is about," Lucien said, stroking his beard. "You are worried for her safety."

"The royal houses of Auris bear some of the most powerful Summoners on the continent," Asteros said.

"And your darling lover is one of the most dangerous weapons ever born into this world."

"Don't you dare call Shalheira a weapon," Asteros roared. "She is a woman. She is a beautiful, complex, fascinating, incredible woman—not a weapon."

Lucien held his gaze. "Weapon or not, she's one hell of a fighter," Lucien said, shrugging. "To keep her locked up here is a waste. You have my opinion, do with it what you want." And, without a word more, Lucien left.

Keries Nightbloom peeled his eyes open, anxiety crawling in his aging muscles as he watched Lyseria fly into the valley. The sickness rumbled within, alive with delight as the person dearest to him dove into danger. His hand itched to grab for his sword, to interfere... to help. But he did not. His subservience to Asteros overrode his instincts, causing the sickness to roar with pleasure once again. His nerves shook, but he held firm.

Lyseria landed in a flurry of steel and shadow, diving into the first two soldiers without hesitation. She stabbed one through the throat, piercing his fur cloak. The other she cut across the stomach and then stabbed through the eye.

The soldiers shouted in surprise, reaching for their weapons.

Keries watched, hand resting on his sword, shaky but firm. He would help her if she needed it.

But she did not need it. She needed no help as the two Summoners threw back their hoods, plumes of flame rising around one, shards of ice forming around the other. Lyseria threw her hands forward, blasting the pair with a wave of umbrakinesis.

The darkness flew like winds in a storm, crashing into the Summoners and knocking them to the ground. Lyseria pursued them, stabbing the Scorcher in a flurry of rage and fury.

She jumped, using an umbrakinetic boost to leap the entire distance to the other Summoner, who was crawling to his feet. Lyseria reached forward, lunging with a dagger.

The other soldiers began to circle around her, nervous but ready.

They knew what they were up against, and they knew that they didn't stand a chance.

Lyseria reached for the Cryostalker. Keries's breath caught as her eyes locked with the Cryostalker's. A single moment of serenity and peace on the battlefield. One could kill faceless, nameless soldiers without hesitation. Yet to kill someone after meeting their eyes... Someone you see, *you truly see*. It was different.

Lyseria paused.

And that was all it took.

The Cryostalker grabbed her arm, sending a shock of ice through her blood, freezing it. Lyseria pushed back, with a boost of umbrakinesis. Something flashed in the falling snow—her dagger. Keries flicked his eyes back to Lyseria, one arm now stiffly pointed off to the side, her remaining dagger in her left hand. There were still nearly a dozen soldiers left—one of which was a Cryostalker. Keries weighed his options, watching the soldiers circle with a predatory air. It had been decades since a Shadow-Swift had been killed. If Lyseria were to be defeated...

No. Keries took a step forward, feeling the boundless power within the Crystals at his waist. *No.* Keries took another step forward, drawing his blade with a steady hand. *No.* Keries shot into the air, phasing into the Unbound instinctually. Lyseria glanced at him, she did the same.

The Frostfall vanished around them, the world now coated in the strange black, smoky residue of the Unbound. The white moon shone brightly overhead in broad daylight, and time seemed to slow.

Keries crashed to the ground beside Lyseria, the sickness melting like snow in flame. Keries advanced, moving quicker than any human ever should, and sliced through the stomach of the soldier closest to him. He whirled, sensing another behind him. Using his free hand, he planted his palm on the soldier's chest, instantly blasting him backward with an umbrakinetic shock. Darkness radiated from Keries. Keries *was* darkness. He stabbed another, and then cut through another, ducking and sliding through the falling snow like a dancer on ice.

And then he locked eyes with Lyseria.

Time stopped. His breathing stopped. The fight stopped. Everything simply... stopped.

Recognition—that was all he felt. A sense of recognition he had not felt in *decades*. And, in that moment, something changed. In those eyes he saw not Lyseria, but Alvaerelle—his daughter.

Something crashed into Lyseria, knocking her to the ground, splattering blood across the white snow.

Someone moved, leaving a blade protruding from Lyseria's chest.

Her bright blue eyes melted away, replaced by pools of amber and shadow—Alvaerelle's eyes. The eyes of a frightened child, staring at her own father with unrivaled terror.

The world faded, and Keries froze. He glanced at his hand, wreathed in darkness, just as it had been on that day so long ago. Alvaerelle was before him, ruined arm hanging the wrong way, her body enveloped in a cloud of darkness.

Someone moved to his left. Something pierced his side.

He did not feel it. He only felt the slight shaking of his armor as it was struck. Even that faded as the seconds ticked by. He glanced down, seeing himself in those plain, rough-spun robes once again. He blinked.

Something hit his armor again, and someone shouted.

A girl moved, screaming, but Keries did not see her. Something hit him on the other side, and he felt a strange cooling sensation run down his spine. Shapes moved, people shouted and screamed. But Keries did nothing. Keries saw nothing.

He only saw Alvaerelle, standing in the frozen night.

She stood before him, her shattered arm hanging uselessly to the side as she limped toward him, a lone tear rolling down her delicate cheek.

Keries reached out with a hand, something of a whimper escaping his lips.

Something pierced his flesh, cutting deep.

But Keries did not feel it. He took another step forward, Alvaerelle did the same. She was sobbing now. Keries felt a tear fall from his own cheek... Distant rains on a foreign field. He should've been knocked to the ground, but, in his trance, he shrugged off another fatal blow, taking a step toward his daughter. Alvaerelle's face flickered, looking as beautiful and innocent as it had so many years ago.

She reached out with her good arm, nearly collapsing as she fell into Keries. But he pulled back. He knew what happened next. He knew what would happen when she took his hand, his own damned hand. The same hand he had run through her hair to stop her crying. The same hand that had dried her tears time and time again. The same hand that had ruined her arm. The same hand that would—

No. Keries took a step back. Alvaerelle fell, dark red blood leaking from an unknown wound. Her body rippled, bones cracking. He took another step back as something hit him in the arm.

Alvaerelle shook violently, her other arm twisting the wrong way with a sickening crunch.

Keries screamed, an explosion of darkness radiating from within.

Figures moved, thrown back by the blast.

Yet Alvaerelle stayed, face down in the snow. Her neck was bent the wrong way. Her legs were ruined, crushed by an unknown darkness, her once-elegant nightgown now torn to shreds. She looked up, her neck bent at a horrific angle. She met his eyes.

Keries took a step forward, his senses failing him as he collapsed before her. He reached out, his hand still wrapped in the black mist. He paused, his eyes landing on his shrouded fingers.

No!

Keries slammed both hands into the ground, drawing upon the Crystals within his cracked armor. He sent a pulse of umbrakinesis through both arms, and then both legs, and leapt into the air. He screamed, pushing through the resistance as he soared into the heavens.

Ice and snow bit at his skin, scratching his tear-stained face. But he did not stop.

Alvaerelle called out below, screaming his name. But he did not turn. If he went back, she would be harmed. If he went back, she would die. If he went back... *He would kill her.*

So he did not. Even as the phantom world faded, and the mountains and clouds returned. He did not go back. He could not go back. Something was wrong, yes. But, if he did, he would only kill her once again. He would only cause more harm, and more pain, and more suffering.

The sickness rolled in like a storm in the distance, only for Keries to realize it had been there all along. Forging these thoughts from the pieces of his memories, trapping him in a prison of pain. The sickness. It was winning. It always had been. But something was different now. Something was... *wrong.*

He didn't care. He never did. He always knew it would win. He never stood a damn chance, not when his opponent was his own mind. He wanted it to win. He *needed* it to. Shouts sounded below as Keries flew. But he ignored them. There was only one place he could go: home.

The Nature of Crystals & the Importance of Faelyn Titansworn

7.22.11-64

*It is often assumed that empty Crystals form something of a
vacuum when exposed to their respective energies. This is true,
though I believe that there is something more to be uncovered in*

the true nature of this vacuum, as well as in the comparison of one Crystal type to another.

Place a Voltarian Crystal in the presence of heat, and it will not react. However, place a Voltarian Crystal in the presence of electricity, and it will absorb it over the course of a few hours. As it is absorbed, it becomes readily available for its respective Summoner to use. Interestingly enough, when placing two Scorcher Crystals near one another, leaving each half filled, virtually no reaction ensues. One might expect the stronger vacuum to absorb the energy of the other Crystal, yet this does not happen, leading me to believe that these Crystals are far more resilient in their holding of their acquired energy than many believe.

Drawing upon a Crystal for the first time is like something of an instinct for the Summoners of Auris. One might expect, then, that it is rather easy to extract energy from these Crystals, and, while I cannot help but agree in some respects, scientifically it is rather challenging to remove energy from the Crystals. I have tried several times to create a vacuum between a full Crystal and one that is empty, yet I have failed at each attempt. Such a result leads me to believe that the trait of extraction is something that is purely instinctual, and that it is passed on genetically.

This makes sense, of course, when one examines the nature of the hereditary laws of Summoners. The purity of the trait in one's blood directly correlates to the strength of their abilities, which is only further proven by the Titansworn's experimentation several centuries ago. Arvendon's Royal Bloodline was purified, ensuring that each child born into the dynasty would be stronger than the last. The Titansworns ordered the Scorchers of their kingdom to mate with one another, producing an influx of Summoners like the world had never seen before. They conducted a similar program with their Whisper-

ers, the second-most prevalent of the Sects in their country's heritage. These programs together offered much insight into the nature of extraction and Summoning itself. Yet no one kept any records of it, for Arvendon feared that, if other nations adopted similar programs, their dominance would be threatened. A fair concern, of course.

From what I can gather, there is a pattern of dominance among the Sects. If two Lesser Summoners of different Sects are to produce two offspring, the chances of them both being of the same Sect— that Sect being the one in which the family's blood is most pure— are exponentially higher than the odds of them being different. Even Stormless who were known to have distant relatives possessing the abilities of a Scorcher were included, which explains why the number of Scorchers in Arvendon is so much higher than it is anywhere else—even Suchara.

Galather the First also took it upon himself to ensure that only the purest of Scorcher Summoners would be allowed to breed into the family. It was Avenos who was predicted to be the last pure Scorcher, for that was when Galather predicted the Scorcher bloodlines would finally be forced to "crossover" to prevent incest —something that he wished to avoid for as long as possible.

Yet he was wrong. Avenos is not the final pure Summoner of the Titansworn Dynasty. It is his son, Faelyn. According to our research of the bloodlines, he is the most powerful Scorcher the world has ever seen—perhaps even among the most powerful Summoners. Lucien claims that I am optimistic, but I think not. Faelyn is something truly special. I thoroughly believe that he stands on nearly the same plane as the Harbingers themselves.

Asteros Silverglade stood in Erydon's grand atrium, looking up from his journal. His eyes settled on a Scorcher Crystal, staring into its enigmatic light. His research on the Crystals had continued without much interruption, though he found himself torn between the Wayfinder's words and the Crystals whenever he did find the time to sit down and continue his work.

Malik leaned against the engraved wall of the atrium, staring blankly at the ground, his oversized sword beside him. He stood still, as if frozen in the warm, stale air of Erydon. His rough face twitched as he glanced at his pocket watch and frowned.

"It's been too long," Malik grumbled, his dark eyes settling on the ground once again as he slid the watch back into his pocket.

"They will return," Asteros said. He laid down his journal, walking toward Malik. The boy remained still, the tension visible in his bulging muscles.

"And if they don't?" Shalheira asked, raising her eyes from the dagger in her hand.

Asteros turned to his lover, staring into her beautiful Sucharan face. "They will," Asteros said, turning away.

Shalheira sighed and turned the dagger once again in her gloved hands.

Asteros closed his eyes, taking a deep breath as he did so. Shalheira disagreed with his decision to push Lyseria into the Initiation.

Malik did not, but he worried for his sister nonetheless.

"Keries is with her," Lucien said, stepping out from his corner in the shadows, a krellin scurrying along the wall beside him. "He watches over her as if she is his own. He won't let anything happen to her."

Malik grumbled once again.

Shalheira flipped the dagger anxiously.

Asteros reached for his journal, but could not find the peace of mind to continue reading. Strange as it was, Malik was right. Lyseria and Keries had departed several hours ago, and, though they knew that the patrol would not have arrived for quite some time, they had assumed that the Initiation would be completed by now.

Asteros indulged in his fears briefly, allowing himself to envision all the things that could have gone awry: Lyseria and Keries dead in the snow, victims of an ambush... Yet, that was impossible.

Keries was one of the best swordsmen in Auris—even rivaling Lucien on the days when his sickness didn't unsteady his hand.

Lyseria herself had become quite the warrior as well. Her light frame gave her a speed and grace that surpassed even Shalheira's. He pushed the thoughts from his head, closing his eyes once again. They would be alright. They were Summoners. They were Shadow-Swifts.

"Malik's right," Shalheira said suddenly, stepping up from her place against the wall.

Lucien advanced, his hand slipping to the hilt of his sword.

Asteros raised both hands, motioning for the pair to settle. "There is no need for unrest, my friends," Asteros said. "Keries confirmed that Lyseria was ready. The only thing she lacks is experience, and our Initiation is designed to give her just that."

"If she is ready, then why send Keries with her?" Malik challenged. "None of us were supervised."

"Lyseria is something of a special case, dear Malik," Asteros said. "Given the magnitude of the task we have undertaken these last few months, it is only natural for one to be nervous, especially one of her age. We are choosing to favor her safety over tradition, I would think that you, of all people, could respect that."

"If you were truly favoring her safety, then why force her to complete the trial in the first place?" Shalheira asked, flipping the dagger once again.

"We cannot afford to keep a liability within these walls," Lucien said. "Not while we are trying to vanquish something as powerful as the damn Tempests."

"Is that what she is then? A liability?" Malik stood straighter, his hand instinctively drifting to his massive blade.

"Yes," Lucien said. "That's exactly what she *was*, yet she is not a liability any longer, rest assured." Lucien paused. "You know, for one so strong in the body, you really are fascinatingly dense in the mind."

"You disrespect me or my family once more this evening and you will find yourself on the wrong end of this blade, I promise you that," Malik growled, advancing.

"Stop!" Asteros hissed, stepping between the two. He pressed a hand on both of their chests, sending a minor jolt of umbrakinesis through both of them—a reminder. "Both of you are unnerved by Lyseria and Keries's absence, I understand this. Yet I promise that *this* is not the way to release your tension. Trust me in this, my brothers."

"We should go," Shalheira said, sliding the dagger back into its sheath. "Something's wrong."

"No," Lucien said, stepping between Shalheira and the hallway she had started toward. "The girl is fine. Keries is fine. In time they will return, and then all will be right in this damned fortress once again, correct?"

Shalheira hesitated. "And if they don't return?"

"They will," Asteros responded, stepping behind her.

"And if they don't?" Shalheira whirled, placing her hands on Asteros's chest. "What if this whole damned Initiation was a bad idea to begin with? What if Lyseria wasn't ready? What if I was right?"

"She is right," Malik said, taking hold of his blade. "We need to go."

"Don't you dare," Lucien said, stepping in front of Malik.

"My sister is in danger, Lucien," Malik said, his voice rough. "You will not stand in my way."

"Even if your sister was in danger, you wouldn't be able to get to her in time," Lucien whispered, his Elosian features twisting into a wicked smile. "You don't even know where she is, and—assuming that something has befallen her—you wouldn't even be able to find her before it was too late."

"I know exactly where she and Keries went. I helped mark the passage for the ambush," Malik snapped.

"Ah," Lucien snickered. "But even so, if she were to have fallen, she would be long gone by now, correct?"

"She is in danger, Lucien," Shalheira hissed, stepping away from Asteros. "Why will you not let us leave? It almost seems as if you want something to happen!"

"I don't give a damn what happens to the girl," Lucien snarled. "I respect the ways of those who came before us. The fact that Keries was allowed to accompany her alone is a mockery of our ancestors."

"Yet you kill without reason time and time again while our ancestors only did so when necessary," Malik said.

"I kill only when it benefits the order. You cannot tell me any different," Lucien said.

"You kill for your own damn enjoyment, and you know it!"

"Do you have any idea of all that I have done for the Shadow-Swifts?" Lucien shouted. "Any idea of what I will do? You haven't any idea what sort of hell-storm we have planned. We aren't just removing the Tempests, we're filling the void they will leave."

"What?" Shalheira shouted. She turned to Asteros, though he remained silent. He knew this was coming. It was beyond his control.

"When we strip Auris of its Tempests, the world will lack stability," Lucien said, his black eyes glowing. "The power vacuum created will be unlike anything this planet has ever seen, and we... We are going to fill that void. We are going to assume control of Auris. We will offer peace where there is chaos, safety where there is danger, and life where there is nothing left but crime and death. We will be the saviors of Auris, and, with the careful manipulation and removal of some of Auris's monarchs, our job will be all completed by the time the skies are cleared."

"You said we would select the new leaders of Auris, not assume their positions ourselves." Shalheira narrowed her eyes.

"I said that we—" Lucien started.

Malik stormed out of the chamber, drawing his sword.

"Where is he going?" Lucien asked.

"I'm going to save my sister," Malik answered, making his way to the backdoor of Erydon.

"Asteros." Lucien turned to him. "Are you really going to let him go?"

Asteros looked to Shalheira, then back to Lucien. "It has been quite a while since they left," Asteros said quietly. "It wouldn't hurt to at least observe from a distance."

"Are you *serious*?" Lucien growled, advancing.

"They might need our help, Lucien," Asteros said. "If they don't, then we turn around and leave them be... But if they do—"

"This is ridiculous." Lucien threw his hands up in disgust.

"Stay here if you want," Asteros said, turning to follow Malik. "But we cannot risk losing Keries or Lyseria."

Asteros knew as soon as he broke through the clouds.

There were only a handful of bodies littering the gulley—not enough to make up an entire patrol. There was no movement on the ground; only the silent snowfall as the sun set somewhere beyond the clouds.

Asteros lowered quickly, sensing Shalheira and Malik beside him.

Keries and Lyseria were nowhere to be found. Only a few spots of blood-soaked snow were still visible. The footprints had already been covered by the continuous snowfall.

They were too late. Regardless of where Keries and Lyseria might be, the Frostfall was too heavy for Asteros to have any hope of retracing their steps.

"Where is she?" Malik asked, his voice wavering. "Could they have gone back to Erydon? Could we have missed them in the clouds?"

Asteros did not respond. He knelt down, brushing away some snow around a particularly bloodied face.

It was an Utryan corpse, as he expected.

"The only corpses here belong to the Utryans." Asteros said, standing up.

"We had to have missed them," Shalheira reassured. "Two Shadow-Swifts against hardly even a dozen Utryans... That's an easy victory, especially for Keries."

"So we go back to Erydon," Malik said. "Easy. Come on." Malik rose into the sky once again, shifting as he did so.

Asteros swallowed, a lump forming in his throat. He knew. He could *feel it*. Something was wrong. But a part of him held on to that glimmer of hope, clinging to it as one holds on to light in a sea of darkness.

Perhaps Keries and Lyseria would be back at Erydon, perhaps...

Numb. There was nothing in Asteros's mind. Emptiness. Numbness. It was as if his entire soul had been stolen from his body, his thoughts torn from his mind.

They returned to find Erydon just as they had left it, with only Lucien and the scholars waiting inside.

Malik paced through the grand chamber of Erydon. Shalheira stood beside Asteros, while Lucien leaned against the wall.

"They will be here soon, right?" Malik asked.

Asteros knew he was searching for reassurance, but there was none to give. If Keries and Lyseria were not here—and given their bodies were not found—there was only one explanation.

"They abandoned us," Asteros said softly.

"*What?*" Malik advanced.

"It's the only possible explanation," Asteros said. "Think about it: We found no traces of them in the gulley, and they *aren't here*."

"They will be," Malik said. His voice was shaky. "They must've pursued the patrol team through their retreat."

"Then why aren't they back?" Asteros asked.

"Because—" Malik started.

"Your sister abandoned us," Asteros said. "She and Keries fled, and none of us should be surprised."

"And what if they didn't?" Malik challenged, his voice rising. "What if they are trapped somewhere? What if they need our help?"

"They are Shadow-Swifts just like yourself, Malik. Containing even one of them would be next to impossible for an Utryan force that small," Asteros said.

"They fled," Lucien agreed. "They deserted our clan."

"Well, then what do we do? We can't just have two rogue Shadow-Swifts running about," Shalheira started.

"What do you propose we do?" Lucien asked, his tone mocking. "They can be *literally* anywhere in these damned mountains. How do you propose we find them?"

"We don't," Asteros said. "We can't find them, not now."

"We are *not* abandoning the search for my sister that easily," Malik growled. "We still don't even know if she's safe!"

"We have a *mission*, Malik," Asteros said. "Aiming to remove the Tempests from Auris is no small task; if we hope to accomplish it, we cannot afford to get distracted by your sister's games."

"They are not games," Malik shot back. "She could be in danger."

"Even if she is, we still have no way of finding her," Asteros said.

Malik continued pacing, making his way over to the wall. He leaned his head against it, taking a deep breath. He lowered himself, turning to sit against the wall. Malik slid down to the floor, holding his head in his hands.

"So we just leave her out there?" Malik asked, his voice unsteady. "We have no idea if she's even safe, and we're just going to leave her out there?"

"Do we have a choice?" Lucien asked, stepping forward. "Asteros is right; we cannot afford to waste any time looking for them."

"We're just going to leave it at that, then?" Malik tossed his hands up. He lowered his head once again.

Asteros watched him. With Keries and Lyseria presumably gone, they couldn't afford to lose another Shadow-Swift, and, if Asteros wasn't careful, Malik would consider leaving as well. Asteros needed to do something... something to ensure that he retained Malik's loyalty.

Keries and Lyseria were mostly unhelpful anyway. Keries was a proficient swordsman, true, but he rarely even raised his blade. Perhaps in time he would return. He knew the magnitude of their plans, which meant that he knew his return would only benefit himself.

But Malik needed guidance, and he needed closure. They needed to move on from this loss quickly—they could not afford to waste any time.

Asteros spoke: "Perhaps there is something we can do."

CHAPTER TWENTY-NINE
LOSS

A fire burned softly in the frozen night. A beacon of warmth in the bitter cold. Frost drifted over the mountains, flowing like water over stone. Asteros watched as a silent tear slid down Malik's face, freezing against his skin before it could fall from his scarred cheek.

The twin moons of Auris shone in the midnight sky, Lotius's pale gray light illuminating the dark mountainscape, Oria's turquoise glow casting the jagged peaks in an ethereal light.

Asteros felt as if he were watching his body from somewhere else. His own indifference to Keries and Lyseria's desertion was not lost on him. Lucien was right—something had changed within him. He only hoped that his ambition did not completely overpower his heart.

"Heavy is the hand that bears the burden of blame," Asteros Silverglade said. In the brief hour before the ceremony he had arranged, he had prepared a short speech.

Malik needed this, and perhaps they all did. Though Keries and

Lyseria were likely still alive, they were no longer a part of their group… and that was a loss in itself.

"I ordered Lyseria to complete the Initiation," Asteros continued. "I pushed Keries to train her. I knew the risks, yet I gave the order nonetheless," Asteros said.

Someone opened their mouth, a sound escaping. Malik.

"I take full responsibility for what happened to Lyseria and Keries," Asteros said. "Though they are likely still on this continent, walking among the living… They are no longer with this clan." Asteros paused. "And so, tonight, we pray for their safety. Though they are still roaming this world, they are not with *us… here…*" Asteros trailed off. "Let us have a moment of silence, to honor all that they have done, and to hope that there is much left for them to do." Asteros bowed his head.

The flame crackled in the icy night. A frozen wind blew across the group, yet the flame burned still, protected by Asteros's umbrakinesis.

"We cannot let this loss be in vain," Asteros said after a moment. "Lyseria's Initiation was meant to prepare her for what was to come, for what we were going to do. For what we *still will* do."

Asteros's eyes remained fixed on the solemn flame, burning quietly on the peak of Telenaris. Erydon was silent below. The usual thrum of burning Crystals extinguished, in honor of them.

"We will continue," Asteros said. "To have only four of us standing atop this peak cuts my soul so deeply that I fear the bleeding may never stop. But we *will* make this right." Asteros felt no shame at the lie. It was a loss, true, but not a great one.

"How?" Malik asked. The boy clung to his greatsword with a childlike desperation, his knuckles white. "How can we possibly make this right? Without their guidance?"

"Your sister has left us, but we must push forward," Asteros said. "I know that she wouldn't want her absence to—"

"She is gone because of you!" Malik snapped. "She is gone,

because of *you*!" he repeated. Frozen tears slid down his rough cheeks.

"I think that I may have discovered a way for us to enter Epirac," Asteros said. "If we keep going, if we complete the Vanishing with this loss to push us onward, her loss will have meant something."

Silence washed over the frozen mountain, the small peak of Telenaris falling into shadow as a cloud cloaked the sister moons.

"How?" Lucien asked, his voice firm.

"The Wayfinder," Asteros said. "His words were veiled, but I think that I have uncovered the secret to opening the door." Asteros paused. "We could not track Lyseria because of the Tempests... Their fight likely went awry because of the Summoners." Asteros looked around, meeting each of their eyes. "Summoners extract power from Crystals, and Crystals are fueled by the Tempests. Think of how many lives we could save! Think about the possibilities... Every Summoner on Auris reduced to a Stormless. Battles that once left thousands dead can now be resolved with steel, rather than spells."

"Everyone would be left powerless," Lucien said.

"Everyone except us," Shalheira whispered. She raised her amber eyes to Asteros, who met her gaze. "You truly mean to do this, don't you?"

"I do," Asteros said. "There would be no more losses like this one. We would be saving thousands of lives each year, just *think* of how it would be."

"So we just forget about this?" Malik asked. "We just ignore the fact that Lyseria could be dead right now, and move on?"

"No, Malik," Asteros said. "We will continue on our path, but we will not forget. Lyseria's absence must push us onward; not all are fit for the mission we pursue, but the four of us... the four of us are *meant* for this." Asteros paused. "We must vanquish the Tempests for the sake of the rest of Auris. All will benefit from what we do, but it is only us four who possess the strength to do it."

"Tomorrow, then," Lucien said. "We go to Epirac, and push onward."

"Onward," Malik said, feeling the word in his mouth.

"Onward," Shalheira said quietly.

Asteros spoke last. He was the leader of this clan. Years ago he had vowed to lead this group to greatness, and that was exactly what he would do, "Onward."

CHAPTER THIRTY
LOST TRUST

Faelyn Titansworn wasted no time. He stormed into his father's chambers, pushing through the massive marble doors, brushing past the guards standing outside the royal rooms. They didn't stop him. There was no stopping him. The Solstice was tomorrow; there was no time to wait.

"Father!" Faelyn shouted, the doors swinging shut behind him.

His father walked through the open door to his study, still dressed in a full suit of orange armor.

"What do you want?" His father glowered, his eyes smoldering in the shadows of the crackling hearth.

Faelyn stood his ground, taking a step forward. His still-damp night wear and disheveled hair likely made for quite a sight.

His father took a step back as his eyes scanned Faelyn.

"I need to talk to you," Faelyn demanded. "And I need you to *actually* listen this time."

"Whatever it is, it can wait until morning. You should be asleep at this hour of night. Besides, I have more important business to attend to."

"Stop," Faelyn said as his father started to turn back to his study.

His father paused, his creased face twisting into a frown. His father's eyes still burned with fury from Pallus's interrogation.

"If this has anything to do with the spy, then I swear by Izara's Shadow Faelyn I'm going to—" his father growled.

"You're going to what?" Faelyn challenged. "Kill me? Beat me?"

His father glared.

"We are all in much more danger than we realized," Faelyn said. "I know that you understand how dire our situation is, so *please* listen to me."

His father took a deep breath, closing his amber eyes. His whole body seemed to shift downward as he exhaled, his long brown hair cascading from his head and down his shoulders. It was then that Faelyn realized something: His father was just a man, like anybody else. A crown on one's head didn't change that fact. His father could be tricked and manipulated just as easily as any other common man. And sending away Arvendon's most powerful Summoners to track down the Blood Sorcerer... His father had made a mistake, but it had been an honest one. That, however, did not excuse his recklessness.

"I met with the Illusomancer again," Faelyn said.

His father flinched, but remained silent.

"At first I disregarded his words, but the more that I've thought about it... Father, if he is working against us, he would've killed me already. But he hasn't. He says that our city is in grave danger. I need you to pull back the Summoners who you sent after the Blood Sorcerer," Faelyn continued. "Not all of them, but at least Delmorian, Surge, and Elric." He paused. "They should already be on their way back anyway, right?"

His father swallowed. "I—" he trailed off, his voice raspy. "I'll send the order soon."

"No, you will send the order now," Faelyn interjected.

"Faelyn, you have to listen to me, they are getting farther and farther north with each passing day. I'm sure they'll be beginning the journey home soon. Hell! They could even be on their way here right now!"

"Which is why it wouldn't do any harm to send your command for their return *now*," Faelyn said.

"I will not stand for this any longer," his father finally said, straightening.

"You've already lost Mother to your stubbornness," Faelyn said. "I know you don't want to lose me too." He took a step forward.

His father's eyes darkened. "You have disrespected me," his father said, his voice like ice. "I understand that you want to help, but you have gone against my word time and time again, and on each occasion you have done nothing but endanger yourself and our family, and I am putting a stop to it. So listen to me, here and now: You are my son, and I am your father. You obey me."

"But—" Faelyn started.

"Faelyn," his father warned.

"You can't expect me to listen if you're just going to—" Faelyn began.

"I am your father," his father repeated. "And, what's more, I am your King. I am ordering you to return to your rooms and stay there," his father said quietly, his voice eerily firm. "Tomorrow night, I expect to see you at the Solstice Feast." His father turned away and waved his hand. "Get out of my sight," he dismissed.

Faelyn turned, not daring to speak up again. His father rarely gave Faelyn an official command... and when he did Faelyn had no choice but to obey. His father was still the King, and Faelyn could not go against his orders.

Faelyn dragged his feet to the door. He opened it and started into the hallway beyond. Defeat was a strange emotion—one that Faelyn hated. His city was likely doomed. His father had just sealed its fate, and now... now there was nothing Faelyn could do.

The Solstice was tomorrow, though Faelyn hardly felt like celebrating. The horrific future Eithor had shown him was in sight, approaching like a fast-moving wave. Faelyn lowered his head as he walked through the halls of Summerglass. It was too late.

CHAPTER THIRTY-ONE
EPIRAC

Ten months ago...

Asteros Silverglade squinted through the falling snow, struggling to see through the Frostfall. Asteros looked to the side, where Shalheira stood at the peak of the frozen mountain, shivering in the cold. Asteros frowned.

She could have partially shrouded herself in the Unbound to stay warm, yet she didn't.

Curious, he thought. He strode over to her side.

She turned away, her arms folded tightly.

"Here," Tsarra Selic called out through the blizzard.

Asteros peered out into the snow, searching for the young woman.

"I think I may have found what we are looking for," Tsarra said. Her silhouette became visible in the distance.

Asteros took a step through the ankle-deep snow, his feet colliding with solid black stone as he walked. The top of Epirac was considerably flatter in comparison to the other mountain. Interestingly enough, unlike the other chambers, Epirac's entrance appeared to be on the top of the mountain, rather than nestled in its side.

Asteros jogged through the snow, coming to the flat peak of Epirac, passing by another figure in the heavy snowfall—Lucien.

Lucien stood beside one of the small pillars that rose from Epirac's peak.

Several such pillars dotted the summit, none more than five or six feet tall, each bearing unique markings. Soran had theorized that they served as nodes for the Rune-Lock, though their purpose was still unclear.

"What have you found?" Asteros asked, slowing to a stop beside Tsarra.

She was barely distinguishable from a bundle of fur, hidden so deeply in her massive coat that Asteros could barely pick out her face.

"Down here," Tsarra said, kneeling.

Soran stood beside her, Eithor approaching from the side.

Asteros didn't miss the heavy silence that fell over the group at Eithor's presence.

The older man glared at the stone patterns that decorated the mountain's surface, hidden beneath the snow, staring at them as if they were the root of all of his problems.

"A two-slip?" Soran asked, brushing aside the snow, revealing two distinct lines in the stone, carved into a square border.

The lines were straight, straighter than most lines on the mountaintop. Each line had a small gap between its edges, forming what looked like a tiny canal.

"Asteros said that it would take two specific Sects to unlock the chamber," Tsarra said. "And here we have two canals in the stone."

Eithor rubbed his snow-ridden beard. "It would make sense."

"The question is how did the Wayfinder know what to look for in his visions?" Soran asked.

"And perhaps, more importantly, why write the code on a stone in Bareholde?" Lucien asked, approaching from behind.

Asteros turned, noting two figures standing in the distance.

Malik and Shalheira.

Asteros opened his mouth, almost calling them over. But he caught Lucien's eye.

Don't, Lucien's eyes seemed to whisper.

Asteros bit his tongue, turning back to the pair. They stood separately, though close enough to know that the other was there. It was almost as if they were bonded in their losses. Though Shalheira hadn't been particularly close to Keries and Lyseria, it was clear that she felt their absence just as strongly as Malik.

"We can ponder the nature of the Wayfinders another time. What matters is that we may have just found our way into Epirac," Eithor said.

Asteros nodded. "He's right; how do these work?" Asteros asked. He recalled reading about two-slips in the past.

"Think of it as a double-layered lock, with each layer requiring a different key," Soran said. "I suspect that spilling enough of the correct blood will allow them to open. Although, if what you have discovered proves true, I think that you must fill one canal with Starburner blood, and one with Revenant blood."

"And if we don't?" Lucien asked, raising a pointed eyebrow.

"Then the seal will not open," Eithor grumbled.

Asteros paused, staring at the empty grooves in the stone square. "What if we have two Revenants?"

"I already told you: Then it's not going to work," Eithor said, turning his haggard eyes to Asteros.

"No, that's not what I meant," Asteros explained. "Would it cause any change to the lock itself? Perhaps loosen some of the ties?"

Soran looked to Asteros. "Ordinarily I would say no. However, given that this lock is unlike anything I've ever seen, I cannot give you a solid answer on that."

"It's almost like it's alive," Tsarra said, feeling the frozen stones with her gloved hand. "The way the lines move and twist yet stay within the square," she said, brushing aside more snow, revealing an almost alien string of Runes. "It's unlike anything I've ever seen..."

"What are you getting at?" Eithor grunted.

"I think that Asteros might be onto something," Tsarra said. "Perhaps a normal lock would be unaffected, but something like this... something that almost seems more *fluid*... Filling both canals with just one type of blood may manipulate the Runes enough to allow us to bypass the lock through other means."

Asteros glanced at Lucien, then shook his head slightly, wondering when he started looking to Lucien for reassurance. But now was not the time for such questions.

Asteros knelt beside one end of the small canal, motioning for Lucien to kneel beside the other end.

Lucien did so, and the two of them shared a look.

Gods, I hope this works, Asteros thought. He drew one of his swords, and pulled off his gauntlet. He could hear Lucien following suit to the side.

Asteros steeled himself and brought the blade to his hand. He closed his eyes and slit the sword across his open palm.

Pain ripped through his hand, crying out into the frozen air. Asteros grunted, tilting his hand and letting the dark red blood drip into the canal. He looked over, tense from the pain, and watched as Lucien did the same.

The tiny canal slowly filled, and Asteros drew upon his Crystals to seal the wound.

Sweet relief swam into his veins as the skin knit itself together.

Wind whipped through the frosty air, blowing pellets of snow and ice into Asteros's exposed face. He sat there, waiting for something to happen.

Nothing did.

They waited for a moment longer, the silence hanging on a razor's edge.

Tsarra sighed, standing up. Soran shrugged, Eithor grumbled. Then, it happened.

Tsarra yelped as the ground began to shake and then move. She fell into the snow, clinging to the rocky mountain top as the very stones themselves shifted in the ground.

Soran cursed, hunkering to the ground as the lines beneath him began to shift as well.

"What's going on?" Shalheira called out from somewhere in the blizzard.

Panic filled Asteros's heart at the sight of her, stumbling over the morphing stones in the distance. "Shalheira!" Asteros shouted, using an umbrakinetic jump to propel himself toward her.

She whirled, slipping to the ground as she sidestepped his dive.

Asteros landed face first in the icy snow, instantly phasing into the Unbound at the bitter cold.

"I'm fine, you fool," Shalheira said, looking down. "Just confused as to why the mountain seems to be moving."

Asteros looked down, brushing the snow off of the rock.

The lines underneath were *bending*, almost looking like rivers in some distant land.

After a moment, the movement stopped. Asteros looked up, watching carefully as Shalheira stood, brushing herself off. Asteros could make out Malik doing the same.

It seemed that it was stable enough to stand.

Asteros leapt through the air, landing in the snow beside the scholars as they rose to their feet. Asteros turned, holding out a hand to help Lucien up.

Lucien took it, his hands somehow seeming rough even through his thick black gauntlets.

"What in Niventia's Light was that?" Eithor grumbled, shaking the snow off his hood.

"Is everyone okay?" Soran asked, looking around.

"Asteros," Tsarra said slowly. The young woman was looking past Asteros, toward some of the... pillars.

Asteros whirled, following her gaze. There, laying in what appeared to be the flattest part of the mountain, lay all eight of the pillars that had been spread out across the summit not moments before.

The pillars were no more than five or six feet tall, and hardly even a foot wide, yet, when arranged in the perfect circle that they now formed, it was clear that they were only *part* of the puzzle.

"Zephyr's Watch," Soran cursed, taking a step forward. He knelt down, brushing aside the snow at the base of the pillars, examining the newly formed lines. "It truly is alive."

"Awake would be a more accurate term," Tsarra said, approaching the ring of pillars. The center of the circle was large enough for perhaps five or six people to fit inside. There were gaps between the eight pillars, though each gap seemed to only be a few feet.

"Fascinating," Eithor whispered from beside one of the other pillars.

"What is it?" Asteros asked, taking a step forward.

"It almost appears as if the pillars themselves have been changed by what we have done," Eithor said. "I recall examining these and finding unique patterns that seemed to have no correlation... yet now... It almost seems as if they were all meant to be together from the start."

"They don't line up, though," Soran said, studying another pillar. "Not exactly, at least. The markings connect, but not without slight... *errors.*"

"It's almost like we're missing some of the pieces," Asteros said, joining them beside the mysterious ring.

By now, the others had wandered to the pillars, though none of them spoke. Malik had hardly spoken since Lyseria and Keries were deemed deserters, and Shalheira... well, Asteros wasn't sure what to make of her. It was almost as if she felt betrayed by what Asteros had told her—or, he supposed, neglected to tell her—about their plan.

"Pieces that do not exist," Tsarra whispered, her eyes widening.

"What?" Lucien asked.

"Draw your blades, everyone," Tsarra said, turning around. She held out her hand expectantly.

Lucien grumbled, handing her the shorter of his two blades.

Asteros passed one of his twin swords to Soran, and Eithor accepted one of Shalheira's daggers.

Malik paused as he unsheathed his sword, almost as if he had forgotten it existed. Something like sorrow flickered in his dark eyes, something like grief. It faded like a fleeting shadow. A solemn coldness came over his face, yet it was different from the kind of stoic indifference that had dominated Keries's features. Where Keries had produced an aura of sadness, Malik bore a sense of icy determination.

Almost like… Lucien, Asteros realized with a start.

"Search for the Stone-Readers," Tsarra said, her voice pulling Asteros from his thoughts.

The other scholars set to work, locating the correct sequences of Runes on each of the eight pillars.

Not more than a few moments passed before all eight of the square Runes had been located.

"Positions, everyone," Asteros instructed, raising his dark blade to the strange cubic marking on his pillar. "On my count." Asteros glanced at the others, who all slowly slid into position, Shadow-Sand blades raised.

"Ready when you are," Lucien said, giving his affirmation before Asteros continued.

Asteros grimaced, wondering once again when Lucien had started to direct Asteros, rather than the other way around.

"Three," Asteros started, tightening his grip on the blade. "Two."

The icy wind whipped through the group, tearing frost and snow across the stones.

Asteros took a deep breath. "One."

Stone and metal screeched, crying out as the blades met their mark.

An eerie stillness fell over the group in the seconds that followed, an almost excited air settling over them as they watched, waiting.

The pillars quivered.

"Get back!" Asteros shouted, jumping a few feet. The others obeyed, yet, this time, the ground did not shift.

The pillars, however, did change. Each one took on a steady white glow, the square Stone-Readers lighting up one by one, slowly activating whatever ancient mechanisms powered them. The small area in the middle of the circle began to shake, at first softly, then more violently.

Asteros covered his ears as a terrible screeching interrupted the howling blizzard wind.

Stone grinded against stone as the ground the pillars had circled began to rise, slowly pushing itself from the mountain, rising above the pillars that surrounded it. An opening appeared within the now-risen ground, forming what appeared to be a small rectangular passage.

The stillness returned as the newly risen stone settled into place, towering over the group at well over ten feet. The rectangular opening appeared to be a doorway of sorts.

Asteros took a step forward, reaching into his armor and producing a Scorcher Crystal for light. The eight pillars that rounded the stone centerpiece lowered quietly, swallowed up by the mountain.

Asteros squinted through the heavy snow, sensing a slight depression in the opening. He drew closer, stepping hesitantly over the now-flat stone where the pillars had once stood. He peered into the rectangular doorway, seeing the curve of the wall first. Then he noted the stairs, leading downwards.

A staircase, then.

He turned around, three Shadow-Swifts and three scholars standing before him. Asteros met each of their eyes, slowly taking in all that stood before him, basking in the moment. *This moment* was the one he had been waiting for... The moment they had all been waiting for.

All his planning... hours spent in that cursed library, researching. Hours spent debating with Lucien, plotting with the man as they laid out what they were to do once they discovered the truth about the Vanishing... once they discovered *this*. Yet here he was. Nearly a year and a half after he had found a way into Herqen. A year and a half after he had learned that there was much more to the Vanishing than anyone had believed. The battles with the Utryans and the Arvendi, the endless skirmishes, the arguments within his own Sect... Lyseria and Keries's desertion... it had all led to this. Each and every moment of Asteros's life seemed to flash before his eyes. Everything had led to this.

Asteros opened his mouth but could find no words to do the moment justice. So he did the only thing he could think of: He turned from the violent Frostfall beyond and started down the staircase.

The Scorcher Crystal blazed in his hand, a beacon in the darkness... something to be heralded in this world of shadow that he was about to enter.

The air was thick, stagnant, like that of the other caverns, yet it was different. Cold. This cavern had been untouched for centuries, untainted by the fury of the Tempests beyond, created in a time far before the Vanishing.

Footsteps echoed behind him as he continued down the long, spiral staircase. The others followed quietly, someone slowly dragging their hand along the dusty, curved walls. Cobwebs decorated the curved corners where ceiling met stone.

Asteros sent out a pulse of umbrakinesis, feeling his way through the stairwell as he walked.

Something waited below... somewhere else. Something beyond their descent. A large room, with something inside.

Several energies reverberated through the pulse, causing him to stumble. He touched his chest, blinking. *What is down there?* he thought with wild curiosity. He blinked, taking a deep breath before continuing onward.

The others paused, but did not question him.

Asteros slowly extended a hand as he took step after step, the steady beat of footsteps the only sound in the forgotten cavern. He twisted his hand, sending out another pulse and feeling the strange energies below.

Dormant. Tired... yet not dead. And they were... *foreign. Strange. Unusual, untouched, unknown to humanity*—or at least to Asteros.

His eyes snapped open, the end of the stairwell rapidly approaching. He lowered his hand, continuing to use the other to hold the Scorcher Crystal out before him.

The curved stairs ended.

Asteros's armored foot sent out a cloud of dust as he planted it on the last step. He lingered there for a moment, hesitantly staring into the darkness beyond.

"We're here," Asteros said quietly, his eyes struggling to adjust to the darkness. He pocketed the Scorcher Crystal, plunging the group into... not the dark... not quite. Asteros blinked a few times, suddenly becoming aware of the shape of the room before him.

It was considerably smaller than the chambers of Herqen and Bareholde. The walls were curved, and the low ceiling was domed.

Asteros looked down, noticing a vein of dark red light woven into the stone floor, just below the step.

His eyes traced the line of blood-red energy through the stone. He lifted his foot, watching with curiosity as the light pulsed, its beating akin to that of a heart. *Strange.*

The vein ran beneath the stairs, seeming to continue on through the mountain below.

Asteros turned, his eyes tracking the vein in the other direction. It continued on toward the center of the room... toward *something*.

Asteros took a deep breath, and stepped onto the room's floor.

A low tone sounded through the chamber.

Asteros jumped back, his heart thundering.

The tone had sounded almost like a low rumbling, yet it was unmistakable, a single note from some ancient force of the mountain.

Asteros looked down, the blood-red vein below his foot growing brighter.

Shalheira gasped. "Over there," she said, leaning over Asteros's shoulder and pointing to the side of the massive, circular room.

Asteros followed her finger, noting the light turquoise vein steadily illuminating in the stone. *Another one...* Asteros looked to the other side, seeing a bright green vein lighting up ahead. Asteros followed the veins with his eyes, watching as the lights advanced toward the center of the room, where there was... *something*. Something large, something dark, something *strange*.

The mysterious forces Asteros had felt were coming from that stone. Even standing this far from it, he could *feel* its power.

Asteros took another step, the tone sounding once again, this time deeper, and longer.

The blood-red vein guided him forward as other strata began to ignite within the stone.

He heard the others step onto the floor as well, gasps echoing from behind.

"Gods above," Asteros whispered, counting the veins. As he neared the center of the chamber, he realized that the room was entirely circular, with the stone—three times the size of a man—in the center.

The entire circular room was decorated with glowing veins, each one protruding from the central stone and shooting out in a different direction... red, turquoise, green, tan, multicolored, violet, and white. Seven in total.

"The Lost Sects," Tsarra gasped, kneeling before one of the veins, tracing it with her finger. "Yet..." Tsarra trailed off.

"There's only seven," Lucien said, locking eyes with Asteros. "There should be eight, right?" Lucien asked slowly.

"Over here," Shalheira said.

Asteros turned to her.

She was looking at her feet, standing between the purple vein and the green one. She knelt, tracing her fingers through the stone. "There's another depression here, another canal. Yet it seems to be unfilled."

"There's another here," Soran called out from the other side of the central stone.

"And here," Eithor rumbled. "Count them, quickly."

"Fourteen in total," Lucien said after a moment, raising his eyes to meet Asteros's once again. "And there are fifteen Sects," he said.

"There are eight lost Sects, yet seven of the veins are unfilled," Tsarra said. "Why don't these numbers add up?"

"And why is one of the veins multicolored?" Shalheira asked, pointing to the vein that glowed with an enigmatic mix of purples, oranges, yellows, and reds.

"That's the Starburner vein," Asteros said, taking a step forward. "It matches the color of their Crystals—according to the Ancient histories at least." Asteros paused beside the violet vein.

Whispers.

Asteros blinked. Had he heard something? He shook off the strange shivers that washed over him and looked upward, toward the large stone in the middle of the chamber.

"What—" Shalheira started. "What is it?" she asked, stopping beside Asteros.

More whispers.

Asteros stopped, turning around. Yet no one spoke. *It was almost like...*

"Whatever it is, all of the veins seem to lead to it," Soran said.

"Or away from it," Tsarra added. "Even the empty ones are connected."

The whispers grew louder, Asteros's stomach crawling as he neared the stone. It was easily fifteen feet tall and six feet in diameter. The stone itself seemed to be made of a sort of obsidian... yet... it was different.

Runes covered every inch of it. Runes of all shapes and sizes. Triangular markings formed a ring around the base, followed by circular markings, which were followed by squares.

Every type of Rune? Asteros thought.

Whispers.

Asteros took another step forward.

Reach out...

Asteros paused.

"What is it?" Shalheira asked, laying a hand on his shoulder.

Asteros shrugged it off, a sudden cold indifference coming over him.

"Step back, Shalheira," Lucien commanded, appearing behind Asteros. "It could be dangerous."

"I can handle myself," Shalheira snapped.

Lucien said something back, but Asteros didn't hear it.

Come closer...

Asteros took another step, slowly extending his hand.

The stone seemed darker than darkness itself, as if it was void of all light.

Reach out... it repeated. The whispers quickened, growing louder.

Asteros closed his eyes, hearing Lucien shout behind him. Asteros's fingers stretched forward, trembling.

Someone moved behind him, but it was too late.

Asteros touched the stone.

Haze. Darkness.

Whispers in the wind. Screams. Flashes of white. Black clouds.

Violet wings in a Silver Sun. Shears of night cutting through the stars.

He inhaled, then exhaled. Then he did it again, and again, and again.

An echo.

Something chasing his breath, like shadows in the night. Something was wrong, something was *different*. Another sound, like a breath of its own, a steady pulse of life. There was a melody to this strange place.

Awareness.

It crashed into him like a Storm Gale's strike. A sudden awareness of something else. Something strange, something more. Something...

"Consciousness is merely a construct of the human mind," a smooth voice whispered—or shouted—he couldn't tell. The voice came from everywhere and nowhere. Both external and internal at the same time. "A projection of our souls' innermost values and desires, cast upon the cold stone of the world we live in, creating what we like to call reality." The voice grew quiet, the steady beat of its breath returning.

"Do you know who said that?" the voice asked suddenly, turning its attention to him.

Nothing had changed, for there was still only darkness in this strange place. Yet, somehow, he could feel the creature's attention.

"It sounds familiar, doesn't it?" the voice asked.

It did.

"It often takes several moments for one to orient themselves in this place," the voice continued. "I was hoping that the words of your former master might help you... *adjust.*"

Haldir's words?

"Ah," the voice mused, its eerily hypnotic tone echoing through the silence, waking his soul yet singing it to sleep all the same. "So you do remember? Don't you, Asteros Silverglade?"

Asteros. That was his name—something that he hadn't realized he'd forgotten.

Golden light flickered somewhere in the distance, weaving a path through the strange darkness. It hovered for a moment, a temporary strand of luminosity in the vast nothingness. The thread of golden light faded.

"What have you…" Asteros stumbled over the words, his phantom tongue twisting around itself. "Where am I?" Asteros asked. He reached out, yet felt nothing. He looked down, seeing only more darkness beneath him.

It was almost as if his body itself had been taken from him. A strange floating sensation wafted through his phantom nerves, as if he were hovering somewhere. But he wasn't. He was sitting. *Curious…*

"Where are you?" the voice started. It was male, though something was strange about it, something distorted. "Or where are we?" The creature moved again, though Asteros wasn't sure how he was aware of its movements.

"Both… I suppose," Asteros said, spinning his—What was he? Remove the body from a human and are they still human? Or are they something else?

"You are on the floor of Epirac, touching the Devourer's Stone," the voice said.

Epirac, Asteros thought with a start. Something about that was familiar. In fact, something about the voice itself seemed familiar. *Curious…*

"Your friends are watching you, wondering why you have suddenly fallen silent. Yet, rest assured, they will not pull you from this place until I let them."

"This place…" Asteros whispered, still unsure of where his voice was coming from. "What is this place?"

"This…" the voice said, solidifying slightly.

It was so familiar, yet Asteros couldn't place where it was—what it was.

"This is the Void," it whispered. "This is somewhere beyond Auris, the Unbound, or even Katauriel. This is the end."

"Katauriel…" Asteros said, feeling the foreign word in his mouth.

Violet wings shifted. Yet there was only darkness, everywhere. He was in two places, yet he was nowhere. It was almost as if Asteros wasn't truly living through this moment. He was almost *remembering* it.

"Fascinating how your kind is still oblivious to the existence of other Realms," the voice cooed.

"What have you..." Asteros tried to speak "What have you done to me?"

"Mmmm," the voice hummed. "Do you recall me citing the words of Haldir, your former master?"

Asteros nodded, or he tried to.

Either way, the creature understood. "And you don't wonder why I referenced such things?" it asked.

Asteros's mind fuzzed. It wasn't that he hadn't wondered... he just hadn't thought to ask. Everything felt slow. It was as if his mind itself wasn't working as it normally did.

"I spoke Haldir's words because I wanted to show you that he was not only correct," the voice whispered. "But that he was wrong as well."

"How—" Asteros started to ask. But his voice was taken from him, stolen like a whisper in a howling wind.

"Such a paradox is not possible on Auris." The voice smiled, somehow. "Yet here... here it is the root of our truest nature. What is wrong is also right, and what is right..." The creature laughed, a dark, crackling sound. "What is right is *especially* wrong."

Asteros turned, sensing movement somewhere.

An image subtly crept into his mind. An image of a man, kneeling before a large black stone, wearing armor of black metal. Someone moved behind him in the image. The man had long black hair, tied back in a ponytail, and a pointed black beard. Sharp features... unnervingly sharp.

Something was strange about the scene, for it was almost as if it were moving in slow motion. It was as if the entire world was coated in a black fog, an oppressive smog that clouded reality itself. Almost like... the Unbound...

"Tenvalisare begins, looming like a storm in the distance," the voice said, shifting and twisting through non-existence.

Asteros flinched. Those words... They were familiar, part of something he had read... somewhere...

"You're a Wayfinder?" Asteros asked, his voice returning to him.

"No, my child." The voice laughed. "I have risen above the very things that they look to for their predictions... I am something more."

"You're a God," Asteros pronounced, the statement feeling like the truth he had always known.

"No. I am..." the voice trailed off. Asteros frowned with his phantom features. It almost seemed as if the voice was confused. It drifted away, sliding into the abyss like rain on stone.

Asteros blinked, feeling *something*.

His eyes opened.

Violet skies. A Silver Sun.

He sat up, looking around, only to find that he was not sitting at all, but floating.

Asteros drifted through the unknown, levitating in a strange world of violet darkness, stars dotting the scene around him. He reached out, staring at his arm.

It was wreathed in a cloud of darkness, rippling and turning like an ocean's waves.

The darkness was snug, yet soft enough that he could move freely.

He glanced at his other arm, seeing the same, strange, sandy substance.

He twisted in the abyss, finding his entire body wrapped in the cloud of darkness, it almost looked like... *Shadow-Sand*. Yet it was unforged, still in its purest state. *Then how...*

"My apologies, dearest Asteros," the voice said suddenly.

Asteros tried to turn, but found himself unable to move once again.

Violet wings closed around him, a cloud of darkness chasing the strange appendages that wrapped around him.

Black enveloped Asteros once again, his body vanishing, cast aside as Asteros was thrown back to that strange place.

Wings boomed in the darkness, the creature slowly gliding toward Asteros... or... *carrying me? To where?* Asteros's mind fuzzed, lost to the fog of the Void once again. His thoughts became thick, his brain slowing, he was gone once again. Somewhere else. Somewhere...

"I—" Asteros started, the image of the man with the pointed features coming into focus once again. "I need to go back."

"You will," the voice assured, the unnervingly firm, masculine security of it washing over Asteros. "With time... time, time, time," it muttered, the wings booming in the distance. "Something one tries so hard to forget, yet something that cannot be forgotten."

What? Asteros thought, twisting his phantom body. He became aware of the restraints, or arms, that carried him. Something... human? Asteros inhaled, his heart somehow syncing with the beat of his breath, his lucidity returning to him slowly, but surely.

"You will not remember this encounter," the voice said. "Not all of it, at least. You will recall bits and pieces, faint impressions, perhaps. But you will not know the extent of what you have learned here today."

The man with the pointed features—Lucien was his name—reached out a slow hand in the other world.

"You must accelerate Tenvalisare: the Unbinding of Auris."

"Tenvalisare..." Asteros whispered, his mind seeming to bend as it absorbed the word.

"The Vanishing was only the beginning, a means to an end," the voice continued, its hypnotically smooth tone bringing a deep haze to Asteros's thoughts. "An end that was never meant to be achieved, an end that always was, is, and will be. Something that you must be allowed to progress, if only so that life may persevere through the fog of death.

"The Vanishing must not be repeated, for the Resurgence is near. A Resurgence of chance, of power, and of luck. A Resurgence that was both accidental and foretold... the centerpiece of a prophecy that is yet to be written."

"Wait," Asteros croaked, sensing a sudden light—awareness. "Wait, don't send me back yet."

Lucien's hand grew closer to the kneeling figure, feeling almost inevitable.

"What am I supposed to do?"

"What was lost will be resurged. The other Sects will return," the voice said, more firmly this time. "You, Asteros Silverglade, bear the blood of a Revenant, a dormant piece of your soul yearns to awaken. My path is set in stone and mist, my hands are bound."

Asteros clawed at the light, its luminescence growing brighter with each passing second. *No. No, he couldn't leave yet.*

"You can still save her."

Asteros froze. "What?" Asteros whispered, memories of a girl, young and afraid, piercing his thoughts. *Lyseria?*

"She is lost, but not gone. You can still save her," the voice repeated, rattling. "When you are ready, you shall return to me, young Revenant... You shall return..."

Asteros Silverglade stumbled back, pulled by Lucien's firm grip. He gasped, his breath coming in slowly.

Lucien cursed.

Shalheira knelt by Asteros's side, laying a soft hand on his shoulder.

Asteros's heart raced.

Someone spoke, then someone else. But he couldn't hear them. Or, he could... but not *really*. Not like he had been able to hear...

"What—" Asteros opened his mouth, his tongue feeling heavy and thick. "What happened?" Asteros mumbled, rubbing his eyes.

The faint glow of the veined floor seemed blinding to him, his eyes feeling as if they had not been opened in centuries. "Where am I?"

Lucien cursed again, then shook his head. "You're in Epirac. You touched that stone even though we told you not to, and..."

"And what?" Asteros asked, the fog slowly lifting from his mind. *What happened to me?*

"Something happened," Shalheira said, her touch gentle. The familiar sense of her hand on his body felt like a warm welcome back to this Realm. Her touch felt like home. In a strange way he couldn't explain, it brought him a deeply satisfying sense of comfort and safety, one that he feared could never be replicated by anyone else. "We're still not sure what exactly it was, but we heard a sound, and then you were just... sitting there."

"Something like a wind, whistling and howling, yet whispering all at once," Lucien said, extending an armored hand.

Asteros took it, allowing himself to be hoisted up by the powerful male's grip.

Lucien paused, his sharp Elosian features unnervingly close to Asteros's face.

Asteros forced himself to meet Lucien's eyes. There was something... strange, something odd about the way Lucien looked at him. There was almost a sense of curiosity, wonder, and... *something else?*

"Is he alright?" Soran asked, making his way over to where they stood beside the stone.

"He should be fine," Tsarra answered. She stood beside the stone, examining its Runes with a deep sense of fascination. "I can't make heads or tails of these Runes... I can't even tell what this stone is supposed to do." Tsarra raised her hand, her fingers nearing the dark mass.

"Don't," Asteros said weakly. "Trust me. Don't."

Tsarra withdrew her hand, wrapping her other hand around it as she did so, as if trying to protect it.

"What did you see?" Eithor asked, the frail rattling of his voice sounding weak and empty in the small room.

Asteros turned to the older man, seeing a sense of hope in his pale eyes. No, not hope. Determination, the determination of a man who had lost both of his sons, the determination of a man who sought revenge.

"I saw—" Asteros trailed off. He blinked a few times, the steady beat of the vein beneath him suddenly becoming apparent to him. He looked down, staring into the dark violet light. *Violet wings... A Silver Sun...* "I saw something," Asteros said, shaking his head. "Someone."

"Who?" Shalheira asked.

"I'm... not sure," Asteros said, rubbing his forehead. He ran a hand through his short black hair, straightening it. "But he said something about... the Vanishing, and something else..."

Lucien glanced at Malik, who watched from the entrance of the room, seemingly paying attention.

"Tenvalisare, he called it."

Tsarra's eyes widened. She started across the room, stopping before Asteros. She grabbed him by the shoulder, her red-brown eyes burning brightly. "Asteros," she said, her voice trembling.

Asteros recoiled a bit, shocked at the sudden touch.

"Are you certain that you heard this person correctly?" Tsarra asked.

"I—" Asteros started, looking away. Tsarra did not break her stare. "I think so, yes." Tsarra cursed, pulling away from him and making for the stone.

"Tsarra!" Lucien shouted, grabbing her by the shoulder.

She halted, trying to twist out of his grip.

Lucien held firm, baring his teeth as he held on to her arm. "What are you doing?" Lucien asked firmly, still unwilling to release her.

"Relax," Tsarra said, shaking her arm off as he let her go. "I'm not going to touch it, I was just going to look at it again." Tsarra prowled toward the stone, a strange sense of fascination in her gait as she walked.

"What's Tenvalisare?" Asteros asked, trying to regain his footing.

"Something that was supposed to happen a long time ago," Tsarra said, kneeling beside the stone. "Yet it never happened, thankfully, for none of us would be here if it had."

"You still haven't answered our question," Shalheira said, stalking toward her. "What is it?"

"And why did this voice mention it when I touched the stone?" Asteros asked.

"Tenvalisare is the *Unbinding* of Auris—meaning that all of Auris would *literally* be cast into nonexistence," Tsarra said, turning to Asteros. Her eyes were grave, yet there was something else in them... *fear?* "I don't know why whatever you spoke to in there mentioned Tenvalisare, but what I do know is that the very concept of it threatens our entire existence."

"How do you know this?" Lucien challenged. "We haven't even found anything in the other caverns that mentions this... Tenvalisare."

"That's because all mentions of it predate the era that those caverns were created in by several centuries... but this one is older, I suppose."

"And, if that is true, then how could you have possibly learned about this?" Shalheira asked, advancing once again.

"I didn't," Tsarra shot back. "It was alluded to but once in the ancient texts of the Freyfall, and, even then, it's nothing more than a brief mention of the possibility of a large-scale Unbinding."

Soran and Eithor glanced at each other, then at the Shadow-Swifts.

"I didn't research Tenvalisare," Tsarra repeated. "But someone I was very close to did."

"Who?" Asteros asked.

Tsarra turned back to the stone, her face falling slightly. She tried to smile, her lips quivering a bit. "His name was Velarus," she said softly. "Velarus Ravamoira. He was my cousin—biologically at least —though he was so much more to me." Tsarra took a deep breath.

"His parents were arrested for crimes against the King, so he was raised by my family, as my brother."

"Yet he's not allowed to continue his research, not anymore," Soran interjected. "I knew him as well."

"He was arrested for trying to warn the people of Freyfall about Tenvalisare," Tsarra said, her voice growing hard. "Six years ago he told me that he found something—a small stone. He found it buried in the sand of a cave on the eastern coast of Auris, next to one of his research outposts.

"Velarus told me that ever since he had touched the stone, he'd been having these thoughts... strange thoughts. Ideas that weren't really his. It was almost as if something were influencing his thoughts, like a Whisperer, almost," Tsarra continued, turning around. "He tried to return to that cave but the stone was gone. It was small to begin with, so he figured it must've gotten washed away during a Tempest." Tsarra paused. "I figured that he had simply gone mad—driven insane by the weight of his studies but..."

"But the visions continued," Asteros said softly. *Violet wings. A Silver Sun...*

Tsarra nodded.

"He continued hearing these voices, saying that they were warnings. He tried to say that Tenvalisare was real, and that it was not a thing of the past, but of the future," Tsarra said, clenching her fist. "He started posting fliers all around Freyfall, publishing his opinions, sewing chaos into the masses—even if it wasn't on purpose. King Theurgi Wickenhardt declared him a heretic two years ago, and locked him in the dungeon for spreading terror and lies through the city."

"But he was right," Asteros said. The floating came back—that strange feeling he had felt when he touched the stone. It was almost as if he had left his body behind. "He was right, what he saw was real."

"How do you know that what *you* saw was real, Asteros?" Shalheira started, turning to him.

Asteros took her hands in his, feeling their warmth, their vibrance.

"Trust me," Asteros said slowly, meeting her amber eyes. "It was real. It had to be real. I know it was."

Tsarra laughed, a weak, terrible laugh. It was the laugh of someone who had given up. "You sound just like him," she said, shaking her head. "He used to say these things, over and over again. 'Tsarra, it was real. Tsarra, you should've been there. Tsarra, you have to trust me.'" Tsarra laughed weakly again, sliding down against the curved stone wall of the large chamber. "It ruined his mind. It'll ruin yours too."

"It told me the other Sects were coming back," Asteros said.

Tsarra paused, her gaze locked on the blood-red vein beneath her.

"I heard him say it: The Resurgence is coming," Asteros said.

"That's impossible," Tsarra said. "The other Summoners were all killed, and all of their energies disappeared."

"We don't know that, Tsarra," Asteros challenged, stepping away from Shalheira. "No one knows what the Revenants did, no one knows what happened here, no one even has a damn clue!" Asteros paused before Tsarra, trying to collect himself. "No one except me." *Where did that come from?* Asteros asked himself.

Tsarra held his gaze, red-brown eyes unyielding in the strange luminescence of the chamber.

"Asteros," Lucien said, approaching from behind. "What was it you said about the other Sects? A Resurgence?"

"Yes," Asteros said. "We were never meant to destroy the other Sects." He looked away. "The Vanishing was never meant to be repeated, it was meant to be *undone*."

"Meaning that there will be more Summoners," Shalheira said softly.

All eyes turned to her.

"Yes," Asteros said, approaching. "There will be more Summoners. Perhaps even Summoners who can help us fix this world."

Shalheira shook her head. "No." She looked down. "No... no... no," Shalheira repeated, shaking her head. "There will only be more conflict, more death. A Resurgence would only return the more dangerous abilities of Summoning to Auris—abilities that are meant to stay in the past."

"Shalheira—"

"I can't do this," Shalheira said, pushing Asteros's arm away. "I can't be a part of this. A Resurgence will bring about a new era of warfare, one with double the Summoners and double the casualties... and think of what it would do to the Stormless."

"Shalheira, you have to—" Asteros started again.

But Shalheira didn't let him finish. "I will not stop you, but I will not be a part of your plan, I'm sorry." She paused. "I told you when we began that I would stop if I felt you were wrong... And, now, I think that this has gone too far."

Asteros stood, dumbfounded.

Shalheira turned, starting up the long spiral staircase to the surface.

Malik stood silently beside the doorway, letting Shalheira pass without a word.

"Shalheira," Asteros called out.

Shalheira did not stop.

"Shalheira, *I* am still your superior!" Asteros shouted. "I order you, invoking my right of command as Leader of Erydon, to stay in this cavern. You will leave only with us, and you will return to Erydon when we do."

Shalheira looked down once again, her hollow eyes flickering in the faint light. "I thought you were better than that," Shalheira whispered, closing her eyes. She turned away, and continued up the stairs.

A heavy silence fell over them.

Asteros stared after her as she disappeared beyond the curve of the stairs.

"We need to see what else we can find here," Asteros said,

waving to the others. "We'll deal with her later. Let's see if there are any inscriptions on these walls, find out if these veins lead anywhere, and see what we can learn about this stone."

The others nodded, scattering around the massive chamber with a newfound sense of purpose.

Asteros grimaced; he knew he had struck a nerve, and they couldn't afford to lose Shalheira—not like this. She would come around... she *had* to. He knew that he should've gone after her, but he did not.

What he had seen in that stone... It was simply too much. He needed answers, and he needed them *now*. Shalheira could wait. He loved her very, *very* dearly. But she could wait—she would have to.

Even as he thought this, he knew what he was doing. He knew that he was putting Shalheira second for the first time since their love had blossomed. He knew what he was risking, and yet he did it anyway.

For now all that rang through his mind as he watched the love of his life disappear were whispers of Violet wings... and a Silver Sun.

CHAPTER THIRTY-TWO

THE CONTACT

Castien Varic watched quietly as the massive gates of Arvendon creaked open. The large stone walls loomed over him, their shadows blotting out the Blazeday sun. Castien watched as the gates slid into place, and the crank stopped rotating.

The fractured Starburner Crystal felt heavy in his pocket. It was useless now that it was empty, but it weighed on his mind nonetheless.

"It's about time we returned," Elric said.

"I suppose you're not used to traveling on foot, are you?" Arthion asked.

"Not at all, my friend." Elric flashed a smile and started into the city.

Archers lined the wall overhead, a Scorcher posted at one of the small towers every so often.

"Strange to think that we haven't even been away for two weeks," Ilyana said as they walked.

Castien turned to her, forcing a smile.

She was going to inform him of their next move soon, for Castien had promised to help her discover the spy within Arvendon's ranks.

"It is," Castien said.

The comfortably uneven buildings of Arvendon stretched out before them along the cobblestone road. The blocks of shops and houses were made mostly of stone or brick, and occasionally a more exotic-colored rock. The Salarin Sea crashed in the distance, closer to them now than it had been for weeks.

Castien smiled to himself; he had missed the sea.

Bells rang distantly, sounding their calls from the ships on which they were stationed. Castien looked around, feeling a strange sense of calm as he reentered his home city. The slightly slanted city looked warm, inviting even. He turned to the left, his eyes following the city's roads up the sharp incline far ahead toward Summerglass Palace.

The white-marble castle shined brightly in the Blazeday, looking much like it must have on the day of Velarus's arrival.

Castien shuffled to the side as a Sunbeam whizzed by.

Ilyana laughed at this.

Castien smiled—for real this time. Sunbeams were much like Wisps, only made of incorporeal heat rather than a strange unknown energy. Sunbeams were far less dense than the useless Wisps in their cover of the land as well, and simply danced through the open air with ease and freedom, rather than clinging to the ground in close-knit patterns.

The crowds milled by Castien, several doing double takes as they realized who had returned. Castien found his smile fading. He did not belong here. Even among a group where arguably only Elric was recognizable, no one looked at Castien.

Someone shouted from a fruit cart nearby, calling out his prices. Castien smiled as he heard the reporters crying out the news. These sounds... They were familiar.

Being back here was strangely welcoming, yet it felt different. It was like Castien was trying to return to a life that he no longer fit into. Or like he was attempting to revive a part of his past that had long since been killed.

"Well then," Elric said, pausing amidst the crowd.

Castien slid up against the Cloudwalker, shying away from the endless swarms of crowds within the city. Many of them wore leather, though those who were wealthy enough wore a colorful fabric of one type or another.

Castien wrinkled his nose. One thing he had *not* missed, however, was the smell.

"I must return to the palace," Arthion said. "The King will be expecting a report from me."

"Aye," Elric said. "I must go to Summerglass as well. I don't know what has happened here over the last few days, but I know that the King likely has need for me." He looked at Castien and smiled softly.

Castien felt a sort of sadness come over him. Most of the last several days had been spent traveling in silence, for Castien was in no mood for conversation. Yet, now that he was having to say good-bye, he found himself wishing that he had gotten to know the Cloud-walker a little more.

"Where will you two go?" Arthion asked, rubbing his gloved hands together and stepping forward. He paused, allowing a sunbeam to zip by before continuing.

"I have a place on the southern side," Ilyana said. Her Elosian features twisted into a smile. "It'll be nice to be home again."

"And you?" Elric asked, turning back to Castien.

Castien fell silent. He needed to put in his notice for the Storm-less Corps, to tell them that he was leaving. Despite the week he had spent walking in silence on the way back to Arvendon, Castien had not changed his mind. He was unsure of what he would do now, but he knew that he could not be a part of the army any longer. This world was changing, and not for the better. It was becoming more dangerous, and a Stormless had no place on the battlefield any longer.

He slipped a hand into his pocket, feeling the shard within.

Maybe finding out what in Calida's Claws happened to me with this Crystal would be a good place to start, Castien thought. He looked back to Elric, quickly letting his hand drop to his side once again.

"I'm probably going to have to find a place somewhere on the southwestern side of Arvendon, at least to start," Castien said quietly. That quarter of Arvendon was well known to be the poorest, though Castien supposed there was no shame in that. He was a Stormless, after all. It wasn't like he could do much better.

Elric laid a hand on Castien's shoulder, meeting Castien's gaze with his emerald eyes.

Castien tried to smile, then looked away.

Elric squeezed his shoulder briefly, then opened his mouth. "I promised you that I was going to help you receive treatment, Castien," Elric said. "I'm going to stand by that promise. The King should be able to spare a Whisperer, on occasion, to help train your mind to better control your emotions." Elric smiled, his blazecrest-shaped nose hanging above his grin. "I'll send for you in a few days, lad. Just don't be too hard to track down, alright?" Elric winked, and turned away.

Arthion approached, the Whisperer offering a warm smile. He extended a gloved hand. "It's been a pleasure to get to know you, my boy," Arthion said, his amber eyes sparkling in the sunlight. "You've shown me that there are more to the Stormless than many believe... and that there is always value within that which may present itself as unimportant." Arthion shook his hand once more, then turned around. "I hope to see you again someday, Castien. May the Gods guide our paths together once again." Arthion walked away, leaving Castien standing in the middle of the busy street with Ilyana.

"You alright, Stormless?" Ilyana asked.

Castien allowed his gaze to linger on Arthion and Elric, tracking them until they disappeared into the folds of the crowd.

"Yeah," Castien said, turning back to face her. "Just..." Castien trailed off. "I'm not sure," Castien said. "It's just weird how quickly this all happened, you know?"

"Yeah," Ilyana said, nodding. "One second, you're just another person in Arvendon. The next, you're on a mission with some of the most powerful people in the world... and, before you know it, you're a nobody again."

"It's strange," Castien said, meeting her gray eyes.

She nodded, her sharp face remaining still.

Castien searched her features, finding a hard sort of reassurance within them. "So, what is it that you need me to do?" Castien asked.

Ilyana looked down, reaching into her blue-gray cloak. She pulled out a small slip of paper that had been folded into a tiny square. "Once you've taken care of everything you need to, go to this address," Ilyana said, handing him the paper. "I'm meeting with my contact tonight. Do what you can to be there by tomorrow morning at the latest, alright?" Ilyana turned away, starting in the opposite direction.

Castien nodded hesitantly. "Wait," Castien called out.

Ilyana paused, swiveling back.

"Are you sure that you don't want me to just..." Castien trailed off. He couldn't go with her. He couldn't start this, not now. If he went with Ilyana, he would become dependent on her not only for a place to stay, but a place to belong. "Never mind," Castien said. "I suppose I'll see you soon."

Ilyana nodded, and turned away.

Castien did the same, looking out into the crowd beyond. It was a little past midday, and he would have plenty of time before he needed to be at Ilyana's apartment.

Plenty of time to throw my old life away, Castien thought, smiling to himself. He slipped his hands back into his pocket, feeling the broken Starburner Crystal once again. *Plenty of time to start again.*

Having turned in his request to leave the Stormless Corps, Castien felt a strange sense of relief. He walked through the dimming streets of Arvendon as the sun slowly set, and the Blazeday dissipated.

Typically, a request of leave with no explanation would not be accepted so easily, though Castien was certain that his presence on the expedition had elevated his position among his comrades to some extent. And, if they did reject his offer, he had no doubts that Elric could use his treatment as an excuse to leave the ranks.

His letter had been brief, and he had delivered it without bothering to say a word to his former squadron. He would say his good-byes, yes, but only after the request was accepted. Castien had no attachment to his new squadron anyway. He didn't even know where his former crew was at the moment.

Yet he had every confidence in his decision. He had thought about it a great deal during the journey home, only straying from the topic when he dared ponder what had happened with the Starburner Crystal. All his life he had honestly seen himself working as an innkeeper, just as his father had. Although that was before... To be an innkeeper now would be rather difficult, given that the family inn was no longer open to him.

He could buy his own, but doing so would require a hefty sum of money that Castien did not have. Castien supposed he could work somewhere in the palace. But no, that would put him right in the middle of the mess of a world that he lived in once again.

He needed something that would separate him from the chains of society. Castien needed something that he could do on his own, something that could make a difference. It was not his concern at the moment, if he was being honest. All he truly worried about was how on Auris he was going to put himself in a position to pick his own occupation in the first place.

The streets were growing darker, and the buildings were becoming less varied as Castien continued to the southern side of the city. Most of these areas were living spaces, and they were somewhat on the cheaper side, though there was a small plaza at the far end of the road which had once been a bustling center of business. Ilyana had likely holed up in one of the apartments in this section of the city, though, when Castien looked at the stone markers on the side of the road, he realized that he still had several blocks to go.

Most of the buildings here were made of dark stone from The Wastelands, augmented with wood lining to call after the architecture of the time before the Vanishing. Window shutters were closing as the sun vanished on the horizon. The city was beginning to wind down, and even the crowds were beginning to thin.

Castien smiled. He should've been worried. He should've been anxious. He should've been *terrified*. Yet, instead, he felt free. It was as if he had been given a breath of fresh air after a lifetime of suffocation. No longer would he be bound by the shackles of the Stormless Corps, and no longer would he contribute to the horrific destruction that was brought about by the armies of Auris.

Castien might not even have to concern himself with being Stormless any longer, given what he had discovered with the Crystal. Unfortunately, there was no way to refuel the Starburner Crystal fragment.

Then a thought occurred to him... The Royal Libraries of Freyfall and Cyfalion: They might have information on the Starburners. Even the Archives of Suchara might suffice. Castien supposed that the libraries in Arvendon would be a more convenient place to start, but they were infamous for holding remarkably little information—at least as far as availability to the public went.

He could travel to Freyfall or Cyfalion and learn what there was to know about the Ancient Sects. He would get to leave Arvendon behind, but...

Freyfall had already aligned with the Blood Sorcerers. An agent had been sent to Cyfalion as well, according to Kels. There was nothing to be done. It seemed that the Blood Sorcerers were effectively beginning their takeover of Auris—if that was what they were planning.

No. Castien needed to stay in Arvendon. Elric had told him that he would receive treatment for his mind, and that was something that Castien figured was at least worth trying.

Castien looked up, seeing another sign ahead. This was where he was to turn, according to Ilyana's note. She had also written that there was a key under the corner floorboard nearest to the apartment, which gave Castien a way to get in if she was not home.

He turned into the dark street, now fully enveloped in the night. Castien looked around, the closed shutters on either side of him reflecting the late hour. He would be wise to get inside soon. Unfolding the slip of paper once again, Castien checked to make sure he had the correct building. It should be the one on the right up ahead, at the end of this small cut-through street.

A lantern offered some refuge from the darkness. The wind whistled softly, matching harmoniously with the distant crash of the waves. Castien took another deep breath, knowing that he was nearing his destination.

A door opened to the side.

Castien hunkered down out of reflex, pressing against the building to his right in the narrow alley. The door squealed, revealing a cloaked figure perhaps forty paces ahead of him. The figure looked out, a familiar gray-blue robe shining in the dim light of the lantern. Castien stayed concealed in the shadow of the building.

Ilyana looked both ways, seemingly missing Castien and turning the opposite direction. She started down through the darkness, a sense of determination in her gait.

Castien slowly peeled himself from the wall, brushing off his dirty leather armor. Castien blinked, and she was at the end of the alley in an instant.

"Damn Dexteris," Castien cursed, breaking into a quiet jog.

Ilyana turned to the left, disappearing around the corner.

Castien picked up his speed, coming to the end of the alley after a minute or so. He looked to the left, spotting Ilyana once again at the end of another alley.

This one was even narrower, perhaps only large enough for three or four people across. The buildings around him were roughly three stories high, and the lanterns were few and far between.

Ilyana turned another corner, going right this time. She appeared to be heading toward the sea.

Castien panted, breaking into another light jog to catch up with her while not getting too close. He wasn't sure why he didn't just call out her name, or simply go to the apartment and wait for her to return. *Something* urged him to continue following her. Perhaps it was in his nature to be mistrustful, even if Ilyana had been nothing but good to him.

Ilyana had to be keeping something from him—everyone always had their secrets. True, Castien had come to like her, but she wasn't exactly trusted by most in Arvendon. Something was off. If he wanted any shot at figuring out *what* exactly was amiss, then he was going to have to follow her.

That's a good rationalization, right? Castien thought. He turned another corner, finding himself deep within the block of apartment buildings. They were made of a dark stone, even further reflecting the twilight shadows in the evening. Castien looked around, seeing a flash of a cloak in the distance up ahead. *She must've used her powers again*, Castien thought, breaking into a run down another long alley. He whipped around another corner, then slid to a halt.

Ilyana was stopped up ahead, standing before a door in the darkness.

Castien stepped back quietly, leaning against the corner, out of sight.

Ilyana knocked.

He heard a door squeak.

"From the sea to the sky," a distant voice said.

"In the blink of an eye," Ilyana said, finishing what was apparently some sort of code.

Castien tilted his head, making note of the phrase.

"It's about time you showed up," the first voice said.

"I was told to arrive just as night fell," Ilyana said. "And that is what I have done."

"Yes, but you were given those instructions before..." the voice trailed off. "There's been a change of plans. Come inside," the voice said. Castien peeked around the corner just as Ilyana vanished into the apartment building.

A dark, gloved hand reached out, pulling the door shut. Castien cursed.

A change of plans? Castien thought. That was... interesting. Though what could he do about it now? Niventia only knew how long Ilyana would be meeting with her contact, and if she came out to find Castien trying to listen in...

Castien had no choice. All he could do was go back to Ilyana's apartment, and wait.

A door squealed open in the night, pulling Castien from the depths of his sleep. Castien rolled over, the small twin bed in the corner of Ilyana's apartment creaking as he did so.

A figure stood in the doorway.

Castien blinked a few times, the dim light of the corridor beyond seemed blinding to him in his dazed state. Castien sat up, watching as the figure closed the door.

The woman leaned against the doorframe and seemed to sag with exhaustion.

"Ilyana?" Castien asked, his thoughts slowly becoming clear as he woke from his slumber. *How long have I been asleep? How long was she out there?*

Ilyana did not answer, though Castien's eyes had adjusted enough that he recognized her blue-gray cloak. Ilyana sniffled, taking a shaky inhale.

Castien frowned. *Am I dreaming?* In the short time he had known Ilyana, he had never known her to show anything but confidence.

Castien rolled to his feet, sliding off the small bed. The apartment had four rooms: a small entryway, a bedroom with a small kitchen, and another bedroom with a tiny bathroom attached. Castien had found Ilyana's belongings in one of the bedrooms—the one connected to the bathroom—and decided that it was implied that he should take the other. Castien had settled in quickly, exhausted from the nearly two weeks of traveling behind him. He had fallen asleep the second his head had hit the pillow.

"Ilyana, what's going on?" Castien asked, his thin underclothes rustling as he stepped toward her.

Ilyana took another shaky inhale, her shoulder still braced against the doorframe. She turned to him.

Castien saw a slight shimmer in her gray eyes in the pale moonlight that drifted through the glass window in the entryway. "Did something happen?" he asked.

Ilyana sniffled again. "I met with my informant," Ilyana said, her voice quiet.

Castien took another step forward, feeling a pit form in his stomach. He had never seen Ilyana like this... he hadn't even thought it was possible for her to be like this.

"He had some news for me," Ilyana continued

"Which was?" Castien asked, laying a hand on her shoulder.

Ilyana flinched, inhaling sharply. She locked eyes with Castien, then looked at his outstretched hand. She nodded slightly, and he lowered it to her shoulder. She opened her mouth to speak, but nothing came out.

"It doesn't matter," Ilyana said after a moment.

Castien frowned.

"What does matter is that we still have a target, and it is absolutely *necessary* that we take care of them tomorrow night," Ilyana said.

"But..." Castien trailed off. "Tomorrow night is the Solstice. Nearly everyone in the city will be at Summerglass—"

"Exactly," Ilyana said. "I was told that we are to make a spectacle out of this. And what better timing than on the biggest night of the year?" Ilyana rubbed her eyes, a cold sense of determination coming over them. It faded quickly, the mask of power melting beneath the weight of what seemed like grief.

Castien laid his other hand on Ilyana's arm, rubbing it softly.

She sniffled, leaning away from his touch.

"It's late," Castien said. He glanced outside, verifying his statement by locating the sister moons of Auris high in the night sky. "You were gone when I arrived at nightfall, and you are only just now returning. Are you sure that everything is alright? You've been gone a long time for a simple exchange with an informant."

"I met with my contact," Ilyana repeated. "He told me the plan, as well as the target, and what my plan should be. I needed to set up our way out before tomorrow evening, and I needed to make sure that everything was in place." Ilyana avoided Castien's gaze.

Way out? Castien thought curiously.

"Who is the target?" Castien asked.

"You don't need to know," Ilyana said. "I will take care of the target. All you have to do is make sure that I have a clear path to them, alright?" Ilyana's eyes turned hard in the pale moonlight.

Castien met her gaze, and nodded slightly. *What could have possibly happened that made her this upset?*

"Wait," Castien said. Ilyana paused halfway to her room, turning around. "You haven't told me any of the plan yet."

"I'll tell you what you need to know when you need to know it," Ilyana said. She turned away.

Castien started after her, forcing authority into his step. "Ilyana," Castien said, grabbing her shoulder.

She whirled around, flipping her arm and twisting out of his grip, locking his arm in a hold against the doorframe. Castien blinked, the sudden burst of speed throwing him off.

"*Don't*," Ilyana growled.

Castien met her gaze, her eyes brimming with tears once again.

"Ilyana, if our mission is truly to remove a Celesian spy from Arvendon's hierarchy, then I deserve to at least know what the basic outline of our plan is," Castien said. "This is dangerous, and I think that I deserve to know where we're meeting, and what my role is." Castien slowly withdrew his arm, then smiled softly.

Ilyana looked away. "We are going to attend the Feast of the Solstice as guests," Ilyana whispered. "You are going to keep a low profile until I get a lay of the land and figure out how exactly I'm going to do this. I'll tell you what to do, and where to meet, and then we'll go from there," Ilyana said. "If there are more spies within the palace, they may try to retaliate. If something goes wrong, we won't be able to take the main road down from the cliff where Summerglass lies."

"So..." Castien trailed off. "If we can't take the road, how are we going to get down? Summerglass is at the peak of a hill, and the road is the only way up. The rest of the hill is edged with cliffs that lead down to the shore."

Ilyana met his gaze. "I told you that I was setting up our way out," she said. "You're going to have to trust me." She turned away once again, this time seeming more determined in her quest toward her bed. "With any luck there won't be another spy... and there won't be any trouble, but we need to have a plan."

Castien watched, almost feeling a sense of longing... yet also frustration at being kept in the dark. Granted, she saved him during the Blood Sorcerers' ambush, but he still felt that he deserved more information than he was getting. There was no reason for her to be withholding all of this information when there wasn't even anything that he could—

Castien stopped himself. Now was not the time.

Ilyana was peculiar in her ways, but she was one of the most powerful Summoners on Auris. And, from what he could tell, her only goal was to earn the trust of Arvendon's people so that she could finally feel like she belonged somewhere. And that... that Castien understood.

He was just going to have to trust her. Ilyana was a smart woman. She was cunning, deadly, and more than a little arrogant. But she was not unwise. Castien had no choice but to believe that she knew what she was doing. And, of course, he could hope that he wouldn't get killed in whatever she was planning for tomorrow evening.

It was the Solstice, after all—the biggest night of the year. Anything could happen.

CHAPTER THIRTY-THREE
SHATTERED

Ten months ago...

Erydon stood silently, hidden in the frozen mountains, far from the prying eyes of society. Snow fell around its walls of stone, a steady pelting of cold and ice on the rock that the Shadow-Swifts called home. Such a peaceful place... A paradise buried in snow.

These stones, once the home of six Shadow-Swifts, were now the home of only four... So much had happened over the past few weeks. And now, after already losing Keries and Lyseria, Asteros had lost something far more important: Shalheira's love.

The three scholars paced in their rooms, quietly. They had no idea how this would change the group, not yet. They only knew that they were on the verge of turning the world on its head.

Asteros Silverglade felt them moving, sensing the motions with his umbrakinesis. He closed his eyes. Asteros stood, numb.

This library, once a source of so much hope and passion, now served only as a reminder of what he had lost. He had found what he sought... but at what cost? This library, once a hearth of inspiration, now brought only feelings of shame. The bright Voltarian Crystals hummed quietly, accompanying the slow beat of Asteros's heart.

A Silver Sun... Violet Wings... Whispers in the wind...

Asteros sighed, rubbing his eyes. The whispers had not stopped. The screams had not stopped. The strange white flashes, and the brief moments of darkness, had not stopped.

Shears of night cutting through the stars...

Asteros cursed, grasping the wall as he doubled over.

The whispers hit him harder each time, coming from nowhere, then vanishing into his subconscious without a trace. They interrupted his thoughts, tainting his mind, twisting his words.

"A part of me is happy to see you like this," a cold voice said.

Asteros flinched, coughing. He turned to the doorway, locking eyes with the woman of his dreams.

Shalheira. Her amber eyes were dark, despite the blinding Voltarian Crystal.

When did that become so bright? Asteros thought, rubbing his eyes.

"Shalheira," Asteros started. "I know that—"

She held up a hand, silencing him.

Asteros quieted, bowing his head.

"First, you drive Keries and Lyseria away," Shalheira said. "And now you claim that you must bring about the Resurgence."

Asteros closed his eyes. A heavy silence fell over the pair.

"Do you expect me to just overlook this?" Shalheira asked after a moment, her voice cracking a bit. "I understand that this was not your original intention, Asteros, I do. But this is still your fault."

Two corpses, stranded on the beach, maimed by a lost storm. Tears. Waves. A living shadow.

"Shalheira," Asteros rasped. He fell to his knees. "If I had any other option, you know that—"

"I know that you will try to convince me, Asteros," Shalheira said. "I know that you will try to win me back. But why even bother?"

Asteros paused, tilting his head. "What do you mean?"

"Everything we did together," Shalheira said. "I understand

now." She laughed weakly, defeated. "I have been thinking, and, after speaking to Lucien, I realized that you never did love me. You never will."

Asteros stood, his face hardening. "What?" he whispered. *Lucien?* He raised a hand to Shalheira's face, but she turned away.

"You only want me on your side so that you can use me to further your own goals," Shalheira said, her eyes distant. "You want to cause the Resurgence and cast Auris into chaos so that you can take control. Although there was one thing that I never understood." Shalheira turned back to him, tears glistening in her beautiful eyes. "Why?" She took a step forward. "You want power, you want control, why? Why do any of this? The life we were living may not have been terribly eventful, but, Asteros... we were happy." Shalheira wiped a tear from her cheek.

"Shalheira," Asteros said, taking a step closer, raising his arms.

She melted into his grasp without hesitation.

He held her warm figure as she wept quietly. "Who put these horrible ideas into your head?" Asteros asked, stroking her soft hair.

"I—" Shalheira started. A sob overtook her, drowning out the words.

Asteros closed his eyes, feeling that familiar warmth at the back of his eyes. Tears slid down his cheeks slowly, the reality of the situation finally crashing into him.

"You know that I would end it for you, Shalheira," Asteros whispered. Even as he spoke the words, he knew that they weren't true. But it didn't matter, he *needed* to get her back. "Everything that I've been working toward, Epirac, the Resurgence... all of it... I would put an end to all of it, for you. Because, the truth is, the reason I was doing all of this to begin with was you. I wanted to give you a life worth living. I wanted to change the way the world looked at our kind, give us a fresh start... I wanted to see the world, and be able to travel through these beautiful lands and not be viewed as a killer, but as a leader, a hero." These were his initial goals, true, but... things had changed. He couldn't help but twist the truth; especially if it helped win Shalheira back.

"You don't have to plunge Auris into decades of war for us to be able to see the world together, Asteros," Shalheira said. "We could cast this armor aside right now, toss these weapons off this damned mountain, take our Crystals, and go."

Asteros's eyes cracked open.

"There's nothing stopping us. No one would know who we are, no one would bother us," Shalheira said.

"We could build a nice little house on the shore, maybe somewhere in The Archipelago," Asteros continued.

Shalheira laughed softly, her warmth melting into him. "Have five kids and show them what life is really all about," Shalheira added, pulling back slightly. "All we have to do is leave. Nothing is stopping us, nothing ever was."

Asteros stared into her face, that beautiful face. He saw hope. He saw something that he had never seen in those amber eyes: peace. He smiled softly, pulling her in once again.

Keries crossed his mind, passing over like a dark cloud. *Lyseria... Violet wings... Echoes... Screams.*

Asteros doubled over, pushing Shalheira aside. His breathing increased, his heart pounding in his chest. Flashes of darkness overcame his vision, resetting his thoughts, dominating his mind.

Shalheira knelt beside him, laying a soft hand on his armored back.

Asteros closed his eyes, breathing in, then out. *Echoes...*

"Asteros," Shalheira said quietly. "Something's wrong, isn't it?"

Asteros looked back to her, met by those same peaceful eyes.

"What's going on?" Shalheira asked.

"Shalheira," Asteros said quietly, standing up.

She stood with him, pulling him into yet another embrace.

Haze... Something clouded his mind. Something was... bothering him. Something was wrong. Something was... *strange.*

"Asteros, you said that you would give it all up," Shalheira started, pulling back once again. "You said that you would drop all of this and leave, if I gave the word."

Asteros nodded.

"So do it," Shalheira said, her head tilting slightly. "Do it, now. Together, you and I can leave this place. We can forget Lucien, we can forget Malik, and the scholars, and..." she trailed off.

Asteros looked off to the side, a strange sense of calm coming over his muscles.

"Asteros, please," Shalheira whispered, pulling him close. "Please," she begged. "That's all I ask."

Asteros stepped back.

Shalheira released her grip on him, hesitantly. Another tear slipped from her glistening eyes.

"Shalheira," Asteros said, raising a hand to her hair. He ran it through the smooth black curls, following his hand with his gaze. "We cannot stop now," Asteros said after a moment.

"Asteros, you said—"

"I know what I said," Asteros cut her off. "But we cannot let all of this be for nothing. We have sacrificed one third of our order for this mission; we cannot let this go to waste."

"Asteros," Shalheira said, her voice shaking. "If we keep going, we're only going to lose more,"

Asteros turned away, his eyes growing distant once again.

A Silver Sun...

"You know that I'm right, Asteros," Shalheira said through gritted teeth. "If we continue, we will only find more death, and more pain. We need to stop *now!*" Shalheira shouted, shaking Asteros.

Asteros turned back to her slowly, his body moving on its own accord. "I'm sorry," Asteros said, meeting her gaze once again.

Shalheira cursed, turning away.

Asteros remained still.

Shalheira slammed her fist onto the table, cracking the wood.

"Shalheira," Asteros started.

Shalheira continued, picking up a book and hurling it at the wall. It crashed into a bookshelf, bringing down several others with it. Shalheira reached for the Voltarian Crystal on the wall when Asteros finally grabbed her hand.

"Let. Me. Go," Shalheira growled.

Asteros shook his head, his eyes hard.

Shalheira twisted, trying to escape his grip.

"You need to calm down," Asteros said. "We still need you."

Shalheira laughed, her eyes red with tears. "So that's what this is about then?" Shalheira said. "You only care about what I do because you still need me to help you in this fight, right? And you only need me because *you screwed up* and lost Lyseria and Keries. How's that, right on the mark?" Shalheira paused. "Lucien was right... All you ever bring to this world is pain and suffering." Shalheira shook her hand, pulling out of Asteros's grip. "Well fine," Shalheira spat. "If all you want me to be is your weapon... well, then you might as well take this." Shalheira drew one of her twin daggers, and slammed it into Asteros's chest plate.

Pain and shock ripped through Asteros's body. He stumbled back, holding the knife where it protruded from his thick armor.

It had broken Asteros's skin, though his armor was thick enough that it hadn't done much damage... Either way, the message was clear.

Shalheira turned, her robe gliding behind her in the phantom winds of Erydon.

Asteros took a step, the hilt of the dagger still protruding from his armor, sticking out haphazardly. "Shalheira," Asteros said firmly, starting after her. "Wait."

Shalheira did not turn.

Asteros continued, following her through the hallway, back toward the main atrium.

Shalheira passed through it wordlessly, her bare feet quietly tapping against the dark stone. She slipped past the armory, grabbing a sash of Crystals and throwing it over her shoulders.

Something awakened within Asteros: a cold, primal fury. Perhaps it was the adrenaline, perhaps it was the love he felt… But she truly was trying to leave, and he could not let her.

"Shalheira, you listen to me, *right now*," Asteros growled, using his umbrakinesis to dash forward and grab her by the shoulder.

She jumped, but he held strong.

"I already lost two of my Shadow-Swifts. I will not lose you too," Asteros said.

"You already did," Shalheira whispered, twisting out of his grip. "You lost me the second you started thinking about the Vanishing." Shalheira turned, but Asteros reached out once again. She was ready.

She phased, dodging his arm before shifting back and elbowing him in the back. She hit one of the armor's cracks, sending a shock through Asteros.

Asteros stumbled to the ground, the force of the fall pushing her dagger deeper into his chest. He tugged on it.

Pain *screamed* through his body.

The dagger was wedged between clefts of his armor. It would take too long to remove safely right now. And, even then, he wasn't sure that he would be able to take it out without causing even more damage.

"I'm leaving, Asteros," Shalheira said coldly, standing over him as he stumbled to his knees. "You can't stop me."

"Yes," Asteros whispered, rising to his feet. His chest burned. Draining a Crystal, Asteros numbed the pain. "I can."

Shalheira ran.

And Asteros ran after her. He still wore his armor, and had several Crystals stored in its compartments. He drew upon these, pushing himself off Erydon's walls, propelling toward her.

She wore no armor, just an ordinary robe, but she drew upon the sashed Crystals.

Asteros saw only darkness as he ran through the passages of Erydon. He *was* darkness. He was a shadow, chasing the final ray of light in his dying life. He remembered the creature in the stone. He remembered how he felt when he was in that place... *the Void.*

There was so much more to this life than they knew. There was so much to be discovered, so much to be found. Yet, Shalheira saw none of it. She wanted no part in his plan. She wanted to leave and never come back. She wanted to hide in the wilderness somewhere, where true responsibility could never find her.

But not Asteros.

Asteros didn't want that life, he never had. He wanted *change.* The world was dying. It needed to evolve, and it had fallen upon Asteros's shoulders to be the catalyst of that evolution.

But that didn't matter. Nothing mattered, not right now. Nothing mattered, except Shalheira. *Whispers in the wind... Screams... Violet wings.*

Shalheira turned another corner, nearing Erydon's back door.

Asteros roared, leaping after her as she jumped toward the crack in the ceiling.

Shalheira screamed, phasing mid-air as she passed through the small gap in the rock.

Two figures of darkness shot out of the mountain and into the night, one fleeing, the other *hunting.*

Snow fell violently, pelting Asteros's face as he dashed through the night, following the love of his life as she flew into the clouds.

She broke through them, the air strangely still above the raging Frostfall, yet Asteros felt anything but peace. Shalheira would not be allowed to leave.

She shot forward, phasing out of the Unbound to lighten the drain on her Crystals.

Asteros took the opportunity. He crashed into her, shifting out of the Unbound as he collided with her robed body. Crystals cracked as they hit. Asteros wrapped his arms around her, locking her in a hold as he drew upon his Crystals, reversing their direction.

Shalheira screamed, kicking him between the legs and tumbling out of his grip. She flew through the air, calling upon her remaining Crystals and continuing.

Asteros growled, shooting after her.

Shalheira shot a bolt of umbrakinesis behind her, narrowly missing Asteros as he followed.

He screamed in the moonlit darkness, the pale glow of Lotius and Oria painting the cloud tops an eerie turquoise-gray.

"Stop!" Asteros roared as Shalheira shot back another bolt of darkness, this one skimming Asteros's stomach. He cried out in pain as the dagger shifted deeper, its hilt still protruding from his chest.

She remained silent, pushing herself even harder through the frozen air. Plumes of darkness trailed her figure, washing over Asteros as he neared her once again.

He would not let her leave.

That night crashed into him once again, the night he had spent with her... that very first one. The night that he had left. But that night was long gone. Nothing would ever be the same. Shalheira would not love him again, not after this. But she would not leave—he would make sure of that.

"I said—" Asteros roared, pushing through the thinning air with all his might. He reached Shalheira once again, grabbing her by the arms and pulling them both to a halt. "...Stop."

Shalheira looked him in the eye, and that was when he saw it.

Fear.

"Asteros," Shalheira whispered, starting to pull away as they hovered over the raging Frostfall below. "Please..." she wept.

Asteros tilted her chin, but she looked away. He followed her gaze, noting that she seemed to be watching the dagger planted in his chest.

Shalheira moved her hand, reaching for something. Her arm wrapped around his back, slipping through the cracks of his armor as she made to unhook it.

He reacted by instinct, twisting her arm and using his enhanced strength to flip her over his shoulder.

Something ripped.

Shalheira tumbled over Asteros's shoulder.

"Asteros!" Shalheira screamed.

Asteros released Shalheira from his grip, hurling her over his back and out into the night, preparing for another chase.

But she did not retaliate. She disappeared into the clouds soundlessly.

Asteros froze, his muscles tense. He inhaled, then exhaled. Then repeated.

A soft clink sounded from his chest. Asteros reached, feeling the dagger impaling his ribs.

Something was attached to it.

He felt the smooth surface of a Crystal hanging from the hilt, and then another. He looked down in horror, his eyes finally settling on the truth.

Shalheira's sash hung from the hilt of her dagger, the rope broken in half. Meaning...

"SHALHEIRA!"

Asteros extinguished his Crystals, plunging into the blizzard. Time seemed to freeze as he fell, his mind empty. His soul was... hollow. Only the pooling sense of dread in his stomach remained.

He crashed into the snowy mountainside, barely slowing himself with his Crystals. He roared, leaping, half buried in snow, soaring back into the air. His frantic eyes scanned the mountainside, his heart pounding in his chest. His breathing seemed to stop, his muscles tensing. *No.*

There. A dark form lying on the rocky slope of the mountain.

Asteros crossed the distance, then lowered himself to the ground, nearing the figure. *No, no, no...* Asteros took a step, his armored foot colliding with harsh stone.

She did not move.

Asteros took another step forward, extinguishing his Crystals. He reached out, his hand trembling.

Her warm figure did not stir as he lay his fingers on her side. She did not move as he brought his other hand up, turning her over.

The once-beautiful face beneath him was barely recognizable. Bones had been shattered, warm blood coating her crushed features in the cold night. Snow fell violently around them, drowning out Asteros's scream.

Everything he had ever done. Everything had been for her. Everything. And now...

A silent scream sang through the night once again. Asteros clung to her ruined corpse. He never wanted to let go. He tore the dagger from his chest, tossing it to the side and bringing her body up against his

She lay limp in his arms.

Maybe if she had fallen with her Crystals... but she didn't. They had gotten stuck on her own dagger as Asteros had thrown her over his shoulder. *No... No... NO.*

She couldn't be gone. She wasn't. It wasn't possible.

"Shalheira—" Asteros whispered, weeping over her broken form. "Please no," Asteros begged. "Please... please..."

She did not move. He knew that it was too late. There was no chance.

She was gone.

CHAPTER THIRTY-FOUR
RUINED SOULS

Ten months ago...

Shattered bones. *A broken body. Violet wings and a Silver Sun...*

Asteros Silverglade lowered himself to the ground, his armored feet landing softly on Erydon's floor. *Shears of night cutting through the stars.* Asteros took a step forward, his bloodied armor cracked in more than one place. He took another step forward.

Echoes.

It wasn't real. It didn't feel real. It couldn't be real. The shocking numbness lingered in his bones for what felt like an eternity, though the events of the night seemed to pass by in but a single second. It was like trying to remember a dream—or a nightmare. But nightmares weren't real.

And this... This was real. Asteros stumbled forward, tossing aside the torn Crystal sash.

It crashed to the floor, sending out plumes of dark smoke as it landed. Asteros didn't care. He felt his chest, where the dagger had been. It was gone.

Dark metal shining in the midnight moons. Falling snow. A Silver Sun.

Asteros closed his eyes, the image of a bloodied dagger lying in the snow beside a broken corpse burning into his mind. He collapsed.

"No," Asteros whispered. Everything was wrong. Everything was very, very wrong. Yet... It was real. It couldn't have been, it shouldn't have been. But it was. "No," Asteros whimpered once again, doubling over as a flash of light blinded his subconscious.

Consciousness is a construct of the human mind.

Asteros vomited. The dark voice whispered in his head, its words echoing through his mind, playing themselves back in one constant, terrible loop. The veins bloomed in his mind, glowing with their strange colorations in the dark cavern. Asteros's vision flashed once again, this time with darkness.

Heat overpowered his body. Ice burned through his skin, tearing at his flesh, raking frozen claws of pain through his organs.

Asteros groaned, curling tightly as he lay on the floor. His head pounded, each beat of his heart sending another echo of pain through his mind.

Tenvalisare begins, looming like a storm in the distance.

Asteros choked, doubling over once again. His twin black blades zipped from their sheaths on the other side of the room, flying toward his instinctual call.

Umbrakinesis exploded around him, knocking chunks of stone from Erydon's walls. Darkness cloaked him, blinding him... hiding him.

"Where is she?" a voice asked as the darkness settled.

Asteros's eyes cracked open, his mind explaining the question as another whisper from the stone. Asteros did not move.

"Where. Is. She?" the voice asked again. It was pointed, sharp. It bit at his mind, piercing his skull, sending a shiver down his spine.

Asteros turned, recognizing the voice.

Lucien Shade stood in the doorway, a shadow over his face. He stood with poise and power. He stood as if he were in control—as if he *should* be in control.

Asteros twisted, his mouth hanging open. "What?" Asteros croaked, groaning as he pushed on the wound in his chest. The skin slowly knit back together at his command, but Lucien had already seen it.

"Where is Shalheira?" Lucien growled.

"I—" Asteros started, trailing off. He sighed, laying his head on the cold stone once again. His eyes closed, a flash of darkness coming over his vision once again.

"Asteros!" Lucien roared. He leaned down, picking Asteros up with his bare hands.

Asteros cried out in pain as Lucien slammed him into the wall, sending yet more stones crashing to the ground.

"Where is Shalheira?" Lucien demanded.

"You did all of this," Asteros whispered.

Lucien dropped him.

Asteros crumpled to the ground, whimpering. "Whatever you told her... It drove her to this." Everything felt fake. Nothing was right. It was as if he were watching the events from a distant window —instead of living them.

"I only told her the truth," Lucien said, turning away. "I saw what happened."

Asteros froze, his muscles tensing. He glanced to his black blades on the floor. They were close.

"I saw the argument," Lucien continued. Asteros relaxed slightly, but kept his eyes on the blades. "I saw her running from you, and I saw your pursuit."

Asteros reached out subtly, preparing a Crystal. His anger grew with each passing second. This was Lucien's fault. Lucien had poisoned her mind, and now... now she was gone because of *him*.

Lucien still faced the other way. "And now..." Lucien trailed off. "You return, and she does not."

Asteros pulled one of the blades to him with a tendril of darkness, acting on the purest of his twisted instincts: rage.

The sword slipped into his hand, and, without a second thought, Asteros brought it up, shoving it toward Lucien's exposed back.

Lucien reacted, twisting out of the blade's reach. He drew his shortsword and longsword, using the latter to knock Asteros's blade from his hand.

Asteros growled, pushing himself to his feet with a blast of darkness. He could've stopped there, but he did not. He had already decided: Lucien was responsible for Shalheira's death, and he had to die.

Asteros pulled both blades back into his hands, the twin swords feeling all too familiar. Asteros glanced at Lucien's stance —defensive.

Lucien had been expecting this, but he had not planned to initiate the attack.

Asteros advanced, dropping to one knee and sliding across the stone floor, one blade raised to block the parry and the other angled towards Lucien's open stomach.

Lucien reacted with inhuman speed, twisting out of reach once again, deflecting Asteros's other blade with his own.

"I don't want to do this," Lucien said.

"Neither do I," Asteros growled. He attacked again, charging with both blades raised, bringing them down in unison.

Lucien was forced to use both of his swords to parry the double-swing, leaving both of their stomachs exposed. Lucien reacted first, kicking Asteros just below the chest with an armored foot.

The umbrakinetic kick shot Asteros backward, sending him crashing into the wall.

Asteros groaned, pain flaring in his back, but he landed on his feet.

"Then stop," Lucien shot back.

Asteros charged again. He phased into the Unbound, slipping past Lucien's counterattack and brushing through the stone wall beside him. Asteros shifted back, bringing down his twin blades from behind.

Lucien flipped his arms, blocking both attacks while facing the other way. He tossed the shorter of his two swords aside, using the now-free hand to grab Asteros's wrist and send a jolt of umbrakinesis through it.

Asteros dropped the blade, his hand stinging from the shock. His bones rattled, but held. No thoughts crossed his mind, there was only focus... because if he let himself think...

Lucien attacked this time, using his longsword to push Asteros's blade aside. Lucien reared back, kicked off the ground with an umbrakinetic boost, and punched Asteros in the chest—*hard*.

Asteros shouted, falling to the ground once again. Lucien had hit where Shalheira's dagger had pierced the skin. Asteros's vision flashed, a dark figure standing over him.

Lucien reached down, picking Asteros up.

Asteros groaned as Lucien charged into the wall, Asteros in hand.

Lucien slammed Asteros into the stone wall.

Pain exploded through his back, bones breaking as Asteros crashed into the stone. Screaming, Asteros summoned his powers and pushed back with a sudden blast of darkness.

Lucien cried out as the pair fell to the ground.

Asteros forced the dark energies into his legs, then kicked off the wall, pushing Lucien into the floor as he did.

The pair skidded across the stone floor, Lucien's head smashing through the ground in several places.

Lucien roared, calling a blade back to his hand.

Asteros leaned back, now on top of Lucien, and did the same. His blade slipped into his grip just as Lucien got a hold of his. Asteros swung.

A deafening *clang* sounded as the blades crashed together. Asteros's muscles quivered.

Lucien's jaw set and his eyes flared. Lucien used an umbrakinetic kick to push himself out from under Asteros, his blade slipping as he did so.

Asteros jumped back in shock, nicked by the corner of Lucien's shortsword.

Asteros panted as the pair circled each other, swords raised. Lucien was breathing heavily, but Asteros was hurting. His chest throbbed, the reopened wound burning from the umbrakinetic punch. His spine wobbled, slowly correcting itself as Asteros drew upon his Crystals once again.

A Silver Sun...

Asteros doubled over, the white flash of heat overpowering his thoughts once again.

Lucien exploited the opening, sliding across the floor with near angelic grace and *slamming* his blade into Asteros's side.

Pain.

All Asteros knew was pain. His breathing grew shallow, warm blood pouring from the open wound as Lucien tore the blade from Asteros's stomach. Asteros opened his mouth, but nothing came out.

Lucien tossed the sword to the ground, standing over Asteros. He raised a cold hand to Asteros's throat and picked him up once again.

Asteros tried to kick, but his legs refused to work. Red, *burning* pain pulsed through his side with each beat of his heart, more pain than he had ever felt in his life. He gasped, Lucien's hand closing around his throat.

"You cannot beat me, Asteros," Lucien whispered, his teeth bared. "I am the best of us, I always have been. You will never be able to beat me."

"You—" Asteros rasped, choking.

Lucien's grip did not loosen.

You can still save her.

The voice was clear as day, booming in Asteros's mind. And finally, in that moment, as the last seconds of his life were being choked away by Lucien's grasp, Asteros understood: The voice had never meant Lyseria... It meant *Shalheira*.

"WAIT!" Asteros screamed.

Lucien paused, his grip loosening slightly.

Asteros gasped, taking in a breath of air. Pain still ravaged his side, but Asteros spoke through it. "Wait," Asteros repeated.

Lucien frowned, dropping Asteros.

Asteros crumbled, falling to the ground with a sickening crunch.

"This is your only chance," Lucien growled. "You killed Shalheira... So give me one reason why I shouldn't kill you right here, *right now*."

"Because I didn't kill her," Asteros breathed. He let out a stifled grunt of pain. "She fell and was killed in the Frostfall."

Lucien tilted his head.

"But... I can save her," Asteros rasped.

"You mean to tell me that she's not dead?" Lucien seethed. "If that were the case, then you wouldn't have returned here without her."

"No," Asteros panted. "No, no. She is dead. But we can change that," Asteros said, meeting Lucien's gaze.

"What?" Lucien leaned in, his hand raising once again.

"We are Shadow-Swifts, Lucien," Asteros said. He let out a loud groan, the pain continuing to tear through his nerves. "Shadow-Swifts are descendants of the Revenants, meaning that we may still be able to access the abilities of our lost ancestors."

"The Revenants are extinct," Lucien said.

"They are for now," Asteros said, breathing heavily. He laid a hand on his side, grimacing. "But I know how to bring them back. I know how to make *us* into Revenants." Asteros paused. He took a deep breath, letting out another cry of pain. "What if... What if we do trigger the Resurgence? What if we do as the Devourer's Stone said?"

When you are ready, you shall return to me, young Revenant.

"Impossible," Lucien whispered. "Why should I believe you?"

"Because I'm telling the truth," Asteros said, meeting Lucien's dark eyes once again. "You've known me for the better part of a century, my friend. Hav—" Asteros doubled over, barely containing his screams of pain. "Have I ever lied to you?" he continued. "And, besides, think about it. If we become Revenants..."

"Necromancy," Lucien breathed. "Revenants possessed the ability to raise the dead."

"If we trigger the Resurgence, and bring about the return of the Revenants, we can bring Shalheira back to us," Asteros said, panting. "Not just Shalheira, but we can find Keries and Lyseria too. We can bring back their families... Win back their trust."

Lucien looked away again, his brow furrowed.

"Everyone that we lost we can bring back," Asteros whispered. "Think about it, Lucien, we would be *unstoppable.*"

"How?" Lucien asked after a moment, backing off from Asteros. "How will you bring them back?"

The Devourer's Stone flashed in Asteros's mind.

"Trust me," Asteros said. He grimaced. "I have a way."

Lucien hesitated. Something flickered in his eyes. Lucien almost looked as if... Lucien handed him a Crystal from the inside of his armor.

Asteros took it, nodding in thanks. The black energy slowly seeped out of the Crystal, knitting the torn skin back together.

"When?" Lucien rumbled.

"Tomorrow night," Asteros said. "After our Crystals recharge, I will take the scholars with me. But you and Malik must stay here, Lucien. If something goes wrong... We cannot risk losing all three of us in this endeavor."

Lucien met his eyes once again, a strange sense of uncertainty in his black eyes. "Asteros," Lucien started. "I could have killed you, and I spared your life, so before you consider trying anything..." Lucien bared his teeth. "I would remember that."

"Thank you," Asteros whispered.

When you are ready, you shall return to me, young Revenant.

CHAPTER THIRTY-FIVE
THE SOLSTICE

Castien Varic stood among the crowd of nobles, in awe as he approached the massive marble doors of Summerglass Palace. The doors were fastened to the walls that extended on both sides, keeping them open for the feast. Ilyana by his side, Castien strode toward the line of guards at the front of the palace.

"Names please," one of the guards said, his vermillion armor shimmering in the turquoise moonlight of Oria. Lotius peeked out from behind a cloud, shining down on the group as well.

Castien's legs still ached from the journey, and the steep walk up to the palace had been taxing to say the least.

Ilyana spoke quietly, telling the guard their names and slipping past them without another word. They were well known anyway, and, besides, only criminals were forbidden from attending the Feast of the Solstice.

It was the longest day of the year and was celebrated as the day when Niventia first descended to Auris from her City in the Stars. Arvendon's annual feast was heralded as one of the greatest festivals of the year, and it considerably outmatched any other royal ball in Auris.

As they approached the steps leading up to the open doors, one of the guards stepped forward.

The absence of Castien's bow left his back feeling unnervingly light. Ilyana had promised that she had stored a bow for him in the palace, and that he would have weapons if he needed them. Until then, Castien would be unarmed.

"Submit yourselves for inspection," the guard called out as they reached the top of the short staircase.

Castien raised both arms, his tight vest feeling painfully constricting. Ilyana had found him a vermillion vest embroidered with gold earlier in the day, assuring him that, if he didn't dress nicely, he would be out of place at the ball.

The guard patted down Castien, his hands running down Castien's thin vest and across his black dress pants that Ilyana had also somehow found for him.

The guard moved to Ilyana, who raised her arms as well. She had recovered from whatever it was that was troubling her last night and looked fantastic—as always. Her hair was tied up in a tight bun, with silver hair pins sticking out in a perfect circle. Her Elosian eyes had been accented with a shiny silver and black sparkle, and her face was covered with a thin layer of white powder, making her seem even paler than usual.

She still wore the same blue-gray cloak, though she had somehow refolded it into the form of an elaborate, stunningly beautiful dress. Silver spirals of fabric rolled across her outstretched arms, lined with blue and black seams at every twist and turn of her perfectly sculpted body. Her right leg was partially exposed, and her dress was fastened up in a way that was meant to highlight her impeccable figure.

The guard nodded, waving them along. Castien looked at Ilyana, who winked. Certainly, she had hidden a knife or two in her dress, though the guard hadn't found them.

The entry hall was extraordinary. Castien had been here several times before, yet he was somehow always caught off guard by its extravagance. The smooth white floor beneath him was spotless, despite the dozens of nobles milling about. Pairs of golden braziers lined the walls, a strong flame burning within each one. Lavish furniture was placed in between these torches. Nobles stood around them, sipping on wines of various colors.

Castien allowed himself a moment to take in the beauty of those around him, seeing vests and dresses of all designs and colors.

A woman with tall, red hair wrapped in a beautiful swirl atop her head passed him, and Castien found himself staring. Pillars lined the walls, stretching up the high ceiling overhead. Conversations echoed around them, the words indecipherable among the almost deafening laughter of the half-drunk nobles.

Ahead of them lay a set of closed doors. *That's the throne room,* Castien thought as they turned to the left. They passed group after group of colorful noblemen, all wearing their best attire for the biggest night of the year. Castien looked down at his black pants and vermillion vest, suddenly realizing why Ilyana had forced him to wear this.

He had never attended the Solstice Ball before, for he had never really cared to go. Given the fact that he had only technically spent a few summers in Arvendon, he shouldn't have felt that guilty. But if this was what he was missing...

They turned right, departing from one long white marble hallway and entering another one. From there, they turned again, following a staircase up to the second level where the ballroom was. Castien gawked at the guests, unable to contain his fascination with their fashion.

Some of the women wore dresses of gold and white that bloomed out in a beautiful bell shape. Others wore tight, Sucharan-style garments that wrapped around their body, partially veiling their faces. Some wore cloaks like Ilyana, which slipped along every curve of the female body, accenting it with sparkle and shine.

The men wore mostly vests of various colors, though some sported thin coats ornamented with buttons and medals. Others wore long capes and cloaks, lined with golden frills and silver buttons.

Ilyana led them closer to the ballroom, taking them to the right as they reached the top of the stairs.

Castien gasped, hearing the distant hum of an orchestra as it played in the ballroom. His heart jumped, the infectious beat slowly making itself apparent. *Music*, Castien thought. It had been so long since he had heard music like this. Only the royals were worthy of the gift of Arvendon's orchestras for most of the year, but, during a time like this, everyone was allowed the privilege of listening to the players in all their glory. Singers echoed the beats, their beautiful voices sounding through the palace with an ethereal allure, humming along to a beat or accenting it with vocalizations of the tunes.

"That..." Castien trailed off. "That's beautiful."

Ilyana tapped him on the hand. "Focus, Castien. Now is not the time for dancing, no matter how beautiful the music may be." Ilyana dodged a drunk partygoer and pulled Castien to the side as they approached the massive doors of the ballroom.

"Why aren't we going in?" Castien asked, feeling almost giddy.

"Have you ever been in the royal ballroom before?" Ilyana asked.

Castien shook his head.

"That's why." Ilyana rolled her eyes. "Listen, your weapons are stashed in a chest in a closet in the hallway in that direction." She pointed past the open doors of the ballroom. "Go that way, turn left at the end, then make the first right and open the second door on the left. It should be unlocked. It's a rarely used storage closet for the servants. If anything goes south, get to your weapons and..." Ilyana trailed off. "Never mind. I'll tell you where to meet me once I figure out a safe rendezvous point, alright?"

"Sounds good," Castien said. "Can we go inside now?"

"Keep a low profile, and try to stay out of trouble. I'm going to do some scouting and figure out the rest of my plan. I'll find you when I'm ready," Ilyana said, turning away.

Castien lingered, feeling a strange sense of dread. Something was off. Ilyana was no longer nearly as upset as she had been the day before. She seemed focused, so focused that Castien was concerned.

Castien started walking forward, the thoughts slipping from his mind like rain on stone as the orchestra began playing another tune. Ilyana turned the corner, disappearing inside the ballroom just ahead of Castien.

Then it was his turn. He turned the corner and gasped, stopping dead in his tracks.

The ballroom must have been several hundred yards long, and at least a few hundred feet wide. Massive marble pillars lined the walls, leading past the huge, checkered dance floor and past the raised landing of tables at the far end of the room.

Castien squinted, making out a speck of a figure sitting alone at the very opposite side of the room. *The King.* Castien looked around, his eyes tracing the dozens of tables along the raised red-carpeted landing all the way back down to the dancefloor.

Long, narrow tables lined the walls, just ahead of the pillars. Endless piles of food were laid about in careful patterns, making up a beautiful display for the guests. Laughter echoed all throughout the huge room, only overpowered by the music of the orchestra.

Castien looked to the right, where upwards of twenty people sat with their instruments of wood and strings. Singers stood beside them, vocalizing their harmonious sounds. Castien felt himself pulled to the dancefloor, where countless pairs of colorful nobles spun.

The tune worked its way through Castien's ears, slipping through his spine and into his body. He took a few steps down onto the dance floor, taking a moment to gather himself. Most everyone was paired up, spinning in well-rehearsed movements.

Surveying the crowd, he picked apart the groups, seeing the social niches that had formed. The political circles of Arvendon were airtight, but word of the Blood Sorcerer's threat had likely already gotten out anyway.

He continued forward, slipping past another pair of dancers. He didn't truly have an assignment at the moment, leaving him free to try and socialize. But he saw the value in gathering information from these conversations. He needed to be alert. Then Castien stumbled, tripping over a stray foot and nearly falling.

Strong hands caught him, keeping him from crashing into the ground.

Castien's eyes snapped open.

Emerald eyes met his gaze.

Castien looked down, observing the rest of the sharp, thin face that hovered over him.

The slender boy lifted Castien up, straightening him and assuring that he was steady on his feet. "Are you alright? You almost fell there." The boy laughed warmly, running a hand through his messy auburn hair.

Castien felt his heart pounding, and his face growing warm. "Y— yeah," Castien stuttered. "I'm fine." Castien straightened his vest. "Thank you," Castien said quickly, realizing that he had yet to thank the boy.

The tall teen chuckled. "It was my pleasure," the teen said, extending a hand. "I don't think I recognize you... I'm Reluraun."

"Castien," Castien said, taking the boy's slender hand and shaking it. He looked down after a moment, realizing that he was still holding on to the warm hand long after he should've let go. He quickly released it. He gazed up, meeting those emerald eyes once again.

Reluraun winked, then let out a deep laugh.

Castien joined him, finding himself giggling like a kid before this beautiful gentleman. He seemed to be around Castien's age, likely only a year younger.

"Oh!" Reluraun exclaimed after a moment, suddenly stopping his laughter.

"Oh?" Castien mimicked, laughing a little.

"That's where I recognize your name from," Reluraun said, his stunning emerald eyes illuminating. "You were on the expedition, weren't you? You were the Stormless?"

"Um—Uh... Yeah!" Castien said, fumbling with his words. "Wait, how do you know about that?"

"Oh, my apologies," Reluraun said, brushing his hair once again. "I am Elric's son. Forgive me, I did not mention my last name when I introduced myself." Reluraun bowed.

Castien felt his face heating, now painfully aware that it was likely bright red. "Ah," Castien said casually. "Yes, I got to know your father somewhat well over the course of the trip." Castien tried to steady himself. The world was spinning slightly, and the music—while infectiously upbeat—wasn't doing anything to help his delirium.

"You still look a little unsteady," Reluraun said, cracking a bright, white-toothed smile. "Are you sure you're alright?" Reluraun extended a hand, his long fingers wrapping around Castien's shoulder once again.

Castien froze, his eyes locked on the hand.

Reluraun laughed, pulling his hand back.

"I'm uh..." Castien trailed off, blushing even further. He cursed himself for being so clumsy with his words. "I'm alright, I promise." Castien laughed, offering a weak smile.

"Words aren't your strong suit, are they?" Reluraun asked, raising an eyebrow.

Castien felt himself smile like a fool. "No, not exactly."

"Well then, maybe I can get you a little something that'll help you," Reluraun said, laying a soft hand on Castien's wrist and pulling him away from the center of the dance floor.

Castien's head spun, the heat of Reluraun's hand pulsing through his wrist and warming his heart.

Reluraun waved his hand, hailing over a servant and taking a glass of pink wine from her tray.

Castien took it gratefully, downing the sweet, fruity liquid in one gulp. Castien lowered the glass.

"So," Reluraun said, leaning against the table with a charmingly casual tilt of his body. "You must tell me the story of how you ended up on an expedition with some of the most powerful people in the world. I mean, I only spoke to my father briefly today upon his return, but it seems like your trip was pretty interesting, huh?"

"Yeah, I guess you could say that," Castien said. He prayed that the alcohol would kick in soon—he wasn't sure if he'd be able to keep his sentences straight in front of Reluraun for much longer. "I didn't do much, obviously. But it was definitely a very eventful expedition."

"Oh, come on now," Reluraun said. "I'm sure you were on that crew for a good reason, and I'm also sure that there's more to you than meets the eye." Reluraun winked again, and Castien thought that he might pass out on the spot.

"I was supposed to detect the influence of a Whisperer," Castien said, his body feeling warm thanks to the drink. "Although there wasn't much to detect, as the whole Blood Sorcerer thing turned out to be real," Castien whispered.

"Yes, I heard as much," Reluraun said. "Faelyn and I have been suspecting that for some time now." Reluraun noticed Castien's blank stare. "Oh, Faelyn Titansworn—the Prince."

Castien gaped. *Reluraun is friends with the Prince?*

"Wow," Castien uttered, his mouth hanging open. He finally managed to peel his eyes away from Reluraun and began searching the upper quadrant of the ballroom for the Prince.

"Oh, Faelyn isn't here tonight," Reluraun said.

Castien turned back to him, intoxicated by his emerald eyes once again.

"He and his father had a... disagreement, I guess you could say." Reluraun continued. "Faelyn seemed to think a good way to stick it to his father would be to miss this, but I don't know."

"Oh," Castien said.

"Yeah." Reluraun nodded, his voice growing quieter. "This Blood Sorcerer situation has hit them pretty hard," Reluraun said.

Castien turned his head, a sudden alertness coming to his mind. *Perhaps there's more to this than we know.* "What do you mean?" he asked, setting his empty glass down on the white-clothed table beside him.

"Oh, you haven't heard?" Reluraun stood up, shifting away from the table. "There was this big confrontation between the King and some nobles," Reluraun said.

"Confrontation?" a voice asked from the side.

Castien jumped, spinning around to find Ilyana standing just a few feet away from him and Reluraun. Castien found his eyes drawn back to her elaborate dress, suddenly unsure of where he should look. He felt his face heat once again. *Tarathiel's Stones! Hold it together, Castien!* he commanded himself.

Ilyana glanced at Castien, undoubtedly noticing his blush. She tilted her head, her Elosian features twisting into a frown.

"Excuse me, who are you?" Reluraun asked, turning to Ilyana.

Ilyana extended a half-gloved hand. "I'm Ilyana Xirel," she said, shaking his hand firmly. "I'm sure that you've heard of me, right?"

"I have," Reluraun said, frowning slightly.

Ilyana withdrew her hand.

"But, if you'll pardon my bluntness, I was having a conversation with Castien," Reluraun said.

"Well, I'm here *with* Castien," Ilyana said. "So, I'd say that this doesn't qualify as an intrusion." Ilyana smirked.

Reluraun's head snapped back to Castien, and his face fell slightly.

"We're not *here* together like *that*," Castien said quickly.

Ilyana groaned, rolling her eyes as Reluraun's smile returned.

"Just repeat what you said about the confrontation or whatever and I'll leave you two alone," Ilyana grunted.

Reluraun sighed, but relented. "A few days ago, a group of nobles started accusing the King of lying and covering up the whole Blood Sorcerer issue. It ended with an arrest and an early end to that night's party." Reluraun paused. "Though since then the prisoner was supposedly covertly released."

"What do you mean?" Ilyana asked.

"Technically speaking, the noble escaped, but given the security of our dungeons the working theory is that someone powerful on the King's Council quietly released him," Reluraun explained.

"Hm." Ilyana paused. "And no one has said anything about the confrontation itself?"

Reluraun shook his head. "The King was firm in his denial, but unfortunately the Cyfali Ambassador was present for the argument, and likely has questions of his own."

Ilyana furrowed her brow, rubbing her chin. "If you wouldn't mind giving Castien and me a moment?" Ilyana said, raising a curved eyebrow at Reluraun.

Reluraun nodded, bowing and backing up. "See you around, Castien." He winked, turning away.

Castien found himself following the young man with his eyes. He was beautiful and seemed to be available. Reluraun seemed just as mature as Castien, perhaps even more so.

"Listen here, Stormless," Ilyana growled. "I can't have you getting distracted, alright?" Ilyana's eyes were hard, yet Castien held them. "I've figured out what I'm going to do... And I've determined a rendezvous point," Ilyana said.

"So you're finally going to fill me in on what's going on?" Castien asked, feigning surprise.

"An argument is soon going to break out," Ilyana began. "Once it does, I need you to go upstairs to the King's floor. Take the long route and grab your weapons on the way. Once you're up there I need you to go to the King's quarters—which are on the northern side of the palace—and cause a diversion to pull the guards away from the doors. I'm not sure where our little spy is going to hide, but I'm willing to bet that most of Arvendon's *important* people will be seeking refuge in the King's rooms." Ilyana took a breath. "Draw them away from the door—I'll be waiting for this—once you do I'll slip inside. Then, you need to get back to the staircase on the Eastern Wing, and go *up* to the next floor."

"Wait," Castien interrupted. "Why would I be distracting the guards? Aren't they on our side? And, second, wouldn't we want to be going down?"

"The King doesn't want any blood on his hands," Ilyana said. "He wants to make this seem as if he had nothing to do with it. So, we need to pull the guards away and make it look like we tricked everyone." Ilyana paused. "And, second, everyone will be going straight for the exit, so we need to be smart," Ilyana said. "Once you're on the next floor, head down the first hallway back toward the central wing, then turn south and stop by the glass windows, high above the main entrance. I'll meet you there, and then I'll lead us to our exit, got it?"

"I..." Castien trailed off. "I think so, yes."

"Good," Ilyana said, turning away. "Oh," she turned around. "And one more thing: My contact informed me that he had arranged a distraction for us, to ensure that we aren't caught by any *retaliators*."

"Another distraction?" Castien asked. "What is it?"

"I'm not sure, if I'm being honest," Ilyana said. "All he said was that people wouldn't even be looking at us by the time we leave the building." Ilyana looked down, then back to Castien. "Good luck, Castien," Ilyana said, a sudden weight coming over her voice. "I'll see you at the rendezvous point."

Faelyn Titansworn sat in his rooms. His legs were folded, the old tome of the Ancient Sects laying on his lap as he half-read it. He absentmindedly skimmed the pages of the section on how the Sects interacted with one another in battle.

The front lines were typically made up of Skin-Shapers and Blood Sorcerers. Behind them were the Stonemasters and Illusomancers, and behind them were the Starburners and Revenants. The lineup made sense according to their strengths and weaknesses, to an extent. Idris had allowed him to keep the book while Faelyn was confined to his rooms, with the hope that he would at least be able to study what he would be working on next until his father decided to lift his punishment.

Faelyn didn't care.

He had been wrong. The expedition crew had been on its way back anyway, and had already partially returned. As he had expected, the Blood Sorcerers had been proven to be real, and the expedition had come back with only more warnings as to how powerful the Ancient Sect was.

Thankfully, Elric had returned. While Surge and Luka were still out in the wilds, pursuing different—yet related—missions, Elric had deemed it necessary to return to Arvendon and ensure that it remained protected.

Faelyn supposed he could find a little comfort in that. Though there wasn't much comfort to be found anywhere these days.

Yet the city was still unprotected. Even with Elric back, Faelyn didn't feel safe. How could he? Between the Blood Sorcerers themselves and the confrontations from the nobles, it seemed as though everything was falling apart.

He hadn't heard from Eithor, not even once. The Illusomancer had given him that veiled warning about the Solstice, and instructed Faelyn to... find him? Faelyn was still confused on that part, for he had no idea where to look for Eithor, and he had no means of contacting him. Yet, either way, it didn't matter. Because, once again, he was alone in his rooms.

The Solstice was tonight anyway. Whatever Eithor was trying to warn Faelyn about would happen, for Faelyn had no say in tonight's actions. *What's the worst that could happen?* Faelyn asked himself. *Another argument breaks out. Someone hurts someone from the King's Council—which would make the bells ring three times,* Faelyn thought to himself.

Faelyn knew the warning about the bells should've concerned him, but that was really the worst that could happen. Besides, in his peculiar state of mind at the moment, Faelyn felt nothing at the thought. Everything was just another movement in his mind... another wave crashing on the shores of his consciousness.

He shut the book, standing up and stretching his legs. He was wearing a white-gold vest with pristine white pants. Just because he didn't go to the ball didn't mean he couldn't still dress up. Faelyn knew that it was silly, but it was a slight ego boost that he felt he was in desperate need of at the moment.

The white-gold coloration was after the colors of Niventia's Solstice, and he wore it in honor of the holiday. Despite himself, he felt no anxiety at missing the party. If something happened, it wouldn't be his problem. Although he did have to admit that he was more than a little annoyed that he had to miss the biggest night of the year.

He paced, stretching his legs and walking back and forth from his bed to his bathroom. Reluraun was out there anyway, along with Elric now. If anything did happen tonight, everyone would be fine. And, as much as he hated to admit it, Faelyn's father was powerful. The King would have no trouble personally defending the palace if he were forced to.

A knock at the door pulled him from his thoughts. Faelyn paused, tilting his head. There were guards posted outside of his doors at all times, preventing him from leaving. *Who could be knocking?*

Faelyn approached the door cautiously, reaching for the handle slowly. He turned it and peeked out.

A familiar gray-robed figure awaited him outside, along with the notable absence of two Arvendi guards.

Faelyn pulled the door all the way open, revealing the wrinkled face that he had come to both fear and revere. Faelyn stepped back, allowing his confusion to show in his posture.

"I thought you weren't going to contact me until I started looking for *you*," Faelyn said.

Eithor stepped forward. "Yes, but due to your confinement in your rooms I thought it only fair to deliver this message myself," Eithor rasped. "May I come in?"

Faelyn nodded and stepped aside. Eithor hobbled inside, his ice-blue eyes still seeming to glow in the dim, candle-lit room.

"How did you get around the guards?" Faelyn asked, shutting the door quietly.

"Oh, you know," Eithor said. He raised his hand and wiggled his fingers. A slight distortion appeared in the air, causing his fingers to appear invisible. "It's not so hard to mislead people when you're capable of weaving illusions out of nothing but air." Eithor grinned and came to a stop in the center of the room. He looked around, taking in Faelyn's canopy bed, and the table in the side of the room, as well as the doors that led to other parts of his chambers.

"Please," Faelyn said, motioning to the table. "Sit down." Faelyn slid into the seat closer to the door, and Eithor sat down in the one opposite to him.

"I come bearing two pieces of news: one good, and one bad." Eithor's face grew grim.

Faelyn frowned, tilting his head. "Are you going to tell me?" he said after a moment.

Eithor took a deep breath. "First, I have freed Pallus, as you may have heard. But I fear that something very wrong may happen at the party this evening. I do not know what it is, and I do not know how to stop it. Yet, what I do know is that, with you there, I think we may actually stand a chance." Eithor's withered face remained steady.

Relief swam through Faelyn's veins. *Perhaps I can trust him,* Faelyn thought. "Thank you for freeing Pallus," Faelyn said. "But what makes you think something bad is going to happen?" Faelyn questioned. "I know that you said something about the bells the last time we talked, but you never explained yourself."

"That is because I…" Eithor trailed off. He looked away, his blue eyes seeming to flicker. "Faelyn, we are running out of time. I don't know what is going to happen, but the longer you're away from the party the greater the danger is. The people need your help. They need *you*. Now come with me." Eithor rose to a stand.

Faelyn remained seated, weighing his options. *He freed Pallus,* Faelyn thought. *He's proven his loyalty to me, what do I have to lose?* Without another word, Faelyn stood, thankful that he was already dressed accordingly.

Eithor opened the door, motioning for Faelyn to lead the way to the ballroom.

Faelyn took a deep breath, closing his eyes. He had been wrong. His father had been right. He needed to face his father and apologize for how he had acted, and he needed to make things right. If he stopped something terrible from happening tonight, he could perhaps regain his father's favor... maybe even his love. But, at the very least, Faelyn could help avert whatever was coming tonight.

"You shot an arrow at my father?" Reluraun cackled.

"And I would've hit him too if he hadn't stopped it with his mind," Castien added, taking another bite of the strange pastry that Reluraun had given him. He had never eaten anything like it before. It was made of some sort of bread, yet it was warm and colorful, with a fruity taste.

"That's wild," Reluraun said, leaning back even farther. He and Castien had found a pair of chairs alongside the long buffet tables that bordered the room, and had opted to sit rather than stand and risk getting bumped into by the increasingly drunk party guests.

"Well, I do like to think that I'm a pretty good shot," Castien said. "He was flying when I shot at him, after all."

"That is impressive," Reluraun admitted, nodding. "Yet that can't be the only interesting thing that happened on the expedition. I'm sure that you saw a little more action than that," Reluraun prodded.

Castien paused. He had already gone over the events of the hunt,

and had briefly explained that Elric had ambushed the Blood Sorcerers' Cave. *Yet...* Castien's hand brushed over the bottom of his vest.
He closed his eyes in relief as he felt the small lump within the vest,
lying just above his waist.

He had decided to keep the Crystal with him at all times. He still
could hardly make sense of what had happened that day... though he
knew that he likely would not get any answers for quite some time.

"We were ambushed by the Blood Sorcerers later on," Castien
said softly. "Though I assume Elric already told you about that."

"He did." Reluraun looked around, the rhythmic beats of the
orchestra sounding through the ballroom.

Castien realized that he had been ignoring them for several
minutes now, and that he had been missing out on tunes that he
may never hear again.

Damn emerald eyes, Castien thought to himself, cursing Reluraun's intoxicating gaze. Castien, despite himself, turned back to
Reluraun. It wasn't often that—

Ilyana, Castien thought with a start. He had nearly forgotten. The
argument she spoke of was clearly yet to happen, for he assumed it
would be unmistakable. He looked around, searching for the blue-
gray dress in the crowd of spinning nobles.

Ilyana was nowhere to be found.

Castien looked farther, scanning the upper landing where all of
the tables and chairs sat. Many of them were filled with older nobles,
or those who had simply grown tired of dancing. He looked past this,
to where the King sat at the center of the longest table, both seats
beside him empty.

"You've fallen silent," Reluraun observed.

Castien looked back to Reluraun, meeting his firm gaze once
again. "My apologies," Castien said. "I—I've never been to one of
these parties before."

"Ah, I figured as much," Reluraun said. "I probably would've seen
you at least once or twice... Maybe even saved you from tripping
again." Reluraun laughed.

Castien felt himself blush once again, though this time he didn't really care. His head was pleasantly fuzzed from the wine. His balance still seemed quite good, and his thoughts were decently clear, if not a little eased. If anything, it was nice to have his anxiety dampened.

"I assume you're a Cloudwalker then, like your father?" Castien asked, quickly shifting the subject.

"That I am," Reluraun said. "I haven't exactly done as many *important* missions as my father. In fact, I haven't actually done any. But the Knyvet Bloodline is strong, and so my powers are strong as well."

"Is your mother a Cloudwalker?" Castien asked. He knew little of Summoning inheritance, but he did know that two parents of the same Sect significantly increased the power of the child.

"She was," Reluraun said.

Castien's face fell a little, though Reluraun seemed unbothered.

"She died a year after I was born, giving birth to what would've been my brother. Things didn't go too well, obviously," Reluraun said.

Castien looked down, unsure of what to say. *What was there to say when one told you that their mother and brother had both died during birth?*

"I'm sorry," Castien said.

"Oh, don't be," Reluraun said. "My father said she and him weren't a great match anyway. Although emotional compatibility doesn't matter much in Arvendon when it comes to Summoners and with whom they choose to have their offspring."

Castien fell silent once again at Reluraun's words. That was something he hadn't really thought about. He knew that Arvendon's Kings had long intervened in marriages, ensuring that the purest bloodlines of Summoners were produced so that the city could remain powerful.

"I was also going to..." Reluraun trailed off.

Castien looked around, sensing the disturbance in the crowd.

Reluraun turned as well, his head angled toward the upper landing where Arvendon's inner circle dined.

"What's going on?" Castien asked, rising from his seat. Reluraun stood up as well. A crowd began gathering around one of the tables off to the side of the King's.

"I'm not sure," Reluraun said, starting forward.

Castien followed slowly. The music halted, and the dancers were slowly drawn toward the upper landing.

There was shouting. Someone seemed to be making a speech of some sort.

Ilyana, Castien thought. *Is this the argument?* Castien looked around, seeing no sign of the Elosian woman.

"...Though the good Nobleman Pallus's words did not go unheard," someone was saying.

Castien pushed his way closer to the front, making out a dark-skinned Cyfali man standing off to the side of the King's throne.

"Pallus was imprisoned for speaking out against your King," the Cyfali man said. "But he escaped his cell," the man continued. "He came to me this morning, and told me something of great importance."

"Ambassador Hallan," the King boomed, rising from his royal seat down the table. "What is the meaning of this?"

"This Nobleman—Pallus," the Cyfali man, who was apparently named Hallan, continued. "He told me that a Blood Sorcerer attacked King Avenos two weeks ago... And that your King covered it up in an attempt to hide it from the public."

Gasps echoed through the crowd as whispering ensued.

Oh no, Castien thought. So, word had gotten out. This information would tremendously hurt the King's image. *By the Six*, Castien thought. *And this is an ambassador leading the confrontation.*

"This is completely false," the King said firmly. "Pallus's words have been *proven* to be false. Why have these allegations not been dropped?"

"You can lie to your own people, King Avenos," Hallan said. "But you cannot lie to my country; I will return to my city tomorrow evening, and, when I return, I will advise that Cyfalion withdraw from all military alliances with Arvendon."

Gasps rang through the crowd.

"*What?*" King Avenos roared.

"The Jaskyan Council frowns upon any sort of deception on the part of an allied leader," Hallan said. "Lying to one's people about something this significant is a crime that we cannot forgive."

"Hallan," the King boomed. "I urge you to consider the consequences of your actions."

By now the entire crowd of the ballroom had gathered around the King's table. If this was the distraction Ilyana was banking on, then it was working pretty damn well.

"You will be hearing from the Jaskyan Council soon," Hallan said, sitting down. "My speech is concluded; I merely thought that your people might finally like to know the hidden truth."

"There is *no* hidden truth," the King shouted. He turned to the crowd, his face red. "My people, have I ever led you astray? Have I ever been dishonest?"

No one spoke.

"Now is not the time to turn on your King," Avenos boomed. His desperation was clear as the sky on a Blazeday.

"Tell us the truth, Your Majesty," someone called from the crowd.

"The truth is out, yet he still won't confess!" another shouted.

"The King is deceiving us!" More cries rang out from the crowd.

The shouts grew louder, and soon nearly the entire crowd of nobles and partygoers was shouting at the King.

Castien's stomach dropped. This was *bad*.

"Hallan!" the King roared over the crowd, turning to the Cyfali Ambassador. "You will be escorted to my chambers, along with the members of my Council."

A squadron of guards advanced from their spots against the wall, taking Hallan's arms as the crowd continued shouting. Food started flying in the air, seemingly thrown at the King.

"Do whatever you wish, Avenos," Hallan spat. "If you harm me, you will feel my city's wrath like never—"

"Take him to my chambers," the King ordered. "I will be close behind." The King straightened his cloak, making to follow the guards, completely ignoring the food being tossed toward his table. He turned to the crowd. "Return to your homes! *Any* further accusations will be rewarded with an arrest. You have been warned," the King turned away. "Guards, ring the bell, and ensure that they leave *quietly*." Without a word more, the King disappeared behind the room's back columns, following Hallan and the guards.

The heavy silence that fell over such a large crowd was unmatched, held together by a King's threat. No one wanted to be the first to talk.

The guards started advancing, motioning for the partygoers to exit the ballroom.

Several whispers broke out. Before long, people were already shuffling out of the ballroom.

A bell rang somewhere overhead, several floors above.

Castien knew the signal. One chime meant to evacuate the palace. Two would've meant that the palace was being locked down. It was well known that a third and fourth chime meant that someone in the Royal Family had been harmed—or worse.

Thankfully, the bell only rang once.

"Castien," Reluraun said, turning around in the moving crowd.

Castien took a step forward, meeting Reluraun's gaze once again. Castien's legs grew weak, anxiety crashing into him once again. He nearly fell, causing Reluraun to place a hand on his shoulder once again. Castien melted into the touch.

"What's happening?" Castien asked, searching for reassurance in the eyes of a boy he had just met.

Reluraun's slender face grew pale, though he forced a slight smile. "I don't know," Reluraun said. "But I'm going to find out; my father is on Avenos's Council." Reluraun furrowed his brow. "This isn't your problem." Reluraun's auburn hair blew slightly in the breeze of the passing crowd. "I know your name, and you know mine. We can find each other later."

"Okay," Castien said, dumbfounded.

Reluraun squeezed Castien's shoulder, and then let go and dashed off toward the upper landing.

Castien turned around and fell into the crowd of colorful nobles as they filed out the massive doors. He passed under the massive crystal chandelier. Castien reached the door when a thought struck him.

Ilyana still needs me, Castien thought. This was Ilyana's distraction, and it had worked. He wasn't sure how she had organized it— or even if she had anything to do with the Ambassador's confrontation—but she still needed Castien's help.

Instead of turning right like all of the others, Castien turned left.

The guards by the door had all run either toward the landing to see what was going on, or toward the exit to ensure that everyone was able to exit safely, so Castien had a clear path.

Left. Right. Second door on the left, Castien thought to himself, recalling Ilyana's instructions. The hallway he was in was covered with a seemingly endless red carpet, and the white-marble pillars that lined the huge corridor were accented with carvings here and there. The hallway went on for quite some time, with windows lining the right side and white walls decorated with the occasional painting on the left. Braziers holding fires also dotted the corridor at regular intervals, of course.

Something moved to Castien's right.

He looked outside, the tiny lights of Arvendon's slanted streets stretching out before him. Lotius and Oria shined brightly overhead in the clear night, the rising moons glowing in the darkness. Castien paused, looking out into the shadows.

The sea crashed to the left, and the fields of Arvendon undulated for miles to the right. The lights in the city glowed brightly, unaware of the disturbance in the palace. The palace was high above the rest of the city, and Castien could see that the exiting nobles were only just beginning to descend the steep zigzagging road that connected the rest of Arvendon to the cliff that Summerglass rested upon.

Something dashed through the night, slipping past the glass window in the blink of an eye.

Castien jumped back, his eyes widening. *It was so quick... Had I imagined it?* Castien stared for a few seconds more, searching for the living shadow. He saw nothing, and turned back to the left. He couldn't worry about it now. This was an unfortunate time for his eyes to be playing tricks on him.

Castien reached the end of the hallway quickly and found himself looking out over a large atrium that spanned not only this floor but the one below and the two above as well. It was a large square, with the railed hallways lining each side of the square on all levels. Countless doors were spaced at regular intervals. Some were rooms for the servants and nobles, others were closets and storage rooms.

He heard shouting down below, where the nobles were undoubtedly flooding out of the building. But Castien ignored this and continued down the hall to the right. He passed dozens of doors in the red-carpeted hallway. The ceiling was lower here, and the atrium to the left was an overbearing presence in Castien's mind. Some guards ran by overhead and below, surely heading for the ballroom.

Castien reached the end of this hallway, and found another much like it to his left, although he was now away from the large atrium. The low-ceilinged hallway had only around a dozen doors, and the torches here were dimmer. It appeared that this was one of the less used hallways.

Second door on the left, Castien remembered, approaching the brass handle quietly. He turned around, searching the various hallways that stretched beyond to ensure that he was alone. Save for a few passing—sufficiently distracted—guards, Castien was safe. He turned the handle and pulled open the door.

The room that appeared to be a broom closet was small, and Castien saw his gear laying in the center of the tiny chamber. Castien leaned down, picking up the bow and quiver Ilyana had left him and slinging them over his back. The weight was comfortable... familiar. He then turned to the shortsword and daggers that looked quite similar to the ones Castien had picked up on the first day of the expedition.

Niventia's Light... The weapons she had found were almost exactly the same as Castien's own. Though his personal bow was still in the apartment, he supposed that this would suffice. He turned back, noticing a pack on the stone floor of the dark closet as well.

Why would she leave me this? Castien thought, picking it up and examining it. It was filled with rations—mostly stormroots and stoneblossoms. *What?* Why would he be needing rations? *How long is she planning on us being gone?* Castien thought, a sense of dread seeping into his mind.

He forced it to dissipate; he didn't have time to worry about this. Ilyana would be waiting for his distraction. Castien turned around, hurling the pack onto his back as well, and shut the door. He broke into a run and dashed for the staircase at the end of the opposite hallway before him.

Castien reached it quickly and climbed the stone steps, two at a time, until he reached the next floor. Turning, Castien scanned his surroundings.

A quartet of guards was jogging away from him, heading toward the center of the palace. Castien narrowed his eyes. They would be running toward the King's chambers, which was exactly where Castien needed to go.

He sprinted after them, careful to keep his steps quiet as he ran. The hallway here was much like the one below, with somewhat narrow walls and a low ceiling. Castien followed the guards down a turn to the left, and then back to the right, and then farther to the north. Before long, he reached one final turn to the left that he knew to be the one right outside the King's chambers—judging by the loud conversations raging just around the corner.

Castien paused, turning around. A large glass window stretched across the wall behind him, a couple hundred feet away.

Something flickered in the night—the shadow once again.

Castien shook his head, forcing the illusion from his mind. He needed to focus. He had been thinking about how he was going to distract the guards, and he had figured out what he thought was the perfect tactic. Taking a deep breath, Castien prepared himself. He placed a pained look upon his face and turned the corner.

"Help!" Castien shouted, faking a limp. "Help!" Castien cried again, limping forward. The short hallway bore a pair of doors to the right—the King's chambers—and a door to the left, which seemed to come from the servant's passages. Around eight guards stood in between the two doors in the somewhat narrow hallway. They were ushering a pair of nobles into the King's chambers.

"Who is that?" one of the guards asked.

Another shrugged as a guard helped the next pair of nobles inside.

Castien looked past the guards, his eyes settling on where the hallway turned off to the left just past the pair of doors and the guards. Ilyana would likely be waiting around that corner.

"Help!" Castien repeated, forcing a look of agony on his face. Luckily, he was shaking from anxiety and flushed from the run here already, so he seemed to play the part pretty well.

"Are you hurt, sir?" one of the guards asked, running toward Castien.

Castien fell into the man's arms, feigning weakness as he was caught by a pair of vermillion gauntlets.

The guard called for the others to help Castien up.

"What happened to him?" one of the other guards asked, his vermillion armor shimmering in the bright light of the hallway.

Turned on his back, Castien could see the large crystal chandelier hanging overhead. He let out another fake groan and allowed himself to go limp.

He heard the rest of the guards run over. *Perfect.* Castien shut his eyes, allowing himself to fall fully to the ground. He waited a few seconds, then opened his eyes.

All eight guards stood over him, looking at him curiously.

"Where did he get the bow from?" one asked.

Another shook his head, extending a hand to Castien.

"Get up, kid, you're supposed to have evacuated the palace by now," the guard said.

Castien took the man's arm and pulled himself up. "Thank you," Castien said, rubbing his eyes and rising to his feet. "I think I'm alright now." He made a point of limping off in the direction he had come from, making sure to grunt every other step or so. Hopefully he had given Ilyana the distraction that she needed.

As soon as he turned the corner, he broke into a light jog and made for the stairs once again. He climbed them quickly, and turned down the first hallway back toward the central wing, taking him directly over where he had been a few moments before.

He turned left and stopped before the massive glass windows, finding the large hallway completely empty save for the torches and chandeliers. Castien turned around, leaning against one of the marble pillars. He looked up, tracing the pillar as it arched toward the ceiling and upheld the tall roof.

Something shifted outside the window once again, a quick *whooshing* following the sound this time.

Castien whirled, scanning the night once again. Lotius's pale gray light clashed with Oria's turquoise glow, and the city's speckled torches still shined below.

This is a positively horrible time to start hallucinating. Castien shook his head, leaning against the pillar once again. He credited the strange sights to his overactive mind, and tried to settle in. He was safe for the moment, and now all he could do was wait.

Faelyn Titansworn screeched to a halt at the entrance of the ballroom. It was practically empty. His stomach fell. He was too late.

The guests were gone, save for a few of the higher-ranking nobles and generals on the upper landing of the ballroom.

Faelyn brushed past dozens of guards, making for the large set of long tables where the few people who remained in the ballroom were huddled. He pushed his way to the front, searching for his father. The King was nowhere to be seen.

Faelyn was able to pick out General Falx from the mix of nobles. "Falx," Faelyn shouted.

Falx stood up, his tanned, scarred face grim.

"What happened?" Faelyn asked. "Where is everyone?"

Falx stepped forward. "Hallan spoke out against the King," Falx said. "He announced that Cyfalion would be pulling out of all military alliances with Arvendon."

"Why?" Faelyn asked, standing up once again.

"He discovered the truth about the Blood Sorcerer, and the Council of Jaskye frowns upon lying to one's people," Falx said.

"Where is Hallan now?" Faelyn asked.

"His Majesty had Hallan escorted to the royal chambers," Falx said. "But not before announcing that the ball would be rescheduled."

Faelyn looked down. *Why now?* he thought. *Why tonight?* The Cyfali revered honor and transparency, but why would Hallan get everyone's attention to make an announcement like that when he knew he would likely be arrested?

A thought occurred to him. It was an unlikely one, that much was true, but it wasn't impossible.

"This might not be what it seems, Falx," Faelyn said. "This wasn't a confrontation, it was a sacrifice."

"What are you talking about?" Falx asked, his eyes suddenly turning hard.

Faelyn looked around, his heartbeat steadily increasing. He felt his Crystals within his vest and at his waist, radiating heat... begging to be used.

"I need to go to my father." Faelyn started toward the corridor, slowly at first, but then picking up to a run once he was through the door frame.

Hallan's announcement was likely meant to be genuine, but it served another purpose: getting the royals separated from the civilians. Hallan had only made such a spectacle out of that announcement for another reason... The announcement was meant to be a *distraction*. Whether Hallan knew that or not, though, Faelyn was unsure.

Either way, if someone was trying to cause chaos in the palace, it could only be because they were trying to accomplish something far more sinister.

He bolted up the spiral staircase, his lungs burning as he did. Faelyn panted, his heart racing, his Crystals glowing within his vest. Faelyn ran.

He reached the top of the staircase and tore open the door. The hallway beyond was in disarray. Guards lay unconscious, while others nurtured fresh wounds. Faelyn cursed, feeling his stomach drop. *No.*

He passed the guards, ignoring the bloodstained walls, and shoved open the doors to the royal chambers, his hands igniting involuntarily. Fire burned dangerously in his closed fists, the glorious power of heat burning through his veins.

The entry chamber was in chaos as well, with guards and generals lying either unconscious or wounded, or both. Faelyn scanned the floor, finding no trace of his father. He looked to the door on the left—his father's bedroom. It was closed. The red carpet beneath him was stained an even darker red from the blood. *No...*

Faelyn felt numb, his hands burning in the dim room. He approached the door on feet that did not feel like his own. Faelyn extinguished his hand, laying his fingers on the golden door handle.

Then he opened the door.

Castien Varic stood pressed against the pillar. He hadn't seen the shadow again and had been catching his breath for the better part of a minute. Unfortunately, his anxiety had more or less made that impossible for him. He was beginning to grow worried. Ilyana had not yet arrived.

His new bow began to feel heavy on his back, almost as if it were warning him that he would need to use it soon. *Gods I hope not,* Castien thought. If he had to fight his way out of this palace... He would be fighting his own country. But Ilyana had promised that her target was a Celesian spy, and Castien trusted her. She was loyal to Arvendon, and she was doing this for the good of the country.

Footsteps—fast footsteps—sounded from the right.

Castien stood up, looking down the long hallway.

Seconds passed, and Ilyana Xirel came bolting around the corner, her once-beautiful blue and gray dress now stained with dark red blood.

"Ilyana! I was beginning to worry," Castien said, his face melting into a smile.

Ilyana kept running, her face a mask of fury and focus.

"Ilyana?" Castien asked. She was nearing him, her Dexteris-enhanced sprint making her speed somewhat alarming. "What's going on?" Castien's muscles grew tense.

"Run!" Ilyana shouted, grabbing Castien by the collar and yanking him along.

Castien's mind went blank.

Ilyana bolted off, boosted by her powers.

Castien's legs already burned as he ramped up to a full-on sprint, trying to keep up with her. "Ilyana, wait!" Castien cried.

The Dexteris zipped away.

He wheezed, following her down the long, massive hallway toward the Western Wing.

Ilyana slowed, but kept running.

Castien grunted, his bow and pack clattering against his back as he ran. The carpet beneath him felt smooth and firm, and Castien swore he could feel the wind breaking around him. Then...

Boom.

Castien froze.

The massive bell's vibrations could be *felt* this high in the castle. The deafening chime rang through his ears.

Ilyana paused as the bell rang for the second time this evening. Castien paled, his stomach dropping. He knew what that meant.

Boom.

A second strike. The palace vibrated, the glass window seeming to rattle.

Boom.

A third strike. Castien's eyes fell to the ground, his muscles growing weak. *No... No, no, no, no.* He looked up, meeting Ilyana's eyes. He could feel it before it happened.

Boom.

Ilyana turned around at the fourth strike. Castien felt his head spin. A fourth strike. That could only mean...

"Ilyana! Who did you kill?" Castien demanded, his voice rising.

Ilyana stepped forward, grabbing Castien's hand. "Listen to me," Ilyana said. "I promise that I'll explain everything when I have time, but right now we have to leave," Ilyana said, lowering her hands. She slipped away, starting to run once again.

"ILYANA!" Castien roared, his muscles shaking.

She stopped, lowering her head.

"*Who did you kill?*" Castien growled. He knew the answer before she spoke. He knew what had happened, for there was only one answer.

"King Avenos Titansworn is dead," Ilyana said softly. "I killed him."

Castien stepped back, shock washing over him like waves on a beach. "But—" Castien blinked, shaking.

"I told you: I'll explain everything once we're safe," Ilyana repeated. "But you *have* to trust me, Castien." Ilyana stepped forward. "If you don't, they'll kill us both."

Castien looked up, feeling red-hot tears coming to the surface.

She had betrayed him. She had known all along, and yet she had never told him the truth. She was a traitor to both Castien and his country.

But—but... She was right. Arvendon wouldn't care that he hadn't known. Arvendon wouldn't care if all he had done was serve as a distraction. He would be killed, just the same as her.

They had no choice but to escape.

Something moved outside.

Ilyana's head whipped to the massive glass windows.

Castien squinted, his emotions boiling. "What is that?" Castien growled through gritted teeth.

A shadow rose in the night, its silhouette clear in the light of the moon. *No, not a shadow*, Castien realized. *A Shadow-Swift.*

"It..." Ilyana breathed out. "It's a distraction."

Faelyn Titansworn stood over the still-warm corpse. A quiet fire burned in his hands, the crackling flame the only sound in the night. Faelyn closed his eyes, feeling cold. A tear rolled down his cheek, sizzling into steam before it reached his chin.

He opened his eyes, tracing his father's arms, then following his figure up to the deep cut in his throat, where warm blood still poured from the wound. Finally, Faelyn let his gaze settle on his father's unseeing eyes... those empty pools of amber staring up at the ceiling.

The King's mouth hung half open, blood dribbling down his cheek. His form was limp, and his beautiful white-gold robes were already stained a dark red.

Faelyn took a deep breath as the fourth strike of the bell sounded through the palace.

Faelyn looked up, meeting his father's sightless gaze again.

Faelyn screamed. Fire exploded in the small room, incinerating the bed, the bookshelf, the end tables. Heat burned through the tiny chamber, destroying everything in sight and shooting out into the rooms beyond.

Faelyn didn't care.

He released his flames, the blaze leaving nothing but ash and tears in its wake. Faelyn stood up, his blood-stained vest and scorched boots scraping against the burned floor.

Grieving could wait. He was going to find the assassin, and he was going to kill them.

Castien dashed through the maze of halls in Summerglass's upper levels, following Ilyana as she wove between the white-marble corridors. His lungs were exhausted, and his mind was racing. He didn't know why he followed her, maybe he shouldn't have... But she was his only way out of this palace alive right now; he had no choice.

Ilyana turned a corner, coming into a lower-ceilinged hallway in the West Wing.

Four guards ran through the corridor. One turned around, spotting them.

"Over here!" the guard shouted. "Sound the alarm!" One of the guards took off in the other direction while the other three charged Ilyana and Castien.

Ilyana gave herself a burst of speed and launched herself at the guards. She flew through the air like a Cloudwalker and raised her butterfly swords—which she must've stashed somewhere in the palace and then retrieved.

She crashed into one of the guards, swords first. Ilyana impaled the guard with both blades, stabbing him straight through the heart. She flipped, pushing off the dying man and tearing her blades from his chest.

Castien watched in horror as she twisted her arm, extending one of the blades and stabbing the charging man directly through the throat.

She turned to the other guard, leaving her blade in her previous victim and drawing a knife from her boot with her free hand.

The guard froze, but it was too late.

Ilyana hurled the knife through the air and hit the man directly in his left eye, killing him.

Castien gasped for air, trying to regain his focus as he helplessly watched the bloodshed.

Ilyana ripped her blades from the corpses and bolted after the fleeing guard, who was running for the alarm. Ilyana was upon him in a second, swiping her elongated sword in his throat before he could react.

Castien nearly fell over, but kept running. He couldn't let this get to him, not now.

"Come on!" Ilyana shouted, dashing for the staircase at the end of the long hallway. Castien kicked into a sprint, passing door after door after door until he reached the staircase.

Ilyana jumped down the marble stairs, crashing into the small landing and rolling.

Castien slid down the steps, then turned and slid down the next set of steps.

Ilyana took the lead once they reached the floor below them and turned down the stairs once again.

Castien heard shouting.

"Go that way!" Ilyana shouted, pointing behind Castien. The next staircase was a few hundred yards down the long, red-carpeted hall.

Castien broke into a run. Ilyana quickly passed him.

Guards shouted behind them, spears clanging against armor and shields as they ran after Castien and Ilyana.

Castien dared to look back, seeing at least a dozen guards racing after them. He cursed, his legs burning with exhaustion as he tried to keep running. The guards would be getting closer, and he wouldn't be able to keep up this pace much longer.

A deafening crash sounded behind him.

Castien spun.

An explosion of darkness shattered the white-marble walls of the hallway. A shadow crashed into the corridor.

The guards screamed.

Castien's mouth hung open as the Shadow-Swift tore through the guards. Two black blades—one short, one long—ripped apart the guards as if they were nothing. Darkness exploded once again, a sickening crunch sounding through the hallway.

In an instant, the Shadow-Swift disappeared through the hole in the wall, leaving a dozen corpses in his wake.

"Come on!" Ilyana shouted, grabbing Castien by the wrist.

Castien snapped out of his trance. "What in Calida's Claws was that?" Castien shouted as they turned down the next staircase.

"I told you: a distraction," Ilyana said, tearing down another staircase. They came out on the next floor, found the hallways to be clear, and continued down the stairs once again.

"Where are you leading us?" Castien managed to ask through his ravaged breaths.

"I'm trying to get us out of here," Ilyana panted. "The palace is on lockdown, but the Shadow-Swift should give us enough of a distraction to slip out." Ilyana spun down another staircase, bringing them to what Castien thought was the third floor.

The staircase ended here, and the pair had no choice but to run to the Eastern Wing once again and take the other staircase down.

More screams sounded below. Cries of "Nyghtmaere"—the Shadow-Swift who terrorized The Highlands a few months before— rang through the palace.

Castien and Ilyana zipped past the torches and chandeliers, the marble pillars whipping by them. Ilyana turned left, then right, and continued forward.

They came to another corner. Castien looked ahead, out the massive glass window of the southern side of the palace. Chaos raged below as people screamed and ran.

Ilyana whipped around the corner, Castien at her side. They both froze.

Ahead, the hallway was long—several hundred yards at least—and there, standing in the very center, stood a teenager who looked as if he had walked straight from Izara's Shadow.

The teen stepped forward, his white-gold vest stained with blood, his long golden hair matted and tangled. Tears streaked his soot-covered cheeks, and his boots seemed to have burned off, exposing his bare feet.

"Stay back," Ilyana commanded, stepping forward and raising one of her swords. She extended the blade, holding a knife in her other hand.

The teen walked forward.

Fire began drifting from the braziers and torches, not into the air, but *toward* the teen.

Castien cursed, as did Ilyana.

The Scorcher was soon connected to a dozen streams of fire. He began to glow as if he was radiating heat himself.

Castien shied back, huddling behind Ilyana as the glowing teen rose from the ground, hovering on the flames.

Fire wrapped around him in a devastatingly beautiful way. The blaze grew brighter, and brighter, and brighter until—

Darkness shot through the window, shattering the glass and sending debris in every direction.

Castien and Ilyana ducked, as did the teen. Castien opened his eyes, standing up.

There, standing in the middle of the massive corridor, cool night air pouring in around him, stood a Shadow-Swift.

Castien's heart pounded.

Ilyana stood up, a knife still clutched in her hand.

The Shadow-Swift wore armor that seemed darker than black, and still held the strange black blades, one longer than the other. The swords were stained with blood, as was the Shadow-Swift's pale face. The Shadow-Swift turned to Castien and Ilyana. He tilted his head, his black ponytail slipping over his shoulder. He raised his dark eyes to meet Castien, his pointed black beard shifting as his lips broke into a wicked smile.

Then, to Castien's shock, the Shadow-Swift turned around and faced the Scorcher teen.

Castien's eyes widened.

The Shadow-Swift launched into the air, black smoke covering the hallway as he flew.

Ilyana pulled Castien away, dragging him in the direction they had come as fire exploded around the corner.

"Where are we going?" Castien wheezed as Ilyana pulled him down another hallway, toward the western staircase.

"That was Prince Faelyn Titansworn," Ilyana breathed. "We have to get out of here. This way." Ilyana released his hand and jumped down the stairwell, leading Castien down the staircase as well.

Castien cursed. *A Shadow-Swift? The Prince? Ilyana killing the King? What in Izara's Shadow was going on?*

Faelyn Titansworn screamed, pushing with every bit of force left in his body as the Shadow-Swift attacked him.

The creature wasn't using his swords, no... It was almost like the beast wanted to make it painful.

The Shadow-Swift grabbed on to Faelyn's face and launched the two of them into the air.

Faelyn roared as he was slammed into a wall, the wind knocked from his lungs.

The world turned dark, strange mists undulating off every surface. Faelyn spun, floating through the air as he slipped out of the Shadow-Swift's grip.

The world flipped back to normal, and the Shadow-Swift was upon him in an instant.

Dark smoke trailed the demigod as he dashed toward Faelyn.

Faelyn cried out as he was tackled once again.

The world seemed to disappear.

Marble exploded all around him. The Shadow-Swift grabbed on to his body and hurled him through another wall.

Faelyn gasped, feeling blood in his mouth as he rolled to a stop.

The Shadow-Swift continued, charging him once again.

The world went numb.

He was losing blood, fast. He would be unconscious before long if he wasn't careful.

Something smashed into his arm, and he crashed into another pillar. He wasn't even sure where he was in the palace; the whole thing was being shredded by the Shadow-Swift.

Faelyn felt himself slipping away, revenge the only word on his mind. His father was dead, and he had let the assassins escape.

There was nothing left to do... except...

Faelyn slid to a stop, the Shadow-Swift landing on top of him, poised over Faelyn with his fists raised. Dazed, Faelyn raised weak hands, trying to protect himself.

The Shadow-Swift's pointed beard twisted as he smiled and brought down his fist.

Something slammed into the Shadow-Swift, whipping him away from Faelyn and sending him spiraling into the columns beyond.

Faelyn gasped, coughing up blood and trying to sit up.

His legs felt somewhat stable; he should be able to walk. He looked around, seeing the destruction on both sides of him.

Cool night air drifted in from the right, where the wall had been destroyed. To the left he saw not one, but *two* figures in the broken rooms.

The Shadow-Swift rolled in the distance, rising to his feet.

Faelyn looked at the closer figure, who spun around.

He wore a white cloak, but beneath that was black armor.

Another Shadow-Swift, Faelyn realized.

The second Shadow-Swift opened his mouth, his graying beard quivering. "Run!" the second Shadow-Swift shouted.

Faelyn blinked, but did not move.

The first Shadow-Swift raised his swords and charged.

The older one drew a singular sword from his cloak and turned to parry the strikes.

The first Shadow-Swift roared, swinging again.

The second parried once again, then turned back to Faelyn. "*RUN!*" he roared.

This time, Faelyn's body obeyed.

Reaching the first floor, Castien slid to a stop. He panted, his lungs and legs burning more than they ever had before. Never had he run so much in his life, and never would he do so again.

He had slipped into a state of survival. He didn't think about what Ilyana had done. He didn't think about what would happen if they were caught. All he could focus on was getting out of this place alive.

"We're almost there," Ilyana said, leading Castien down the next hallway.

The halls here had smooth marble floors, and the ceilings were much taller.

Castien gasped, staggering down the hallway and tumbling to a stop at the end.

Ilyana continued to his left.

Castien heaved another breath, his thoughts coming in slow waves. There was a window at the end of the hallway. He paused, watching as Ilyana approached the window and used her sword to break the glass.

She turned, waving for Castien to follow, and slipped out into the night.

Castien took a deep breath, and stumbled forward, his feet aching. He was almost there. Another hundred feet or so.

Something slammed into him, knocking him to the ground.

Castien screamed, fumbling around beneath the weight of his attacker. He spun, his back on the cool marble floor.

Prince Faelyn Titansworn knelt atop Castien's chest, his amber eyes burning with rage.

Castien cried out, kicking and thrashing, but Faelyn held strong. Castien tried punching the boy, but his arm was slammed to the floor, sending a horrible shock of pain through his body.

Faelyn paused, hovering over Castien. He raised his hand, a steady flame burning within.

Castien shouted.

Faelyn brought his hand down, roaring with delight as he pushed the fire through Castien's skin.

Heat. Pure *heat* seared through Castien's veins, scorching his muscles and bones.

Castien screamed. His arm sizzled, the skin burning and hissing.

Faelyn laughed, forcing another wave of heat through Castien's body.

Castien's head grew heavy, his bones growing weak. He was being burned from the inside out. He wouldn't be able to hold on for much longer.

Thud.

The heat ceased.

Castien peeled his eyes open, the pain still searing through the skin of his left arm.

Faelyn fell to the side, knocked unconscious.

Ilyana stood over him, the hilt of her blade raised where Faelyn's head had been.

Castien sat up, the pain numbing slowly. His arm still screamed with fire, but Castien could barely feel it. The rest of his body felt hot—too hot. But it didn't matter. He *had* to escape.

Ilyana helped him to his feet, sliding his uninjured arm over her shoulder and helping him walk. Each step stung horribly, and his arm felt dangerously numb, but Castien pushed on.

Ilyana kicked aside the stray glass and jumped down the small ledge, landing on the grass beyond the palace safely. The ocean beyond crashed rhythmically against the shore far below.

Ilyana helped Castien to his knees.

He slid out of the window, sparing one final glance at the unconscious Prince—or King, he supposed—as he fell into Ilyana's arms.

Ilyana guided him through the darkness, leading him toward the cliffs.

Castien's thoughts were a jumbled mess, and even walking seemed overwhelming to him. He could slowly feel his consciousness slipping away. He wouldn't be able to stay awake for long.

What felt like seconds later, Ilyana was attaching some sort of straps to him.

Castien leaned over, his eyes half open. He looked down at the ocean at least a hundred feet below, and watched the dark waves move beneath him.

Ilyana was saying something, but he wasn't listening. Something about how she had set up these ropes and straps the night before, and how they were supposed to rappel down to the bottom.

Castien faded in and out of consciousness, finding himself watching Ilyana strap herself to something. At one point he was in her arms, the wind in his hair as they drifted down... down... *down...*

Hours passed like seconds. The events of this evening... the King... the Shadow-Swift... the Prince... they faded from Castien's mind, washed away from his conscience like lines in the sand.

At some point he and Ilyana were on solid ground once again, though it had clearly been some time. The moons were lower, and the glow of the little stars in the sky was beginning to falter.

Waves washed quietly against a shore, and sand was suddenly beneath Castien.

He heard someone sigh, and fall down beside him. Ropes dangled above him, swinging alongside a steep, jagged cliff.

Castien tried to open his eyes farther, but could not. He tried to sit up, but he was *so tired*. His arm hurt, his chest hurt, his head hurt. His legs were burning.

Have I been running? Castien found himself thinking, his eyes cracking open once again. His heart was a slow and steady beat, a calm rhythm of peace that provided some stability for his lost mind in the dark night.

A face appeared over him, watching him curiously. The worried countenance shifted into something like relief as Castien reacted.

It was a woman, with sharp Celesian features.

"Ilyana," Castien whispered.

She turned back, her eyes tensing.

Castien wanted to ask her something. There was something that they were supposed to do tonight, something that must've happened. And yet... "Ilyana... The Celesian spy," Castien said. There was a Celesian spy in the palace, and they were supposed... supposed... "The Celesian spy," Castien repeated. "Who was it?" Castien rasped, feeling his eyes flicker once again. He forced them open, finding Ilyana's face as she opened her mouth.

"It was me," Ilyana whispered.

Castien closed his eyes, the words washing over his soul as he let the darkness take him.

"It was me."

CHAPTER THIRTY-SIX

THE VANISHING

Ten months ago...

Asteros Silverglade stood in the frozen wind, the pillars of Epirac's gate quivering. Night was falling rapidly, an icy cold coming in with the darkness.

Tsarra, Soran, and Eithor stood at his side, quietly watching as the stones rose once again, revealing the hidden door to Epirac.

"You need not worry," Asteros said quietly. The wind howled, his words echoing through the mountains.

The scholars said nothing as the ancient stones screeched to a halt.

Asteros took the first step, the others following slowly. He had not told them why they had come tonight, nor had he told them why Lucien and Malik had stayed behind. He had no intention of explaining himself. He simply wanted someone there to pull him out if something went awry.

The stairwell felt shorter this time, almost as if his grip on reality was fading as he neared the stone.

A Silver Sun... Violet wings... Whispers in the wind.

Asteros closed his eyes, drifting through the darkness.

A face appeared to him, pasting itself in his mind's eye before he could react. It was beautiful. No—it had been beautiful, once, but it was not any longer. It was ruined, crushed by the force of a thousand stones... crushed by a fatal fall from the clouds.

Asteros's hands went cold, feeling the broken body beneath him once more. *Eyes that didn't see... A heart that didn't beat. Cold wind in the frozen night.*

Asteros flinched, blinking as he reached the bottom of the staircase. His body went numb, his mind vacant. There was no salvation for him, not in this world, but maybe...

You can still save her...

"Stop," Asteros said, holding up a hand in the darkness.

The scholars froze, mere steps from the bottom.

"You are to watch from a distance, and only pull me back if I command you to," Asteros said. "Do you understand?"

"Yes," Tsarra whispered, her voice steady.

Asteros nodded, and took a step forward.

The tone sounded again, the blood-red vein lighting up beneath his outstretched foot. The strata began to light up, the second tone sounding as Asteros took another step.

The chamber illuminated, red, turquoise, tan, green, multicolored, white, and violet igniting in the darkness. Asteros took a deep breath, his body moving on its own accord.

Approach...

Asteros obeyed. The stone loomed over him, its long shadows cast on the rounded ceiling by the glowing veins in the floor.

Asteros said nothing, the scholars said nothing... for there was nothing to be said. There was nothing left to say. There was nothing left in this life, not anymore. Keries and Lyseria's desertion had been one thing, but Shalheira... Asteros closed his eyes, seeing her ruined face in the darkness once again.

A gentle tear welled in his eye, pooling until it overflowed, and slid down his cheek. Asteros could see only the shadow of a woman falling in the night. She landed quietly on the dark stone of the mountainside—broken, shattered.

Come closer... young one.

Asteros took another step forward, the low hum in the back of his mind growing louder. The whispers returned, voiceless, soundless, yet ever present. They were indecipherable, though he felt as if he knew what each and every one of them was saying. It was almost as if he shared an understanding with them, an understanding that things were not as they should be... that the world needed to be corrected.

Asteros took another step.

A Silver Sun... Violet Wings... Whispers in the wind... Echoes...

Asteros took another step. The whispers grew even louder, now shouting into his mind, pushing him forward. Even if he had wanted to resist, he doubted that he could have. It was too late.

He reached out, his bare hand drifting through the air with an impossible slowness, and closed his eyes. Cold, dark stone met his fingers, and the world disappeared.

Haze. Darkness.

Whispers in the wind. Screams. Flashes of white. Black clouds.

Violet wings in a silver sun. Shears of night cutting through the stars.

He inhaled, then exhaled. Then he did it again, and again, and again.

An echo.

No. Something was wrong. Something was different. This moment... he had already lived through this moment. Asteros turned, his phantom body refusing to materialize beneath him. He saw nothing in the darkness, felt nothing as the awareness collided with him once again.

"Something is..." Asteros called out, his voice sounding eons away. "Something is wrong."

Wings beat in the distance, growing closer. Asteros drifted toward them, unseen currents pushing him in the direction of whatever it was that approached. *A Silver Sun... Violet wings...* The wings grew near, arms of sand and darkness wrapping around Asteros, restraining him.

They carried him away, like the wind carries a stray leaf during a Cyclone.

Asteros squirmed, the thing's grasp tightening. Asteros tried to open his eyes, glimpsing a flash of light. Darkness enveloped him once again.

"Consciousness is merely a construct of the human mind," a voice whispered.

Asteros grimaced, groaning as he twisted through the darkness. Something tugged at his face, his whole body beginning to tilt as they continued their flight. *Those words...* Asteros strained, listening, but the voice grew distant, fading away like the fires of a dying blazecrest.

"That voice," Asteros said. "I've heard those words before..."

Something moved in the darkness.

"I've—" Asteros's voice vanished, stripped from him in an instant. He doubled over, shocked, but the creature did not release him.

The creature's wings continued beating, nearly on pace with its strangely slow heartbeat. Its sandy armor shifted, twisting and turning with each breath the thing took.

Asteros tilted once again, his stomach lurching, his head spinning. *Why am I here?* Asteros thought, his mind moving with a painful slowness. *Why did I...* Asteros's own thoughts trailed off, the image of a man in black kneeling before a stone projecting itself into his mind. *Me...* Asteros thought, laying eyes on the man before him. His body looked strange, almost foreign. *That can't be real, can it?* Asteros tilted once again, his mind slipping through his fingers.

The creature stopped.

Asteros floated, his arms and legs suddenly feeling as if they were no longer there. The image of the man and the stone disappeared, replaced by only darkness once more.

A Silver Sun appeared.

Asteros cried out, falling back. The blinding silver light knocked him sideways, sending him spiraling into the night. He lurched to a halt, crashing into a phantom wall. The Silver Sun moved, drifting away into the darkness, sliding ever farther from his form.

It stopped, then began to move upward, floating into the heavens with a strange slowness. Asteros tried to blink, but realized that he did not need to. He did not need to do anything. Here, he could simply *be*.

The Sun settled, casting its enigmatic light on Asteros. He looked down, finding himself kneeling on black stone once again. This was not Epirac... no. It was someplace else, *something* else.

Violet wings eclipsed the fallen sun, their ever-present beating growing closer once again.

Asteros jumped, cowering beneath the sandy winds of darkness in this strange place, hoping to hide from whatever it was that approached. Asteros paused, realizing that he had been holding his hands in front of his face, though he still could not feel them.

A golden thread of light materialized, poking through the darkness and weaving its way through the Void. Asteros watched as it twisted and turned, carving a path in the endless night. The golden light began to fade, then winked out.

"I have been waiting," the voice whispered suddenly. It came from everywhere, yet nowhere.

Asteros turned, darkness surrounding him once again.

"I knew you would return, and here you are," it said.

"You..." Asteros trailed off, the world slowly coming into focus. He was laying down, somewhere. Asteros shifted, his head feeling heavy. His hands felt leaden, though in a way they still did not seem to exist. *Curious.* "You told me that I could still save her,"

Asteros said automatically, his phantom lips moving before his mind.

"Ah." The voice seemed to smile, the wings shifting in the darkness. "And you can."

Asteros released a breath, his head falling to the dark stone again. Tilting...

"But not yet," it added.

"What?" Asteros growled. The world flipped, and suddenly he stood on his feet. He held out his hands, expecting to feel the familiar weight of his swords in his palms. He looked down, and they were there. Snow fell in the empty void around him. He looked back at his hands, the world twisting once again. *How...*

"You cannot control this place, Asteros, though your instincts encourage you to try," the voice said. "Your mind has been removed from its body, and your consciousness has now been separated from the world it knows... you are as you will be when you die—save for the presence of the memories I allowed you to take with you to this place."

"So am I..." Asteros started, feeling very light. "Am I dead?"

The voice laughed. "No," it said after a moment. "Not yet, at least."

"Who are you?" Asteros asked, finally steadying himself in the vast emptiness of the Void.

"An inconsequential question in the grand scheme of things, as I'm sure you're aware," the voice rumbled. "Yet, I know you well... So I understand why you wish to know."

"I would rather know with whom I am speaking when I am in a world so foreign and strange because, if nothing else, being able to put a name to your voice—"

"Would give you some measure of realness to this realm of chaos, yes, I understand," the voice finished for him. "I was in your position too, once. Yet now... now I am here." The world tilted again. "Now, I am the one known as the Emissary."

"Emissary?" Asteros asked.

"I am a messenger," the creature—the Emissary—said. "Yet, unlike most emissaries, I was also once a warrior," the Emissary continued. "Though that was a *very* long time ago."

"You've been speaking to me," Asteros said, tilting his head. "You've been whispering into my mind."

A Silver Sun... Whispers in the wind...

"Ah," the Emissary mused. "I am glad to hear that you have been receiving my messages. You are among the few who have been."

"I—" Asteros trailed off. His mind seemed to be trying to piece something together, it was almost as if it were trying to open a lock that had no key. Suddenly, his mind flashed back to the very first thing he had seen when he arrived; it felt as though the thought had been pushed into his mind, in a way. "I heard you, again," Asteros said. "When I returned, I heard you repeating the very same words that you said to me upon our first meeting."

"That is because you saw yourself, Asteros," the Emissary said. "It matters not *when* you enter the Void, but *where*."

Asteros turned once again, feeling the cold sand of the creature's armor on him.

The wings continued to beat. "You see, you entered the Void through contact with the Devourer's Stone, the same as I did."

"So when we were flying..."

"I was taking us somewhere else, somewhere far from where our first encounter occurred, somewhere safe," the Emissary whispered, his voice moving through the darkness.

Asteros felt heavy, his body falling through the night once again. *Shalheira.* "How do I bring her back?" Asteros asked, a strange coldness coming over him.

The creature stopped, turning to him. Asteros glimpsed the violet wings once again—sprouting from a humanoid figure who wore armor of black sand.

"You do not," the Emissary said, the darkness around Asteros suddenly twisting once again. "At least, not until you bring back the Revenants."

"The Resurgence," Asteros breathed, the clouds of darkness around him beginning to take shape. Epirac formed around him, although... something was *off*. The chamber was of the same dark stone, and the darker-than-dark Devourer's Stone stood tall in the center, yet

"The veins," Asteros realized.

"They are empty." The Emissary nodded.

Asteros took a step, his illusory body feeling light in this fabricated world.

"They are yet to draw in the powers of the Sects that will be lost," the Emissary said.

"What are you talking about?" Asteros turned, meeting the shadow before him.

The Emissary held no form in this world, instead materializing as a simple mass of black smoke, somehow transparent despite the dense fog within.

"Where have you taken me?" Asteros asked.

"I have taken you exactly where you need to be, Asteros Silverglade," the Emissary growled, drifting through the massive chamber. "I have taken you to the Vanishing."

Voices rose from the distance.

Asteros turned, tracking their origin to the staircase—the same staircase he had come down not moments before. *Or was it centuries ago?* Asteros wondered, but the thought disappeared as the source of the voices came into view. Asteros squinted as four figures walked into the massive chamber, the low tone sounding on the leader's first two steps, just as it had with Asteros's.

"This is it, then," the first one said. Asteros noted the man's armor: black and sinewy, almost immaterial... similar to the Emissary's. "This is the Stone."

"Aye," the second man said, stepping forward as well. He held a violet Crystal in his hand, *a violet Crystal*. Asteros took a step forward.

"Well, then what are we waiting for?" a third voice called, a female figure pushing past the other two. "We are here, why wait any longer?"

"We hesitate because we know not what we are on the verge of unleashing," the fourth one said, standing beside the woman. This one sounded older... almost tired. "This is unknown territory, my dear. This cavern may even predate the days of the war. A bit of caution will do us no harm."

"It may very well do us in," the woman snapped. "Who knows how long we have until they find us."

"*She* has promised us protection. And, besides, they will not find us," the first one said calmly.

She?

"They do not know how to open the lock, even the Rune-Writers will not be able to decipher it." He stepped forward. "We have all the time in the world, my friends."

"Even so, you'll understand if I feel the need to expedite our mission," the woman said.

"She's right," the second man said. "We are the last Revenants who bear the key to this door, if something does happen—and we fail—then there's no one left to finish the job."

"I worry only for the four of us, should this not go in our favor," the fourth one said. "What does it matter if they even know what we did if we are not here to see it?"

"They will know what we have done," the first said, approaching the Devourer's Stone. "Besides, if what I have been told is true, this will take several days, if not weeks."

"How can we expect to defend the mountain for that long?" the second one asked.

"We won't have to," the first said, producing a red Crystal from a pouch in his armor as he examined stone, nearing it. He flinched.

Asteros heard the whispers once again, feeling them tug at his mind. The first man seemed to hear them as well...

"How are we even supposed to do this?" the woman asked.

"I'm not sure," the first man whispered. "But it seems that I am supposed to..." he trailed off, raising a hand to touch the stone.

Asteros flinched, the man's hand slowly colliding with the dark mass.

A low rumbling overtook the mountain, shaking the entire cavern. To Asteros's surprise, the man's eyes suddenly snapped open, his hand still on the stone. *How was he still conscious?*

"Everyone, with me!" he shouted, raising his other hand and pressing it against the stone. The rumbling grew louder as the others approached.

Without hesitation, the second man placed his hands on the stone, nearly collapsing on impact.

The woman followed suit, and the fourth man—though he hesitated—finally did the same.

The rumbling grew progressively louder, turning into a violent roar.

Asteros cried out, his phantom body falling to the ground.

The Emissary laughed, his shadow spiraling through the chamber with an animalistic delight.

The stone shook, and began to glow. Asteros crawled to his feet, watching as the darkness within the stone seemed to ignite.

The Revenants cried out.

A deafening explosion sounded through the mountains, knocking Asteros and the Revenants away from the stone, scattering them across the room.

Asteros groaned, straining to get a look at the mass of darkness.

The stone rumbled, and then a bright white light exploded from the top, shooting through the ceiling and into the night sky.

The Revenants cursed, stumbling to their feet and rushing toward the stone, which was now glowing brightly with the white light. The roar of the white beam was almost deafening. "Wait!" the first Revenant shouted as the others charged the stone.

The white beam stabilized, but did not slow down. It continued shooting out of the chamber, shining with the light of a Scorcher's blaze, burning with a horrifying screech. "It's working," the Revenant said. A subtle red tint came over the beam as it burned through the sky.

Asteros watched as the red light trickled down the beam, dribbling into one of the grooved canals of the chamber, filling it with blood-red energy.

"Gods above," the first one cursed, holding the red Crystal in his hand. The Crystal's light began to fade.

Asteros peered through the massive hole in the roof of the cavern that the stone had created as the others gathered around the first Revenant.

Countless Summoners flew overhead, explosions of fire and darkness colliding with each passing second.

A beam of pure light shot across the sky, crashing into a massive white symbol.

A Rune, Asteros realized. The Rune moved through the sky, carried by something, or *someone*.

A stone broke off from the nearest mountain, and hurled through the air, knocking the Rune-Writer out of the sky. The stone then shattered, cleaved in half by another beam of light.

Red shot across the night sky, hitting a group of flying soldiers. The soldiers multiplied, then multiplied again and again until there were hundreds of them hovering in the sky.

The red beams tore through each one as if they were nothing.

Illusomancers, Asteros thought. The soldiers were not really there.

A winged beast flew across the sky, wicked claws growing from each of its horrific hands, cleaving through the illusory soldiers. The claws retracted, and the wings shortened. The creature grew a massive spiked tail and whipped through the night, using it as a weapon. *Skin-Shaper.*

The red beam arced in the air, returning to a hovering robed figure. The figure seemed to twitch, then began to drift away as a slight red mist drained from his body. *Blood Sorcerer.*

Asteros looked back to the cavern.

The blood-red vein continued to fill, though it was hardly even a hundredth completed; this was clearly a slow process.

Asteros watched as the Skin-Shaper flew directly into the white beam, trying to cleave it in half with its massive tail. The creature screeched, disintegrating as it came into contact with the force of pure destruction. Asteros stumbled back.

"It will take many days for all of the various energies to be absorbed," the first Revenant said after a few moments. "The stone must draw every last bit of energy from the skies in order to remove the Tempests, and then it must drain the Crystals themselves, channeling the energy through the stone and into the mountains."

Into the mountains?

"It will remove the Summoning powers from the outside world, stripping this wretched place of its Tempests and its Summoners," the first one finished.

"Yet the people will still live, the war will continue," the older man said, his withered face now dimly lit by the red strata.

"Indeed." The first one nodded, his sharp features coming into view. "But just think of it. A human without Summoning... Who would've ever thought such a thing would be possible—"

The scene halted, melting away into dark smoke as if it had never existed.

A human without Summoning...

"No..." Asteros whispered, the dots slowly connecting in his mind. If there had never been humans without Summoning, then that could only mean... "That's *impossible*."

"It is more than just 'possible,' dear Asteros, it is the truth," the Emissary said. "*Every single person* on Auris is a Summoner. Many of them simply had their energies stolen from them." The Emissary paused. "Those you call 'Stormless' are in truth those who belong to the Lost Sects, though, without the correct Crystals, they are currently powerless."

Asteros felt sick, his stomach tingling, a shiver running down his spine.

"As the days passed, and the Devourer's Stone took in the energies, the Crystals began to disintegrate, leaving those who were once powerful Summoners with nothing but dust and blood."

Asteros's mind seemed to be frozen, as if he couldn't process the knowledge. It seemed impossible... Tsarra, Eithor, Soran, his parents...*everyone* was a Summoner. Their access to their powers had simply been stolen from them by the Devourer's Stone in the Vanishing.

"What happened?"

"The Revenants did not realize that their own Sect would be destroyed as well," the Emissary said, another scene forming before Asteros's disbelieving eyes.

He was inside Epirac once again, though it was clear that days, if not weeks, had passed since the last scene.

The Revenants leaned against the walls, exhausted and sleep deprived. Open food containers and waterskins lay scattered across the floor, which was now lit up with seven different veins. White, tan, red, multicolored, green, turquoise, and gold.

Violet is missing, Asteros thought with a start. *But gold has been added?*

The face of the first Revenant was illuminated by the violet Crystal in his hand.

The Crystal flickered.

The man sat up, looking at the Crystal. He blinked, the Crystal flickered again. "No," he whispered. "We have a problem."

The others rushed to his side, watching as he held out the Crystal.

The white beam took on a new tint, one of a dark violet.

"It's..." the woman started.

"It's absorbing our power," the second one whispered. "*She* lied to us," he breathed. "No... No, no, no, no, we have to stop this."

Who? Asteros took another step forward. *Who are they talking about? Who is "She"?*

"We can't," the oldest one breathed. "It's too late."

"No," the first one said, stepping forward. "No, it's not."

"Endon," the older man said, reaching out. "What are you doing?"

"I didn't become a Harbinger just so that I could stand by and watch my own Sect's destruction," the first one—Endon—said.

Asteros's eyes widened. This was one of the few names he recognized from the Ancient Times.

Endon... This man was a Harbinger... *The Harbinger of the Revenants*—the one who brought his Sect's power to Auris.

"Endon," the woman said. "What are you trying to do?"

Endon raised his arms, his sharp face curving into a twisted, focused smile. "I'm going to stop this," Endon said. He raised his hands, unleashing a horrific roar as torrents of dark violet energy exploded from his arms.

Asteros stepped back, shielding his eyes.

The white beam sputtered, shaking as Endon's purple darkness collided with it.

Endon roared, the other three Revenants crying out as they were knocked to the ground. They screamed for Endon to stop, but he did not.

Endon's body began to disintegrate. He reached out, laying a hand on the stone. He stiffened as something rose overhead in the frozen night.

The Silver Sun... Asteros realized, his eyes meeting the glowing white-gray mass overhead.

Endon's eyes widened.

Asteros watched as Endon shifted his power, guiding it away from the beam, and toward the Silver Sun.

Violet energy crashed into the Silver Sun, piercing through it, dancing around it.

A golden moon shined overhead, glowing brightly behind the tortured sun. And in that moment, watching one of the Ancient Harbingers themselves, Asteros understood.

Purple light crashed into the golden moon, a slow silver wave forming on its edge.

The Emissary laughed once again, flying around the room as the golden moon—Lotius, Asteros realized—began to transform into a metallic silver.

The Silver Sun began to dissolve, Endon's divine powers draining away the last of its energy and transferring it into something eternal, something immovable: one of Auris's moons.

Then, he turned to the Devourer's Stone, and he attacked it.

Asteros fell to the ground, a massive shockwave exploding from the stone as Endon unleashed the full might of a Harbinger on the creation.

The white beam flickered, then flashed one final time before vanishing.

Asteros shielded his eyes, then peered past his phantom hand, searching for Endon.

Endon was gone, leaving behind only a strange purple mist that slowly melted into the Devourer's Stone.

Asteros turned to the other Revenants, watching as their violet Crystals turned black, their armor solidifying into black steel.

The former Revenants cursed, reaching out.

Asteros watched with fascination as a plume of darkness shot from the woman's hand. Her power now mirrored Asteros's.

Then, without a second more, the scene disappeared.

Asteros's face fell. "I..." he trailed off. "I don't understand."

"The Revenants were destroyed by the Devourer's Stone: the key artifact that is responsible for the Vanishing—the artifact that you are touching right now," the Emissary said. "Though not all of their power was lost to the stone, for Endon was able to sever the curse before it fully took effect; he transferred the energy of the Revenants into one of Auris's moons, Lotius, thus saving the Revenants from losing their power. The result was instead a dilution of their power, transforming them into a new Sect: the Shadow-Swifts."

"And the other surviving Sects? The Voltarians, the Scorchers, the Cloudwalkers, and so on?" Asteros asked.

"They were fortunate enough to have been spared, for the spell was only half completed when Endon froze the curse," the Emissary said. "By nothing more than chance, when the stone was completing the curse, the random order it chose placed the surviving Sects after the Revenants, and, due to Endon's interference, they were preserved."

"And Endon himself?" Asteros asked, his voice echoing.

"Mmmmm," the Emissary hummed, drifting through the shadows. "Endon sacrificed himself in order to put an end to the Vanishing, fusing his power with the stone while losing his life in the process."

Asteros's body turned once again, seeming to fall through the darkness in no particular direction. His head spun, his mind racing, yet he could do nothing but watch as he was tossed through the Void once again.

"How—" Asteros trailed off, the spinning stopping gradually. "How do you live with this?"

"The tilting?" the Emissary asked, his voice rising in pitch a bit. "You get used to it, eventually."

Asteros rubbed his imaginary head with fake hands, then looked around with unseeing eyes once again.

"Wait," Asteros said, a low rumbling sounding from beneath him. "What's happening?"

"I am bringing you closer to Endon's power," the Emissary said, the beating of his wings steadily overpowering the rumble.

"You mean to say..." Asteros started, feeling the strange sense of restraint come over his body once again. "His power is still here?" Asteros breathed.

The Emissary hummed in confirmation, the rumbling growing louder with each passing second. "The Harbingers—the ones who brought the powers of Summoning to Auris—are not as you believe them to be," the Emissary said. "The Harbingers were far more powerful than regular Summoners, but, when a Harbinger dies, their power does not die with them..." the Emissary said. "Their power stays behind, waiting to be claimed by another.

"This very mountain is the outlet of the Revenant's power," the Emissary continued. "Each lost Sect had their powers redirected to one of the mountains in The Highlands. These mountains are protected by an otherwise unbreakable seal meant to keep the energies from escaping. Though, if you were to loosen the seal powered by the stone, perhaps they could be unlocked... And, with time, the lost Tempests could return as well."

"The..." Asteros frowned. "What is the Devourer's Stone?"

The Emissary did not answer.

Asteros twisted, trying to meet its eyes. "How was it able to absorb the energies of Summoners? And why did it simply redirect them? If it was capable of taking in the energies, why didn't it simply destroy them?"

"There are some things about the nature of the Devourer's Stone that we still do not understand," the Emissary said. "It is my hope that your insight will give us some answers."

"Us?" Asteros asked.

The Emissary seemed to pause for a moment. "There are others allied with myself who are seeking the same knowledge... Others who wish to discover the secrets of the past."

"Is—" Asteros started. "Is that why you guided me here? To help you find such knowledge?"

"I guided you here so that I could begin the Resurgence," the Emissary said softly. "And soon, with your help, that will be accomplished." The Emissary paused. "Dyvnire—the Silver Sun—will follow soon after."

"What is Dyvnire?" Asteros questioned.

The Emissary paused. "It is the product of our plan," the Emissary said, turning his phantom head. "The stone will create it, if directed properly. Everything is as it should be, you need only to fulfill your destiny, Asteros Silverglade."

Asteros found himself standing once again. Epirac returned around him. Present-day Epirac.

Tsarra, Soran, and Eithor whispered to one another by the staircase as Asteros rose to his feet. They remained still as Asteros reached forward.

He hesitated, trying to resist—to take a moment to think everything through—but found his thoughts washed away like sand in the sea. There was nothing he could do.

"It is too late, Asteros," the Emissary whispered.

"You said that I could still save Shalheira," Asteros said, somehow finding his voice in the darkness. "You said..." His voice gave out. "You said that I could still make things right."

"I am afraid that bringing Shalheira back is quite impossible, at the moment," the Emissary said. "But, if you trust me, and if you bring about the Resurgence, then you may just stand a chance."

Asteros almost listened. Asteros almost followed through with his grief-stricken plan, but there, standing in Epirac's chamber once again, Asteros realized the weight of his task, and he now understood that the Resurgence must be stopped.

This was wrong. Everything was wrong. Coming here had been a mistake, the greatest one he had ever made. If the Resurgence were to begin, the rising tensions throughout Auris would escalate to war. The Stormless would become Summoners, and where each man would normally only be capable of killing only a few others... Each would become infinitely more dangerous. Without the Stormless as pawns, the Summoners would tear one another apart. Thousands— no, *millions*—would be killed. Asteros's muddied mind could not discern much, but he knew this: He must stop the Emissary.

Asteros clenched his muscles, trying to resist. But it was too late.

Asteros's hand touched the stone. He screamed.

The Emissary roared, its attention turning to Asteros. Yet, by some miracle, Asteros held on. His mind fused to the idea of resistance, forging a bond that felt unbreakable.

White light exploded from the stone.

The scholars ran into the chamber, calling Asteros's name. They were knocked to the floor, sent sprawling across the cavern as the explosion intensified.

Asteros roared, tightening his grip on the resistance.

The Emissary pushed back, wings of violet darkness and armor of black sand grinding against stone and metal.

The veins flickered, then began to drain, the light slowly fading from them. *No*, Asteros thought. *No, no, no, NO!*

The Emissary laughed—a horrific, bloodcurdling sound. And then it happened.

A white beam shot into the sky, the six other colors of the lost Sects slowly wrapping around it.

The Resurgence was beginning. The plans of the Emissary were coming to fruition.

Asteros cried out, flying backward. He crashed into a rounded wall, falling to the ground. With a turn he realized that he had not crashed into a wall, but into a wall of *energy*.

There was a circular white barrier surrounding Asteros and the stone, keeping him from escaping. Which meant... *The Emissary has trapped me here.*

Rage. Pure, unrivaled rage filled Asteros's veins. The Emissary had tricked him, and now he was preventing Asteros from escaping safely.

But, even here, Asteros still had his power. He still had his Crystals, and when he reached out... He could feel the infinite supply of Revenant energy stored within the mountain.

Asteros raised his hands, calling upon the power within his body. He grabbed ahold of the white beam that was shooting into the sky, and he *pulled*.

The white light disappeared, falling from the night sky like the sun at dusk.

Asteros contained it, holding it in place, cloaking the stone in its terrible light.

Yet Asteros found that he could not move. His hands were fixed in their position, his eyes locked on the glowing white stone before him. Yet, despite his frozen state, Asteros was able to complete the spell; he wrapped his power tightly around the stone, sealing the Resurging energies into place.

The Emissary pushed back, his battle cry ringing through the mountains, but Asteros held strong.

Asteros could still feel the energies slipping away; a part of their power had already escaped.

"It has already started, Asteros," the Emissary mused. "The seals have been broken. Stormless around the world will begin to feel the *pull* of their power. You cannot stop this now."

"No," Asteros said softly. "But I can delay it," Asteros growled. "You tricked me, and now you won't even let me *leave*... If you're going to keep me here, then I'm going to do everything in my power to *slow you down*."

"It is only a matter of time now, Asteros," the Emissary said. "Soon you will understand why I have done all of this. But, no matter what you do, there is no stopping what I have already begun."

"Then why won't you let me *leave*?" Asteros snapped.

The Emissary laughed. "Because I wasn't just after the Resurgence," the Emissary said. "I was seeking to capture *you*." The Emissary laughed again.

Asteros grunted. "Why?"

"You will soon see," the Emissary said, its voice soft. "Resist the Resurgence if you must." Violet wings began beating, and the Emissary's voice grew further away. "Fight against my power if that is your desire, you will remain trapped here either way... But, when you're ready to learn the truth, come and find me." The Emissary's voice faded away, leaving Asteros alone in the darkness.

He tried to move once again, finding his muscles frozen. His power still held against the stone, slowing the escape of the energies to a soft trickle, but it was not enough. Despite his efforts, and despite his strength...

...The Resurgence had begun.

CHAPTER THIRTY-SEVEN

POWERS UNLEASHED

Ten months ago...

Lucien Shade took step after step as he descended Epirac's spiral staircase. He knew what had happened.

What struck him as interesting was the fact that the brief flash of white light had come from within the mountain, yet, when Lucien had examined Epirac's peak, he had found no gaps in the stone... The mountain had already proven itself capable of moving itself, so why wouldn't it be able to reforge stone that had been destroyed?

Violet wings and a Silver Sun... Lucien grimaced, pausing. He leaned his head against the dark stone wall, taking a moment. The whispers faded, as they always did, but the influence lingered. Though, after all this time, Lucien was used to it.

He neared the bottom of the staircase, the air strangely cold.

A low rumbling became apparent as he neared the cavern, and, when Lucien rounded the last turn, he saw why.

An orb of white energy surrounded the large stone in the center of the chamber, and there, trapped inside of it, was Asteros Silverglade.

Lucien cursed, taking a step forward. No sound accompanied his steps this time; there was only the low rumbling of Asteros and the stone.

Asteros held his hands up against the stone, purple energy exploding from his palms, wrapping around the chamber and seeming to contain something within the stone. *Curious...*

A cold steel blade pressed against his throat.

Lucien paused, his eyes scanning the chamber. The veins were slowly fading, yet there was still enough light to see two figures lying on the ground—both male. *Which meant...*

"Hello, Tsarra," Lucien said calmly, turning his head slightly to the side.

Tsarra leaned against the wall, dagger raised to Lucien's throat. She stepped out from her hiding place slowly, keeping the dagger against his skin.

Lucien shifted slightly, but did not resist. He could have phased and killed her, had he wanted to, but Tsarra's boldness had piqued his interest.

"What are you doing here?" Tsarra growled, her red-brown eyes hard.

"When one sees an explosion of white energy followed by the brief appearance of a strange beam that seemed to be piercing the sky, it can only be expected that they would investigate such things, would it not?" Lucien asked, his pointed features curving into a smile.

Tsarra frowned, her hand quivering.

She's nervous, Lucien noted. His eyes slid back to the other two figures, who were beginning to stir.

"What is that?" Tsarra asked, tilting her head back to the translucent energy barrier around Asteros and the stone.

"I was hoping you could tell me," Lucien said, taking a cautious step forward.

Tsarra flinched, but let him move, though she did not lower the dagger.

"Although I suppose the more important question is this: Why did you think I would know what it was?" Lucien asked.

"I have been suspecting that you know far more about all of this than you've been letting on," Tsarra growled, her voice shaking as she pressed the dagger against his throat once again. "You've been playing all of us from the start."

"Oh, Tsarra." Lucien laughed. "You expect far too much of me."

"No. No, Lucien." Tsarra shook her head. "I think that everyone else has simply been expecting far too little."

Lucien smiled, raising a finger to the dagger, lowering it slowly.

"What I haven't been able to figure out is why," Tsarra said, apparently realizing that her efforts to intimidate Lucien were futile.

"Your friend Velarus is not the only one to have touched one of those stones, Tsarra. I have come in contact with one as well," Lucien said, smiling once again as he took a step forward. He neared the white barrier, staring through the translucent energy shield with a sense of fascination.

Asteros seemed completely and utterly frozen, yet the barrier rippled and twisted with each passing second, as if it were almost alive.

Lucien turned, looking at Soran and Eithor, who twitched on the floor, barely conscious.

Eithor flickered, his entire body seeming to glow. Lucien blinked, and suddenly found himself staring at three mirror images of the old man. Two of them dissolved into turquoise frost.

Illusomancer... Lucien thought. *Now that's interesting.*

Soran seemed to be in pain. Lucien approached, watching curiously as Soran's hand moved, the skin rippling like waves in the ocean. Wicked claws grew from the fingers, and the hand lengthened, glowing a strange shade of green. It returned to normal, and Soran slumped to the ground once again.

Skin-Shaper, Lucien thought. *I should expose them to the stone... They would be completely under her control.*

"What happened to them?" Lucien asked, turning back to Tsarra, who stood near the staircase.

She raised a hand, a slight red mist slipping from her fingers. *Blood Sorceress.*

"The same thing that happened to me, it seems," Tsarra said.

"Fascinating," Lucien breathed, stepping toward her.

Tsarra raised the dagger once again, and Lucien halted. Tsarra backed toward the steps, keeping her dagger raised.

"Where are you going?" Lucien growled, tilting his head.

"I don't know what's going on here," Tsarra said, fear finally breaking through her even voice. "I don't understand what *that* is," she said, pointing at Asteros. "And I don't understand... *this*," she said, the red mist returning to her hand. "But I do understand this much: Something is changing here. Something is happening to Auris, and whatever happened in this chamber today... I can't be a part of it, at least, not like this."

"Tsarra—"

"No!" Tsarra cut him off, the dagger shaking. "Don't." She held up a hand. "Please, don't try to stop me. I know that you could kill me with nothing more than a thought but... please..."

Lucien sighed, reading her face. He frowned, his mind running through the possible outcomes. "Where will you go?" Lucien asked.

"North," Tsarra said. "I don't know what it is, but *something* is pulling me there. Something is calling me, and I shall heed its summons. With any luck, this will be the last time we see each other," Tsarra said, taking another step up the stairs.

"I wouldn't count on it," Lucien said, turning away. He heard Tsarra let out a breath and listened quietly as she started up the long staircase. Lucien kept his head lowered, he knew he would regret what he had just done, but... Perhaps a part of him still held on, somewhere...

He turned back to Asteros, whose face was fixed in a focused glare, teeth bared. Lucien stared at the fading veins in the stone, then at the scholars—who were now Summoners. Finally, he looked back at Asteros, staring at his friend through the rippling currents of violet energy.

The Resurgence had begun. Asteros was trapped. The Ancient energies had been unchained once again.

Lucien sighed, taking a step forward. He stared at Asteros, shaking his head. "Oh, Asteros," Lucien whispered. "What have you done..."

EPILOGUE

Ten months ago...

Lyseria Krelek stood in the frozen cave, listening. Someone was here. Someone had found her. A part of her was relieved. Maybe she wouldn't die here. She had barely survived her failed Initiation, yet she had survived it nonetheless. If she could live through that, she would live through this.

Keries had abandoned her, fleeing the skirmish, zipping from the scene like a snowflake in the wind. She knew that he had some sort of strange condition that affected his mind, but he had abandoned her when she needed him most, and that... that had nearly gotten her killed. During the fight, she had taken a cudgel to the side, and lost no small amount of blood.

It didn't matter. She had used the last of her Crystals to heal her frozen arm and bleeding core, and escaped by dashing into the blizzard. A part of her was thankful that Keries had abandoned her. She knew that she was likely presumed dead, which meant that she was finally free from the rule of the other Shadow-Swifts. Though the fact that her Crystals were now empty—and that she had very little understanding of how to fill them—had proven to be an issue.

So she had waited, sitting in this cave, hoping that someone would find her. Either that, or she would eventually freeze from the cold, which wouldn't be all that bad either.

Yet someone had found her.

Snow crunched beneath footsteps.

Lyseria instinctively tried to draw upon her empty Crystals, only to be met with a frustrating emptiness. She cursed, drawing her twin daggers from their sheaths and crouching behind a particularly large boulder. The inside of the cave was mostly black rock and frozen ice, with massive stones scattered around. She shivered in the cold air, listening as more footsteps approached.

They stopped.

Lyseria paused, craning her neck as she listened.

One singular figure continued walking forward, their footsteps soft and light.

She knelt down, thinking. Whoever it was who was entering clearly knew that someone was in here. She wouldn't be surprised if Asteros had developed some sort of method for tracking Shadow-Swifts, but for anyone else to find her would be near impossible.

"Are you sure this is the right cave?" a smooth voice asked.

Lyseria stiffened. There was something strange about the accent. It was soft, almost like certain syllables were brushed over, rather than enunciated. Yet the accent was not rudimentary. In fact, there was a strange sense of elegance to it.

"I'm certain," said another, firmer voice. "This is the one."

Lyseria tightened her grip on the daggers.

"We know of your presence, young one," the voice called out softly. "We mean you no harm, I assure you of that much. We have been sent to assist you."

Like they expect me to believe that...

The man stepped forward, a nonthreatening air settling over the chamber.

Lyseria braced herself as the ice crunched.

He was close.

She shivered from the cold, readying her dagger. She yelled, jumping out from behind the boulder and thrusting her dagger toward the approaching figure. Lyseria locked eyes with her attacker, meeting a pair of eyes nestled above strange face wrappings. She froze, though this wasn't the same as her hesitation with the Cryostalker; her dagger was stuck.

She frowned. She looked back, still frozen in place. Her dagger was being held by the man's cloth-wrapped hand, a strange golden aura cloaking his fingers. *He is stopping the dagger... with his hand.*

"Well," the man said, his gold-brown eyes melting into a friendly smile from behind the cloth wrappings. "This is quite a surprise." He lightly pushed Lyseria's dagger away.

She took the blade away from his hand, the golden aura fading from his fingers after a few moments. "How did you..." Lyseria trailed off, stepping back. "Who are you?"

"Are you a Shadow-Swift, my child?" the man asked.

Lyseria flinched.

The golden aura reappeared around the man's hands at her sudden movement, but he stayed still.

He has good reflexes, I'll give him that, Lyseria noted. "I..." Lyseria started. "I am a Shadow-Swift," she said firmly. Lying wouldn't have done her any good, especially considering that her Shadow-Sand armor had already given her away.

"Interesting," the man said. He reached back, pulling down the white cloth that covered the lower half of his face. The man who met her eyes was a bit older than she expected. Though he was still young, for there were no wrinkles on his strangely smooth face.

Lyseria glanced past him, noting that there were seven others behind the man, each wearing the same clothing.

"Forgive me," the lead man said. "My name is Enzo." He extended a wrapped hand. "I have been sent to locate and assist someone in danger, and it appears that that person is you."

Lyseria blinked. He said it so plainly, as if it were nothing. *Yet...*

"How did you find me?" Lyseria asked slowly, lowering—but not sheathing—her daggers.

"We were led to this cave by our visions, young one," Enzo said.

"Visions?" Lyseria asked, raising an eyebrow. Keries's lessons sped through her mind, her body subconsciously preparing for another fight.

Enzo smiled once again. He turned, pacing through the small ice cavern. "We are not like your kind, dear child," he said. "We come from Elan Taesi, the island off of Auris's western coast."

"How did you stop my dagger?" she asked.

Enzo grinned, showing off twin rows of bright white teeth. "I told you," he said, his voice soft and smooth. "We are not like your kind." He turned around, the other members of his group still standing at the cave's entryway. He started toward the exit, wrapped feet crunching lightly on the ice. "You're going to want to come with us," Enzo said.

Lyseria noted the curved blade hanging at his waist. It was strange... *foreign*. Unique.

"Who are you?" Lyseria asked again, sheathing her daggers and taking a step forward.

Enzo turned, the bright sun blinding her as she tried to read his face. "We're Wayfinders."

To be continued...

The Fire King, Book 2 in the STORMLESS Series will be released late 2023

REFERENCE GUIDE

TEMPESTS

Auris does not experience ordinary weather patterns... Instead, there is a collection of seven Tempests that blow across the land (switching daily) dominating the sky and dictating many aspects of life on the continent. The Tempests are deadly, violent storms, and most will not survive if caught in one unprotected. Due to this, roughly a thousand years before our story begins, one of the Lost Sects known as the Rune-Writers created wards to dampen the effects of the Tempests. These wards cover only a small portion of Auris, and all of the continent's cities have been built within their protection. However, the Tempests do not come without their advantages... Each Tempest (save for one) serves to recharge the Crystals of one of the Sects. The Tempests are listed below.

- **BLAZEDAYS:** Blazedays are the warmest of the Tempests, and are characterized by intense heat, a blinding sun, and the presence of sunbeams.

- **CYCLONES:** Similar to Cyclones in our Realm, Cyclones on Auris are dangerous windstorms that consist of breezes and gusts strong enough to knock many off their feet.
- **FROSTFALLS:** While similar to snowfalls in our Realm, Frostfalls can range from violent blizzards to light ice-rains.
- **MISTVEILS:** Mistveils are a form of *very* heavy fog in which many are unable to see more than a few feet in front of themselves.
- **SLICK-DAYS:** Slick-Days are a mixture of moderate rain and high winds, leading to many surfaces becoming "slick."
- **STORM GALES:** Storm Gales are rather similar to thunderstorms in our Realm, though Storm Gales are far more dangerous. They consist of powerful winds, heavy rain, and frequent lightning strikes.
- **WISPWINDS:** Wispwinds are the only one of the seven Tempests that does not recharge a Sect's Crystals. These are characterized by swarming (yet harmless) orbs of white energy with thick, immaterial tails. Visibility is drastically reduced on these days, though the Wisps cause no harm to people or animals.

THE SEVEN SECTS OF AURIS

Auris has ordinary humans—called Stormless—though the land is also inhabited by Summoners, humans who possess magical abilities. Summoning is passed on genetically, with the potency of each parent's bloodline dictating the Sect that the child will belong to as well as how powerful they will be. Though two parents could be of different Sects, their offspring will only possess one Sect's powers (usually whichever Sect runs more strongly in one's blood).

Each Sect was founded by one of the Ancient Harbingers. The Harbingers were Ancient beings from the Planes of Genesis who came to Auris bearing the gifts of Summoning. These demigods held incredible power, and were responsible for founding each of their individual Sects.

All Summoners gain their power from Crystals, which they typically carry with them. These Crystals serve as vessels of the power offered to Auris by the Tempests, and are capable of absorbing the energy released by the Tempests and allowing Summoners to use said energy to power their abilities. These Crystals grow outside of the wards, though only very rarely. They refill slowly, over the course of the day. They also transfer one Tempest's energy into a usable form for Summoners, as Summoners cannot draw power directly from the Tempests themselves. The Sects, their abilities, and their corresponding Tempests are listed below.

- **CLOUDWALKERS:** Telekinesis, Wind Shaping, Flight - Cyclones
- **CRYOSTALKERS:** Cryokinesis, Greater Weapon Conjuration - Frostfalls
- **DEXTERIS:** Enhanced Physical Speed, Reaction Time, Strength, and Coordination - Slick-Days
- **SCORCHERS:** Pyrokinesis, Lesser Weapon Conjuration - Blazedays
- **SHADOW-SWIFTS:** Umbrakinesis (Ability to Manipulate Darkness), Transcendence (Ability to temporarily remove themselves from their current Realm, transporting themselves to an underlying one) - ???
- **VOLTARIANS:** Electrokinesis, Storm Conjuration (On a small scale) - Storm Gales
- **WHISPERERS:** Limited Thought Reading, Emotional Manipulation - Mistveils

THE EIGHT LOST SECTS

Around a millennia ago, eight of the fifteen original Sects disappeared alongside the arrival of the Tempests in an event known as "the Vanishing" for unknown reasons. The eight Lost Sects were known to be extraordinarily powerful, even when compared to the seven remaining Sects. The eight Lost Sects are listed below.

- **Blood Sorcerers:** Sanguimancy (Blood Manipulation), Corporikinesis (Control over one's own body, and others)
- **Illusomancers:** Hallucikinesis (Ability to create and control illusions)
- **Revenants:** Unbinding, Necromancy, Tainted Umbrakinesis, Greater Weapon Conjuration
- **Rune-Writers:** Rune-Writing (The ability to imbue written letters with divine power that can serve various purposes, such as locking, warding, trapping, etc.)
- **Skin-Shapers:** Shapeshifting
- **Starburners:** Dynamokinesis (Energy Manipulation), Lumokinesis (Light Manipulation), Starfire Summoning
- **Stonemasters:** Terrakinesis (Ability to control most elements of the earth, including rocks and the ground itself)
- **Wayfinders:** Divination (Ability to predict the future), Very Limited Dynamokinesis

GLOSSARY

ARVENDON: Capital of Etherus

ASARI: Country in the Southwest of Auris

ASHOS: Volcanic island in the middle of The Archipelago

AURIS: Continent where most of the story takes place

AYRIA: Small city in the South of Asari

BAREHOLDE: Mountain in The Highlands

BLAZECREST: A medium-sized flying creature famous for its ability to ignite its own feathers

CALIDA: The Goddess of deception and transformation

CELES: Capital of Elos

CLOUDCATCHERS: Siege weapons capable of shooting large, weighted nets to bring down Cloudwalkers

CRYSTALS: Vessels of power that absorb and transform energy from the Tempests into usable energy for Summoners

CYFALION: Capital of Jaskye

DESERTSPINES: A plant with a sharp outer shell, and a sweet fruit inside native to Asari - edible

DIVEBRISKS: A species of fish native to the Salarin Sea, these fish tend to leap from the water and flash their reflective wing-like scales before diving back into the ocean

DUNESAILS: A new, revolutionary vehicle created in Suchara to make crossing the Dunes of Despair easier.

ELAN TAESI: Island-sanctuary of reclusive Navesian monks

ELOS: Country in the northeast of Auris

ERYDON: Shadow-Swift fortress in The Highlands

ETHERUS: Central country of Auris

FIRESNUFFERS: Arvendi device operated by Cloudwalkers used to extinguish or redirect incoming flames

FREYFALL: Capital of Utrya

GOLDENLEAF: Small town in southeast Etherus

GREENBRANCHES: Trees native to Jaskye

GREENVINES: Rapidly growing vines native to Jaskye... They often grow on Greenbranches

GREYFUR: A four-eyed, four-legged predator native to the North. Its thick, gray fur protects it from the bitter cold of the Ice Fields

HARBINGERS: Ancient Summoners of Divine Power who came from the Planes of Genesis, bringing magic to Auris. Each of the fifteen founded a Sect, passing on their gifts before returning to Genesis

HELIONN: The God of the sun

HERQEN: Mountain in The Highlands

HIRANE: Small city in southern Utrya

HYTHE: Small town in northwest Etherus, on the border of The Highlands

ICE-BLADE: Commonly conjured weapon of Cryostalkers

ICEBLOOMS: Plant grown in northern Auris - edible

INCENDIARY: A flammable mixture of liquids used as fuel for most lamps and torches

INCENDIARY CANNONS: Powerful weapons capable of shooting flaming hunks of metal toward targets

IZARA: The Goddess of death, darkness, and decay

JASKYE: Country in the Southeast of Auris

KRELLIN: A twelve-legged insect with a hard shell... they are very common in the Northern part of Auris

LESSER SUMMONER: A half-blooded Summoner, or a Summoner whose bloodline is weaker than that of a Master Summoner's.

LOTIUS: One of Auris' Moons, it has a pale gray coloration

MASTER SUMMONER: Pure-blooded Summoner who comes from two parents of the same Sect ... they are considerably more powerful than Lesser Summoners

NAVESIAN: The primary religion of Auris, mostly followed by those in the North and the East of the continent

NIVENTIA: The Goddess of life, light, and prosperity

NREKUMAS: Scaled beast of The Wastelands

ORIA: The Second of Auris' Moons, it has a blue-green coloration

ORRINSHIRE: Small town in northern Elos

PHASING: Another word for shifting

RUNES: An ancient language created by the Rune-Writers that allows written letters to be imbued with unparalleled power

RUNE-LOCKS: Rune based locks that are virtually impossible to bypass

SANDWORMS: A species of worm that live in the deserts of Asari - edible

SHIFTING: The switching of a person (usually a Shadow-Swift) from Auris to the Unbound

SECT: A class or "order" of Summoners characterized by specific abilities

SHADOW-SAND: Sand-like material from the Unbound... the only substance capable of shifting with Shadow-Swifts (can be condensed and forged into weapons and armor)

SHOREBEANS: A plant grown in southern Auris - edible

SNOWFIN: A large, thick-skinned fish native to the Northwest of Auris

SNOWPROWLER: A large, aggressive snow cat that dwells primarily in The Highlands

SPARKCOILS: Electricity-conducting wire systems usable by Voltarians.

STONEBLOSSOMS: A plant grown in central Auris - edible

STORMLESS: Ordinary people that are not Summoners

STORMROOTS: A bitter plant that grows in central Auris— edible

SUCHARA: Capital of Asari

SUNBEAMS: Harmless wisps of heat-energy that float through the air on Blazedays

Sunbird: A type of bird with eight angelic, luminous wings. These birds are said to be the children of Niventia

Tarathiel: God of the land, stone, and the mountains

Telenaris: The mountain in which Erydon is hidden

The Archipelago: An island chain surrounding the volcano: Ashos on the southern tip of Auris

The Highlands: A massive region of mountains in the central-northern part of Auris consisting of virtually inhabitable, treacherous mountains

The Planes of Genesis: A mythical Realm from which all powers of creation and Summoning began

The Unbound: A parallel/underlying Realm to Auris that is still partially connected to Auris

The Vanishing: The unexplained event that led to the disappearance of The eight Lost Sects and the arrival of the Tempests

Utrya: Country in the Northwest of Auris

Umbrakinesis: Manipulation of dark energies

Wards: Rune-powered shields that serve a various purpose

Zephyr: The God of time

ACKNOWLEDGMENTS

Working on this story has been one of the greatest experiences of my life. Taking it from a rudimentary first draft to the finished copy that you now hold in your hands could not have been done without a lot of help. First, I would like to thank my mom and dad for being my number one fans right from the start. You two were the ones helping me turn my dreams into a reality. Dad: Thank you for always helping me take the next step in the writing process... for helping me look for agents, and for helping me explore the world of self-publishing once we shifted gears. Mom: Thank you for reading through countless versions of this story and always giving me your best feedback, for helping organize my trip to New York for the Writer's Digest Conference, and for helping me become the best version of myself.

I would also like to thank my editors: P.J. (Tricia) Hoover and Samantha Wekstein. Your feedback was instrumental in helping me make my book into what it is now. Thank you to Daniel Berkowitz for your help with our website design, and thank you to Jeff Brown: our illustrator. I also want to thank Shaun Loftus and her entire team for their help with the publication and marketing of my book.

Thank you to my grandma: Linda, for reading several versions of this story and always providing me with insightful feedback. Finally, I want to thank all of my friends and classmates who I would relentlessly bounce ideas off over the time that I was developing this book.

ABOUT THE AUTHOR

 Nick is just seventeen years old. He lives in Indiana with his mom, dad, older brother, and two dogs. While Stormless is his first "real" book, it is far from the first story he has told.

He has always been fascinated with reading, and once he began middle school, he thought he'd try writing. As he learned and grew as a student, his writing also improved. He connected with other readers and writers in his grade, compelling him to work even harder on his writing.

He juggled tennis, golf, writing, and reading throughout middle school and built an impressive academic resume. And, of course, he always loved (and still does love) to kill a few hours on PlayStation gaming with friends. However, beginning in high school, he started to take writing more seriously. After finishing his freshman tennis season, which would ultimately be the only season he played in high school, he began formulating a new story.

Fast-forward nearly a year, and after spending all summer relentlessly working on his tennis skills, injuries forced him to stop. He soon realized, however, that this was an opportunity to begin working on the project he had been so carefully putting together in his head. And so, starting in the fall of 2021, he began writing *Storm-less*. He woke up early every day to work on the project before school, and by May, he was finished. He was paired with an editor on

Reedsy, and after spending the summer working with her and revising his work, *Stormless* was nearly complete.

Since then, he has begun working on a new, untitled project while continuing to tighten up *Stormless*. He has recently started a social media account to connect with other writers! He doesn't plan to stop writing stories, writing is his passion, and his dream is to one day share his stories with readers around the world.

Even with *Stormless* books one and two nearly completed at seventeen, this is still a lofty goal. Still, his journey as a writer is just beginning.

facebook.com/nickstitleauthor

instagram.com/nickstitle_author

amazon.com/stores/Nick-Stitle/author/B0BZQ8KFCN

bookbub.com/authors/nick-stitle

twitter.com/nickstitle

ALSO BY NICK STITLE

www.ingramcontent.com/pod-product-compliance
Lightning Source LLC
Chambersburg PA
CBHW022013300726
48970CB00003B/869